Anselm Audley was eighteen in June 2000. Having studied at Millfield School, he is now at St John's College, Oxford, reading Ancient and Modern History.

HERESY

Book One of
THE AQUASILVA TRILOGY

ANSELM AUDLEY

EARTHLIGHT

SIMON & SCHUSTER

London • New York • Sydney • Tokyo • Singapore • Toronto • Dublin

A VIACOM COMPANY

To my parents

First published in Great Britain by Earthlight, 2001
An imprint of Simon & Schuster UK Ltd
A Viacom Company

1 3 5 7 9 10 8 6 4 2

Simon & Schuster UK Ltd
Africa House
64–78 Kingsway
London
WC2B 6AH

Simon & Schuster Australia
Sydney

A CIP catalogue record for this book is available
from the British Library.

ISBN 0-7432-0950-8

Typeset in Bembo by SX Composing DTP, Rayleigh, Essex
Printed and bound in Great Britain by The Bath Press, Bath

ACKNOWLEDGEMENTS

Aquasilva has been a long time in the making, and thanks to all those people who have helped it along at various stages and stopped me going mad while writing it: my parents and my sister Eloise; Dr Garstin, Naomi Harries, Gent Koço, Polly Mackwood, Olly Marshall, John Morrice, John Roe, Tim Shephard, Poppy Thomas. Special thanks to James Hale; no-one could have a better agent.

Equatorial circumference
as calculated by the Oceanographic Guild
65,397 miles

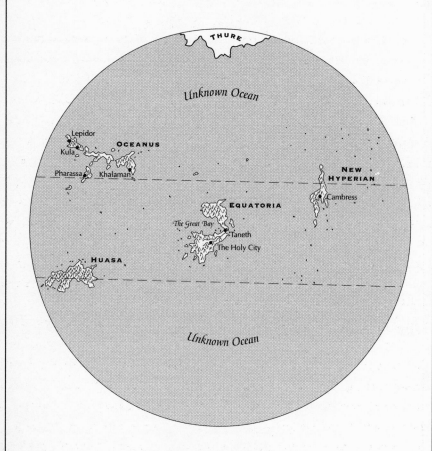

Continents

NOTE: *Aquasilva is a much bigger world than Earth, with a diameter of about 20,000 miles; the continents are therefore drawn larger than life for legibility.*

Kreon Eirillia
Cartographer to His Imperial Majesty
Orosius Tar'Conantur

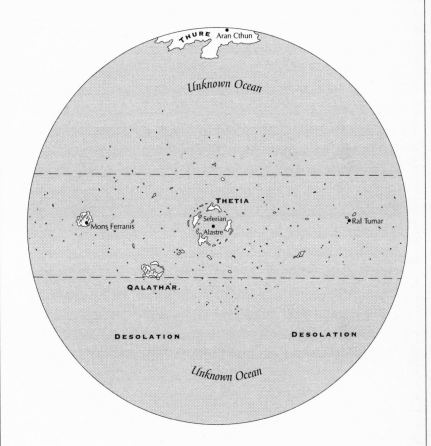

Archipelago

NOTE: *Aquasilva is a much bigger world than Earth, with a diameter of about 20,000 miles; the continents are therefore drawn larger than life for legibility.*

Part One: The Journey

CHAPTER I

'IRON! IRON!'

The shout drifted up through the forest out of the tumult ahead, near the entrance to the gem mines. Birds settled in the branches of the cedar trees shrilled and rose from their perches. I urged my horses on, the wheels of the chariot stirring up clouds of fine dust from the path behind me. Then I pulled on the reins, slowing the chariot down as the path twisted abruptly round a tree.

Ahead of me the trees gave way to grass, falling away down the slopes of the foothills. To the right was the stone wall around the compound of the gem mines, its guard towers deserted. I could see a large knot of people in the entranceway where the gates hung wide open. What were they doing there? Had there been an accident? A riot? That was all we needed.

As I slowed down in the empty space of the killing field around the mines and wheeled the chariot round, they spotted me. I stopped the chariot a few feet from them.

A tall man, one of only a few wearing robes rather than labourers' tunics, stepped out of the crowd as they turned towards me, excitement showing on his face. It wasn't a riot, then, or an accident.

'Escount Cathan, it's fortunate that you have arrived; may Ranthas be with you.' His beard was cut quite short, and his oiled hair was overlaid with powdery dust. His face was thin and gaunt, his eyes deep-sunk but alight with the same interest as the others'.

'What's all the commotion, Maal?' I asked. 'What's so important that work's been interrupted, with the ship due to arrive any day now?' Any day now, that was, as long as the coriolis storm out over the ocean dissipated soon. It was the second this month, and the ship had already been delayed once.

'Master, we have found iron! The priest of Ranthas who offered to help our mining operations has discovered a huge seam of the red ore!'

I almost refused to believe him at first. Iron? Had we been sitting on top of one of the most valuable commodities of all for these last few ailing months and neglected it? Iron was in short supply across Aquasilva; the floating islands simply didn't hold enough of the ore to meet the demands of the steel foundries – and, ultimately, of the continents' armies. After flamewood and its derivatives, iron was the most highly prized of all the raw materials.

'Is this certain?' I demanded, keeping my face impassive. I didn't want to show too much excitement in front of the mine workers.

In answer, Maal called to someone in the throng. There weren't as many of them as I'd thought at first; about twelve or fifteen people were clustered there, mostly overseers and foremen. Someone at the back tossed a lump of rock over their heads. Maal deftly caught it and handed it to me.

One of the horses whickered as I turned the rock over in my hand, noting the grey-black crystals in it.

'Is it mineable?'

'The priest thinks so. He's in the mine with Haaluk.'

'Someone come and hold the reins,' I said. One of the men moved over and took them, and I stepped out of the chariot.

'Take me to the priest,' I said to Maal. 'The rest of you continue with your work.'

A path opened for me to pass through them. Maal led me across the court inside the palisade. There were buildings along one side, and the opencast trenches on the other. Opposite us yawned the black hole of the mine entrance. I wasn't particularly fond of going in there – I hate caves – but this was important, so I'd have to try not to think about being underground. This gemstone mine was the principal reason for the existence of Clan Lepidor, the northernmost of the fifteen clans on the continent of Oceanus, and by a small margin the northernmost continental clan in the world. There hadn't been a city here before the Tuonetar War, but a hundred and fifty-eight years ago a prospecting party had discovered rich gem seams and shortly afterwards a group of Oceanian and Archipelagan refugees had settled in the area and founded a new clan.

We were rather lucky, in fact – there were rich fishing grounds nearby, and the mountains gave better than usual protection from the storms, allowing a lush forest to grow up along the coast. I was glad of that – it made Lepidor territory a lot less bleak than the lands of some of the more southerly clans, which were too exposed for trees to grow there, and hence were very depressing places to be.

My House had been in power since its founding, after some distant ancestor or other had performed an extraordinary service for the city and the other Houses had unanimously chosen him to lead them. At least, that was the official story. It sounded rather dubious to me, and I guessed the reality had been somewhat less honourable. Still, that was history now, and my father, Count Elnibal II, was known as one of the most upstanding of the present fifteen Counts of Oceanus.

The problem for us at the moment was that over the last few years the price of gemstones had been dropping and the mine had become less profitable, and in recent months the Count and the merchants had been struggling to make ends meet. We could survive, of course, without the mine: there was fertile farmland along the coast and extensive fisheries for food, and the forests would supply us with wood and keep some exports going.

But without the gems there was nothing worthwhile to trade, and so Clan Lepidor would degenerate into a farming combine, not fit to be called a clan. And since I didn't want to inherit a mere combine, nor see my clan's fortunes plummet, I'd been as worried about the future as anyone.

Until now. My head was suddenly full of possibilities. If there was enough iron, and it could be exploited, we'd be rich again as soon as the first cargo was sold in the markets of Oceanus's capital Pharassa. We might even be able to sign a contract with a Great House to carry it across the ocean to Taneth, Aquasilva's trading capital. It was a long journey, and I knew it was much more dangerous, but the iron prices would be much higher there.

I ducked under the wooden framework of the gateway and into the tunnel of the mine, lit by three flamewood torches. I heard two voices a little way ahead.

'. . . Seam extends out for hundreds of feet, I tell you.'

'I know the rock around here, Domine, and there's no possible way it can.' The voice of the mine's manager, Haaluk-Itti, coarser than the smooth, modulated tones of the priest of Ranthas. Haaluk had been exiled from Mons Ferranis two years ago after a quarrel with a merchant, and would spend another year supervising Lepidor's mines before we lost him again to his homeland. It would be a pity: despite his abrasive bitterness, he was a good manager.

'Ah, Escount Cathan,' the priest said, as he saw me. His face was in shadow.

Haaluk, who was standing with his back to the entrance, swung round. 'Doubtless you've heard,' he said. 'I have found myself forced to disagree with Domine Istiq, despite all his wisdom, on the extent of the deposit.' Priests were always called *Domine*, a title from the old tongue.

'What's the difference in your estimates?' I ask Haaluk.

'His are twice as large as mine.'

'Is the mine workable with your figure?'

'By all means. The Domine will tell you,' he said gruffly.

'My calculations are rough guesses, you understand,' Domine Istiq said, 'but I would estimate you have enough here to sell ten thousand corons' worth every month, for more than a century and a half.'

I attempted to calculate the resulting profit figures in my head, but failed. I was never very good at mental arithmetic, although I could work sums out easily enough on paper.

'Your annual expenses amount to around two thousand, Escount Cathan,' Istiq said. 'Eight thousand left over, at least four remaining after other expenses such as tithes and a merchant's cut.' A sideways reminder there that we'd have to pay their dues to the Domain temple again, dues that had been waived this last year to help our survival. Lepidor's Avarch, while not native-born, had been in charge of the temple for twenty-six years and was more of a Lepidorian than a priest now; he was always very helpful and considerate.

'Those calculations are made with Haaluk's estimates?'

'Yes. With mine, you can go on mining for three centuries.'

I wasn't worried. 'Either way, we get back in profit.'

'You'll need to hire trained iron miners from Pharassa, and they're much in demand. A contract as well, with some merchant from Pharassa or Taneth.'

'Don't forget the Cambressian Admiralty,' I said, remembering the third possible market, but Istiq looked doubtful. 'Will you come back to the city for supper?' I added.

'Thank you for your offer, but I'll stay here a while longer to see if we can find out the exact extent of these deposits.' Istiq bowed, and I returned the courtesy before turning round and making my way back up the tunnel, cursing as I almost cracked my head on one of the wooden support beams. Maal followed me.

I blinked as we emerged again into the bright sunlight of the yard, now resounding again with a dull thudding sound as the gem miners broke up the ore with flamewood hammers, melting away what wasn't pure gemstone. At least, that was what I remembered my tutor telling me. I found the whole mining process even less interesting than theology lessons; it had nothing to do with the sea.

'Will you be going back to the city now, Lord Cathan?' Maal asked.

'Yes,' I replied. 'Work should continue as normal for the rest of the day. Haaluk is to come to me with some figures this evening. I need some hard facts before I take any action.'

Actually, it was my mother, effective Regent in my father's absence, who would make any decisions. Not yet of age, I wasn't experienced enough to take full charge of the Count's duties while my father was away, and so I sat on the dais with the First Adviser whispering Countess Irria's advice into my ear. I'd actually been trying to pay more attention to statecraft lessons since my father left, because it was galling not to know enough to take my own decisions.

I went back across the courtyard and under the gate, noting that its towers were once again occupied by watchers who could survey the surrounding hillsides for traces of barbarian raiding forces. Not that they were likely to find any – there was only one pass into the mountains within the city's territory, and it was well guarded, as were the coastal approaches.

The man to whom I'd entrusted my chariot handed me the reins. I hadn't taken my wrist guards off, so I curled the reins around my forearm, flicked the whip, and moved off along the path down to the city.

It was an exhilarating feeling, rushing along the road behind the perfectly trained two-horse team, and the speed more than compensated for the jolts as the wheels went over loose stones or shallow potholes. The road was beginning to show signs of disrepair, and I saw one or two holes big enough to lose a wheel in. It would need a team of road masons with proper tools to carry out repairs – that was, if we had enough money for the flamewood. Well, the iron should solve that problem, I reflected.

The path straightened when I reached the main valley, and I passed between huge cedars interspersed with stretches of clear land. Once or twice I passed horse-drawn woodcarts manned by lumberjacks, carrying logs from the logging sites on the slopes. Then the road curved round and the trees fell away as I came out opposite Lepidor.

The city was built on a promontory, with a lagoon to the east, my right, serving as the city's harbour. To the west the coastline curved away, a long vista of farmland and stands of acacias, gently sloping down to a long sandy shore. Shining stone-built walls erected across the end of the promontory protected the city: I could see the houses of the Land Quarter just beyond them.

Lepidor wasn't a big city; the last census, carried out for tax purposes two years ago, had shown just under two thousand citizens. What it lacked in size, however, it made up for in cleanliness and the quality of its architecture. I'd seen most of the other cities on the continent and, even allowing for my loyalty to Lepidor as my home, I thought it was the best of communities, its buildings the most beautiful.

Every building inside the walls that ringed the outside of the promontory was built of the local white stone, and many stretched to three storeys. From every roof, above the colonnaded windows of the first floor, a verdant garden sprouted, rooted in earth that had mostly been carried up by hand; there were some things that even flamewood couldn't do. One or two of the larger dwellings had small domes on their roofs.

In the surface harbour, also protected by walls, I could see warehouses and wharves, the masts of nine or ten fishing ships, and over to one side a small domed building – the top of Lepidor's undersea harbour, where mantas docked and Lepidor's single home-stationed undersea warship was kept.

I raced across the green open space that lay before the city and through the gates of the Land Quarter, the outermost of the city's three districts. The guards, both of whom I recognized, waved cheerily, and I waved back to them as I sped through. I had to slow down inside the gates, but at least the main street led almost straight through to the gates of the other two quarters – Palace and Seaward. All three districts were circular, and protected by their own set of walls – they had to be, for proper shielding from the storms. That was another reason I was glad to live here – because the storms were less severe, our walls could be lower and weren't the dark, towering monstrosities of some other cities.

I passed the internal gate into the Palace Quarter, where the main marketplace and official buildings were, as well as my home – the Palace.

The royal Palace – more of a mansion than a Palace, really – stood at the end of the main street, only a couple of hundred feet away. Both sides of the street were lined with shops, each one with an awning extending out of its front. Their counters were spread with wares, whose holders nodded cheerily at the slow-moving chariot. I manoeuvred my horses round the fat, green-robed bulk of the merchant Shihap, who was bargaining furiously with his friend the shield engineer.

'A fine day, is it not?' Shihap called, turning from his haggling. 'You look happy!'

'Believe me, I am,' I said, 'and so will you be when the money begins to flow again.' The story of the discovery would be all over the city by nightfall, so it wouldn't do any harm if I planted the first rumours of it. I spurred the horses on before Shihap had a chance to enquire further: let whoever Haaluk sent to spread the news have the pleasure of telling the citizens what had happened.

I slowed twice more to greet people before I reached the small square in front of the Palace. The stables were hidden away on one side, against the outer walls, downwind of course, and I handed over the chariot to a servant who ran out to take the reins. I unknotted the thongs of my wrist guards and left them in the chariot, along with the whip. My father didn't like riding equipment lying around in the Palace.

Two guards sat inside the gate of the Palace, as usual gambling with copper coins. They waved me cheerily past and into the small court of the Palace. It wasn't more than thirty feet across, with a flight of stairs leading up one side and plants growing in spaces between the paving stones. At one side was the door to the banqueting hall and council chamber, and the servants' door was set in the base of the stairs. Again, it was much smaller than, say, Lexan's Palace in Khalaman, but it was far more friendly – and, for me, home.

I ran up the stairs three at a time, almost hitting my head again on the beams that supported the tiled roof.

'Where's my mother?' I asked the first servant I saw in the whitewashed hallway at the top.

'In the upper council chamber with the First Adviser, master.'

I slowed my pace to a fast walk along the tiled corridor. Voices came from within the closed door of the third room on the left, and I knocked.

'Who's there?' came my mother's rich contralto voice.

'It's me,' I said.

'Come in, then.'

I pushed open the cedarwood door and went inside. The council chamber was a large room with a whitewood table in the centre. This was the secret council chamber; open meetings were held in the main hall, because we'd never been able to afford a proper conclave room. There were twelve chairs around the table, one with a red canopy. My mother was sitting in it while the First Adviser sat in the first chair on the right-hand side.

'What is it?' my mother asked, seeing straight through the composed look I tried to keep on my face. In her youth she'd been accounted beautiful and, now past forty, she still looked impressive. Her long hair, an unusual dark blonde, was tied up at the back, and she looked proud and regal. She wore a long gown of white and green.

'I drove past the mine while I was exercising my horses. They've found enough iron there to give us a—' I tried to remember the figure '—four thousand coron profit for the next century.'

'Iron?' Atek half-rose from his seat. Our First Adviser was my mother's cousin, three years younger than her. He'd come with her when she married my father because her father, Atek's guardian, had had enough of his nephew's wild reputation. I'd never seen that side of him, and all my mother's relations agreed that he'd turned into a sensible man and a good adviser. He'd been employed as my father's First Adviser and chancellor since his predecessor's death two years ago. I didn't like to be disrespectful to the dead, but I preferred Atek to the dour, vinegary Pilaset. Atek was brown-haired and broadly built, though I'd noticed he was getting fat due to lack of exercise. He wore a white robe with red decoration, belted at the waist.

'Iron,' I confirmed. 'Domine Istiq and Haaluk are quite certain, although they can't agree whether the supply will last one and a half or three centuries.'

'How come we never discovered this before?' Atek said, sinking back into his chair, his expression dazed.

'Because we've never had a trained miner-priest before,' my mother said. 'That was a section of the hill we'd never tested before he arrived.'

It had been sheer luck that we'd gained Domine Istiq's service in the first place: he'd been one of three survivors from a manta that had been destroyed by a whirlpool off Islesend Cape three months ago. Once he'd recovered, he'd offered to do some prospecting in our mine to keep him busy until another manta arrived from his original destination, Mons Ferranis, to collect him. I hadn't had much contact with him, although it had been one of my undersea probes that had detected his powerless escape ship floating out towards the open ocean. It had been a triumph for me, though, because I'd at last proved to my father that all the time I spent in the sea or with the oceanographers did have some value.

'I ordered Haaluk to have some definite figures for us this evening,' I said. 'Domine Istiq would rather stay out there until nightfall, as he always has.'

'You did well,' my mother said, a warm smile lighting up her face.

'We have to send word to Count Elnibal,' Atek said, coming to the same conclusions as Istiq had. 'We'll need to sign a cargo contract with some merchant of Taneth or Pharassa, to carry the iron to the foundries.'

'Could we set up a smithing industry here?' my mother wondered aloud. 'If we made the iron into weapons before shipping it off, the profit would double.'

'It'd make us a major target for pirates, though,' Atek reminded her. 'Until we have the money to build proper defences, it would be better merely to sell the iron. I will suggest that course to your husband.'

'Where do you think is the best place to sell the iron?' I asked.

'Taneth,' Atek said immediately.

My mother agreed with him, and I was fairly certain that my father would have the same idea. Of the other two possible markets, Pharassa was closer, and safer, but the prices were comparatively low since there was very little demand there. Oceanus already had an operating mine so there wouldn't be much of a market for our metal in that place, either. The other possibility was the one Istiq hadn't seemed to like the sound of: Cambress, on the continent of New Hyperian. But the journey there was almost twice as far as the one to Taneth, and the profit margins would be far smaller.

Also, the route to Cambress passed very close to the territory of our deadly enemy Count Lexan of Khalaman.

'Who do we send?' my mother said. 'Elnibal only left two weeks ago, and the council never lasts less than a month.'

'This one might,' Atek said. 'The Halettites are pressing on the borders of the cities on Equatoria, so many of the Counts there will be anxious to get home.'

'Which means we must decide before the trading ship arrives. Whoever goes will have to be quick at Pharassa and get passage on one of the military mantas making the courier run from there to Taneth.'

'I should go,' Atek said.

'I need you here,' my mother reminded him.

'There's no one else we can send.'

'There must be. What about entrusting a package to someone who was planning to go anyway?'

'No one of high enough stature. None of the bigger merchants were planning to go.' Atek looked at me suddenly. 'On the other hand, as long as he is escorted, Cathan could go.'

I felt a thrill; I'd been hoping against hope that somebody would mention me, and wondering whether I should suggest it myself. I knew before she spoke that my mother wouldn't like the idea, though.

'No!' she said. 'He's supposedly in charge in his father's absence; without him everyone will know I'm ruling, and that'll hardly endear us to the Domain.'

'Everyone knows already,' Atek reminded her. 'Besides, his brother can serve as a figurehead.'

'His brother is only five years old, or had that fact escaped you?' my mother said sharply. 'What if there's another storm like the one three months ago, and Cathan's ship was sunk as well? What do I tell my husband then?'

'If Elnibal gets no word, he'll have to make the journey to Taneth again, at the time of year when Lexan and our other enemies can take advantage of any weaknesses, and that *will* be far more dangerous. Either I or Cathan must go. There aren't any alternatives.'

'I would prefer it if you went, Atek,' she said after a pause.

I decided this was the time to speak up for myself, before my mother decided in favour of Atek.

'Mother, I'll need experience of Taneth before I go to my first Council meeting. And of Equatoria. All of Courtières's sons have already gone.' Courtières was one of our allies.

My reasoning was sound, I knew, and my father would have given me leave without hesitation. But my mother was always so overprotective!

I saw her looking at me as Atek nodded sagely.

'Is your heart set on going, then?'

'Yes!'

I saw a brief flicker of doubt on her face. But then she said, 'Very well.'

I was too conscious of my dignity to leap in the air and shout something, but inwardly I was pleased as could be. Clan heirs needed to have seen some of the rest of the world before they succeeded to their posts and I felt that so far I hadn't seen enough.

I was due to spend a year or two away from home quite soon, to learn how politics, trade and religion actually worked, get a grounding in oceanography, and find out how to sail mantas and surface ships. It was an apprenticeship that all clan aristocrats' and leading merchants' sons went through, but so far there'd been no indication of when I was going.

Not that I'd need to learn anything about ships or oceanography. I'd spent nearly as much of my life in the water as on land – which was why my father was concerned that the rest of my education was falling behind. But he'd never been able to keep me away from the sea for very long.

The furthest I'd ever been from Lepidor was Pharassa, Oceanus's capital, two years ago – I could have gone to the Great Conference with my father last time it happened, three years ago, but I'd been ill. Pharassa was a mighty city, but it was still on my home continent of Oceanus, and I'd never crossed the ocean.

And the obvious destination across the ocean was Taneth, one of the two greatest and richest cities on all Aquasilva, where it was said a manta entered or left port every hour, and a sailing ship every five minutes. Taneth was Aquasilva's merchant capital, and somewhere I'd always wanted to go.

'Who shall we send as escort?' Irria asked.

'Someone who has crossed the ocean, someone we can trust.'

'Hasn't one of the acolytes from the temple been called to train in the Holy City?'

'I believe so. A promising young man who's been to New Hyperian and Equatoria. We'll send two guards with them. I'll arrange it with the High Priest.'

'Do it now,' my mother ordered. Atek stood up, bowed to both of us, and left the room, closing the door again behind him.

'It will be a long journey,' the Countess said. 'And going by sea, there is very little to do. Learn what you can from the acolyte, both about the world and the faith of the Domain. If he proves to be a fanatic, don't let yourself be taken in by his teaching. There should be a balance in the world, and sacking the lands of those who don't conform, as the priesthood does, is not right.' She stood up and went over to the window.

'Atek is right, you've seen too little of the world. What you've seen of the priesthood is all that is good about it. We are too small a city to warrant anything more than a temple with four priests and ten acolytes. But in the capital and the other great cities, and in the priesthood's lands around the Holy City on Equatoria, there are thousands of warrior priests. They're zealots – priests who can fight better than most other men, who believe in the cleansing power of fire and the sword. The Prime sends them out against those who don't believe in Ranthas. Cities and whole peoples have been destroyed by them. They're called the Sacri, the Sacred Ones.' My mother almost spat out the last words. I'd never seen her so emotional – she was usually very calm and collected, except on the few occasions when she argued with my father.

I tried to make sense of what my mother was saying. 'Who does one worship, if not Ranthas?'

'Before I tell you, you must swear never to reveal what I disclose to you to anyone, or even hint that you know about it. Not even to your brother. Most certainly not to the acolyte.' She seemed nervous, in a way I'd never seen before, fiddling with her girdle.

'Swear on what?'

'On clan honour.'

'By my heritage and the clan of my birth, and by the continuation of our House, I swear to keep what I know learn secret and hidden from all the world,' I said. Then I waited.

'What is the Domain's religion based on?' she asked.

Confused, it took me a second to answer. I'd been expecting her to tell me something, not ask a blindingly obvious question.

'Ranthas, the embodiment of fire from which all life comes.' I took the passage directly from the primers the Avarch had used to teach me.

'And his gift to Aquasilva is? Tell me from the Catechism.'

'Flamewood is Ranthas's gift,' I recited, one of the homilies drummed into everyone as a child by the priests of the temple. Learning them had to count as the most boring thing I'd ever done. 'It gives heat and light and power to Aquasilva, and through it the will of the God is channelled. Through flamewood we cross the seas, and keep away the storms. With it we make war and peace, all by Ranthas's bounty.'

'Fire is an element, isn't it?' she said.

'Of course. Fire, Earth, Air, Water, Light, and Shadow, but Fire is the dominant one, and the one that holds Aquasilva together, with its dominion over Light.'

'And it's the only one that endows men with the gift of magic, to heal and destroy?'

'Of course.'

'So why do none of the other elements have gods, or magic? Flamewood may be vital, but we need water to keep us alive, air to breathe, and earth to grow our crops in. And without shadow there is no night.'

'Fire is the Creator,' I said stubbornly, still unsure of what my mother was talking about.

'Cathan, fire is but one of six elements. Each of the others has its own deity, its own magic, its own power. Some are potentially far more powerful, and far kinder, than the Fire-God. Don't we live on the surface of an endless ocean that makes up most of Aquasilva? That ocean is the domain of Thetis, Goddess of Water. The Void, the heavens beyond the storms, surpassing even the oceans in size, is the home of Shadow, and its spirit Ragnar. Then there is Earth, and its ruler Hyperias, after whom New Hyperian was originally named. Althana, Goddess of the Winds, and Phaetan, God of Light, are the other two. All of these have a history of worship as old as fire itself, and once they were freely tolerated. The Thetian Empire was founded on the worship of Thetis.'

Her voice was no less compelling for the heresy of her words, but I found what she was saying a staggering concept to take in.

'Anyone found worshipping the other elemental deities is burned alive in the main square of their city. Even to know of them is dangerous.' My mother's voice had descended to a whisper. 'I don't ask anything other than that you keep what I have told you in mind, and that you look upon the works of Ranthas in the knowledge that other powers can accomplish the same thing, without needing to be supreme.'

'This is the opposite of everything I have been taught,' I protested.

'Teaching is the key to control,' she said. 'Remember your oath to the clan.'

'I will,' I promised, standing up.

Her voice rose to its normal pitch again as she, too, stood up.

'You must prepare for your journey, and bid farewell to your friends.'

'And my brother.'

'How good of you to remember him,' my mother said, opening the door.

We walked out into the passage beyond and headed for the open door at the far end of the corridor, which led out onto a small roof garden overlooking the sea. The sky was virtually cloudless: only small white wisps marred its azure expanse, and the sea rippled beneath a light breeze.

That night I found a small scrap of paper with a passage in my mother's handwriting lying under my pillow. At the top she had written an instruction not to take it with me, for to be caught with it was death.

I memorized it before I dropped it in the furnace, though.

From a chronicle written by the last Thetian High Priest of the old religion.

. . . And so it was that I stood by my brother's memorial, looking out over the empty ocean towards the continents that had once been green and were now shattered wastelands. I have often wondered if this would have happened if my father had lived, but then I remember the incessant wars between ourselves we went through before all this. We have lost a world, but now we have a chance for a lasting peace and a new beginning. I only hope that Aetius's shade can rest in peace, and that we shall stay true to the vision so many have died for. I will never be able to fight or wield magic again, and even now I cannot walk up from the harbour without Cinnirra's help. Although I may recover some of my strength, it is my son and my

nephew who lead Thetia now, and I hope that they will have the chance to forge a
better world than I have ever lived in.

Hail and farewell,

Carausius Tar'Conantur.

It didn't sound like the writings of the Carausius we'd been told about, brother of the arch-demon Aetius who'd plunged Aquasilva into a terrible war. I wondered what my mother meant by it, and where it had come from.

CHAPTER II

The quays of the surface harbour were still glistening wet from the last storm when I boarded the trade barque *Parasur* two days later, along with most of my escort. Suall, a gorilla-like guardsman, was carrying all the luggage, while his more normal-sized companion Karak sauntered along behind. Three small chunks of iron ore, wrapped in canvas, lay at the bottom of my bag, the safest place I could find. They were the precious samples we'd need to negotiate a contract.

As we walked across the slippery stone surface, the *Parasur*'s captain appeared at the top of the gangway and beckoned us to come up; I noticed the planks shaking as I stepped on them – it seemed Bomar didn't have the money for repairs any more than we did.

'Welcome on board, Lord Cathan. It is an honour to have you travelling on my ship.'

'Thank you.' I nodded to Suall, who grinned and took the bags down the aft companionway that the ship's master had indicated. Bomar was a lean, spiky man, with a beard that was quite short for one of his station, and he was dressed in a brown robe that had seen better days. He'd commanded the *Parasur* for as long as I could remember; it was the ship that made the regular run along the coast to buy the monthly cargoes of gems from Lepidor, wine from Kula, and various other products from the small settlements on the islands along the route. These would then be sold for a higher price in Pharassa, although the profit margin for the gems had been dropping rapidly recently and Bomar had been muttering about not coming any more. However, with the news of the iron mine's discovery, he'd doubtless been calculating the possible gains he could make. Although we couldn't use his ship for transporting the ore, Lepidor's population would grow, and he'd have more people to sell to.

'Could I ask, sir, where is the priest? It is imperative that we leave as soon as possible, or we won't make the anchorage at Hulka before nightfall.'

I turned and scanned the harbour, wondering where my travelling companion had got to, then saw two red-robed figures walking quickly down the street that led to the wharves. One was the frail figure of the old Avarch, Lepidor's High Priest; the other, carrying a bag over his shoulder, had to be the acolyte, Sarhaddon.

As they quickened their steps, coming around the edge of the basin, I looked back at the Palace again, where the bushes on the sea-balcony waved slightly in the breeze. I could see my mother standing there, dressed in a dark green robe, with the small shape of my brother Jerian by her side. She didn't wave, but I saw her incline her head, and I waved in response.

'I am very sorry we're late,' the Avarch said, as he reached the foot of the gangplank, pushing Sarhaddon up it with a gentle hand.

'It's no trouble, Pontifex, I assure you,' Bomar said deferentially, moving smoothly aside to let Sarhaddon on board. 'Pontifex' was an Avarch's title.

'I don't believe you,' the Avarch said jovially. 'May Ranthas be with you.' He turned to Sarhaddon, who was leaning over the rail across the gangway from me.

'And with you too, Sarhaddon. It's been a pleasure teaching you, and I'm sure you're destined for great things in the Holy City. Come and visit us before they make you Prime.'

'Prime' was the title of the most senior priest of all, higher even than the Exarchs who had supreme power over each continent in the Domain. Evidently Sarhaddon had shown ambition for them even to joke about such a thing. But if the Avarch liked Sarhaddon, I couldn't help feeling that I would, too. The Avarch was one of my tutors, and the most interesting of them, even if his subject was boring.

The Avarch waved and walked away along the wharf, calling down blessings on the workers labouring there. Almost immediately Bomar ordered the gangplank pulled on board and the mooring ropes untied. Sailors ran across the deck as the harbour cutter's trailing rope was attached to the *Parasur*'s bow, ready to tow her out into the open sea.

'Let's be going!' Bomar called, and the beating of a drum sounded from ahead. I walked forward to the bow as fast as I could and leaned over the gunwale to the right of where the prow reared up, the mast-rope securely fastened to it. Ahead, the tug-cutter was increasing its stroke, the oars beating faster on the port side as the ship turned to face the harbour entrance. As we moved out across the harbour, I looked back at Lepidor again, at the workshops and taverns around the harbour. The familiar sights seemed even more vivid now I was leaving them for three months – I'd never been away for that long before – to go to the other side of the world.

One or two people standing on the dock waved to me as we cleared the harbour entrance, then the cutter fell away and *Parasur*'s captain ordered the sail set for Hulka Anchorage. The boat began to rock with the motion of the small waves, but that wasn't a problem: I'd never been seasick.

'It's always rather daunting, leaving home,' said a voice to my left, 'but look on the bright side: you'll probably be back here soon. *I* may never return.'

I turned abruptly, to find Sarhaddon standing there, a friendly smile on his face. The hood of his acolyte's robe was thrown back, revealing an alert, lively face, brown hair and dancing green eyes.

'Who are you? . . . Heavens, I should know. You're Cathan,' Sarhaddon said, 'Getting forgetful in my old age.'

I laughed. 'If you're old, what does that make the Avarch?'

'Good question,' the acolyte countered. 'A ghost of a ghost?'

'Do such things exist in higher theology?'

'I wouldn't know. Still, he's a nice old relic.'

My first impression had been right: I liked Sarhaddon. The acolyte had a quick wit and levity. He promised to be enjoyable company on the long weeks of the voyage.

'How old are you, then?' I asked.

'Twenty-three. About. Shall we find somewhere drier to sit?'

The spray driven up every time the ship's prow plunged into a trough was coming uncomfortably near us. We left the bow and went along the port gangway, avoiding the sailors, and hoisted ourselves up onto some canvas-wrapped bales of cloth. From this vantage point we could see the coastline ahead, and Lepidor city gradually slipping away to starboard.

'Why are they sending you to the Holy City?' I asked.

'Because—' he imitated the pompous tone of a prelate, '—I've shown exceptional prowess in my studies. Or so they say. Actually, it's because a distant relative of mine is Fourth Prime, and wants all the supporters he can get to enable him to skip a place on the ladder and move up to Second when the old Prime finally dies.'

'The Prime is dying?'

Sarhaddon shifted his position, glaring at a loose rope that seemed to be trying to hit him on the shoulder.

'Yes. The current personification of Ranthas has reached the span of his years and will be drawn up to join the gods soon. Meanwhile, for the less exalted mortals, there will be a struggle for places.'

I was fascinated by this glimpse into the private world of the priesthood, collectively known as the Domain. It was a side of them I'd never really thought of before, but which confirmed what my mother had told me yesterday. It seemed like blasphemy even thinking about it.

'How will the new Prime be chosen?' I asked.

'That's a secret even I don't know,' Sarhaddon said. 'I might when I get to the Holy City, but suffice it to say that in the end one of the Exarchs or an Under-Prime will end up on top, or be voted there, chosen by the powers, whatever. It will probably be quite a hardliner, one who feels that the Domain has grown too lax in its treatment of heretics over the past few years. Not an extremist, though.'

'So then they'll crack down harder on any traces of heresy.'

'Probably. I personally have no time for the zealot wing of Ranthas's worshippers. They're generally narrow-minded fanatics. Heresy should be rooted out, of course, or how will the world function? But it isn't necessary to go looking for it in every nook and cranny.'

Sarhaddon sucked in his cheeks, giving his face a hollow look, and rolled his eyes. 'Ye are heretics here, cut off from the light of Holy Ranthas! You will be cast into the utter darkness beyond the world, and eaten by the daemons of the Circles of Death! If they can stomach you, that is!' Sarhaddon collapsed into laughter, and so did I. Two of the sailors nearby looked at us curiously.

'Are they really that bad?' I said, when I could talk properly again.

'Worse!' said the acolyte. 'They're truly terrifying.'

'We're just rounding the headland to the south of Lepidor,' Bomar called down from the deck above us, leaning over the rail. 'If you landlubbers want to take a last look, it had better be now.'

I rushed to the rail and watched as the white walls and towers of the city slowly slid out of sight behind the scrub-covered promontory. Two men collecting the eggs of seagulls from its rocky crevices waved to the *Parasur* as we went past. Then Lepidor was out of sight, and I'd had my last glimpse of my home city for at least three months. We wouldn't be out of clan territory for a couple more hours, though.

Sarhaddon was, like me, a bit pensive when we'd rounded the headland; although he was originally from Equatoria, Lepidor had been his home for more than five years, according to Atek. The Avarch had explained that young acolytes, even those who had the potential to rise to high office, were always sent off for a period of instruction in a remote temple, to learn the basic tasks of the priesthood.

'This should be an interesting voyage, though,' Sarhaddon said, a few minutes later. 'Much better than when I came out, when I only had a gruff old stick for company.'

The sun was sinking behind the mountains of the interior, and the sky was darkening sharply through shades of red and blue to dark purple, when we finally stopped for the night, beyond the end of clan territory. Bomar's boat was capable of night sailing, of course, but along the next section of the coast a huge coral reef, stretching way out into the open ocean from the continent's shore, made navigation in the dark virtually suicidal. I remembered there'd been a plan three or four years ago to blast a channel through the reef. My father had been quite enthusiastic, but the oceanographers had pointed out that the end might well snap off and drift out to sea, where it would be even more dangerous.

The *Parasur* glided into a small bay, its edges protected by promontories and with a beach stretching up towards a small forest. A thick stone wall had been constructed around the landward side, similar to a city boundary.

'It's an aether wall,' Bomar said, when I asked him about it, as the ship lay anchored in the clear water of the lagoon, and the crew were relaxing below. 'Sharp eyes you've got. The mountain people round here are an unfriendly bunch, even worse than near Lepidor, so your father had the stockade erected to protect the crews from night attacks. We always lay in here, and I've only ever once had trouble from the screaming savages since it went up.'

'We won't have any trouble with them tonight,' one of the sailors said, brandishing a sword. 'They use iron for weapons; no match for a good steel blade like this one.'

'If you stay awake, that is,' Bomar said to the man as he went below. 'Well, gentlemen, I'll show you to your cabins. They're the best on the boat, but I'm afraid they're not much. Are you used to sleeping on board ship?'

'Not recently, but it's not a problem,' I answered. Every time I'd left Lepidor before, it had been on our manta, never on a surface ship. But I had spent a few nights at sea in the training boats. My father didn't like it because it was so dangerous if a storm came up.

Sarhaddon shook his head. 'I came out on a manta,' he said.

'There's very little difference from a bed on land unless the weather's bad. Would you care to join us for supper on deck? We'll dine on the fish some of my men caught this morning.'

'How do you eat when you haven't had a chance to do that?' I asked.

'Either we land and go hunting, or we eat dried fish, which is just as bad as it sounds.'

Bomar led us down the companionway at the base of the quarterdeck and along a narrow passageway with five doors leading off. Sarhaddon was in one of the passenger cabins – a small, poky cubicle with a tiny porthole. I, on the other hand, would take over Bomar's cabin, the starboard half of the great room at the end, twice the size and much more comfortable.

Suall and his companion, who would be sleeping in the crew's quarters, had dumped our bags earlier; they were now on deck, playing cards.

Supper was eaten in the cabin opposite mine – the port half of the end room, which boasted a faded carpet on the floor and some battered wooden furniture. It was lit by flickering oil-lamps in wall sconces, and I could hardly see anyone's face, let alone what I was eating.

While the food for officers and crew was being prepared by the ship's cooks, two crewmen who'd been instantly nominated by all their fellows, Bomar's deputies – first and second mates, sailing master and purser – sat around the table and told each other various tall stories of their or their friends' exploits. Each new fantasy was greeted by a chorus of derisive cheers; I felt that the best one was the helmsman's tale of an incident on a pirate ship off Ethna Island. Apparently they had sunk a small trader, but had then been spotted by a Cambressian frigate. When the pirate captain had made a run for it, the frigate had given chase, but then had been lured onto a hidden shoal on the south coast of the island. The resulting plunder had kept the pirates in business for several months.

When it came, the meal wasn't as good as I was accustomed to at Lepidor, but it was passable. Afterwards the talk turned to women. Sarhaddon didn't seem disturbed by the sailors' ribald discussion, but then, only a few priests were required to be celibate – the Sacri, the Inquisition and cloistered priests.

There was no trouble from the tribes that night, and when we sailed out of the bay in the morning I thought it had been as if there were no such people.

'What will you learn in the Holy City?' I asked.

The *Parasur* was making its way through wavelets off the easternmost point of Haeden Island, on which lived members of our clan, Lepidor, as well as people of our ally, Clan Kula. To port, I could see a bleak, rocky shoreline rearing up into mountains a short distance inland; huge piles of boulders spilled down from the mountainsides right into the sea, bare and stark. The shoreline was composed mostly of cliffs, their stone grey and black. I couldn't see any vegetation or animals for miles in either direction, although inland cloud covered the tops of the mountains, and there was no way to see up there.

Bomar interrupted our conversation, strolling over from the brazier on deck, which he had been watching intently.

'You can see Mount Hesion today,' the captain said, pointing through a gap at the base of two mountains to another, which divided sharply about ten thousand feet up, two gaunt spires thrusting high into the air a further five thousand feet or so. 'A friend of mine in the Kulan Marines told me there's an ancient castle in the saddle between the peaks.'

'How ancient?' Sarhaddon asked.

Bomar shrugged. 'Judge for yourself – the tribes have been in control of that area since the War. They used to use it, apparently, until a lightning storm shattered the walls and the main tower when they were sheltering after a raid.' He opened his mouth to say something else, then spotted a rock ahead and sprinted up to berate the helmsman.

'Interesting diversion,' Sarhaddon said. 'Proof of the power of

Ranthas, though. Punishing the barbarians for their refusal to follow him.' Despite the number of storms, lightning strikes were very rare around Haedon, and, according to my father, all around the Haeden-Nurien storm band as well as the Pharassa-Liona band below it. It was just another peculiarity of the storms.

'Why would anybody dispute Ranthas's power?' I asked as we sat down, as usual, on the bale of cloth below the poop deck.

'There are some still who believe in the other elements, who dispute the omnipotence of Ranthas and His acts. The very few, but the fear is magnified out of all proportion by the Sacri commanders and the zealot High Priests. It's only in the Archipelago that there are more heretics than believers.'

'Do they pose a threat to the Domain?'

'Skies above, no!' Sarhaddon said. 'It's wrong to dispute the supremacy of Ranthas, fundamentally wrong. That's their sin. But in themselves, that apart, they aren't a threat. The priesthoods of the other four elements fight amongst each other; there is no organized structure or proper alliance between them. Most of them wouldn't harm the Domain anyway, as the Exarch in Pharassa told me. The problem is that the Domain believes dissent is dangerous, so prefers to try and wipe them out rather than convert them to the true path. But every heretic burnt means another generation will hate us.'

'Is this a widely held view?' I asked. A large seagull had landed on the ship's side and had fixed its beady eye on us. We stared back at it, and a moment later if flew off.

'In the provinces. Not on Equatoria itself, I believe. There aren't many heretics there, but it's where the Holy City and the sacred places of Ranthas are. They send in the Sacri and Halettite armies to crush outbreaks of heresy there.'

I remembered what my mother had said. Unintentionally, Sarhaddon had confirmed every last word. But surely, if Sarhaddon and the High Priest in Pharassa could regard the heretics as mere deviants to be converted, they weren't really such a great problem?

'So what *will* you do, or learn, in the Holy City?' I said, repeating my question of a few moments before.

'I'll study the writings of the Prophets of Ranthas, the teachings of the Elders, and the interpretation of other sacred texts. Also, the Holy City is the only place where they teach the ceremonies and secrets necessary to become an Avarch.'

'Mostly academic study, then.'

'There's also a physical training programme, to purify the body. At least, that's what they say. I think it consists mostly of hunting down the most beautiful slave-girls, judging by the inspectors they send out. And those who demonstrate exceptional ability and are blessed by Ranthas can become Mages, able to channel far more of the power of the gods than ordinary Avarchs.'

'I saw a mage in Pharassa, I think, a few years ago.' I vaguely remembered seeing an unusual-looking priest among a group of high-ranking dignitaries. I was only six at the time, though, so it wasn't a very clear memory.

'They wear flame-coloured robes.'

'Yes, it must have been a mage, then. He was in a procession, next to the King of Pharassa.'

'I even know his name,' Sarhaddon said, and grinned. 'That mage is called Itaal. He wormed his way into the King's confidence and has been whispering in his ear ever since. An utter reprobate, and he has a harem of several dozen beautiful slave-girls.'

'Is he supposed to?'

'Not according to the Prophets. But some teachings of the Prophets are ignored these days, by everyone except the fanatics. Common sense, really. What's the point of staying celibate, even if you are in the service of Ranthas?'

'To purify the mind?' I suggested, jokingly.

'It's a lot less pure if it has no outlets for the distracting thoughts that occur from time to time,' Sarhaddon said, half seriously. 'Of course, some of them claim to be so pure they can ignore such feelings. Those are the dangerous ones. Often they're zealots. The worst one is a Sacrus called Lachazzar: he's the effective commander of one of the three Sacri chapters. In addition to being unpolluted by worldly thoughts, he believes that the Domain should use its armies to enforce religion far more strictly. In effect, he wants the Domain to rule the world.'

'How much power does he have?'

'You're learning fast, Cathan,' Sarhaddon grinned. 'Too much, but at present the Second Prime and the Commander of the Sacri keep him in check. Since the Second Prime will almost certainly be elected the new First Prime, Lachazzar's influence will be contained. With luck, after the choosing he'll be sent off with a hundred Sacri and told to convert all the tribes in the interior of Huasa.'

'Is that the Domain's equivalent of exile?'

'More like death, actually. At least, from what the Cambressians told me. The barbarians over there are the strongest ever encountered. Outside the territories of the clans themselves, no one dares venture down the coast without a squadron, or into the interior without an army.'

'Despite their seeming holiness, the Domain has ways to get round everything, then?'

'Everything,' Sarhaddon said. 'It's really a very large empire with tiny chunks of territory spread out all over the world, which uses its channel to the gods to further its own interests. There aren't many who actually put Ranthas first.'

'Which type of priest do you intend to be?'

'I don't intend to be a fat, power-grabbing prelate, put it that way,' the acolyte said, gazing out over the tossing blue-grey waves and the wheeling seagulls. 'Nor a bigoted, narrow-minded Sacrus or Inquisitor. What of you, though? Do you intend to stay as Count in Lepidor all your life?'

'What else would I do?' I said. But Sarhaddon's question had set my mind working, and I began to wonder what it would be like to choose. 'Lepidor is my clan and, however small it is, it needs government, needs a good ruler. I hope I can be that ruler; if I'm not, then my brother will be.'

'Haven't you ever wished that your life wasn't mapped out that way? I always had the freedom to choose, and even now I've decided to become a priest there are a lot of options open to me.'

'The nobility aren't supposed to have freedom of choice but, yes, I have wondered what it would be like not to be tied to Lepidor. I'd join the Oceanographic Guild straight away, I suppose.' Was I less adventurous, I wondered? Or was it something else?

'Maybe you've had the sense of duty so firmly instilled that it confines you without your awareness. Still, from now until you ascend to the countship you'll live some life in the open world, spend your year as a merchant apprentice, some time learning to command.'

'My brother's the lucky one: he has a choice of everything, as you did.'

'Still do. About all one can't do in the Domain is become a Merchant Prince. And in five years' time, if your father decides to pass you over, think of it.' I bridled slightly even at the suggestion, feeling that I alone was allowed to speculate about that sort of thing. But Sarhaddon smiled, and I realized he didn't think I would be.

'By then you'll be Second Prime, of course?'

'*Second*? Nothing less than Prime for me, my dear chap!'

'In five years?'

'Less!' Sarhaddon's cry of glee alarmed some of the sailors, who, as usual, looked at their strange passengers curiously.

We reached Kula, capital of the only other clan on Haeden, just before sunset on the fourth day after leaving Lepidor. Kula city was the same size as Lepidor city, but built on an island, linked to the mainland by two causeways that enclosed the surface harbour. There was a small ship in the harbour as well as the fishing fleet, but what drew my attention was something that definitely wasn't a commonplace sight: a war-manta drawn up along a makeshift jetty on the ocean side of the town. Work parties were scurrying about on its blue surface, and I saw three or four huge rents in the polyp armour-plating. The green and silver flag of Cambress hung from a short flagpole, limp in the sultry evening heat.

It was a hot, windless day, and we'd been becalmed most of the morning, delaying us enough to lose Bomar the chance to finish all his work in Kula in a single day.

'I'll give everybody enough money for supper ashore. It's too late to trade tonight, we'll do that tomorrow morning,' Bomar announced, standing on the poop deck, his eyes darting curiously to the Cambressian manta. 'Will you two need it?' he asked us, obviously expecting that we wouldn't.

Sarhaddon began to reply, but I cut him off.

'No, we won't. What time do we sail in the morning?'

'Late morning, about four hours after sunrise.'

'We'll see you then,' I said, pulling Sarhaddon along with me off the ship and on to the quay.

'What's all this about?' the acolyte demanded.

'There's no need to spend travel funds on a night in an inn. Count Courtières of Kula is an old friend of my father's, and even though he's away I know his son. We should be welcome at the Palace.'

'I see. I bow to your good sense here. Which way is it?'

'Isn't it obvious?' We were standing on the quayside immediately in front of the gate from the harbour to the city. Ahead of us a wide street ran up to a busy market square. Beyond that was a building with a five-storey tower, the Count's pride and joy: it was the tallest building on Haeden.

The stalls we passed going along the main street were packing up for the night, their owners moving merchandise inside and taking down the awnings. Few paid us any attention. The situation was the same in the main square, where all the traders were departing, leaving the two marine guards in front of the Palace gates standing vigil over the bare frames of the stalls and a few cats rooting around in the debris.

'Good evening, Master and Acolyte,' said the guard on the left, a young man I didn't remember from my stay here the previous year, although that wasn't surprising – the storms had been so bad most of the marines had stayed put in their barracks across the street. 'Master' was a title used for strangers whose rank one didn't know but guessed was higher than one's own. 'May we be of assistance?'

'I am Escount Cathan of Lepidor, and this is Acolyte Sarhaddon,' I said; 'Escount' was the title given to a Count's heir. 'We're here to visit Escount Hilaire.'

The guard's eyes widened, but his companion nodded and said, 'Enter, please. The Escount is entertaining the commander of the *Lion*, but he will welcome your presence. Meraal here will take you to him.'

'F – follow me,' the other guard said, leading us inside the open gates and into a large atrium off the small courtyard beyond. As we walked through the stone-floored corridors, I relaxed; this was the place outside Lepidor that was most like home, and I had memories of many happy days spent here while the Counts were conferring. I hunted, swum, and practised arms with the Count's second son, Carien. Carien was a year older than me, and already embarking on his years of experience as a merchant's apprentice in Taneth.

'He's in here,' Meraal said, stopping outside a bronze-bound wooden door, from behind which came the sound of men's voices, loud and jovial. Evidently Hilaire was entertaining the Cambressians right royally. Meraal knocked on the door tentatively.

'What is it?' called a voice, quite high for a man's. I recognized Hilaire's tone.

'Escount Cathan of Lepidor is here, Your Honour.'

There was the sound of steps, and the conversation faded into silence. The door was flung open, revealing a thin, brown-haired man of twenty-six in a royal white robe.

'Welcome, Cathan!' he cried warmly, ushering both of us in. 'Too long since I saw you. Who's your friend?'

'Acolyte Sarhaddon. My "escort".'

'He's welcome, too.' The Escount's eyes narrowed. 'Escort to where?'

'Taneth.'

'You must tell me why you're going all that way in your father's absence. But first, the introductions.' Hilaire made a sweeping gesture, taking in the other three men in the room, all of whom were sitting around the table.

'Xasan Koraal, Captain of the Cambressian manta *Lion*, his deputy Ganno, and the trade representative Miserak of Mons Ferranis.'

All three inclined their heads while I studied them as politely as possible. Xasan was a powerfully built man with unusual sandy hair and a ready smile; his deputy Ganno was black-haired and narrow-faced. Miserak was the astonishing one, though: his skin was far darker than that of either of the Cambressians, and his face was a different shape. I knew the Mons Ferratans were black-skinned, but I'd never seen one before.

The Escount clapped his hands to summon servants, and ordered more chairs. When they arrived glasses of wine were poured, and we sat down as Hilaire demanded to know what we were doing.

CHAPTER III

Hilaire listened avidly as I told him about the iron find, and the reasons for the journey to Taneth. The presence of the Cambressian commanders ensured that everyone who mattered would soon know, but since Bomar's sailors would in any case be spreading it around as gossip, that wasn't a problem. Nothing that concerned trade ever stayed a secret for long.

I watched Hilaire, detecting hope of more profit in his gaze. The iron would put Lepidor on the map and Kula would benefit too, since more ships would call in on their way up the coast. The Kulans would be jealous, though: Lepidor would graduate from being a typical obscure clan – like Kula – to one of the biggest resource producers in Oceanus. I thought how lucky it was that Kula wasn't significantly more powerful, militarily or otherwise, than Lepidor, and that Count Courtières was my father's oldest friend.

'Are you going to look for a permanent contract in Taneth?' the Cambressian captain, Xasan asked. 'With one of the Great Houses?'

'I think so. The First Adviser said that's what my father will want to do.'

'You as well, young man,' Miserak, who had so far remained silent, said. 'Get involved in these negotiations. Learn how it all works. Nothing beats a good deal.'

'Before you leave,' Xasan said, 'I'll give you a list of the Houses that would be best for this. Most of them have no scruples at all and wouldn't hesitate to cheat you or bend the contract. There are only a few that actually honour their contracts to the letter, and they tend to be the biggest, although not the flashiest.'

'Thank you for that,' I said gratefully. If Xasan's information matched his good intentions, it could save us hundreds of corons and several weeks of searching.

'Pardon me for asking,' Sarhaddon said to Xasan, after a second of silence, 'since you must have been asked this already, but what happened to your ship?'

I'd been as curious as he was.

'Attacked by someone, we were,' Ganno said, in a strange rough accent I'd never heard before. I wondered if he was Cambressian at all.

'There was an underwater storm surge out to sea, about a week ago – you probably felt the tail end of it up on the Lepidor coast,' Xasan explained. 'We were caught in the deep ocean and nearly pulled down; we only survived by the skin of our teeth and through Ganno's skill at the helm. As soon as we could, we headed back towards the land to avoid any more that might be brewing, and find some safe cave to surface. There's only one on that part of the coast, and we searched for a whole day, but the place was nowhere to be seen. Eventually we spotted the mouth of the Lyga River. It's hardly perfect, what with the currents and eddies, but there was nowhere else, and the *Lion* was still taking on water. We mounted a watch, because the natives round there are none too friendly and they'd sell their souls to get their hands on a manta.'

'Turned out it wasn't the natives we had to worry about,' Miserak put in. 'It was another manta that attacked us.'

'Another manta?' I said, wondering who would dare to attack a ship of Cambress, even thirty thousand miles away from Cambress itself. One simply didn't mess with them; they were the best sailors in the world, from what I knew.

'Bigger than us, it was,' Ganno said. 'Two hundred and fifty yards wingtip to wingtip, and with darkened windows. Black armour, too.' That threw me: I knew that manta armour was always blue – the colour of the polyp is was made from – so how could you get black armour?

Xasan continued. 'Because we weren't expecting a sea attack, and our sensors were directed at the land, we didn't see the thing until it was only a few hundred yards away and charging up its pulse cannon. Our own cannon were damaged, but the watch got a torpedo off; I didn't see if it hit. Then the black thing started pounding us in earnest, trying to wear down the shields. And they even called on us to surrender, the hellspawn.'

All three took up the story after that, and I spent most of the time trying to piece together what had actually happened from the three accounts. The *Lion* had been hit in four places, and serious damage done to its armour. The attacking manta had also fired torpedoes at the Cambressians, and then, for no apparent reason, had turned away and headed back out to the depths, soon disappearing in the gloom.

'I've never heard of anything like this black manta,' the Escount said. 'Only Pharassa and the Domain operate mantas in these waters, and why would they build a black ship and attack the Cambressians? Pharassa and Cambress are at peace, and it would be suicide for Pharassa to make an unprovoked attack. It's possible the manta was Imperial Navy, but that seems doubtful, because it's too blatant for them even though they hate Cambress. As for the Domain . . . they don't paint anything black.'

Ranthas's colours were red and orange; the Domain believed in Light and Fire, and that all darkness contained evil.

'What language did they speak?' Sarhaddon asked. 'When they hailed you, I mean.'

'Archipelagan – same language as everyone else. Maybe a bit of an odd inflection, but I couldn't tell you where from.'

'All I can say is that I'm not coming this way again without company,' Ganno said.

'Will Cambress send a squadron to investigate?' I asked.

'Cambress will send a squadron if the Great Council and the Admiralty stop quarrelling for long enough to give the orders,' Xasan said dryly. 'At present it takes hours of discussion to get them to agree on what day of the week it is.'

'Worse than the Halettites,' Miserak agreed.

The Halettite Empire was the major power over most of the Homeland continent, Equatoria – the only continent whose interior was inhabited by civilized people. From being a small colony in the years after the Scattering they'd risen to conquer the rest of the heartland.

In recent years the Halettites' expansion down the Twin Rivers, Ardanes and Baltranes, towards the sea had been cause for concern. Their territory now bordered that of Taneth itself. Fortunately for the rest of us, they had no deep-water ports or manta yards, and no fleet to speak of. The Tanethans, with their fifty-plus war mantas, controlled the rivers' mouths, and stopped the Halettites going any further, while the Thetians poured money in to maintain the status quo. Even from what little I knew about the region, I dreaded the thought that they'd ever break out.

But, most importantly, they were fully supported by the Domain in all their conquests and attacks, to the extent that, as Sarhaddon had said, elaborating on the matter later, Sacri fanatics frequently fought beside the Halettite armies against heretic settlements in the remote Equatorian highlands.

'Have they campaigned recently?' the Escount asked.

'Not recently, but there's some bad news for the rest of us. Reglath Eshar has returned from exile.'

Hilaire's smile disappeared, and he reached for his gem-studded goblet. 'Reglath? Prince Reglath, the brother of the King of Kings?'

'The same. He appeared in a remote fishing town far in the south-east, outside Halettite borders, and when the King heard he welcomed him back with open arms. It's said that Reglath has changed, though, that he's lost what humanity he ever had.'

'Precious little *that* was,' Ganno said.

'Who's Reglath Eshar?' I asked tentatively, looking from Hilaire to Xasan. I was reluctant to display my ignorance but I was anxious to know what they were talking about.

'You haven't heard of him?' Xasan shifted position on his couch, pulling a fold of his tawny-coloured captain's cloak out from under his chest. 'I suppose Lepidor has nothing to do with Haleth, so their affairs wouldn't concern you. They will now that you intend to deal with Taneth.'

The Cambressian captain told me that Reglath Eshar was the present Halettite King of King's blood brother. No one knew exactly where he was from, and he hadn't been heard of before six years ago, but he'd proved to be an excellent soldier. He had won several battles for the King of Kings of that time and, with his conquest of the last refuge of the Galdaeans, his fame had threatened to eclipse that of his blood brother Alchrib, the heir to the throne. A year ago, Alchrib had murdered his father and assumed the crown. Assassins had been sent after Reglath, then on another campaign, but he had eluded them and disappeared. Alchrib had proclaimed Reglath's exile, but not ordered his death. Since then, nothing had been heard of Reglath.

'Why has Alchrib welcomed him back, though?' Aurelius asked.

'Surely Reglath poses a threat to his brother's power?'

'It may be that Alchrib believes he can keep Reglath under control, or that they've struck a bargain of some kind. The danger for the rest of us is that Reglath is the best commander the Halettites have. Taneth and her satellites will be in even more danger.'

'Surely only the small clans, not Malith or Ukhaa?'

'If the Halettites move against them, it is possible that Malith or Ukhaa will fall, after a long siege. And if Malith falls, the gateway is open for the Halettites to threaten Taneth. Taneth is impregnable, of course, because it's on an island and the Halettites don't have a fleet. But their territory could be severely pared down, and upriver trade restricted.'

'All this assumes, of course, that the Halettites believe they can threaten or attack Taneth,' Miserak said. 'The King of Kings is canny enough to realize the importance of Taneth's trade to his people. As are his allies the Domain. More likely, he'll demand a heavy yearly tribute, the Tanethan merchants will pay it, and life will go on as before.'

Tribute was an accepted substitute for war and control, used all over the world. It was expensive – Pharassa's demands had nearly ruined Lepidor a few years ago – but, I supposed, better than war. I knew that merchants, with the exception of arms dealers, didn't prosper in wartime. Since it was the merchants who ruled most of Aquasilva's clans, generally the clans would pay a tribute to any oppressor – usually either the Halettites or the Thetian Empire – and go on with their business. Both parties would benefit: the merchants from keeping their peaceful trade, and the receiver of the tribute from the money.

Small states on Equatoria often considered it beneath their dignity to pay tribute, and would refuse it and consequently be destroyed – I wondered how they could be as blind as that, and not see how out-matched they were. Any rational Aquasilvan put profit before pride, with the possible exception of Halettites and Archipelagans.

'It would be the first time the Halettites have show sense,' Xasan said. 'Usually they can't see past the end of their swords.'

'Cities in the interior are one thing, Taneth is another. And they do have little niceties on their side like elephant cavalry, which the Halettites are no match for, and the support of the rest of the world.'

'Is the rest of the world sensible enough?' Sarhaddon said, drinking deeply from his wine glass. I hadn't touched my own yet, and I took a few sips so as not to seem impolite. It was 'guest wine', the best in the household, reserved for when important strangers came visiting. That the Escount had brought out his best wine for a mere manta captain showed how far the shadow of Cambress reached.

'We should be,' Xasan said, then added, 'if we'd stop squabbling.'

Miserak glowered briefly at the Cambressian, but I felt he held no rancour, and was merely making a point.

'Over who owns Mons Ferranis, possibly?' said the Escount. 'In addition to your internal disputes.'

'That's a sore matter with us at the moment,' Ganno said, 'and likely to be for a while. I don't doubt that if Taneth is threatened, though, the Admirals will stop their quarrelling and do something to help.'

'I think we're worrying ourselves too much,' Xasan said. 'Even if the Halettites attack Malith, *and* if they refuse the tribute, it will be ten years or more before Taneth is in serious danger. And in ten years, a lot could happen.'

'And what's that supposed to mean?' Miserak asked sharply.

'Nothing much,' Xasan replied cagily.

'I propose a toast,' Hilaire said loudly, 'To peace, prosperity and the confusion of the Halettites.'

'I'll drink to that!' Miserak said, draining his goblet in a long draught.

The conversation continued after that on matters of far less importance, mostly concerning the intricacies of trade. Servants came in and lit oil lamps, raised on marble columns, as the evening drew on; outside the windows, the few remaining noises from the harbour ceased.

Later on, we ate supper in the count's personal dining hall, a larger room than the one we'd been talking in, its floor tiled with geometric patterns that I could remember staring at during an interminable diplomatic event several years ago. The food too was honoured-guest quality, and a welcome relief from fish. It was traditional that one didn't serve fish to sailors in port, because they ate so much of it while at sea and were grateful for the change.

'When will your ship be leaving tomorrow?' the Escount asked Sarhaddon as we sat around the table.

'Late morning sometime, after Bomar's finished his business.'

'Oh, you're with Bomar, are you?' Hilaire grinned. 'He demanded an audience with me on the way up, complaining he'd been short-changed by one of the merchants. It was just a zero in the wrong place in his ledger. Well, I'll offer you hospitality for the night, of course, and send a servant to wake you up an hour in advance, if you're not up already.'

'If you don't mind, Lord Hilaire, can we turn in now?' Xasan said, yawning. 'It's been a long day, and there are more repairs tomorrow. I'd offer to take you people on to Pharassa, except the *Lion* won't be in fighting trim for another four or five days. Oh, and I'd better draw up that list, as well.'

'Bring writing materials,' the Escount said to a slave, who hurried away and returned soon with a piece of scroll paper and a quill pen, which he handed to Xasan. The Cambressian captain propped the tablet on his knee and began to write.

'I'll put them in order of size; a bigger concern usually has more money to keep its ships in trim. House Hiram is the biggest, and the second largest House in Taneth. They trade all over the world. The second is House Banitas, only slightly smaller. Third, House Jilreith, who only trade to the east and north; no concerns in Huasa, Thetia or the interior of Equatoria. Fourth, House Dasharban, a new House on the way up that should go far. Fifth, House Barca. They're old and were almost ruined by years of mismanagement, but they have a new House Head with a reputation for honesty. Anyone you ask who lives there will know where the Palaces of all five are. Jilreith and Barca can be hard to contact, as they both have strongholds along the Delta.'

'Thank you, again,' I said.

Xasan stood up, and the rest of them followed.

'May you strike a profitable bargain, and prosperity shine on Lepidor.'

'May your ship win all its battles, and prosperity shine on Cambress.'

'*And* Mons Ferranis!' Miserak said, glaring again at Xasan's back. Both of them erupted into laughter, no doubt helped by the amount of wine they'd drunk.

Servants guided Sarhaddon and me to large, well-appointed chambers looking out over the sea. I knew mine well: I'd stayed here several times before, and I was too tired to do much more than simply fall asleep.

I'd had two glasses of wine the night before, I realized in the morning; it was dangerously close to my limit, and I was lucky to be awake at all. Neither of the Cambressians were anywhere to be seen, nor was the

Escount, even several hours after dawn, but Miserak was sitting on a bench in a corner of the kitchens when we went down to grab some provisions. Despite having had a large number of drinks the night before, he seemed perfectly clear-headed.

'Watch out for that black manta, boys,' he said amicably as we turned to leave. 'You'll be going past that river mouth. Oh, and there was something Xasan was too proud to admit last night. Since I wasn't one of the crew my pride isn't damaged, but don't pass this on.'

'What?' Sarhaddon asked. I noticed him wincing slightly as a shaft of sunlight from one of the windows fell on his face. He'd had a lot more to drink than I had the night before.

'That ship was commanded by a woman. The voice that called on us to surrender was definitely female, and we heard another woman's voice in the background. They were both a bit muffled, but definitely belonged to women.'

'This gets even more peculiar,' Sarhaddon said after we'd taken our leave of Miserak and the Palace, and were walking back through the early-morning bustle to the harbour. 'The Archipelagans are the only people outside Mons Ferranis who have women warriors of any kind, and they're all ceremonial temple guards, like the rest of their army.'

'Do the Mons Ferratans have women warriors?' I asked, startled, trying to visualize such a thing.

'The Mons Ferratans are a strange lot. They have an elite corps, consisting entirely of women, that guards their most treasured asset. But, while they *would* have reason to attack a Cambressian manta, if they thought they could get away with it, we're three months' journey from Mons Ferranis here. The Mons Ferratans have no interests up here, and they'd never have slipped past all the patrols guarding the cities without being noticed. None of it makes any sense.'

We walked out through the harbour gate to the accompaniment of screeching gulls and saw the *Parasur*'s sails being hoisted.

'Looks like we're a little late for Master Bomar,' I said, spotting the *Parasur*'s master waving urgently from his deck. 'Better hurry up.'

I nearly slipped up on a fish carcass and Sarhaddon bruised his knee on an anchor, but we made it around the harbour's edge and up the *Parasur*'s gangway in record time.

'What have you been dawdling around for?' Bomar demanded.

'It's still half an hour to when you wanted us to be here,' Sarhaddon said.

'To hell with that! We have to get well past the mouth of that devil-cursed river by nightfall! I have no intention of losing my ship to a fleet of the minions of darkness!'

Ahead, Kula's cutter was already attached by its tow rope, and Bomar's first mate gave the order to cast off. Suall, my gorilla-like escort, was helping the sailors. Kula was friendly territory, so he hadn't needed to accompany us. Pharassa would be a different matter.

'We're clear!' the first mate shouted.

'Row!' Bomar yelled at the Kulan cutter commander, who gave a cheery grin and barked an order to his crew. I could see Bomar almost jumping with impatience as the *Parasur* swung slowly round and was pulled out of the lagoon. We took up our accustomed places on the bale and watched the scenery go past. The harbour smells – of rope, pitch, caulkers and fish – gradually faded as we drew abreast of the entrance. Out at sea Bomar hardly paused to throw the pouch across to the cutter with the pilot's fee in it before heading the ship south-west at full speed.

The *Parasur*'s crew had evidently been talking to the Cambressian manta crew the previous night and, clearly, they'd all been drunk. It seemed natural that the Cambressians would exaggerate the enemy's strength to lessen their shame at being caught unawares, but they'd taken their tale-telling to ridiculous lengths. Doubtless the story would be all over Pharassa when they docked and then no master would sail up-coast without an armed escort, which would hardly be good for trade.

If the sailors' accounts were to be believed, the *Lion* had been attacked by at least ten black mantas, all with huge numbers of pulse banks and sixteen torpedo-launchers. However, as the water was very shallow many of their projectiles had missed, because any sane man knew that fighting inshore was very difficult, even for servants of evil bloodsucking creatures that were accustomed to seeing in the dark. The Cambressians had rallied bravely and severely damaged three of the enemy, causing them to melt away into the night, with chilling howls and the sound of unearthly music coming through the water.

'Amazing how things can be exaggerated, isn't it?' Sarhaddon said thoughtfully, as we ploughed on under the midday sun, now sitting under one of the awnings always rigged up at this time of day when the sun became too harsh to stay out under. 'If we hadn't heard the true version last night, from Xasan and from Miserak, how would we know what to believe? For all we know, Reglath Eshar's reputation as a commander could stem from a single charge in a single battle, which was built upon by rumour and magnified out of all proportion, so that now enemies flee at the mere mention of his name.'

'Sailors are a superstitious lot, and more prone to exaggeration than others,' I said, thinking about his words. 'I would think a hard-headed merchant would be able to scale the story down and guess how it actually was, realize that the *Lion* wouldn't have survived against three mantas, let alone ten.'

'I don't know. Perhaps,' Sarhaddon said, his eyes staring into the distance out over the restless sea. 'But now you have seen how stories – and myths – begin. Maybe in fifty years' time Xasan and his crew will be shining heroes of a long-ago era who battled valiantly against a devil's horde until Ranthas sent a thunderbolt down out of the sky and saved them. Or something of the kind. Maybe they will become prophets of Ranthas and someone will invent a Prophecy of Xasan. That is what's wrong with the Domain, as well. We make up prophecies, did you know that? Any Magus who starts prophesying is locked up immediately and his sayings recorded, then altered to suit the Domain's plans. That's why so many of them say *Destroy all heretics*. Some Magi even invent their "foretellings" quite cynically.'

'Don't the zealots disapprove?'

'They don't disapprove of *anything* that gives them an excuse to hunt down more heretics. They are interested in the purity of Ranthas's faith, certainly, but they only want to turn their attention to the Domain itself once all heretics are wiped out. Lachazzar's different; he thinks that the house has to be put in order first, but he really *is* on the lunatic fringe.'

'You paint a stark picture of the Domain,' I said, looking at Sarhaddon, seeing only his profile still gazing off into the distance. He was prone to these periods of thought and pensiveness, and when he was like this I could see what he was really like. A dreamer, I'd concluded two days ago, only one with his feet planted in the real world.

'It seems to be the truth. I just hope I can make a difference, do something to change it and bring something of the mysticism that has been lost back into it. Without killing hundreds and thousands of people, as Lachazzar would prefer.'

Sarhaddon's voice was taking on an almost soporific tone, lulling the senses. I made a conscious effort to shake off the creeping drowsiness this induced until I could feel again the motion of the boat and the rushing of water beneath the hull.

'Do you think you can?' I asked, not wanting to disturb Sarhaddon's calm.

'If I can rise high enough, perhaps I will be able to reform a city. As Prime, I would make the Domain what it was meant to be, an organization for worshipping Ranthas and educating men.'

After a long pause Sarhaddon shook his head and tore his gaze away from the far distance. Around us the sailors were sitting in small groups, gambling. They played with wooden counters because their voyage wages were either already spent or in Bomar's hands. Bomar snored on a pile of canvas under an awning on the foredeck. Only the helmsman and one other were on the deck, and three up in the crow's nests, changing shifts at regular, and short, intervals.

'What do you make of the black manta, then, Cathan?' Sarhaddon said. 'Creatures of the night, renegade Pharassans, Thetian operatives, Mons Ferratan assassins, Domain fanatics? You haven't said much about what you think, only asked questions.'

'That's because you've been solving the problem for me.' I was only wearing a tunic, yet I still felt uncomfortably hot. I took a swig of the diluted lemon juice that was drunk to relieve thirst on board ship.

'Only speculating.'

'You know much more about the way the world works than I do,' I said. 'This mysterious feud between Mons Ferranis and Cambress isn't the talk of Lepidor; we've hardly even heard of it.'

'Why should you? High politics over on the other side of the world. I'll explain what's happening later; it requires an ability to think clearly, which the heat saps away.' Sarhaddon leaned back against the planking.

'You keep on thinking about it, I'll listen until I can find a reason why anyone would attack a Cambressian manta in the dead of night and then run off again.'

'Hopeless!' Sarhaddon threw up his hands in despair. 'Does your brain vegetate when you spend your life in a Palace?'

*

That next day and night Bomar pushed his men to the limits, dropping anchor in the harbour of the tiny settlement of Korhas, a friendly tribal fishing village, three or four hours after sunset. In the morning the village headman, who was clearly pure tribesman, like most of his population, came down to greet us. Bomar apologized for our late arrival but, curiously enough, there was no reaction of horror or fright when the headman was told about the black manta. He simply nodded his wizened old head sagely, bargained some fruit and supplies for a little of Bomar's cargo, and wished us well on our journey.

We encountered no trouble of any kind the next night and on the morning of the fourth day after leaving Kula, the seventh out of Lepidor, we rounded Vextar Island and sighted Pharassa.

CHAPTER IV

The city known as the Jewel of the North was built on a large island a few hundred feet from the mainland shore. White houses, many with columns and porticoes, started at the water's edge and heaped on each other up the sides of the central hill, growing richer and more opulent as they went higher. Each one was surmounted by a roof garden of luxurious greenery that put Lepidor and Kula to shame, and in many of the gardens flagpoles bore the devices of their owners' families. On the flat land at the eastern end of the island a huge, monumental ziggurat rivalled the hill and dwarfed everything else in sight, rising more than two hundred feet above the street. It was surmounted by two identical shrines, from which thin columns of smoke rose into the blue sky.

Behind the island I could see a vast complex of wharves and docks, including a yard big enough to build arks, that held hundreds of ships; I could see their masts even from this far way. More ships than visited Lepidor in six months were entering or leaving the harbour, under the watchful eye of two squadrons of six galleys flying Imperial dolphin banners.

And the vast metropolis that glittered before us in the sunlight was only half the size of Taneth of the Delta, if accounts were to be believed.

At the entrance of Pharassa's surface harbour we were met by a cutter manned by sailors in coarse green tunics. The boat was identical to those in Lepidor and Kula, which wasn't surprising; after all, they'd been built in the same yard to the same specifications.

The officer commanding the cutter waved to Bomar and shouted to him to throw his tow rope down. Bomar obliged, and soon we were being pulled across the harbour. I was struck by the similarity to Kula: the harbour of Pharassa was also a lagoon formed between the island and the shore. The difference was the scale: Pharassa's harbour stretched hundreds of feet along the city's shoreline and took up a large proportion of the landward side. Wharves extended from the shoreline, each with room for five or six ships to dock at, and behind the wharves were ranks and ranks of warehouses.

About halfway along, a large pyramidal building caught my attention, rising six or seven storeys above the water, balconies stretching all the way around the outside. This was the Imperial Naval Headquarters for Oceanus, and the command centre for the Pharassan clan navy, surrounded by moored ships of the line and frigates of the surface fleet. I'd been taken on a tour of the complex last time I came, and I remembered my awe at the sheer size of some of the ships, as well as at the huge tunnels and caverns beneath the island that provided cargo space and connected the military headquarters to the undersea harbour on the other side. Pharassa's harbours had been built centuries before the fall of the Thetian Empire, centuries before even the Tuonetar. Now they were home to the largest Imperial squadron outside Thetia itself – last time I'd been here it had consisted of twenty-eight ships of the line, nineteen frigates, numerous smaller craft and twenty-one mantas.

I turned my attention away from the pyramid as the cutter towed us right through the harbour's mass of shipping, ranging from scows hardly bigger than the cutters to Merchant House arkships, white-sided, six-masted titans towering even over the pyramid.

'From Taneth, that one,' Bomar said as we passed one of the arkships, a black, green and red flag flapping from its foremast in the breeze. Two seawood-powered tugs pulled it serenely through the water, other ships moving out of the way. Its master, standing haughtily on its poop, wore a rich blue robe. 'That peacock on the deck will be her captain, not even a member of the House. Shows you how rich they are down there.'

The harbour smell was once again all-pervading, even stronger than in Kula. Above the din of shouting and ships unloading, I could hear hammering from the shipyards along from the military harbour, together with the clink of metal on metal. Two mid-sized merchantmen were towed past on our port side, separated from each other by mere inches, heading for the sea. Their masters appeared to be arguing fiercely across the narrow space of water in between, while interested crewmen looked on from bales of bleached cloth stacked high on the deck.

Another vessel, a five-masted ocean galleon with an orange-and-yellow Merchant House flag, swung across our bow, provoking a stream of curses from the cutter's commander. After half a minute or so of tirade, the galleon's master deigned to look over the side and stiffly apologize for any inconvenience. That, according to Bomar, was another Tanethan ship, belonging to House Foryth.

The *Parasur* finally slipped into a berth between two other similar coasters, one almost deserted; her crew were evidently enjoying the delights of Pharassa. The other was loading goods, to the accompaniment of much cursing. Her captain waved cheerily to Bomar; I guessed they were acquaintances.

When the ship had been secured, Bomar walked over the Sarhaddon and me where we stood in the waist of the ship. Suall and the other guard were carrying the bags again.

'You've been good passengers. I wish you well in Taneth, Cathan, and may Ranthas smile upon you. The same to you, Sarhaddon, in the Holy City. And I look to see your father, the Count, coming back with news of more prosperity for Lepidor.'

He saw us down the gangplank and then returned to his business. I looked back at the *Parasur*. It hadn't been a bad journey, I reflected. In fact, it had been interesting. Especially the stop in Kula with the Cambressians.

Then Sarhaddon pulled at my arm and we set off along the docks.

'Where are we heading for?' I asked.

'First, the military harbour. The fleet runs the fastest regular service from here to Taneth, carrying official government dispatches and ambassadors. Passage doesn't cost anything for high-ranking people like you, and I can pretend to be one of your entourage. After that, if the courier manta isn't leaving today, we'll need to think where we're going to stay. What about the Lepidor consul here?'

'We could try him,' I answered, 'but I can't stand the man. He resembles nothing so much as a crocodile lurking in the reeds. My father gets on with him, but I'd rather sleep in a fishmonger's.'

'I can understand. Well, that leaves three options. The mantas go once every six days, so I hope we don't have to wait too long. A week's delay could mean we miss the Aquasilvan Council, and your father will be on his way home. But, unless we're lucky enough to get a ship this afternoon, we can either stay at the Palace, the Temple, or at an inn. I wouldn't recommend the third: our funds aren't up to staying somewhere relatively safe, and while you may be trained in the arts of battle, there are toughs here who have thirty years' experience.'

'What does the Temple have going for it?'

'It's fairly luxurious, free, and you'll get to know more of the Domain there. Ah, here's the military harbour.'

We were now walking between the city itself and the walls surrounding the fleet base. I could see the heads of patrolling sentries above the parapets, along with the muzzles of one or two pulse cannon. A few dozen yards ahead a long line of timber carts coming from the opposite direction were turning in through the gates of the military shipyards, supervised by a group of men in silver breastplates and plumed helmets, carrying swords at their sides.

'Leave this to me,' Sarhaddon said when we reached the gates. He turned to the officer in charge of the small detachment and asked, 'Where could we find out about the Taneth run?'

The officer turned and his gaze flickered up and down, taking in Sarhaddon's best set of acolyte's robes and my own dark red robe with its patterned sash.

'Who are you?'

'Escount Cathan of Clan Lepidor and escort.'

'Warrants?'

They were certainly on their guard here. I reached inside my pouch, its leather strap finely worked in silver thread, and produced a scroll bound with the clan seal of Lepidor. It was my proof that I was who I claimed to be. I'd need it to secure passage on the manta and entrance to the Council in Taneth.

The officer took the scroll, which wasn't sealed, and scanned it. He seemed to find it acceptable, handed it back, and pointed inside the gates.

'Harbour Master Goraal's office, first on the left once you're inside.'

'Thank you,' Sarhaddon said. I nodded thanks as well, and we moved past the two alert scale-armoured guards and through the cool arch of the gates. Inside, the compound was a hive of activity.

Pharassa's military harbour compound hadn't changed at all since I'd first seen it about three years ago. Warehouses and sheds were built up against the outer wall, their interiors like dark caves stacked with arms, cordage, sailcloth and timber.

A broad quay ran along in front of us, perhaps forty feet wide and bustling with activity – carts transporting wood, detachments of marines, seamen lugging bales of canvas past. Beyond that jetties enclosed double berths for the ships themselves, which varied greatly in size. One or two had just arrived or were getting under way, with men scurrying around on their decks, but for the most part they were manned only by a few sleepy watchmen. Down at the far end were the bones of a ship on the construction slipways.

A few yards further down, a wide stone bridge led out to the pyramid, which had a fountain now by its main door, shooting out crystal-clear water – that hadn't been there before, I remembered, and wondered how they could have such clear water in a harbour. A group of men were heaving a handcart with a statue on it over to the pyramid – more decoration for some admiral's study?

The harbour master's office was similar to a merchant's booth: the front was cut away to form a counter, with the harbour master sitting behind. Three or four scribes were busily working at aether consoles in the room beyond. The counter was shaded by a brown awning that had obviously seen previous service as a sail.

There were three or four people waiting already. I guessed from their clothes that they were all sailors or officers, so Sarhaddon and I stood behind them while the two guards waited off to one side. The first person seemed to be taking an agonizingly long time to agree on some small matter about a cutter. Eventually he reached an agreement and stomped off with the peculiar rolling gait of a man who'd been a long time at sea and had only just landed. After him the others in the queue dealt with their business quickly, and it was a welcome relief when we got under the awning at last: my robe was a little too warm for standing around in under the hot sun.

The harbour master was a large man in a rich dark green robe, his blond beard unfashionably long.

'Escount Cathan of Lepidor would like passage on the courier manta to Taneth,' Sarhaddon said. It was normal, indeed expected, to have someone act as mouthpiece and aide for one of my rank, and Sarhaddon seemed to have taken the place by default. Anyone would have been preferable to Suall.

I handed the scroll over again, complete with the Lepidor seal and

signatures of Countess Irria and First Adviser Atek. Harbour Master
Goraal scrutinized it more carefully than the officer at the gates had, but
eventually he nodded approval and handed it back.

'Count Elnibal's son, are you?' He spoke directly to me.

'Yes.'

'He came through a few weeks ago, on the way to the Council. Is this
your entire entourage?'

He frowned, looking around for anyone other than the two of us.

'My entire entourage, plus those two guards,' I said. 'And all the
baggage.'

'You believe in travelling light, I see. Since I assume you're hurrying
to reach the Council before it breaks up, you're in luck. *Paklé* leaves from
gantry twelve tomorrow morning; be at the undersea harbour three hours
after sunrise. You won't be needing accommodation here, I assume?'

'We don't know where we're staying,' Sarhaddon was saying, 'since
we only just got in.'

'You'd be best off at the Palace, but we can put you up in the senior
officers' apartments. None of them actually live there, they all have
Palaces on the hill. Come back by sunset if you need our help. Your seal
will get you through the gates tomorrow.'

Sarhaddon thanked him and we left the military harbour.

'So, we have to find one night's accommodation,' Sarhaddon said
when we were standing at the bottom of the street leading into the city
– the main road, not the one going through the harbour districts.

'Any suggestions?'

'The Palace is most comfortable. At the Temple . . . well, it's hard to
say. They always like to make sure the aristocracy looks on them with
favour. The Exarch isn't a bad sort, either, for a political appointee. He's
the one who thinks the heretics are unimportant.'

We turned from the wide, crowded street onto a broad avenue that
was still more crowded. A large group of richly dressed men on horseback
were riding up the middle, towards the Palace. Struggling along behind
them was a cart stacked high with wine barrels.

'I think we should follow them,' I said. 'If they're going to the Palace,
we turn straight back around and head for the Temple. Most likely, with
the King and his Heir in Taneth, some of the younger sons and the
Council are taking the opportunity to hold drunken parties.'

'Do all the nobility here do that?' Sarhaddon asked lightly. He may have been far more streetwise than me, but I did know, at least, what the Pharassa island aristocracy got up to. Not that it was much of a trade-off: they weren't a particularly interesting bunch.

'The third son here in Pharassa is an inveterate womanizer. Normally there's someone to keep him in his place, but this year the Heir has gone to Taneth with his father, so I suppose the safeguards they'll have put in place didn't work. The second son's no use either – he's a religious maniac who's into hair shirts and the like.'

People of all nationalities thronged the streets, rich and poor alike, and opulent stalls lined the sides. We passed from the lower part of town, heading up the hill, into the quarters of the more reputable trades: the silk merchants, the goldsmiths, jewellers and wine sellers. People's clothes began to get smarter and of better quality, with trimmings instead of bands of different colours.

Thalassa's architecture was subtly different from Lepidor's and Kula's. There were a lot of fluted columns, and the buildings tended to be square, without domes. The main marketplace had apparently once been a political meeting place, and I could remember being shown an inscription above the door of an ancient strongroom: *Republica Pharassae.* Republic of Pharassa. It had been destroyed by Aetius two hundred years ago – according to the Domain. After what my mother had showed me, I wasn't so sure any more.

When the horsemen rode in through the front gates of the towering Palace at the top of the hill, its five-storey towers and elegant architecture dominating the city, I stopped.

'I'm not staying in the Palace during one of their wild parties. However comfortable and luxurious it may be, it isn't worth the hassle of being called a country squire by those wastrels in their drunken orgies.'

'You sound quite bitter,' Sarhaddon said, looking at me.

'I must have a puritanical streak. I've never felt an inclination to drink to distraction.' Actually, that wasn't the reason at all.

'A saving grace, that, when I remember some of the priests in Taneth. Come, we'd better head downhill again. We're in the wrong part of the city for the Temple.'

Not that one couldn't see the Temple from virtually anywhere, I reflected as we approached it, the gigantic bulk of it looming high above us. Lepidor's Avarch had told me that all the Domain's temples were built to the same pattern: a huge ziggurat, its size and height reflecting the wealth and prosperity of the city, with a large compound of smaller buildings stretching out around its base. The ziggurat at Pharassa was a three-stage one: a massive first storey, going about eighty feet up, then, on top of that, a broad platform, followed by second and third storeys of fifty and twenty feet respectively. On top of the third were the twin shrines, their outer walls gleaming with gold decoration. All the levels were reached by a massive staircase that ran up the front from the courtyard at the structure's base, and by two secondary sets of steps that ran up the side of the ziggurat and joined the main staircase in a sort of gatehouse construction at the top of the first storey. It was a breathtaking monstrosity, and I couldn't help but feel humble beside it.

As we watched, a procession of red-robed priests emerged from the two shrines at the top and began making their way down the central staircase with slow, measured steps.

Sarhaddon squinted upwards at the sun, which was directly above them, more or less; the glare made it hard to see. 'The midday blessing,' he said. 'It's traditional in the ziggurats.'

We approached the buildings of the compound, their outsides forming a solid wall, with the only gate leading into the central courtyard. Through this two streams of people were moving in both directions. Mostly they were of the poorer classes: workers and small tradesmen. They were paying, or had just paid, their daily respects in the courtyard. The richer inhabitants of Pharassa – the majority of the merchants and higher-status artisans – would pay their respects later on, when the day was cooler and there weren't so many people around. *Religion by rank*, I thought cynically.

We passed through the massive gates of the temple with their huge painted-brick gateposts and into the crowded courtyard. Sarhaddon pointed across it to another, smaller, gate to the left of the ziggurat stairs. 'That's the entrance to the priests' area,' he said. 'First, though, we have to pick our way through this lot.' The crowds were constantly moving and jostling each other in their efforts to reach the altars in the middle.

'Perhaps it would be better to go around the sides,' I said. 'It's less crowded there.'

We walked around the back and along the left side of the courtyard: the walls cast only a little shadow on the ground, as the sun beat down mercilessly from overhead. The procession we'd seen leaving the shrines on the ziggurat's summit was just disappearing down the steps against the building itself, which I could now see led down inside the wall that separated the temple complex from the outer courtyard.

'Well, well, I wonder what they're doing here?' Sarhaddon said as we approached the door. I didn't know to what he was referring, but as I looked around I saw what he meant.

Standing at the door to the temple complex were Sacri warrior priests, the first I'd ever seen. Two guards watched over the entrance, each wearing a white trousered robe and shirt and, over that, crimson-lacquered armour. Each held a lance in his right hand and a shield resting on the ground by his left. Their helms, also lacquered crimson, were surmounted by plumes, but below eye level their faces were covered by a cloth of the same red, hiding all but the slits of their eyes from view. I felt an aura of menace about them, and was glad we'd never had them in Lepidor.

'What's your business?' one of them demanded, in a voice that seemed to lack all inflection – a cold, inhuman voice, I thought.

'I am Acolyte Sarhaddon of Lepidor, escorting Escount Cathan of that city to stay in the Temple.'

'We were not informed of your arrival. Do you have proof?' His voice didn't even rise as he asked the question, and I shivered.

Sarhaddon glanced at me, and once again I pulled the scroll out and handed it to the Sacrus. 'May Ranthas be with you, Escount Cathan, and His light shine on your visit here,' he said before handing it back a moment later, and motioned us through. He turned and barked an order to a novice waiting inside, who promptly ran off. 'Someone fit to receive you will be here soon.'

When we were within the small amount of shadow offered by the gate, I raised an eyebrow questioningly. But Sarhaddon motioned me to silence, and I wondered if he was nervous. Inside was a smaller courtyard surrounded by a colonnade; to the right I could see the staircase leading up the ziggurat's face. Two- and three-storey buildings loomed up against the base of the great building, with more on the other sides. The novice disappeared into the darkness of the colonnade opposite us. After a moment there was a flurry of activity, and two priests emerged with four or five acolytes in tow.

'Greetings, Escount Cathan,' said the head priest, a powerfully built man with a pronounced aquiline nose. His robes, while they were the red that was specified for priests, were of high quality, and his belt was inlaid with gold thread. 'I am Temple Master Dashaar, and my companion is Guest Master Boreth. I hear you're seeking accommodation.'

'Where better to stay?' I said, unsure of myself.

'Of course. It is obvious that you are already one who walks in the light of Ranthas.' The way he'd said the phrase, it sounded like something dashed off, repeated by rote. 'Is Acolyte Sarhaddon your escort?'

'He is.'

'Then he will be accorded the full respect due to a member of your entourage.' Dashaar frowned. 'Are these your only companions?'

'I travel light.' Suall and Karak, it seemed, were beneath his notice.

'Come, we mustn't keep you standing in the sun,' Dashaar said. 'Come inside, and we will find quarters suitable for your rank and arrange for Etlae to receive you. The Exarch is away at the moment, I'm afraid, in the Holy City.'

Who was Etlae? As I walked inside with Dashaar and his companions, and the acolytes relieved Suall and Karak of the bags they carried, I wondered at Dashaar's effusive welcome. The man was a slippery, smooth-talking 'mouthpiece', I could see that. But was it customary to fawn over all nobles, however minor they might be? This welcome certainly went beyond what I'd received in the Palace – but why, for a clan heir from what even Pharassans regarded as the back of beyond? I'd need to keep my wits about me.

Once we passed under the shade of the colonnade and through a wide door into the interior, I was astounded at the opulence of the place. It certainly matched the interior of the Palace here in Pharassa, and surpassed anything in Kula or Lepidor. The floors were mosaic or polished white marble; the walls were decorated with tasteful, costly frescoes and the columns were of gilded cedar wood. Even the vault of the roof above our heads was painted in shimmering colours. Incense lamps burned at regular intervals, their smoke pervading the whole building with a sweet, dreamy smell. One could lose oneself in this kind of luxury, I reflected.

Dashaar led us upstairs to a large ante-room and invited us to sit down in cushioned chairs. Wine was quickly brought and poured into golden goblets studded with semi-precious stones.

I see you are admiring our decorations,' Boreth, a smaller man than Dashaar but no less unctuous, said. 'This temple is built to glorify Ranthas, and what better way to honour Him than by lavishing the greatest attention on the places associated with him?'

'Who are these, Dashaar?' a peremptory voice demanded. Everyone looked surprised, and Sarhaddon left his chair and sank to one knee. I was no less amazed when I caught a glimpse of the speaker, who had emerged through a doorway that led to an outside room – there was a light breeze coming through the gap.

The speaker was a woman, tall and angular, dressed in the white and gold of an Exarch. Her face was partially obscured by a veil, but it didn't hide iron-grey hair piled up in a bun behind her head, and sharp, set features.

'You may rise, Acolyte. Greetings, honoured guests. I am Etlae, Third Prime of the Element, Over-Priestess of the North.'

My eyes widened, and I made the obeisance demanded by one of my station to a Prime. A *Prime*, no less, even if a female Prime – a Prime of the element Fire rather than the god himself. What was she doing here in Pharassa, I wondered?

'I . . . am Cathan, Escount of Lepidor.'

'What brings you to the temple rather than the Palace?'

'I preferred to avoid the bravos who have the run of the Palace in the King's absence,'

'Wouldn't you rather be up there with them?' Did I detect a trace of humour in her voice?

'No. Being a provincial, I'm not accustomed to riotous parties.'

'I see,' she said, scrutinizing me. 'And for how long do we have the pleasure of your company?'

She had the manner of a tutor questioning a small child about some misdemeanour, which I found more than slightly galling. Had we made the wrong decision in coming here?

'Until tomorrow.'

'Good.' She turned away. 'I hope to see you again at supper tonight.' Without a word she swept away through a door on the far side of the next room, her robes swishing behind her.

'Does she live here?' I asked, breaking the uneasy silence that fell after her departure.

'She's normally in Taneth,' Dashaar said with what could have been a touch of acerbity, 'and rarely honours us with her presence.'

An Over-Priestess of the North who only infrequently visited her area of responsibility. Was this a pattern repeated elsewhere in the Domain, I wondered? Was absenteeism the norm? Dashaar and Boreth engaged us in meaningless conversation for a while, until a novice in a brown robe appeared and hesitantly announced that a suite had been prepared for the guests. Boreth snapped a dismissal and the young man fled. Then, all smiles again, Boreth asked us to follow him. We went through more of the palatial corridors and up another flight of stairs, where Boreth held a door open and allowed us to pass inside, down a short passageway and into my rooms.

The apartments I'd been assigned put my rooms – indeed, the entire Palace – in Lepidor to shame. Ornately woven matting was spread over the polished tile floor, and the walls were covered in bas-reliefs and hangings obviously executed by master craftsmen. More incense burners stood in the corners, though the air was not as spice-heavy because the rooms led out on to a wide portico with a view over the complex. I was glad of that; after a few minutes in the Temple I had found the all-pervading scent oppressive. How could anybody stand it day after day? The two guards and Sarhaddon would sleep in the rooms in the corridor, and share a washroom; I had one of my own.

'Are these guest quarters?' I asked Boreth, Dashaar having excused himself before we left the antechamber.

'Yes, they are reserved for visiting secular dignitaries such as yourself. Will you be needing to leave the Temple?'

'The Escount has some business he needs to conclude in the city,' Sarhaddon said promptly. 'We'll return later in the afternoon.'

'I'll arrange for word to be left with the guards. Supper for the Temple chapter, should you wish to attend it, will be after sunset in the Exarch's refectory, although it's unlikely he himself will be there. You are also invited to the sunset ceremony in the High Shrines. Is there anything else you require?'

'No, thank you.'

Boreth bowed and closed the door behind him. As our two guards occupied themselves in their own chambers, Sarhaddon shut the door of the main room and leaned against it, shaking his head in amazement.

'What is it?'

'I remembered the Temple here as being fairly luxurious,' he said, lowering his voice and signalling me to speak as quietly as possible.

Fairly luxurious, I thought? And why the secrecy?

'Nothing else is the same. Dashaar and Boreth are new; neither of them were here when I was. Boreth is from Taneth, by his accent. The place is swarming with Sacri, all hiding in the shadows.'

'I didn't notice any, except the ones at the gate.'

'You don't keep your eyes open; you were too busy staring at the decoration like a stunned ox. And the Prime is unnerving.'

'Do you think someone's listening?' I said, my gaze scanning the room, then added, 'She makes my flesh crawl.' She had been rude enough to me that I didn't care if she somehow found out my adverse opinion of her.

'You're right, there almost certainly is someone listening. Honoured guest quarters, and there'll be an acolyte crouching in the rafters listening to everything we say, so that the priests can discover any convenient secret. Anyway, *you said we have to see your father's consul.*' His last words carried an emphasis whose meaning I grasped after a moment's confusion.

'Of course we do. He'll need to be told before he gets to hear from the gossip.'

We made our way back down through the corridors towards the gate, twice losing our way in the twisting passageways. The second time, we went down a flight of stairs that Sarhaddon remembered led directly to the main courtyard, only to find our way barred at the end of the hall by a stout door. Sarhaddon cursed softly and we turned round, but just as we passed a curtained chamber to the left we heard the sound of voices. I froze.

'Won't the Exarch in Cambress object?' said a man's voice.

'The Cambressian Exarch won't be a problem,' Etlae said. 'He's come down with a sudden illness and he'll be unable to attend to conclave for the new Prime's election. If the Cambressians didn't insist on picking their own candidates, they would be less of a nuisance. He's the only one who could stop Lachazzar now, but, rest assured, he won't be there.'

'Good.'

Sarhaddon dragged frantically on my arm. We didn't slow to a walk until we reached the courtyard, and once we'd cleared the outer gates of the Temple we ran again until we were back in the anonymous safety of the city.

CHAPTER V

We walked in silence along the central street again and into the main market square, a huge plaza seven or eight times the size of that in Lepidor and crowded with stalls. Some of them were practically permanent shops, with silk roofs fluttering in the breeze and pavilions with their floors carpeted. Even the smaller ones showed a degree of wealth unheard of out on the coast.

Although the stalls were dispersed over a large area, the aisles between them were packed and filled with people. More than once we were crushed back against the sides of a stall when some merchant rich enough to afford an escort was making his way through.

'Why are we here?' I said to Sarhaddon when the third such man came past and we narrowly missed overturning a cloth merchant's wares. The man shook his fist at us and then at the passing dignitary, calling down curses on everyone equally.

'In case anybody wondered why we left in such a hurry, or spotted us and tried to follow,' Sarhaddon answered. 'There's no way anybody could track us through this.'

'Where are we heading for?'

'I've no idea,' he answered. 'This place is a little too public to discuss anything.' He thought for a moment, then said. 'We should head for one of the gardens in the rich merchants' quarter; we'll blend in there, and nobody will question a Count's son's right to enjoy the peace and quiet.'

'We seem to have missed out on peace and quiet lately.'

'Too right, too right.' I thought he seemed distracted, but that wasn't surprising.

We eventually escaped from the throng of the market square and made our way up a smaller, less crowded version of the central street until we came to a walled expanse of green on the left-hand side. A pleasant smell of greenery and flowers replaced the pungency of the rest of the city.

'This is the street entrance,' Sarhaddon said. 'There'll be a guard. Just put on your most noble air, tell him who you are, and look commanding.'

In the event, Sarhaddon's strategy proved perfect for dealing with the singly smartly turned out watchman who lounged near the gates of the park. I supposed the occupants of the quarter would have their own entrances around the back, and could pass inside without scrutiny. However, I was sure they couldn't have any old riff-raff wandering in, possibly with intent to harm members of the exclusive society of the district.

Inside was a profusion of greenery, fountains and splashing pools, with more than one small tower with a private chamber inside. I felt more at home than at any time since I'd left Lepidor where there was much more room between the buildings and there were a lot of open spaces. The gardens in Pharassa's lower town had been built over centuries ago, and it felt somewhat uncomfortable and sterile.

'It seems these towers have a lot of uses,' Sarhaddon said, looking inside one and spotting a woman's scarf carelessly discarded on a small staircase leading downwards. In others I heard the muted sound of voices conferring in hidden chambers, loud enough for their presence to be noted once inside, but quiet enough to be inaudible to a listener outside. Pharassans probably saw these gardens as the place to conduct business that wouldn't stand up to official investigation, I reflected. Would there be spies listening in? Surely the merchants wouldn't allow that.

We eventually found one of the towers that wasn't in use. The below-ground chamber was small but refreshingly cool, and its only furnishing was a stone bench around the sides.

'So, what's all this about?' I demanded.

'Put simply,' Sarhaddon said grimly, 'some traitors are scheming to make Lachazzar the new Prime.'

'*Lachazzar?* As in the heretic-burning, sword-wielding fanatic you told me about?' Sarhaddon had been emphatic about Lachazzar's position on the lunatic fringe. How could people be considering him for Prime, then?

'The same. It seems he has supporters in high places.'

'What was all that about removing the Exarch in New Hyperian?'

'The Cambressians – in other words the whole of New Hyperian – appoint their own Exarchs,' Sarhaddon said, pacing across the circular floor of the chamber like a penned bull.

I knew that, although I couldn't remember from which of my tutors I'd heard it. They'd won the power to do so twenty years ago, when the Domain grew too pushy and interfering. The Cambressian Admirals – their leaders – imprisoned all the priests and Mages in their territory, and threatened to send an expeditionary force against the Holy City itself. That must have been when the Halettites were weaker, I reasoned, because now the Holy City was considered unreachable by a hostile army.

At that time the Domain were too weak to enforce their decisions, so in the end they caved in and allowed the Cambressian government a fair amount of control over the temples in their territory, including the right to control appointments to Avarchates and Exarchates. Because of that, the Exarch of New Hyperian, one of the most senior of all the Exarchs, second only to those of Taneth and the Holy City in importance and power, was usually an independent figure. And with Cambress's fleet backing him up, his power must be quite considerable.

'The present one is no exception,' Sarhaddon finished. 'He's a moderate and sensible man, and his support could sway the election. If – as I understand from that conversation – he's been poisoned, then the Sacri from New Hyperian won't be there to influence the choice of Prime. Without their support and the Exarch's presence, the moderates will lose a lot of power. You can see what'll happen in that case.'

I didn't know or understand much about politics outside Oceanus, despite my father's best efforts to teach me. But even I could see what Sarhaddon meant.

Thousands more would die, and the Domain's hands would grow heavier. Moderate Avarchs would be replaced by zealots intent on rooting out the slightest trace of original thought. And even New Hyperian could be affected, although I found it hard to imagine an organization as scattered as the Domain having too much power over Cambress. Still, Cambress's naval ascendancy – stronger even than Taneth's – had lasted for centuries, but they hadn't gained even a modicum of control over the Domain until a few decades ago.

New Hyperian . . . the manta! Xasan's attacker, the black manta! Military matters were something I *did* understand.

'Then the Domain could have been behind that attack on Xasan and the *Lion*.'

Sarhaddon swung round suddenly in mid-step, his eyes lighting up. 'Ranthas's fire, Cathan! That could just be it! Perhaps Xasan stumbled on something when he was here, something to do with the plot. Even if he tried to conceal it, they could have found out he knew.'

'Or perhaps it was a diversion, intended to focus the Cambressians' attention up here,' I suggested.

Sarhaddon looked puzzled. 'What would they want to divert Cambress away from?'

'Shady goings-on in Equatoria? Moving large numbers of Sacri around? It's only a guess.'

More likely they're afraid that someone will see a connection between any strange happenings, so they're inventing some ghosts to cloud the trail. Whatever this plot, it reaches all the way across Aquasilva.'

I felt myself gripped by a cold fear. These people had poisoned, or intended to poison, the Exarch of New Hyperian. It seemed unlikely that they would baulk at doing away with a troublesome princeling and acolyte who'd learned of their intentions.

'But there's nothing we can do except get killed, so why involve ourselves?'

'We can warn your father when we reach Taneth. He can then pass the warnings on to the rest of the Council, and perhaps they can do something.'

'Will he believe us? Will they?'

'Perhaps it's a shot in the dark, but it's the only way anyone will ever find out. Although even then it may be too late. The last I heard, Prime Halezziah was fading fast, and had only weeks to live. He could die before we reach Taneth – for all we know, he could already be dead. It's a week upriver from Taneth to the Holy City, and another week to here.'

'Do you have any idea how the Prime is actually chosen?' I asked.

'It's some kind of election, with all the Exarchs and the three Under-Primes voting.'

'How many Exarchs are there?'

Sarhaddon stood still and looked thoughtful. 'Ten: Oceanus, Thetia,

New Hyperian, Equatoria, Huasa, the Archipelago, Silvernia and the Isles, and the Exarchs of the Sacred, Inquisitorial and Monastic Orders.'

So with only thirteen voters, the absence of a single Exarch, especially a widely respected one, would have an impact.

'How many of those are likely to support Lachazzar?'

'That's what I'm not sure about. This is only guesswork, of course, because I don't know exactly how things work, or how strong the alliances are. But the three Order heads are almost certain to vote for a hardliner, the more zealous the better. The Archipelago, too. New Hyperian and Oceanus are both liberals, probably the Silvernian as well. And the Second Prime is bound to vote for himself.'

It seemed fairly even, then . . . as long as New Hyperian was there. But if Etlae's plot were to succeed, he wouldn't be. Was there anything we could do, in any case? It was an internal Domain affair, over which even the Aquasilvan Council had no jurisdiction.

Sarhaddon started pacing again, and I thought for a moment. 'Wouldn't it be better just to forget we heard anything?' I said.

He stopped abruptly, and looked at me with a confused expression somewhere between puzzlement and surprise. 'Why?'

'All we'll be doing is drawing attention to ourselves – or to my father. The Council can't do anything, and even the Cambressians can't threaten the Domain the way they used to.'

'So you'd say we should just let this go.'

'Would you rather lose your head?'

'Scared, Cathan? What about the thousands of people who'll burn if Lachazzar succeeds?'

'How can we stop Lachazzar succeeding the old Prime, though? Warn the Cambressians? If Halezziah's as ill as you say, we'll almost certainly be too late. Then Cambress will want to know how we found out. And once Lachazzar is Prime, there'll be nothing we can do anyway.'

'I suppose you're right,' Sarhaddon said. It didn't make me feel any easier or more comfortable, just sordid at having rated my own family's survival above that of thousands of others. But what *could* we have done?

Sarhaddon, being a mere acolyte, wasn't invited to dine with the ziggurat's Chapter that evening. He had been whisked off to supper in the refectory by another acolyte who was a few years younger, and I was left to find the Chapter suite by myself. It wasn't an easy take – there were surprisingly few people around.

I set out from my room with a vague idea of where I was going – Boreth and Dashaar were both otherwise engaged – but within a few minutes was totally lost. I reflected gloomily that my sense of direction seemed to be even worse than my arithmetic – and I hadn't thought that was possible.

I finally met someone in a narrow, tiled corridor on what I hoped was the first level. Even though it was after dark, there were hundreds of lights – supplied, I'd been told, by a system of pipes that ran within the walls, sourced from an underground oil reservoir – and the wood-panelled and tapestry-covered walls reflected the light and turned it inwards. It was warm and actually rather friendly, I thought, very different from the grandeur of the daytime. I was still lost, though, and I was wondering what had happened to the ziggurat's couple of hundred residents when a girl came out of a side door a few yards ahead. She was clutching what looked like a bread roll and some dried fish. She saw me and groaned.

'Curses! Of all the bad luck . . .' Then she peered more closely, and I saw guarded hope on her face. 'Who are you?'

'Lost,' I admitted.

She pushed a clump of untidy red-brown hair away from her face with the back of her hand and heaved a sigh of relief. 'You're only a visitor. Where are you going?'

'The Chapter Rooms.'

'Exalted company. Bunch of hypocritical, stuck-up time-servers who shouldn't be running a kennel, let alone a ziggurat,' she said scornfully. 'I don't care if that offends you – after all, what have I got to lose?'

'I'm not Domain,' I said, wondering who she was. She was about my age, perhaps one or two years older, dressed in a shapeless brown novice's robe. She was also as tall as me, and broader across the shoulders as well – although that wasn't hard, because I was as thin as a rake and fairly short.

'I hadn't guessed, of course. You don't look like you own the world. Since you're not one of them, I can be perfectly civil to you. If you'll just let me dispose of these—' she held up the bread and fish '—somewhere, then I'll be happy to show you where the piggery is.'

'Piggery?'

'I'll tell you in a minute.' She brushed past me and disappeared down the corridor. I turned round and saw her surreptitiously looking out into the next corridor. Then she vanished around a corner. A moment later she was back.

'So much for fasting. The Chapter dine on ice-deer meat brought all the way from Silvernia, but the novices have to purify their bodies by fasting. Oh yes, that's exactly the will of Ranthas.' She paused, breaking off the diatribe. 'Sorry, I forgot. I'm Elassel Sandriem.'

'Cathan Tauro,' I said.

'Title?' she asked, setting off in the direction I'd been heading earlier.

'Escount. How did you know?'

'Only people with titles or vast amounts of money eat with the Chapter. You were either going to be an aristocrat or the heir to some company or other. They don't bother with people whose coffers aren't bulging or who have no influence.'

'Why are you a novice, if you hate the Domain so much?'

'My stepfather, who's a priest, is doing six months' missionary work in the interior, so he enrolled me as a novice to keep me out of trouble until he and my stepmother get back. I think he was hoping I'd find a vocation, but he won't be that lucky.' Her tone suggested that the stepfather would regret enrolling her in the first place as well.

'What are you doing here?' she asked, taking me up a flight of steps. I saw a statue I recognized from earlier, and realized I'd been on the wrong level.

'I'm on my way to Taneth. We discovered iron ore, so I'm taking the news and some samples to my father at the Council.'

'Which clan are you from?'

'Lepidor,' I said, as we crossed the ziggurat's main corridor, twelve or fourteen feet wide, and went up another passageway, more sumptuously decorated still. The sound of someone playing a lute drifted out of another side corridor and Elassel stopped abruptly. I didn't stop in time, and bumped into her.

'Sorry,' she said, turning round as I stepped backwards. 'I've never heard that player before, and I thought I knew all the lutenists in the Palace.'

I paused for a moment, wondering what she meant. 'You mean you can tell who's playing just from hearing them?'

'Of course,' she said, as if it was the most natural thing in the world.

'It helps that I've heard them all play at some time or another. Most of them aren't very good, but whoever that is has a gift.'

'And what about you?'

'I'm the best of the novices, and better than most of the priests. It's the one thing I can do without tripping over my feet.'

I hadn't met anyone as direct as her before – nor anyone my own age, except Courtières' third son who treated me as an equal – and I found it rather refreshing.

'This is it, by the way – the Chapter rooms are just round the next corner. I won't go any further, because there'll be Sacri guarding it, and they give me the creeps. A pity you're not staying, I could do with some company. Goodbye.' She smiled at me, and then hurried off in the direction from which we'd come. I stood there in puzzlement for a moment, wondering why she seemed familiar. I should have asked her where she was from.

But I was already late. I didn't want to offend the Chapter, so I went on the way she'd indicated, and into a wider corridor with a pair of bronze-plated double doors at the end. Two Sacri stood impassively in front of them, wearing exactly the same armour and uniform as the ones I'd seen earlier.

'You are Escount Cathan?' the left-hand one said, in the same chill, dispassionate tone as the one who'd spoken to me earlier. Did they train them to speak like this?

'Yes,' I said, suddenly aware under their blank scrutiny that my belt was slightly lopsided. He said nothing for a minute, then opened the door. 'Follow me.'

The crimson-armoured warrior-priest took me along a vaulted hall festooned with antiques and through another impressive door. We emerged in a high-roofed room, its tall windows covered by scarlet curtains.

Seven or eight priests and one priestess – Etlae – were sitting round a large, polished dark wooden table. Dashaar, who'd spoken, stood up and asked where my escort was. He said that Boreth had been sent to find me, but that he'd been distracted on the way – or that was what I thought he said. Dashaar dismissed the Sacri and showed me to the remaining free seat, two places along the oval table from Etlae. The table laid for the meal was a work of art, with china and crystal that surpassed anything we had in Lepidor.

As the five courses were brought in, each successively more extravagant than the last, I remembered Elassel's remarks about the piggery. I could see what she meant. All of the Chapter ate with gusto, and looked as if they did this regularly. There were exceptions – Etlae, who limited herself to small portions of the less exotic dishes, and one other priest, tall and gaunt, who ate virtually nothing.

The conversation, after they'd asked me about the iron mine and what I was doing – I claimed not to know the exact extent of the deposit – was mostly about political matters, and I didn't understand most of it, although I tried to remember as much as I could. Some of the priests were rather condescending, which I found irritating, but I wasn't really concentrating. Only towards the end of the meal did the Chapter's talk turn briefly to something that caught my attention.

The Treasurer had been talking windily for some time about the ramifications of some trade agreement that the Domain had established with a clique of Tanethan Great Houses, to better regulate the trade into the Holy City – it sounded to me like they were creating a monopoly.

'And of course, the next step is a deal to ensure the safety of our people travelling to and from the continents,' he said.

'Why would we need that?' asked a white-whiskered, jowled old man who seemed to be only half awake. He was the Chancellor, which I knew was an honorary position given out to retired Avarchs.

'Because of the attacks,' the gaunt man said. He didn't quite add, 'you fool' but it was implied. 'Several of our brethren have been abducted or killed in attacks at sea.'

'Have they had any leads yet?' one of the others asked Etlae.

'No,' the Under-Prime replied. 'A group of renegades, terrorists, perhaps. The Inquisition's efforts are hampered by the fact that it is their people who keep disappearing. I am sure we will find an answer soon.' Her voice carried a note of finality – she didn't want any more discussion on that subject.

She couldn't stop me wondering, though. Attacks at sea? I wondered if there could be any relation between those attacks and the black manta. Maybe the black manta was a culprit there as well.

Afterwards, before I went back to my quarters, Etlae suggested that I might like to stay another day, to be a guest of honour at the ziggurat's Feast of the Summer Flame, and catch a Domain frigate-manta that would be leaving the day afterwards – it would be faster, so I'd only lose a day in Taneth. I politely declined her offer, remembering that time was running out, and also that it was Domain priests who were being attacked. Travelling on a Domain manta didn't seem safe. Besides, I felt I was safer in the hands of the Imperial military than I would be with the priesthood. I didn't mention the matter to Sarhaddon.

The next morning we ate breakfast in our quarters, then left the Temple by the back door. The route that way was quicker, Sarhaddon insisted, and cleaner than going through the main streets and down to the harbour.

Followed by our two bodyguards, we slipped out into the early-morning bustle of Pharassa's artisans' quarter, which, while busy, was less crowded and dirty than the central thoroughfares. Here was where the artisans' workshops were – goldsmiths, furniture makers, stone carvers, luthiers – anything you cared to name. If we'd had more time I'd have stopped and gone into one or two of the scientific-instrument makers we passed. I needed an aether spectrometer for water analysis – Lepidor's oceanographers didn't have one, nor did the instrument shop back home. I would probably have time to find one in Taneth, I supposed, although my father might not be best pleased. He didn't actively disapprove of my informal apprenticeship to the oceanographers, but I knew he was worried I wasn't paying enough attention to learning how to rule. Maybe Sarhaddon had been right, and I wasn't the right person to succeed my father.

As we crossed a street that led back through the merchant's quarter and past the ziggurat, to the road we should have taken, I saw a confused mass of people filing through the streets, and for the first time heard shouting above the noise of the artisans.

Sarhaddon stopped abruptly. 'Riot', he said, listening intently. 'That's unusual, so near the ziggurat. I'm glad I remembered this short cut, otherwise we'd have been caught in the thick of it.'

A few minutes later we entered the marine quarter, around the under-sea harbour. I felt more at home again – here were the oceanographers, the aether engineers, the offices of the seawood harvesters. Almost every building had a sign of one or other of the marine trades outside it, and those that didn't were living quarters for those who worked here.

Scientists tended to live in the marine quarter as well – strictly under Domain control: there were too few of them to have their own quarter, and oceanography was the most similar trade. Although, of course, the oceanographers were more important. Keeping track of the shifting currents and undersea storms across Aquasilva's vast oceans was vital to trade and survival. I'd never actually seen an undersea storm, thank heavens, but I knew how destructive they were.

After a few more minutes' walking, the noise of the riot fading behind us, we reached the undersea harbour. All I could see of it above ground was a five-storey circular building with a spire on top, its base surrounded by a wall. There were guards on duty at the gates, but they were only there to stop troublemakers and they didn't ask us our business.

As we crossed the compound, heading for the main doorway, I looked up at the blue sky that was dotted with wispy clouds – the last glimpse of it I'd have for two weeks. Still, we'd be at sea: it wasn't as if we were going into a cave for a fortnight, without any water around.

The two guards followed us through the doors and into the building. The ground floor was just the top of the real structure, and held the entrances to the passenger elevators and the stairwell. We pushed our way through the crowds and went down two levels to staircases to the broad sweep of the control deck. There was a wide-open space surrounded by aether displays, official booths, and consoles. I could make out, above the heads of the crowd, the areas devoted to each continent, and finally found the Imperial military in a large section of their own.

'Are you Escount Cathan?' asked a thin-faced young man in the dark green uniform of a lieutenant who was standing by the desk. He had to talk loudly to be heard over the din in the confined space.

'Yes,' I said, producing the official pass. A moment later he handed it back.

'I'm Lieutenant Ierius, operations officer of the *Paklé*. If you'll follow me?'

He took us over to a twin-shaft that had no people around it. A moment later, when the lift – a platform with a rail round it – glided down through the ceiling, I realized it was for military personnel only. There were only a couple of ratings using it, apart from the lift operator who stood by the panel at one side.

'What level, sir?' he asked Ierius.

'Fifteen.'

'Right.' There was a slight lurch, and for a moment I felt my stomach dropping away from me. Then we moved off, leaving the bright ceiling lights and the official bustle of the reception are behind, dropping down into the hub of Pharassa's central harbour. It was one of the biggest, I knew – twenty levels below ground, and docking gantries for sixty-one mantas. Here at Pharassa the continent shelved away under the city, so much of the undersea harbour was free-standing, not built into the rock like the one at my home in Lepidor. Only Cambress, Taneth and Selerian Alastre were bigger: Taneth had ninety-six gantries. And even that wasn't as big as the one in the Thetian capital, Selerian Alastre, which Lepidor's marine historian had told me had more than a hundred.

As we descended, level by level, a few people got on and off, but not many. The navy didn't have much to do at the moment – apart from catching that wretched black manta – so there weren't many of its people around the undersea port.

'Why's your ship called the *Paklé*?' I asked Ierius as we went through level eleven without stopping. 'I've never heard the name before.'

'She's named after a fabulously beautiful woman, some ancient emperor's consort or other. The admiral chose it – personally, I think it was his mistress's pet name.'

Ierius grinned what would have been a cheery grin if it wasn't for a scar across his lip that made him look, I thought, positively sinister.

The elevator stopped. I thanked the operator and followed Ierius across the almost empty expanse of another lobby, this one far smaller. Its walls were transparent, giving a view out into the murky depths, illuminated by searchlights, with the occasional bulk of a manta visible. We went through a door and along the gantry – through the transparent roof of which I saw the *Paklé*.

She was a standard Jewel-class war-manta, her dull blue hull, punctuated by the white lights of portholes, stretching off into the gloom. Below and to my right I could see the port wing, its curled tip showing the slightly lighter underside, then widening as we walked away from the hub.

Standard for her designers, perhaps, but for most people – certainly for me – the mantas were the most beautiful things – by which I mean the most beautiful ships – ever built. Like their namesakes and distant ancestors, the manta rays and stingrays, they moved gracefully through the water with slow wing beats, crossing the vast gulfs of the ocean at speeds of up to fifteen hundred miles a day. It was a pity, I'd always thought, that they couldn't go very deep – no more than seven or eight miles, a tiny distance when you considered that Aquasilva's world-ocean was eleven thousand miles deep. Even the deepest recorded dive – made by an oceanographic research ship fifty years ago – had only been ten miles.

We reached the end of the gantry, where another officer was waiting somewhat anxiously.

'There you are, Ierius,' he said curtly. 'Captain Helsarn's frantic. He wants to leave now.'

'We've got another half-hour or so,' Ierius said, puzzled, as he ushered us through the door.

'Well, somebody's put the fear of Ranthas into him – literally, because there a mage-priest on board.'

'Is everyone here now?'

'Everyone we're taking.' At the end of a short passageway we emerged into the manta's well, the galleried chamber that linked all the manta's levels, from the cargo bay a deck below us to the observation room two decks above.

'Will you want to go to the observation room, to watch us leave?' Ierius asked me.

'Yes.' I didn't want to miss the chance to see the whole of the undersea harbour.

Ierius ordered a rating to take Suall and his companion to our cabins, to leave the bags there, and himself took us up to the upper deck before excusing himself to return to the bridge.

The observation room was the only room on the ship with an actual – not aetherized – view in all directions, and many of the ship's passengers seemed to have gathered there. Most of them, I could tell from their clothing, were military officers or high-level Pharassan bureaucrats, but I thought one or two of the others were important merchants, and Sarhaddon pointed out one in Great House colours.

We found a place by a window on the port side – facing towards the undersea harbour, with the bright lights of the hub and the spotlight-illuminated shapes of mantas above and below us.

A few moments later the manta's deck shuddered slightly, and I knew that, two decks below us, the seawood reactor had been linked to the wings and drive systems. Then there were two muffled thuds and another shake, as the gantry doors were closed and the *Paklé* was disengaged from the docking clamps. Very slowly, the manta began to drift away from the undersea harbour, gradually turning until we could no longer see it from the port side and had to move to the stern. Then the wings began beating, slowly, then slightly faster, and I could see the whole of the undersea harbour hanging in the clear waters, with the rock of the island as a backdrop.

I watched as it receded, until even the vague, indistinct shapes had vanished into the gloom behind us, and we were out in the Sea of Life.

After that, I only went back to the observation deck to watch as the *Paklé* rounded Cape Lusatius and we passed out of the Sea of Life into the unbounded expanses of the Thetis Ocean.

It was there, at the extreme edge of Oceanus's land, that the black manta attacked.

CHAPTER VI

I was just leaving the observation room when the manta shook violently, and the deck dropped away from under my feet. I was caught off balance, lost my footing, and slid downwards towards the observation windows about three yards away.

For a moment I stared down, paralysed by terror, as I slid towards the window, wondering if it would hold. But my fear was replaced by relief and a flash of pain as I hit the wall instead of the window above it. A second later the rest of the people in the room were lying in dazed heaps where they had fallen. Outside the windows, the aether shields flared a bright blue as they were turned on. Then they faded into the background.

'General Quarters!' the comm system boomed. 'All hands to battle stations!'

The manta slowly righted itself, and the floor was level again. I wondered what could have caused the massive lurch – the manta had nearly tipped over on to its side.

I picked myself up and tried to brush my clothes down. The room kept lighting up as the aether shield received more blows. Who was attacking us? Who would ambush a Pharassan manta within the navy's patrol area?

'Where do we go?' I asked Sarhaddon, who had collapsed in one of the padded chairs that dotted the room. I could feel my heart thumping in my chest, but I felt more confused than afraid now.

'Stay here,' Sarhaddon said. 'Sit down. I'm not going to sit blindly in my cabin wondering what's happening. At least here we can see.'

The *Paklé* wheeled round, turning away from its heading into the deep ocean to arc in towards the rock of the Cape. As I saw the underwater crag head-on, growing ever-larger in the aether-enhanced view ahead, I shivered. The rock at this depth was bare and black, and utterly lifeless, a wall of forbidding darkness stretching off in both directions. It was like the desolation of the deep ocean – a cliff on which the sun had never shone, where no animal had ever swum or walked.

The I saw our attacker, and gasped at the same time as Sarhaddon. I heard shocked cries from some of the merchants, and curses from the military passengers, who I saw were rushing towards the door, heading for the bridge to offer their services.

It was the black manta, nearly twice the size of *Paklé*. It was without a shadow of doubt – as far as I was concerned – the one that had attacked Xasan. No lights shone from its smooth black surface, and looking at it was like looking into a darkness infinitely blacker than any night. Beside me Sarhaddon was reciting, almost gabbling, prayers from the *Book of Ranthas* in a fervent voice. Others in the room began joining in, although I hesitated for a second.

Then the ship shook again, and as I saw what could only be described as bolts of darkness hurtling towards us through the water from the other vessel, I too turned to Ranthas for comfort. Maybe there were other gods, but Ranthas was the only one I knew, and if He had given the Domain power, he could surely help us now.

Bright globules of aether and orange flame pulses were now coming from *Paklé* as it returned fire, I saw through the starboard side windows. But they simply vanished when they hit the utter blackness of the other craft's surface.

The *Paklé* was now only a few hundred yards from the rock foundation of the continent, and its forbidding surface filled the whole viewscreen as we shot past the other manta. Then the Pharassan manta turned, and we were heading around the dark, jagged point of the Cape, perhaps trying to put the rock itself between us and our attacker.

Whatever the captain's motive, his manoeuvre failed. Within a minute, a violent concussion sent me sprawling on the floor again, and our manta began slowing down.

Since we were on the uppermost deck we couldn't see what the black manta was doing when it was below wing level. But within seconds we realized where it was.

'Prepare for boarding! Hostile forces on intercept course!'

Boarding was the customary way of finishing manta battles, I knew.

Once a manta's shields were down and its weapons disabled, an attacker would try and board, then kill or capture the crew and tow the defeated manta back to the victors' base for repair and future use.

The passengers' prayers grew louder as they heard the muffled thud when the two ships connected. Then a crewman burst in, shouting, and threw a bundle of swords on the floor.

'Fight for your lives!' he cried, and the voices fell silence. 'We're under attack by a ghost ship! Prayer won't help you, but these might.'

'You err, my son, but I will forgive you.'

I and everybody else in the room turned towards the speaker, who had appeared behind the crewman. He wore the crimson robes of a Sacri warrior-mage.

I suddenly remembered what the officer in the doorway had said. This must be the Sacri mage-priest! Maybe there was hope, if these men were as powerful as I'd heard. Even if they did burn heretics, this Sacrus could save our lives right now.

'Exalted One . . . I . . . I didn't realize!' the crewman stammered.

'I will help you in the fight. Take me to where the demons are trying to board.'

As it turned out, that wasn't necessary. A few seconds later I heard the indistinct sounds of a fight from somewhere down below.

Although I preferred to spend most of my time at sea or with the oceanographers, my father had tried his best to train me to fight. I was so slightly built that I didn't have the strength to match an opponent blow for blow in the proper way, but I was good at the lightning technique, which relied on speed and agility.

I leaned forward and snatched up one of the blades the crewman had thrown down – standard two-handed marine swords, single-edged and slightly curved. I must have stirred the other passengers into action because a moment later everyone else did too, some testing the blades with the critical eye of warriors: merchants though they were, I guessed they'd done military training at some point.

I was glad they couldn't see how I actually felt as the fighting moved down the corridor below and the manta echoed with the sounds of men killing and dying. My stomach had tied itself into a ball, and my chest was pounding and tight.

Searing flames were the first thing I saw as I followed the crewman down the wide staircase from the observation room into the main corridor below.

There I saw a knot of uniformed crewmen struggling with, and losing ground to, a larger group of forms armoured from head to foot in black, their faces covered. Even as I watched, one of the crewmen was picked bodily out of the group by what seemed like a black cloud, and screamed as he was flung a few feet down the corridor in the other direction.

I stood rooted to the spot, unable to flee as my mind was shouting at me to, held by my own fear. I'd never fought in earnest before.

A firebolt hit one of the black-armoured figures, sending flickering lines of fire across his armour and surcoat, and knocking him backwards. Two more turned towards the mage-priest, their swords glinting coldly in the light of the aether roof-panels as they advanced. Another firebolt bounced harmlessly off empty air, striking the corridor wall and scorching it.

Two of the boldest passengers attacked the black-armoured figures, their borrowed swords hammering at the black armour, which seemed able to withstand almost anything. One figure turned his blade and brought the flat of it heavily down on one of his attacker's heads, knocking him to the ground.

I tried to move my legs as the two figures advanced, one sweeping three people out of his way with a blow of his mailed fist. A white glare exploded just in front of his face as the mage-priest struck out with a borrowed sword that was dancing with orange flames. This time it did cut through the armour, slicing into the figure's arm, and a grunt of pain came from beneath the black helmet. But he continued to advance towards me.

I stabbed out in blind panic, aiming for the crack in the armour. My sword hit something hard and then struck flesh. The figure staggered away but I saw the other one lunging and I let go of the sword, instinctively pulling back.

Another passenger threw himself bodily against the second of the two figures, whose comrades were still dealing with the *Paklé*'s crew. The man's face contorted with pain, but the figure was still pushed off his feet, and the two fell headlong.

'Well done!' the mage-priest gasped, his face running with sweat. 'All of you.' More fireballs streaked from his fingertips towards the black-armoured attackers, some finding their marks.

I felt someone grip my arm and turned to see Sarhaddon, clutching a crossbow, offering me another sword.

'Don't use the crossbow yet!' the mage-priest said as the crew rallied and the invaders fell back. 'It may infuriate them, and they aren't trying to kill. I'll protect you if you'll keep any away who get too close.'

I wondered whether the Sacri really were so evil, if this one was anything to go by. He had no obligation to help us, but he was standing in the front line, working tirelessly in defence of his fellow passengers and using up his precious magic to protect us.

The crew's rally proved brief, and the last of them went down under clubbing black blades. Six or seven of the black figures started forward to aid their companions.

'Remember your orders!' a woman's voice shouted from behind. 'No casualties except the priest.'

'Etlae?' Sarhaddon said disbelievingly. 'Traitress!'

I didn't see one of the black figures stop and level an aether crossbow at the priest. All I took in was that the mage-priest suddenly staggered in mid-cast, blood spraying from his chest, and collapsed backwards. I stared blankly at the rictus of hate frozen on the priest's face as he died, blood running from the corners of his mouth, his crimson robes wet with blood. The commanding presence of just a few seconds before was gone, replaced by a bloodied, pathetic heap of crumpled robes. I felt ill.

'Surrender!' one of the black figures called. 'And we will spare your lives and free you. That includes you, Acolyte. We aren't pirates, and we don't mean any of you any harm. The priest was our target.'

Sarhaddon and I glanced around at the other passengers. After a slight pause, one powerfully built merchant-warrior threw his sword down.

'Not worth death or slavery any more, friends.'

His words sparked off a metallic clatter as the seven or eight remaining passengers in the corridor divested himself of their borrowed weapons. It took a second for me to realize what was happening, then I followed suit. The merchant was right: there was no point in fighting any more, not against these odds.

Two of the black figures strode forward and scooped up the weapons, while a third indicated for us all to go back up into the observation room. Sarhaddon and I obeyed, the acolyte only briefly glancing down at the lifeless body of the priest.

Inside the room, one of the black-armoured figures motioned for us to stand over by the windows. My stomach was still tight and constricted with fear. Would the attackers keep their word? Pirates had been known to massacre whole ships' complements to leave no survivors behind to tell tales. My head felt light, and I realized I was breathing in shallow gasps; while I no longer felt sick, I didn't feel any less afraid. Was this how you were supposed to feel, or was I the only one who was scared?

Three more figures strode into the room. Even though all three were wearing full scale armour and masked helmets, I could see that two of them were women: their shape and slimness in comparison to the rest gave them away.

'Your voyage will not be further disrupted,' the man said; his accent was refined and cultured, and he sounded more like an aristocrat than a pirate. 'Our healers will attend to your and the crew's wounds, and you'll be on your way again shortly.'

'Who are you?' one of the passengers demanded.

'You don't need to know that. Any of you who are wounded, however slightly, please see the healer who will be here shortly. My men will stay here until we leave to ensure that no unfortunate incidents occur.'

One of the women leaned over and whispered to the man. After she'd finished, he pointed at Sarhaddon and me, and said curtly, 'You two, come with us. Now.'

I looked at Sarhaddon, who simply shrugged. He didn't seem at all concerned, and I wondered how he really felt. Was he afraid too?

We followed the three figures down the stairs from the observation room, a brief distance down the corridor and into the deserted dining room. The pressure on my chest and the fear had increased again, if that was possible. Once they were in the dining room, both the women pulled their helmets off, and I immediately recognized Third Prime Etlae, her grey hair gathered up to keep out of the way of her helmet. She still radiated her aura of command; however, it was the other woman–girl, more like – who drew my attention.

She couldn't have been any older than I was, possibly younger. She had straight jet-black hair tied tightly back away from her face, and I could tell from the shape of her face – high cheekbones, a narrow chin – that she pure-blood Thetian. Like me. And even though her face was set, and her expression cold and aloof, I found her beautiful. The grey eyes that returned my gaze, had not a scrap of warmth in them, and I felt she was measuring me up like something at an auction. It wasn't very pleasant.

'You two are a problem,' Etlae said, in an irritated voice. 'Why you couldn't have taken the hint and missed this ship I don't know, but you're here and you recognized me. That makes you inconvenient. However,' and she held up a hand to silence Sarhaddon, who had tried to speak, 'we aren't in the business of killing innocent bystanders.'

Had the riot been meant to stop us, then? And what she'd said last night – how could I have been so blind as not to see what she'd been implying?

'Especially those who are brave enough to fight us as you did,' the man said. 'Misguided you may have been, trying to defend a Sacri butcher, but you tried.'

'Butcher?' Sarhaddon said.

'He was a particularly unpleasant specimen. Condemned two hundred people to the stake while serving as a Judicator in Huasa. However, that isn't important.'

'What *is* important,' Etlae continued, 'is what we will do with you. Sarhaddon, you could be a lot of trouble to us now. Are you sensible enough to realize this is a power struggle you'd best stay out of?'

Evidently Etlae was unaware that we'd overheard her conversation with the unknown man in the ziggurat at Pharassa. Otherwise, I suspected, she wouldn't be half so merciful. I offered up a silent prayer to Ranthas, thanking Him for that.

'I have no wish to become involved in Domain politics, Holy Mother.'

'Good. Few people are as forgiving as I am. You will swear an oath on Ranthas and on your vows as His servant never to reveal anything of my involvement in this affair. We will also help you to forget as much as possible of what you have seen. In any case, within six months or so this knowledge will be of no concern to anyone. Do you agree?'

There was a brief pause, then Sarhaddon nodded.

'Yes, I do.'

Etlae produced from her pocket a talisman in the form of leaping flames; I recognized it as the one adornment that all priests wore, Ranthas's symbol, and on which they swore their oaths. Oaths on a flame talisman were considered the most binding of all, even overriding promises to the dying, to one's clan, or to one's House.

Sarhaddon swore a similar oath to the one I'd taken back in Lepidor the day before I left. Then Etlae opened the door and ordered the black-armoured soldier to escort him along to the mind-mage.

They had a mind-mage? This was very creepy indeed; I didn't like the sound of it at all. Mind-magic was a discipline limited to the Inquisition. I wondered if there was an Inquisitor on board, and why, if there was, he wasn't with Etlae.

The door closed again and Etlae turned back to me.

'The mind-mage will also ensure that everyone goes to sleep for half an hour or so once we leave, in case anybody should try to follow us,' she said. 'You're a different problem from Sarhaddon.'

I felt very alone, standing facing the three black-armoured figures, one intimidating, one concealed, and the third unreadable. It was frightening to think that these three – or Etlae on her own – had my future in their hands. I tried to reassure myself, but failed.

'You aren't under the Domain's control, you see,' the man said.

'I could order you to swear an oath and forget, but you will always keep your memory of the infighting that is causing this; you may already have guessed what's going on,' said Etlae.

I hadn't, in fact, until she mentioned infighting. Then I did see what was going on. She didn't realize that I knew it was no ordinary disagreement, but a power struggle at the highest levels, and again I was thankful for that.

'The Citadel.'

It was the girl who had spoken, for the first time, her voice clear and lilting but almost as emotionless as those of the Sacri – like the voice of the King reading a proclamation. Etlae turned to look at her, and I wondered what the girl was talking about, and what the Citadel was. There was only one Citadel I knew of, and that was Selerian Alastre, the Thetian capital. The name meant Citadel of the Stars.

'You can't be serious, girl! Whose side are you on?'

'Ours, of course, Holy Mother. However, didn't you say earlier he was Elnibal of Lepidor's son?' Etlae didn't look like she could ever been anybody's mother, she was so thin and spiky.

'I did, but what does that have to do with it?'

'Whose side is Elnibal on, Etlae?' the man said. 'Ravenna has a point here. He would be a valuable recruit, and it might save us some time.'

Their discussion now totally excluded me, so I tried to take my attention off the matter by wondering what they were up to. Ravenna must be the girl's name, I thought: how appropriate. Hair black as a raven's feathers – and the evil eye of the bird, too.

It was obvious to me now that there was some serious Domain faction-fighting going on, and Etlae's faction was not only poisoning Exarchs but even killing off opposition to put their candidate on the Prime's throne. That was surely the only reason for this mysterious attack and all the business of concealment. As for Etlae's remark about six months, presumably by the end of that time she would be too powerful for any of this information to harm her.

But why, if Etlae was working for Lachazzar, was she killing off the Inquisitors and Sacri who were his allies?

Ravenna suddenly walked over to me, a slight frown on her face. 'Don't move,' she said. For a moment she touched my cheek lightly with fingers as cold as her expression, then drew away and walked back to where she'd been standing. The other two looked at her curiously.

'I think he has potential,' Ravenna said. 'He could be a powerful asset.'

'You're very keen all of a sudden, Ravenna,' the man said. 'Interested?'

She turned a withering look on him. 'Imagination, Uncle! I mean he could be as powerful as I am.'

I felt a chill again. Another mage? Whose mage? The Domain didn't have female mages, they were too chauvinist. And what did she mean about me?

'Are you serious?' Etlae said sharply.

'Quite. Look at the colour of his eyes – nobody has turquoise eyes naturally. He could be amazing, though, if we could train him. I'd have to do a proper test to find out, of course.'

'I'm not sure I want two of you walking around the place, Ravenna,' the man she had called 'Uncle' said. 'One's bad enough. But, if you say so.'

'You'll have to come back with us,' Etlae said. 'It'll mean a year away from home, but the alternatives are being thrown in a dungeon or made an acolyte, and I don't think you or your family would appreciate either of those.'

I stared at her in dismay. How was I to pass word on to my father?

'Can I go to Taneth first? The message I carry is vital for Lepidor's survival, and I'm the only person who can tell my father.'

'You go on to Taneth and it risks everything. We can't allow it.'

'I can't just vanish, leaving my father to go all the way back to Lepidor and then out again to agree a merchant contract. He's in Taneth now, and it's not the time of greatest pirate activity. We'll lose months if we can't agree a contract now, and maybe even go bankrupt.' I risked adding something prompted by what they'd said. 'What use is my father as an ally is he's bankrupt?'

There was a long silence as Etlae seemed to confer with herself. But finally she said, 'You're right. However, we'll have to take some precautions to ensure you don't slip away from us. I can promise you you'll enjoy your time at the Citadel; your father certainly did. I'll also give you a verbal message that you *must* take to him. Understood?'

'Yes.'

'Ravenna, could we use your talents for a moment?' the man said, reaching into a flat pouch that hung at his belt. He fished around for a moment, then produced what looked like a flat metal bracelet. 'Just channel into it after he's put it on.'

'Of course.'

He handed the bracelet to Ravenna, who walked over to me again. 'Hold out your left hand,' she ordered. I didn't need any more prompting: the presence of the other two was coercion enough. Ravenna slipped the silvery-grey bracelet over my hand on to my wrist, then touched it with her finger. I felt a slight tingling and the metal turned a darker shade of grey. It fitted well enough not to slip down but not so tightly that it would rub.

Ravenna stepped away, leaving the slightest hint of perfume in the air.

Etlae said, 'Tell your father, *The Elders greet him, and are anxious for recruits.*'

'"The Elders greet him, and are anxious for recruits",' I repeated, wondering what she meant.

'Don't tell it to anyone else, especially not Sarhaddon. You won't have any trouble from him, and if he asks, tell him you took an oath on your inheritance. In Taneth, we will come and find you. The bracelet will remind you of the message, tell us where you are and make it very difficult for you to tell anyone except your father what has happened. Now come and join the others.'

The two women pulled their helmets back on again and left the dining room, escorting me along the corridor to the observation room. The healers had finished and only two black-armoured soldiers now kept guard.

I'd no sooner joined the others than a terrible drowsiness came over me, and I felt an overwhelming urge to lie down and sleep.

The *Paklé* hadn't been badly damaged, so when the passengers and crew awoke it wasn't long before we were under way again. The passengers were shocked by the attack, and the crew were dispirited for days – I thought they were probably depressed at the ease with which the black manta had broken through their defences and captured the ship. The military passengers loudly declared their intention on their return to pressurize the Admiralty to step up patrols and try and find the pirate bases. But I doubted whether anything would actually be done.

What really interested me was the way the other passengers treated Sarhaddon after the attack. Many came up and expressed their regrets at the terrible incident, and for the rest of the voyage he and I – by association, I supposed – were treated by them as the most important people on board. It was faintly unnerving, and also showed some of the power of the Domain – I think they were afraid they'd be interrogated or accused of complicity in the attack. The ship's chaplain received the same treatment. As the Domain's only representatives on board, the chaplain and Sarhaddon were the only people who the Domain would believe if they held an inquiry.

There were no more incidents during the rest of voyage, although the company at dinner was rather subdued. It might have been shock, or perhaps pretended mourning for the mage-priest. We met no other ships, although that was to be expected, given that we were crossing twenty-five thousand miles of ocean in a shipping line a thousand or so miles wide.

The journey was, in fact, fairly boring, and I spent a lot of time reading, playing cards and talking to Sarhaddon – there wasn't much else to do. I spent quite a lot of time when I was on my own wondering about some of the people I'd met: Elassel and the Chapter, Xasan and Miserak, but chiefly Etlae, Ravenna, and their mysterious companion – what they were up to, who exactly they were, what was this Citadel place?

I only realized later what it was that most intrigued me.

The magic Ravenna and the others had used wasn't fire magic. The only flames in that corridor had come form the mage-priest. Our attackers' magic had consisted of things like throwing crewmen down the corridor with black clouds, and deflecting flame-bolts in mid-flight.

Shadow magic?

The lights on the manta were turned up and dimmed to maintain a semblance of day and night during the voyage, and it was still dark when I woke up on the morning we were due to arrive at Taneth. The precious iron samples were still in Suall's bag, and my mother's letter was safe in my own. I'd be saying goodbye to Sarhaddon today, after the acolyte had delivered me to my father in the Royal Palace in Taneth. Sarhaddon would travel on, down the river, to the Holy City. Once he arrived, it would be entirely possible for him to spend the rest of his life there. I hoped that Sarhaddon would rise in the hierarchy and be posted out; aside from the friendship I felt for him, a Domain priest was always a useful ally.

'We shall be arriving at Taneth within the hour,' the captain announced over the comm. 'You will need to have your papers checked by the Sea Guards, and there may well be a Domain welcoming committee – I am sending a message ahead as required by regulations, so you may be taken to the ziggurat. Taneth will be displayed on the aether table in the observation lounge, for those of you who haven't seen it before. I hope that aside from the attack you've had a good journey. Helsarn out.'

The Taneth defences were watertight, it seemed: we'd been hailed and asked for identification by two patrols during the night and now, as we slowed down among the other mantas heading in to Taneth, there was another naval vessel off to port, keeping a watchful eye on the ships approaching. I wondered what they were afraid of – Taneth had never been attacked either from land or sea.

Leaving my luggage in Suall's care near the well, I joined Sarhaddon in the observation lounge where a glorious image was displayed on the floor aether-panel of the place where we were about to arrive. It was my first proper view of the trading capital of Aquasilva: Taneth, City of Gold.

CHAPTER VII

I'd seen pictures of Taneth before, of course, but never in three dimensions. The image on the huge aether pad set into the floor was a complete replication of Taneth and its surrounding islands. I was amazed they had enough spare power on the manta to generate something this complex – the aether generator depended on the ship's main seawood reactor for its power, and I didn't want to think how much energy this used up: the image was almost five yards long and three or so wide.

It was the city rather than its surroundings that caught my attention. Built in a narrow corridor of calm between two storm bands, Taneth had no need for the looming walls and circle plan of every other city on Aquasilva. The hilly islands that dotted the strait around it were covered with verdant forest, with houses showing here and there in clearings – Great House retreats, Sarhaddon told me.

It took me a few moments to grasp the sheer scale of the city, though. Taneth covered eight or nine islands that formed a small cluster, most of them – or so I guessed, comparing them with the scale given around the side – two or three hundred yards long, and every one covered by buildings, with what seemed like long rows of trees running down every street; larger oases of greenery, I supposed, were parks or gardens. The large island in the centre was over a mile long, and some of the buildings there dwarfed all but the largest structures in Pharassa. The ziggurat alone was about three hundred feet tall. And the buildings weren't white but a warm golden colour.

'Where did they get the stone to build all this?' I asked Sarhaddon.

He shrugged. 'Brought it downriver, I suppose, or maybe quarried some of the other islands.'

I stood and stared at the rest of the image – the huge bridges connected each of the outer islands to the main one, the hundreds of ships in the surface harbours between them. There were so many ships it made Pharassa seem like Lepidor.

But then, Taneth was in the centre of the world.

'Where's the undersea harbour?'

'Under each of the islands,' Sarhaddon replied. 'There's so much cargo space needed that they've hollowed out all the islands for warehouse space, and built a small harbour in each one. We're coming in to Ademar or Kadreth Island – those are the two military harbours, if I remember rightly.'

My gaze remained fixed on the Taneth panorama on the floor until we reach the edge of the harbour. Out of the window I could see the shapes of the islands emerging through surprisingly clear water, each one with the spindly arms of an undersea harbour protruding from bedrock that had none of the untamed wildness of the Cape – it had all been cut and formed into warehouses, sea-ray bays and other structures. All the edges were rounded and smooth.

Then, as I looked down to the bottom of one of the undersea harbours as we passed it, I realized something else.

Taneth was built on solid rock. The islands actually rose up from the base of a shelf a few hundred feet below. There was no open ocean below this city. Instead, like Lepidor, it was actually on a continental shelf. Towards the southern end of the strait, where we were passing, the water was deeper but still had a seabed. I hadn't realized before that the northern and southern parts of Equatoria were actually the same mass of rock.

The *Paklé* glided in on slow, small wing-beats towards a gantry in the mid-levels of one of the islands. When we got as close as a hundred feet or so, the wing-beats stilled entirely and the manta's momentum carried it gently towards the docking gantry. A few minutes later we made contact, and there was a muffled thud as the clamps were engaged.

'Doors are open,' announced a crewman from below.

Within five minutes of our docking, customs officials, the Taneth Sea Guards, were in the well, checking the passengers for wanted pirates or criminals. They recorded our names and our reasons for travel. As far as I could see, it was a pointless exercise, because once in the city people could go anywhere. But Sarhaddon pointed out that almost everybody either arrived or left the Equatorian continent through Taneth, so this was one way of keeping track of how many foreigners were on the continent. Apparently both the Domain and the Council of the Houses insisted on the census. And on Equatoria, outside Halettite territory, the Council and the Domain held absolute sway.

Surprisingly, though, there were no Domain priests waiting for us.

I wondered if Etlae had cleared the way, pulling strings so that news of the attack was ignored. Or perhaps the Domain's efficiency had been decreased by their infighting. Either way, nobody seemed to care about the dead priest and Sarhaddon and I encountered no more than the usual number of officials as we made our way up through the undersea harbour to its surface entrance.

Emerging down the steps from the cool, moist atmosphere in the manta and harbour, the dry heat of Taneth itself hit me like a hammer. I hadn't really thought about the temperature difference, but Taneth was almost on the equator and, without all the storms that beset most other cities, was far drier as well. I felt as if the heat was sapping my strength almost immediately. The air was mixed with smoke and stirred-up dust, but even through that I could smell the difference. The air of Taneth smelled of plants that didn't exist in Oceanus and of warm breezes driven up out of the storm bands from the jungles of northern Equatoria.

'You'll get used to it,' Sarhaddon said. 'I believe each continent smells slightly different. Except Silvernia, that is, where it's so cold that your nose freezes and drops off if you so much as poke it out of the window. Or so I'm told.'

'It's warm here, at least.'

'You may find you have to wash more often while you're in Taneth. One's skin dries out quickly.'

I could well believe him.

'Thanks. Where do we go now?' I looked around at the small, bustling plaza we had emerged in. It was surrounded by elegant buildings of sand-coloured stone with arched windows and a broad colonnade that extended out beyond the buildings at ground-floor level. I noticed that everybody leaving the harbour had headed for the colonnades, and there were very few actually in the centre area, except under the trees.

'We need to find the bridge to the next island. This is Ademar, and I don't think it has a direct link to the main island. We walk, of course; no transport except litters and handcarts is allowed in the city. By order of the Council. In this city the Council's word is law and there's no appeal. Unless you're a priest, of course.'

'Which Council?' I knew there were two Councils in Taneth – the Senate, with all the merchant lords, guild masters and the leaders of Taneth's three clans on it, and the Council of Ten.

'The Ten, of course. The Senate is just a run-of-the-mill body that approves things like going to war. The Ten actually runs the city in the name of the Great Houses. The merchant lords are the only ones who really matter here.'

I remembered my father telling me that the 'Tanethan Republic' was nothing more than a glorified oligarchy, and what Sarhaddon said confirmed that. I could see it even as we walked through the colonnaded streets, sometimes down their galleried sides, sometimes under the shade of the trees in the middle. A Great House head was carried along in his litter, heading for the undersea harbour, and in front of him strode four burly men with whips and sticks, clearing everyone else out of the way. I saw a master oceanographer and an admiral pushed back against the wall while the small cavalcade went past. The ordinary Tanethans seemed to accept it as part of life, though, just moving aside and then continuing on their way.

'Where are we going now?' I asked.

'To the Palace to find your father. Then I'll go to the ziggurat and find out when I'm to leave. There's a regular Domain ship downriver to the Holy City, and it's free, for priests at least. Anyone else has to pay a surcharge.'

'How are we going to find him? There're over two hundred Counts staying in the city: how many people are going to know where any of them are at any one time?'

'Only the senior Palace officials. The most irritating form of life, because they consider everybody's below them. Your diplomatic pass should get us inside, although the security'll be tighter than a tribesman's purse strings. After that – well, you know more than me about what happens at the Conference.'

'I've never been to one before.'

'You know what happens, thought, don't you?' Sarhaddon beckoned to Suall and the other guard and we set off along the long, colonnaded passage of the bridge. Each of the bridges from the central island formed the boundary of one harbour, I realized; the only ships that could travel between the harbours were those small enough to pass through the arches of the bridges, like the wherries and barges that were tied up by the landing field's docks.

'My father explained what's *supposed* to happen, but I got the strong impression that most of the time they sit around drinking and telling each other stories about the skirmishes they fought when they were younger.'

'What do the younger ones do?' Sarhaddon said, grinning.

'Go out and fight skirmishes, presumably. The Conference is a wonderful idea, and as old as time, but there's nowhere near enough business to keep them occupied for a week, let alone a month.'

'I'd think the Halettites were a cause for concern,' Sarhaddon said, frowning. It was unusual for me to know more about something than Sarhaddon, and a change to be telling instead of asking. I was looking forward to seeing some of the Conference first-hand; elder sons rarely went until their fathers were too old or had too much on their hands to travel. It would be useful experience for when I went myself, although as my father was only forty-six that was unlikely to be for some time yet, Ranthas willing.

'The Halettites are only a cause for concern to the Equatorian Counts and the King. Apparently most of the rest couldn't care less, and are only interested in matters that affect them.'

'Fools,' Sarhaddon said absently. 'They'll regret it when the Halettite armada descends on them.'

'Will it? The Halettites've never been able to operate anything bigger than a fishing fleet.'

'I suppose not. The Domain doesn't want them to, and the Tanethan fleet will always keep them away from Taneth and the shipyards here.' Taneth had the only shipyards in southern Equatoria, I knew.

'Couldn't they build their own mantas?'

'They haven't the expertise, or the undersea harbours to moor at even if they did. The only possible way they can build mantas is to take Taneth, and nobody's ever managed that.'

'There's always a first time.'

'I doubt it'll be now, unless the Halettites have bought the entire Senate. And since that would need more money than there is in the whole of Haleth, that's unlikely.'

After Sarhaddon had dismissed the idea of treachery, we walked across the rest of the bridge in silence. I saw a fair number of people on it: labourers, artisans, soldiers, housewives, many wearing clothes as rich as their station and purse could afford, the artisans displaying guild badges on their tunics. Their speech was heavily accented and slow to my provincial ear – we spoke the island dialect in western Oceanus, a much livelier and more expressive dialect than the Tanethan.

At the other end of the bridge we emerged again into the bright sunlight, past a guardhouse whose occupants scanned passers-by alertly from the shadows. How unlike the guards in Lepidor or Pharassa, I thought, dicing in their guardrooms or at home with their mistresses, supremely confident that nothing would happen that would need more than two of them to sort out. Taneth was the glittering capital, bit I could see there were other sides to it, not least that it was a city permanently on the brink of war.

'This is Isqdal Island, I think,' Sarhaddon said. 'Or maybe Laltain. Anyway, the bridge to Federation Island is just round the other side.'

A wide road ran right around the edge of the island we were one, whichever one it was, separating the housing and shopping areas from the warehouses and docks. It was paved with large rectangular cobbles of the same sandy stone as the rest of the city, with large covered drains running along either side.

The buildings on the island side, away from the docks, were all fairly similar to each other and to Oceanus's: not too smart, three storeys high, with the characteristic colonnades, and smaller, arched galleries on the top floors that hadn't been present on the island we emerged on. There were still roof garden on top of every house, which had given the city its forest-like feel when viewed from above on the shipboard aether pad. The plants I could see now, both hanging down from the roofs and set along the street, were different, lighter green, with fronds rather than leaves, more suited to the drier climate of Taneth.

The streets were crowded and noisy; everyone seemed to be talking at the tops of their voices. The smell of docks, cordage and tar overhung everything like a vast miasma, making breathing a somewhat unpleasant experience. The people didn't seem particularly clean, either. I didn't like Taneth as much as I'd thought I would; I was finding the reality very different from the glittering city of legend.

Sarhaddon pointed up the street to where it curved away around the end of the island. 'That way, I think,' he said. 'Don't blame me if we're wrong, though. And don't be afraid to push, either; nobody moves aside for you here unless you've got two brawny footmen in front.'

'How can anybody stand living here all the time?' I asked.

'Beats me. I feel the same way as you do, but the Tanethans can't understand why anybody *wouldn't* want to live in a city of this size.'

I collided with someone who seemed to have materialized in front of me. The man directed a stream of curses over his shoulder but otherwise didn't turn round, leaving me momentarily nonplussed.

'Your mother was a goat and your grandfather had congress with a camel,' Sarhaddon said to the man's back, moving on. The next time I answered for myself, but my insults were too uninventive and hesitant for the other to take any notice. People didn't shout at each other in the streets like this back home.

'You have to question their ancestry,' said Sarhaddon. 'Put a farm animal or two in their family tree. The other way is to imply that they're not good merchants. Tanethans generally only care about their purses or their moneymaking ability. Oh, and never insult a Great House member unless he insults you first, and even then shut up if he's a house head or heir. Anyone else, it doesn't matter.'

We made our way along the street and found the bridge that led from Isqdal (or Laltain) Island to the central island that Sarhaddon had called Federation, although the acolyte didn't know where the name came from. This second bridge was even more crowded than the first one, and I saw more higher-status people going along it.

Federation Island, the big island at the heart of Taneth, was built on an altogether larger and grander scale. The houses were taller, their colon-nades better decorated, their doors protected by cedarwood porches. The road around the edge was in fact a wide avenue, flanked by four rows of leafy trees that turned the central section into a green tunnel. Some of the buildings had first-floor cafés and bars, again galleried or shaded by trees – those showed the pleasant side of Tanethan life.

Even the warehouses and the docks on Federation were smarter and better maintained than those we'd passed earlier. Many of the ships docked there were pleasure craft, liners or spice carriers, with the occasional five-masted cruiser tied up against the quay, its awning-covered decks deserted. This wasn't the main harbour section, I realized, just the luxury-yacht marina. We turned inland at the first major road, another grand tree-lined avenue, this time on two levels: a walkway edged with a parapet ran along on top of the ground-floor colonnades on each side. Brightly striped awnings extended from every building, some covering cafés, others with signs above announcing the trade of the occupants. I must have gaped as we walked along, overawed by the scale of the city, the number of people around, and the magnificence of the buildings.

The street ran directly up the hill, and as we got nearer to the summit, after crossing another wide road, the buildings changed again. I'd thought Taneth couldn't get any more splendid, but it did. These were Palaces, each one detached, each one more elegant than the last and more highly decorated, each owner showing off his wealth in as many ways as possible. They were set very slightly back from the roads, screened by trees. A line of fountains ran down the middle of the road, and two more lines were set outside the trees, providing a welcome relief from the miasma of the lower city. There were far fewer people around, and I felt more comfortable again, perhaps helped by the fountains' spray drifting through the air.

'We're above the market district. There are the homes of the Great Houses,' Sarhaddon explained. He pointed down and to their left. 'Just down there is the main market square and the road leading directly up to the Palace. Most of the less rich who need to come up here use the main road, so nearly all the people in this street are working for one or other of the Great Houses. The banner on the front of each mansion tells you which House owns it, if you know the colours. I can only tell you a few – that red-and-white one is Canadrath; the orange and yellow is Foryth; purple and yellow are Hiram . . . weren't they on Xasan's list?'

'I think so,' I said, looking around like a country yokel on his first visit to the town. The list was at the bottom of my bag, and I couldn't be bothered to bring it out.

'Midnight blue and silver, I wonder who they are?' Sarhaddon said, continuing his running commentary as we reached the looming walls of the Palace. The house the acolyte was pointing to looked as though it had seen better days. Its decorations were faded, its shutters scuffed; even the flag looked a bit moth-eaten.

'Fallen on hard times, whoever they are,' I said. Could Great Houses fall, I wondered, and cease to exist? Or had the Houses not changed since the beginning of the city? The first seemed more plausible – surely the Tanethans, of all people, would have not time or space for failures.

I could see the tops of the towers of the Palace behind a high surrounding wall that was obviously built for defence and seemed out of place in this smart district so far from the city's edge. However, as we walked along the road around its base, I could see the masonry crumbling slightly in places. The well looked more like an ornament than a practical feature. Besides, if an invader reached this far in, Taneth would be already lost. Or perhaps it was there to keep rioters out.

The Palace's main gate was at the very top of a road that ran dead straight down to the end of the island. Looking down it, I could see a huge square, surrounded by buildings, where not an inch of bare ground was visible. That was the market square, I supposed.

A small queue of people was waiting in the gateway as guards blocked the entrance, enquiring why they wanted to come in.

'Better wait in the queue,' Sarhaddon said. 'These are Council of Ten troops: for them nobody's so important they can breeze past.'

Suall and his companion fell in behind us as we waited. I felt unpleasantly hot, because while the guards and the front petitioners stood in the shade, all the rest of us were outside, unprotected from the draining heat. Were Tanethans more used to it, I wondered?

I was profoundly glad when our turn came at last. Once again, I left Sarhaddon to do all the talking.

'Business?' the guard officer, a tall, fork-bearded man, inquired curtly.

'The son of the Count of Lepidor requests admittance.'

'Lepidor? We weren't informed. Do you have proof?'

I produced the diplomatic pass that the Pharassan military had given me for the manta, and the Regent's letter, and handed them to him. The guard read them, then turned and called to a subordinate, 'Do we have the Lepidor seal impression?'

'I'll just get it. Which continent?'

'Oceanus, isn't it?' the officer asked me. I nodded.

The subordinate was back a minute later with a scroll on which crude representations of the emblems of each of Oceanus's cities were displayed.

'It matches,' the officer said after a moment's scrutiny. 'Go on across the courtyard into the large antechamber. One of the officials there should be able to tell you where your father is. I'd send a man but I haven't got one to spare.' He waved us through, and we were finally inside the Palace.

We crossed the courtyard, which was planted with orange and lemon trees and had ground-floor colonnades built against its walls, and went in through the bronze-covered cedarwood doors. The familiar Palace scent of incense was there again, the heavy fragrance of luxury and comfort.

A bored-looking official was sitting behind a desk at the far end of the hall, filing his nails. 'He should know,' Sarhaddon said, and we walked across to enquire where my father could be found. However, we'd reckoned without the arrogance of Tanethan officials. The man interrupted us before we had a chance to speak.

'What are you two vagabonds doing in here?'

I was aware that I hadn't dressed my best, but surely I didn't look that bad? On the other hand, beside this peacock of an official . . .

'My father is the Count of Lepidor,' I retorted, annoyed at the way the Tanethans seemed to look down on everybody.

'And I'm the Halettite King. Who let you in here?'

'The guards. Who know a diplomatic pass when they see one.' I wasn't quite sure why I'd added what was almost a direct insult, but I hadn't come this far to be throw out by a pansified court official. The man went almost apoplectic, however.

'How dare you imply I don't know my job? Let me see this diplomatic pass!'

I was about to give it to him, but the man snatched it from me before I could pass it over.

'This is from the Imperial Navy.'

'Written by an Aquasilvan official like yourself.'

'You're treading on dangerous ground,' Sarhaddon hissed at me.

'It's not valid here. You're not on Oceanus now; Thetia has no power here.'

Was the man determined to obstruct us? And if so, why? What possible significance did I have for this official? Unless he was one of Etlae's . . . but that was an internal Domain matter, and how would it help Etlae to keep us out of the Palace?

'If you would be so kind as to call the Count, he might be able to clarify things,' I said, trying to be reasonable despite the man's teeth-grating rudeness.

'Out of the question! This Count, whoever he is, doesn't want to be bothered by vagabonds while he's at the Conference.'

Looks like he already is, I thought angrily, *if this specimen is anything to go by.*

'Guards!' the man called. I felt a stab of fear and looked anxiously at Sarhaddon. But at that moment another man came into the chamber.

'What is this commotion?' he demanded. The newcomer must have been in his forties, I thought, with a broken nose and deep-sunk eyes. Not a man I'd like to cross. He was wearing an orange robe, with a gold chain around his neck. On some it would have looked ridiculous, but this was not a man who could be called ridiculous by any stretch of the imagination. He looked like someone who was used to getting his own way, and not one I'd have cared to offend.

'Two vagabonds trying to bother a Count, High Councillor Foryth.'

'By all means eject them, then.'

'Unfortunately, we aren't vagabonds, High Councillor,' I said coldly. High Councillor? Did that mean he was on the Council of Ten? He was certainly a House member; Foryth had been one of the richer-looking Palaces we'd passed on our way up, with its orange and yellow flag. That might explain the orange robe.

'Who are you, then?'

'The Count we're trying to "bother" is my father.'

'We'll see about that soon enough. Right now, the Conference is in session, and I'm in a hurry. Detain them, and find out later.' Foryth started to stride away towards the far doorway.

'*Not so fast, Tanethan!*'

My heart almost stopped from sheer relief. If it wasn't my father, it was one of the only other two people at this conference who would recognize us and weren't our enemies.

'Not content with trying to rob me, you're now trying to throw my ally's son into prison. Leave them alone, Tanethan.'

'Will you keep out of this, Oceanian!' Foryth snapped. 'I couldn't care less who they are. Guards!'

The guards who'd been standing silently at the edge of the room since the official's summons hesitated, unsure who to go for.

The person who'd interrupted Foryth moved out of the doorway, and into my field of view, facing the High Councillor. Tall and burly, Courtières, Count of Kula, towered a good six inches above the Tanethan. He held the High Councillor's gaze with supreme assurance.

'Tanethan, I don't care who you are or what your position is. You've tried to cheat me, and now you are up to more tricks. I would suggest that you call off the guards and try not to incriminate any other Oceanians today.'

'I am not a good enemy to have, Oceanian.'

'Nor a good friend, it seems. I'll refrain from telling the King that the High Councillors are cheating the men he's trying to get aid from. You for your part can leave these two alone.'

The High Councillor met Courtières's calm stare with a look of pure hatred, then jerked his head to tell the guards to leave.

'You have made a mistake today, Oceanian. I would hope you don't live to regret it.'

'You'll need our aid when the Halettites are at the gate, Tanethan. Just because we're provincials, that doesn't give you a licence to offend us.'

'I could have you all thrown into prison regardless, but I'll be generous today. This once,' the Tanethan said as he turned on his heel and stalked off through yet another doorway, not the one he'd originally been heading for. I wondered why.

Courtières turned his gaze on the official, who stammered an apology, then smiled with a presumably false warmth and gestured for Sarhaddon and me to follow him.

'Shouldn't I be going?' Sarhaddon whispered.

'Wait until later, when my father can get you a safe-conduct to the Temple.'

'Sorry about that,' Courtières said, as we walked along the relatively empty corridors of the Palace. His voice matched his frame: deep and confident. 'Why are you here, anyway? Good afternoon, Acolyte . . .'

'Sarhaddon.'

'You were at the Temple in Lepidor, weren't you?'

'Y – yes I was,' Sarhaddon stammered, seeming amazed that the Count of another city remembered him from a brief visit. I knew Courtières's phenomenal memory from experience – he could remember me stealing an apple from the kitchen during a visit to Kula when I was four years old.

'So what brings the two of you here? Your father certainly isn't expecting you.'

'Good news.' I grinned at him, glad to be on safe ground and with friends at last. 'You know that mining priest we rescued a few months ago, the shipwrecked one?'

'Istiq, wasn't he? He was helping you look for more gem seams.'

'Exactly. He started looking up around the north end of the mine, where we'd hit bedrock, and found something far more valuable.'

'Iron?' Courtières guessed. 'You found iron?'

I nodded.

The older man's eyes widened. Then he clapped me on the back.

'That *is* good news, for myself as well as for your father. You'll certainly have a clan to rule now – no more uncertainties about the future. Clever of you to come all the way to catch him before he leaves as well. I know your mother will have decided, but you must have had something to do with it.' Courtières was very generous as well, and far freer with praise and compliments than my father.

As we walked through the corridors, Courtières told me a little about what had been happening at the Conference, mostly concerning the growing Halettite threat after Reglath Eshar's return. It felt comforting to be in familiar company again: Courtières was my father's oldest friend and lifelong ally – together with Moritan, the enigmatic ex-assassin turned ruler, they made up one of the five main factions of Oceanus.

I didn't know why Courtières hadn't been in the actual conference room, but we caught up with the Counts as they were flooding out of the hall after a full session. Courtières shouted out my father's name, and disbelief gave way to delight on Count Elnibal's face as, with Moritan by his side, he headed over towards us, leaving his enemy Lexan glowering in the background.

CHAPTER VIII

My father near-crushed me in his customary bear-hug, then stood back and looked critically at me.

'What are you doing here?' He had been a soldier and was never inclined to beat about the bush. Rather like Courtières, although my father would have been even less diplomatic with the High Councillor.

I was so eager to actually tell him that once we'd moved out of the way, I forgot entirely the words I'd planned during the long, boring hours on the *Paklé*. 'Iron! We found iron in the gem mines. Tons of it, Domine Istiq estimated three hundred year's worth,' I blurted out. Disbelief battled with jubilation on my father's face. He wouldn't ask if I was being serious or not, because he'd realize I hadn't come halfway across Aquasilva to tell him jokes.

'Do you have the samples?' He looked around. 'Let's find somewhere private before Lexan and his slithering minions start listening in.'

'Along there,' Moritan said. He pointed down a mosaic-floored hallway that led out of the pillared reception area we were standing in.

'Aren't these rooms infested with spies?' Courtières said doubtfully.

Moritan grinned.

'I'm sure the King appreciates us knocking out his spies all the time,' my father said dryly.

'Shouldn't spy on us, then.' Moritan was a small man with short-cropped black hair, darting blue eyes and the demeanour of a hungry wolf. 'Not if he wants to get any money out of us.'

'He shouldn't offer such low interest, either,' Courtières said. The third door along the corridor was ajar, and he pushed it open and went in. It was a bare antechamber, its whitewashed walls only relieved by a thin border. The room was illuminated by light coming through a window that looked out onto a courtyard.

I introduced Sarhaddon to Father, who scrutinized him carefully for a moment, then nodded in approval. 'My thanks for keeping my son in one piece, Acolyte.'

'It wasn't easy when he was fighting the pirates,' Sarhaddon said. I glanced down at the dark grey band on my wrist, remembering the words of the message and the warning not to let Sarhaddon know anything.

'Pirates?' Moritan lifted an eyebrow. 'On the Oceanus run?'

'I think we'll wait for a full explanation until later,' my father said, closing the door and gesturing for the rest of us to sit down. He glanced meaningfully at Moritan and pointed towards the window. The little ex-assassin — he was smaller than me, which made him short in anybody's eyes — moved silently across the room, then leaped in a single fluid motion onto the window ledge. He jumped back down again a moment later, giving the all-clear sign, then ran his hand all the way along the border and the join between the floor and walls. Twice he stopped to jam small scraps of cloth into spyholes. I envied his skill and economy of movement. His jump onto the sill had been perfectly timed and executed; if I'd done that, I'd have brained myself.

'No Council or Royal spies listening in now,' Moritan said. 'Ridiculous, this place, you can't even fart without a report on it being sent to the Council of Ten. Not like at home, where we can tell Lexan's greasy toadies a mile off, and all the spies in the Palaces are working for us.'

'Most of them,' Courtières reminded him. Moritan made a throat-cutting motion with one hand, and then sat down in the remaining chair.

'I've brought some samples,' I said, rummaging in my luggage, which I'd retrieved from Suall. He was now waiting outside with the other retainers. 'Mother said you'd probably want to contract a Taneth merchant to sell the ore here, rather than in Pharassa for a lower price.'

'She's right, although I baulk at having anything to do with these Tanethan racketeers.'

I finally found the pouch with the samples in it, having scraped my knuckles on something sharp and unidentifiable, and tipped the nuggets out into my father's hand. He handed some round to the others, and examined one critically.

'Haaluk and Istiq assure me it's good quality,' I said, anxious to reassure him.

'Seems it,' Courtières said shortly, rubbing his sample with a meaty finger. I was on tenterhooks, though, waiting for my father's verdict.

'Seems good. Three hundred years, you say?'

He quizzed me for details of exactly what the priest and the mine manager had said about it, even after I'd handed their letters to him. As a ruler, I was supposed to remember the details, and in the past he had often grilled me on whether I'd remembered lessons or not. I could recall what people said well enough, but figure – even though I could work them out satisfactorily – and lists eluded me, and my memory of the profit margins Haaluk and Istiq had predicted was woefully inadequate.

When I'd finished, my father nodded his approval, and I relaxed a little.

'You did the right thing, bringing this all the way here, and I think a Tanethan merchant is the answer,' he said, looking round at the rest of us. 'Which gives us another problem, my friends, as there are upwards of a hundred and fifty Great Houses to choose from.'

'The hundred and fifty best cheaters in Taneth,' Moritan muttered.

I might be able to help again,' I said nervously, looking in the bag again for the list the Cambressian captain Xasan had scribbled down for me on a piece of paper. 'We stopped off in Kula on the way. There was a Cambressian naval captain there, whose ship had been attacked by the pirates. He seemed trustworthy, and he gave me a list of five of the most honourable Great Houses.'

'You *have* been busy,' my father said. 'Excellent foresight. Which houses?'

His praise was never fulsome nor easily earned, and I was pleased that I'd received it twice in five minutes.

'Hiram, Banitas, Jilreith, Dasharban and Barca.'

'That narrows it down to only five big-time thieves,' Moritan commented. 'Don't look any more closely, or you'll be chasing shadows.'

My father fixed him with a look of amused annoyance.

'Do you have anything useful to contribute to this discussion?' he said.

'Jilreith are clients of Foryth, who are one of the most powerful houses, and also the biggest criminals.'

'Then don't even think about them,' Courtières said. 'Not only is Lord Foryth an evil, manipulative swine, but he doesn't like Cathan. Not

Cathan's fault, I assure you. Foryth tried to cheat me this morning – that is why I wasn't in the meeting, I went looking for him – and when I found him he was causing more trouble.' I noticed that Courtières didn't mention exactly what trouble, possibly to stop my father challenging Foryth to a duel. He always lost his calm completely if anyone threatened me, my mother or my brother.

'I'll take your word for it.' My father always trusted those he called friends absolutely, a trait that wouldn't have been advisable in Taneth. On Oceanus, though, the boundaries between friends and enemies were very clear-cut. There were fifteen Counts: three in each faction, and the alliances had been steady for decades. In Taneth, from what I'd heard, pacts were made to be broken.

'Can anybody point us towards any of the others?'

'Dasharban, I think, are in the Domain's black books,' Sarhaddon said after a moment's pause. 'It could be another house beginning with D, but I think it's them. If it is, they aren't a good proposition, especially if you don't want the Sacri to investigate you.'

'Dasharban's out, then.' Courtières said flatly. My father nodded agreement.

'Unless anybody knows anything about the other three, we'll have to try them. There are no more Council sessions today, and we've already had lunch.'

As we left the room, Sarhaddon said, 'If it's not too much trouble, I need to go on to the ziggurat.'

'Of course not,' my father said. 'My thanks for having escorted Cathan here, and I hope your career goes well. You'll always be welcome to stay in Lepidor.' He reached into a pocket of his dark green robes and extracted a money pouch.

'We Oceanians are not Tanethans: we always pay for services rendered. It's not much, because at the moment we aren't that rich, but if it helps you find a powerful mentor or something in the Holy City, I'll be happy.'

'Th – thank you, Count Elnibal,' Sarhaddon said.

We shook hands on parting outside the Palace, and wished each other well. I wondered if I'd see him again.

'Arrogant charlatans!' my father muttered fiercely as we walked away from

the Banitas mansion. 'If they're trustworthy, then I'm the Emperor of Thetia.'

I said nothing: my father in a temper was a forbidding figure, not someone I cared to provoke further. We had sought a contract with both Hiram and Banitas over the past three hours, and failed both times. Hiram had been civil enough, and had a genuine reason for turning us down: one of their mantas had been taken by pirates, and they simply didn't have the ships to make a run to Lepidor, in an area where they didn't have any present links. My father had grudgingly agreed, afterwards, that they were probably being truthful and doing us a favour by not taking us on when they couldn't really cope with us.

Banitas were another matter: although they had been recommended by Xasan, they didn't seem honourable at all, and their thinly veiled hostility was not only insulting but, to me, inexplicable. It was similar to the official's and Foryth's earlier in the day. But why would a house refuse custom like that? They must have known it would given them a bad name among provincial counts. Their excuse had been a blatant lie and it was that, more than anything else, which had annoyed my father. It seemed Moritan had been right.

'Well, we might as well try the last one, Barca,' my father said wearily, as we stopped some distance along the street from Banitas's mansion. The three retainers who we'd brought along as servants were standing a little way away. 'It can't do any harm, and we can call another council if this one fails.'

The sun was well past its zenith and the furnace-like heat of midday had abated enough for people to be walking out of the shade. My father ordered one of the servants to stop a passing bearer and find out where the Barca mansion was, and what their colours were.

'They're just near the top of the next street along,' the retainer reported. 'Midnight blue and silver.'

Midnight blue and silver? I wondered. Hadn't that been the flag on the dilapidated house I'd passed with Sarhaddon on our way up? If it was, I didn't have much hope of our getting a reliable contract there. Perhaps, though, if they were desperate they wouldn't be quite so arrogant. What had Xasan said? Years of mismanagement, but there was a new house head now?

It was the Barcan house that we'd seen earlier, although it looked somewhat less run-down now that the sun's full glare was not on it. Like all the mansions, it had a ground floor elevated a few steps above the street, its windows few but large and high-silled so that those passing couldn't see inside easily.

The door opened as we approached, and an old man dressed in worn blue livery appeared. Old though he was, his beard and hair were well-trimmed, and his eyes still sharp.

'Are you here to see the master?' he asked, masking well any curiosity he felt.

'If he's home,' my father said, his usual calm self again – at least on the outside. I thanked Ranthas that Courtières was not with us; he really didn't know what the word 'subtle' meant, even in dealings with other potentates. He'd insulted our old enemy Lexan in public on numerous occasions, and the King had called him to task for it several times.

'He is. Come in. Who shall I tell him is here?'

'Elnibal, Count of Clan Lepidor in Oceanus, and his heir.'

The old man waved us into an antechamber that, while it wasn't in the best condition, completely belied the house's Tanethan exterior. Light, gauzy curtains covered the entranceways, and instead of having the usual Tanethan patterns on them the walls were painted a vivid rust-red, with a wave-motif border at waist level. The tiled floor was covered by a sandy-coloured matting rug. It was like stepping into another world – but which world? The style and decoration were like nothing I'd ever seen.

I noticed that the doors to the interior courtyard were open, showing, to my surprise, an immaculately kept garden overflowing with palm trees and other tropical plants, a fountain burbling in the centre.

Having brought us, along with the servants, inside, the old man strode off through a side door, and a minute later we dimly heard the sound of his voice.

A few moments later, the door opened again and the Lord of House Barca stepped forward and bowed. We returned the gesture, and as he greeted us I studied him.

He wasn't more than thirty, I guessed, only a few years older than Sarhaddon. He had the characteristic Tanethan features in abundance: olive-brown skin, high cheekbones, a prominent, aquiline nose and green eyes. His dark brown hair was curled but not oiled, he had no beard, and he was wearing a robe he'd obviously just put on, judging by the rumples in it. It was copper-red with a bronze-worked belt.

'Welcome to my house, Count Elnibal. I am Hamilcar.' His voice was a mellifluous tenor, and I'd heard so many Tanethans speak today that I was getting used to the Tanethan accent.

'Long may your house prosper, Lord Hamilcar. I am Elnibal of Lepidor, and this is my elder son Cathan.'

'What business do you seek with me?'

'I am seeking a contract to transport iron.'

The formalities were over, but even before the last lines Hamilcar's face brightened. He looked careworn, I realized, like one who had given up hope, and my father's words seemed to bring a ray of light into the house.

'Let us move somewhere more comfortable. If you will follow me?'

He led us through a door on the opposite side and into what I thought was a receiving chamber, even more astonishing than the hallway. There was more of the matting on the floor, as well as plants all along the wall that had windows. I stared in amazed interest at the walls: they were covered in frescoes of sea scenes done entirely in shades of blue. On a podium in one corner was a sculpture of a dolphin, perhaps a foot long, covered in worn and battered lapis lazuli. I wasn't very good on art styles, but I was sure I'd never seen anything like it before.

Hamilcar noticed the direction of my gaze and said, 'It's ancient Qalathari, Eighth Dynasty, from a temple destroyed in the War.'

My eyes widened. Eighth Dynasty? I didn't know that much about Qalathari history, except that the Thetian Empire had been the Eighth Dynasty, and they'd lost the throne two hundred years ago. The dolphin must be terribly valuable – how could Hamilcar have acquired one, if he was so poor? Maybe it had been a family heirloom.

As the old man ushered our escort out into the courtyard, Hamilcar indicated for us to sit down. When the old man returned, he said, 'Bring refreshments for our guests – the Cambressian wine, and summon Palatine here immediately.'

He turned his attention back to us, the hope on his face replaced by a cautious optimism, but now every inch the House merchant brokering a deal. 'A contract to carry iron, you say, from Lepidor to . . .?'

'Here, I was thinking.'

'How much, and how often?'

'My manager estimates production should be up to eight hundred tonnes of refined iron a month within a year, although we have to set up the infrastructure. The first cargo will be in about four months.'

'Eight hundred tonnes – that would need two bulk transports working full-time on the run. The price of iron is high at the moment and it rarely slumps, so we're talking about nine to ten thousand corons a month on average. Twenty per cent cut for House Barca?' My father nodded, and Hamilcar continued to tot up figures in his head with a speed and competence that made me green with envy. 'Two to two and a half thousand for me leaves seven to seven and a half for you.'

The Tanethan merchants mostly used percentage deals – selling the goods on the producer's behalf for a share of the profits – rather than buying everything outright and selling it for a higher fee. This reduced the risk of their going bankrupt over the loss of entire cargoes to pirates or the elements. I'd been told that once a contract had been signed and copies deposited with various authorities, the Tanethans always kept to their word. Houses which cheated their customers were dissolved by the Council of Ten, who were terrified of losing business, but having seen the Tanethans' behaviour so far today I was amazed that anybody trusted them on anything.

The discussion was interrupted by the return of the servant, bearing a tray of drinks.

'Palatine's on her way, my lord,' the old man said, putting the tray down on a low table with legs decorated in gold-leaf. He poured out dark red wine into glass goblets – even in difficult circumstances these Tanethans possessed luxuries that matched any city ruler's prized treasures – and handed them round. I'd never seen their like before, either, and I wondered if they too were Qalathari, or Qalathari-style. And, as I discovered a moment later when I started my second glass of the day, they knew what a good vintage was.

'Palatine's acting as my secretary while the real one is ill,' Hamilcar explained. 'One of my ships found her adrift on some wreckage, and brought her back here. She has no memory of where she comes from or who her parents were, although she's clever and well-educated.'

As I put my goblet down steps sounded in the antechamber, and Palatine came into the room.

It was lucky that I had, because otherwise I'd have dropped it.

The moment I saw her I knew she reminded me of somebody I knew very well. But it was several seconds before I realized exactly who, during which time she was staring back at me.

Her hair was light brown, which was unusual for an Archipelagan – most had dark brown or black hair. Her skin, too, was much paler than that of anyone else in the room. It was her face that fascinated me, though. She wasn't particularly pretty, but there was nonetheless something about her face that held the gaze. And, unmistakably, she looked very similar to me.

I wasn't my father's blood son – he had told me eight years ago, when it became obvious to me that I resembled neither my parents nor any of my grandparents or close relatives. What was more, I had a narrow, finely chiselled face and a slender frame – characteristics limited to pure-blood Thetians and Exiles. There weren't many people in either group.

Palatine's eyes were dark grey rather than blue-green, and there were the obvious differences in a woman's face, but her face was definitely more similar to mine than that of anybody I'd ever met.

'Palatine,' said Hamilcar, looking curiously at me, 'this is the Count of Lepidor and his son, Cathan. Count, Escount, this is my secretary, and friend, Palatine.'

Palatine sketched a bow, as if she was used to doing so – something else unusual, because that was a male greeting – and sat down on a seat next to Hamilcar. But as the bargaining continued, my mind wandered, and I reverted to the old pastime of daydreaming about my origin, one that I'd often used in boring tutorials when younger. My father – Elnibal, of course – had told me that he'd found me in the ruins of a ravaged village deep in the jungles of Tumarian, in the Archipelago, while he was fighting there as a mercenary the year before he became Count. My real parents, he said, and the rest of the village, had been killed by the bandits they were chasing. Since my father had told me, I'd often wondered who they had been, or what they'd been like, but it was only idle fantasy. Instead of being brought up in the danger of the jungle, I was the heir to a city, and happy, so I never really concerned myself with my real parents.

But now, with the sudden appearance of someone else, about my age, who looked so similar yet, frustratingly, had no memory of who she was, I was disturbed. Could she be a relative? If so, how had she turned up here with no memory of her past?

And then, just as Hamilcar asked me a question and I had to tear my mind away from the problem, I remembered something else. Any name ending in -tine was unusual, and the only ones I'd ever heard had been those of Thetian emperors and empresses.

My father signed a contract with Hamilcar as the sun set, in the presence of four witnesses, as required by Tanethan law. Moritan and Courtières witnessed for my father, and the heads of two other Great Houses, Telmoun and Eiza, were summoned for Hamilcar. After Lord Telmoun had left, Hamilcar invited all of us and Lord Eiza, who was obviously a friend of his, to stay for dinner.

It was quite a merry affair, considering that there were two groups who were almost complete strangers to each other. Hamilcar seemed almost ecstatic, but when he told us the story of how his house had fallen so low, it was easy to see why.

'Our troubles began twenty-two years ago,' he began, having just finished his fourth glass of wine. 'That was the year of the Archipelagan Crusade, the year the Domain destroyed Paradise. At least that was what my mother called it: I've never been to the Archipelago myself, but as you can see from the house, I have a passion for the place and its history. Especially Qalathar.'

So that was the strange style I didn't recognize – Qalathari.

'You don't want to go,' my father said. 'Not now. I went there before all the carnage, when I was seventeen. Truly parts of it were close to paradise, but what's left is just a memory.'

Moritan nodded sanguinely, his eyes already unfocused – he didn't appear to have much capacity for drink.

'House Barca had a lot of interests in the Archipelago, and after the Crusade there was nothing left. My grandfather loved the Archipelago, and he died of a broken heart the year after. That left my father in charge, but he wasn't up to the job of rebuilding, and for five years we struggled along, gradually losing customers and capital. My uncle Komal began to siphon off a large percentage of the remaining profits, and he gave us a bad reputation. My father didn't find out until it was too late. He tried to rein Komal in, but he wasn't strong enough. Komal murdered him, and took over the House. My mother and I were banished to a decrepit fortress we owned further up the Strait, and for another twelve years

Komal bled the House white. He didn't live here, which is how I had the chance to decorate it with what little we had.'

Hamilcar's mother had nurtured him on revenge, until eventually, eight years ago, Hamilcar had been able to depose Komal. But Barca were reduced to two loyal customers. Neither of them was very lucrative, and while Hamilcar had tried to reform the House, he hadn't succeeded in getting any new customers. Until today.

To me, Hamilcar seemed very detached and distant when speaking of his family, as if the events he was narrating had happened to somebody else and he had no emotion about them.

Later on, Palatine quizzed me about myself, and my family, and Lepidor. She was lively and cheerful, although she seemed frustrated by the loss of her memory. She had a ready wit and an easy laugh, and I enjoyed her company almost from the start – although it was just friendship, and never would be anything more.

Things were looking up, I decided as we left that evening, Lepidor's future secure. We had found what we had come for, and my long journey hadn't been in vain. I felt very satisfied and content, and my father's earlier bad temper had entirely disappeared – he was almost jocular.

Moritan commented that Hamilcar had no soul. Courtières looked at him straight-faced and said, 'But, my friend, neither do you.' They were both hopelessly drunk and burst into gales of merriment. My father fixed them with a jaundiced eye.

'You'll wake the street,' he said.

'What does it matter?' Moritan said. 'They're all crooks.'

'Even our host?'

'He doesn't have a soul,' Moritan said very solemnly, 'so he can't be a crook. Courtières said so.'

I thought that, surely, somebody with the kind of fascination for a place that Hamilcar had for Qalathar would have a soul, but it wasn't an important point.

I hadn't drunk half as much as either of them, because I can't hold my drink at all. Anything in excess of two glasses of wine or thereabouts made me collapse, without any of the intervening feeling of goodwill.

Over the next few days, I attended some of the Conference meetings with my father (although they were for the most part mind-numbingly boring and consisted of the King trying to extort money from all and sundry in order to finance anti-Halettite plots). The real work was done outside of the meetings, when small groups of Counts would confer and work out proposals to put before the full conference in voting sessions, or agree trade pacts between themselves.

I told my father of Etlae's message five days after we'd arrived.

'So soon?' he said. 'If the Elders have requested you, Cathan, you must go. You'd have spent your next year away there anyway.'

I didn't protest: when my father made up his mind, it was final, although I was not happy that I wouldn't see Lepidor again for another year. I did, however, ask him all the questions I could about the place.

'It's an academy, built on one of the islands of the Archipelago. I went there myself, when I was your age. They'll question everything you believe in there, but I can vouch that they're the best teachers you could have.'

That was all my father would say of it, and no more.

I also became friends with Palatine during that fortnight in Taneth, and we spent a lot of time together, much of it exploring the vast hive of humanity that was Taneth. It was an endless treasure, there was just so much of it, and I was curious to find out what all the different parts of the city were like, and what happened there. We visited every island, as well as the market place, a lot of cafés, the ziggurat – although Sarhaddon had already left – and the oceanographers. I managed to find the water analyser I hadn't had time to buy in Pharassa in a poky instrument shop on Laltain Island – which wasn't the one Sarhaddon and I had walked across on the first day – and we didn't see anything more of House Foryth.

But for all Taneth's wonders, I decided it would not be a place I ever wanted to live, or spend more than a short period in. Towards the end of the two weeks I started missing a friendly, empty ocean to swim in – the waters around Taneth were fairly clean, and those a little way out in the strait wonderful for swimming, but they were very crowded.

The day we were due to go, with my belongings already packed, we went down into the city one last time, expecting not to see each other again for a long while. I would be away in the Archipelago for a year, Palatine would be in Taneth, and even when I returned I'd spend most of my time in Lepidor.

★

We never noticed the two figures following us as we made our way through the artisans' quarter on Isqdal Island. I heard a blow and Palatine's cry of pain, but before I had time to do more than turn slightly, something hard cracked into the back of my head, and I fell into darkness.

Part Two: The Citadel

Chapter IX

I came to in a confused daze, and it took me some time to work out which way was up; my head felt like it was stuffed full of wool, and I couldn't see anything at all. Panic gripped me – had I somehow gone blind?

Eventually, I managed to reassure myself that I hadn't, but it was completely dark and the only thing I could tell was that I was on a manta. After a childhood spent in searays and the recent month of voyaging, I recognized the deep, low hum of the flamewood engines immediately. But whose manta was I on? I wondered where it was, and whereabouts in it I was.

I was lying on the floor, but when I tried to sit up I found my hands were tied in front of me with something rough and itchy. Then a flash of pain shot through me; my head seemed to have been split open. The chamber felt close, and confining. I'm not claustrophobic, but utter blackness and a sense of confinement would be enough to make anyone nervous.

There were occasional creaking noises, the usual sounds of a manta at cruise depth, but above that there was another noise, one that I couldn't at first pin down. It wasn't a part of the manta creaking; it was too regular. After a few moments I realized it was the sound of breathing. There was someone else in the room. I craned to see if I could work out where they were but was rewarded with another flash of agony. After that I lay back on the floor, feeling gradually more uncomfortable as my head cleared itself. My arms were cramped.

The breathing changed rhythm, becoming faster and irregular; whoever it was was waking up. Was it someone I knew? The last thing I remembered was a street in Taneth and being hit on the head – and recalling that had taken me considerable effort. Palatine – that was it! I'd been with her when we were ambushed. Did that mean it was her lying some unknown distance away? I hoped so: the prospects of being confined in pitch blackness with a total stranger, even if they were also tied up, was not one to lighten my heart.

I needn't have worried. A muffled curse sounded from somewhere to my left, in a voice I recognized, followed by,

'Where am I? This place is blacker than Ragnar's heart!'

'Who's Ragnar?' I asked.

'Who's that?' Palatine said. 'Oh, it's you.' She groaned, evidently making the same discovery I had, that her head had been hit very hard with something solid. 'I haven't the faintest idea who Ragnar is. Do you know where we are?' She spoke Archipelagan – the common language – with a noticeable accent I'd never heard before meeting her.

'On a manta, at depth,' I replied. 'Other than that, I haven't the foggiest.'

'I don't like being hit on the head,' she said, a trifle unnecessarily in my view; that seemed rather obvious. 'Somebody owes me an explanation.'

'I doubt whether whoever put us here is the type to apologize,' I said.

Despite my flippant comments, I was afraid – with almost the same fear as when I'd been facing the black-armoured pirates in the companionway of the *Paklé*. Only this was worse because I was helpless, and also because I had no idea where I was.

'Who is it, do you think?' Palatine said. She sounded calm, but there was a slight wobble in her voice; I guessed she was just as afraid as I was.

'Who put us here? Either the Domain or Lord Foryth – they're the only two I can think of, unless it's some enemy of yours or Hamilcar's. I'm assuming they're not friendly.'

'Hamilcar has a lot of enemies, including Lord Foryth. Now, why does Lord Foryth dislike you?'

I told her what had happened in the antechamber of the Palace; Palatine listened in silence.

'If he's responsible, then we're being used for someone else's game. What about the Domain?'

I told her as much I dared about the incident with Etlae, Ravenna and their black-armoured marines, and wondered how she could remain so rational and analytical. I'd been near to panicking until she came round.

Now, for some reason, I felt reassured.

'If they've done this, then, we won't come to any harm?' she said.

'I don't think so. But why kidnap us from the streets of Taneth, tie us up and throw us into some dark hold? They were expecting me, and I'd have gone along anyway.'

'But if we were taken because of you, I think we're safe. Your father's a Count and has the ear of the King of Oceanus. I can't see that Foryth would risk an outcry merely to avenge himself on someone who annoyed him. It wasn't even you – it was Courtières.'

Another frightening possibility came into my mind, one that swept away the superficial calm Palantine had induced. 'My father expected me to leave today – if it's still the same day – and not to see me again for over a year. If Foryth had learned of this, he could kidnap us, do whatever he wants, and my father would believe all the time that I was in the Archipelago. By the time he noticed I was late, the trail would be cold and Foryth'd be able to deal with anybody investigating.'

'Dead hostages are no use, Cathan. Trust me, nobody's about to throw us overboard.'

'How can you be so sure?' I demanded, amazed at her self-assurance.

'I'm always sure,' she said simply. 'At least, most of the time.'

I resisted the urge to laugh.

That 'I am always sure' summed up Palatine. Even as a stranger and a prisoner in what was, for her, a strange land, she never once lost confidence. I wasn't sure whether it was a personality trait or whether she'd been trained. And if so, why *was* she so highly trained? It was the kind of training one gave to a ruler or an assassin. She wasn't an assassin, I felt sure of that. A ruler, then, but of where? The Domain were fanatically against female rulers.

'What do you know about this Domain squabbling?' she asked me a moment later, and for what must have been a few minutes – I couldn't really tell – I told her everything I knew about the Domain, Etlae, and Lachazzar. I welcomed the distraction: it was infinitely preferable to lying in the darkness wondering what would happen next.

I was just coming to the limit of my knowledge, repeating things I'd already mentioned, when there was a sharp bang and a series of creaks from somewhere outside the room, sounds caused by people moving about rather than the ship's motion.

A moment later there was another series of creaks, nearer at hand, and a rush of cool, fresh air, and I could feel that someone else was in the room. We were still in utter blackness, though. Why did all the lights need to be off?

I sensed that whoever it was loomed over me, and I tensed, dreading the next few seconds, expecting the touch of a knife.

There was a knife, but it didn't draw anybody's blood. Whoever the figure was sawed quickly through the ropes on my wrists, then moved over to Palatine and did the same. Gratefully, I eased my cramped arms down – and grimaced as severe pins and needles set in.

The smell of perfume reached me at the same time that Ravenna bent down and whispered in my ear, 'Not even a word of thanks from you, Cathan?'

'My thanks?' I said, aggravated. 'For bashing me on the head, tying me up and throwing me into a pitch-black hold without even a hint as to who'd done it?'

'Is that all the gratitude I get? How ungenerous. I'm going to blindfold you, because after being in the dark as long as this your eyes will need to adjust. You can stand up, by the way.' She wrapped a band of cloth around my eyes and fastened it at the back.

As she moved over to Palatine I felt a great rush of relief, glad that my fears had been groundless. I was also curious to know why we'd been treated like this, not to mention annoyed.

I pushed myself upright, but my first try at standing up was swamped in a wave of dizziness and pain, and I slumped down on the deck.

'Not as strong as your sister, are you?' Ravenna said mockingly.

'Wrong there, I'm afraid,' Palatine said. 'I'm not his sister.'

'There's a strong resemblance between you.'

'How can you tell in the dark?' Palatine demanded. 'You can't even see me.'

'Even if I hadn't seen you in Taneth, how do you think I've untied you if I can't see in here?' she said, with a hint of a laugh in her voice.

I tried to stand up again, and this time succeeded, with Ravenna's help. But when I tried to take my weight off her arm, I almost stumbled, and had to swallow my pride and lean on her – not an altogether unpleasant experience, if my head hadn't been swimming. Palatine must have had a harder skull, as she was able to walk unaided.

'Take my hand, not-a-cousin,' Ravenna said to her, 'or you'll walk into the wall.'

'My name's Palatine.'

'*Palatine?*' Ravenna said, walking forward slowly, pulling the two of us along with her, 'That's an unusual name. Who gave it to you? I'm sure I've heard it before.'

'I can't remember!' Palatine said, for the first time sounding irritated.

'I'm surrounded by fools and incompetents today.' I wondered what they were talking about; Palatine *was* an unusual name, but no more so than Cathan – or Ravenna, for that matter.

The door must have been quite narrow, because we had to turn sideways on to get through. Once we were in the room next door, which felt bigger, Ravenna guided me a few steps more and then sat me down on what felt like a bench seat.

Then my eyes, even behind the blindfold, were dazzled by a sudden explosion of light.

It was quite a while before they let me take off the blindfold, during which time a healer attended to the gash on my head, gave me a foul-tasting potion to drink and washed the blood out of my hair. When the blindfold was finally taken off he shone a light in my eyes, then nodded and said, 'You'll be fine, just a bruise for a few days.'

I was sitting in the admiral's cabin of a manta that I guessed was much bigger than the *Paklé*. The room was spacious and well lit, running along one side of the manta. The floor was covered in decorated matting, and the room was lavishly furnished, with a table, several comfortable chairs and enclosed bookshelves and pictures on the walls. There was only one other person in the room besides the healer, Palatine and Ravenna: an older man.

'Welcome aboard *Shadowstar*, Cathan and Palatine. I am Ukmadorian, Provost of the Citadel of Shadow.'

His voice was languid and precise; he had been Ravenna and Etlae's companion the last time we had met. His brown beard was streaked with grey, grown long in the Halettite fashion. He actually was, I realized a moment later, a Halettite.

He must have seen my surprise, for he said, 'I have no allegiance to the

Halettite Empire; I've lived in the Archipelago these past seventeen years.'

'Isn't Shadow one of the forbidden cults?' Palatine asked. She had a rather strange expression, I thought, as if she was distracted.

'Yes, it is. You seem worried.'

Palatine shook her head, frustration showing on her face. She was fiddling with a pencil. 'I'm sorry, but I don't know who I am or where I came from.'

It had taken me the time of the whole of this exchange to understand exactly what Ukmadorian had said. If he was a follower of Shadow . . . I remembered what my Mother had told me before I left Lepidor.

'You're heretics, not Domain at all!'

'Well done,' Ravenna said. 'Took you long enough to work *that* out.'

'What about Etlae, then?'

'Etlae is a heretic in the highest ranks of the Domain. Our spy, if you like, in their Councils. She isn't coming back with us to the Archipelago but going on to the Holy City to attend to our affairs there.'

Heretics in the Holy City? That hardly sounded plausible, although I supposed an organization as large as the Domain would have its share of traitors. But if these were heretics and my father knew of them . . . did that mean he was a heretic, too? And why had he never told me?

'Is my father a heretic?' I asked.

'Yes,' Ukmadorian said. 'He spent a year at the Citadel when he was seventeen. It is the way we keep the ideas alive. Most families have been sending their children to the Citadel since they were founded.'

'Could we possibly deal with something else first, Uncle,' Ravenna said, 'before we tell them exactly what they've let themselves in for? Such as why Cathan owes me an apology.'

She was single-minded, that was for sure. And beautiful, but with a tongue like a knife. I was a little in awe of her, but that awe was fast turning to dislike, mainly due to her constant taunts.

'I'm terribly sorry about your confinement,' Ukmadorian said off-handedly, 'but it was for your own safety. You see, the men who knocked you out weren't our men. We don't know who they were, but after they ambushed you they dragged you into a nearby house and tied you up, and Elements know what they'd have done if we hadn't been following you as well. To be brief, we surprised them and managed to snatch you back, but we had to run for the harbour with them chasing us. We threw you into the locker there, because it's the safest place on the ship and if they boarded they wouldn't find you. We could well have been searched by a warship further up the estuary, and we didn't want to risk them finding you. So, if you accused Ravenna of having kidnapped you, I'm afraid you *do* owe her an apology.'

'I'm sorry,' I said to her with bad grace, trying to ignore her look of triumph. I wondered what I'd done to offend her.

'He was perfectly justified,' Palatine said, 'and could you please explain what exactly is going on? I don't mind staying a year at this Citadel, because I was really only a guest of Hamilcar's, but I haven't got the faintest idea what's going on. Except for what Cathan told me earlier.'

'How do we know you're not a Domain spy?' Ravenna demanded, before Ukmadorian could speak. The older man gave her an irritated glance, but said nothing and then fixed his gaze on Palatine.

She spread her hands, and gave Ukmadorian what I thought was a resigned look. 'If you want to believe that, there's no way I can convince you otherwise. All I want is to get my memories back – it's no fun not knowing who you are.' Her voice became urgent. 'I'm *not* working for the Domain, you'll have to believe me.'

Ukmadorian looked at her, brow furrowed, for a long time. Then he said, 'I don't think you are. However, it always pays to be on the safe side. Your friend Cathan has had no trouble with his bracelet, so neither will you.'

I hardly noticed the inert grey band on my wrist any more. But when were they going to take it off?

Twenty minutes or so later, with both Ravenna and Ukmadorian seeming satisfied, at least for now, that we weren't working for the Domain, they unlocked the door and led us along the passage, up two flights of stairs and into the observation room.

This was the ship that had attacked us off Cape Lusatius: no ordinary manta was this big. *Shadowstar* was a battle cruiser, which the Ocean Code defined as being any ship over a hundred and fifty yards long. There was an image of it in an aether tank against one wall – the unearthly black sheen had gone, and the ship was once again the deep blue of an ordinary manta. I noticed more weapon ports than were usual, and a spare set of air converters near the stern.

What really drew my attention, though, was its overall shape and lines. *Shadowstar* was – or had been – a Thetian ship, and from the size of the air vents I guessed it was quite old, fifty years or so. Mantas had long lifetimes – the hulls themselves lasted for centuries unless damaged by enemy action, and the interiors could be modified as new inventions came into use.

The crew I saw were, with few exceptions, Archipelagans, their faces finer boned than those of any continent-dwellers, their skin olive. They waved cheerfully at Ukmadorian and Ravenna as they went about their duties. I was fascinated by them – these were the first Archipelagans I'd seen, and I was sure they were my people – and Palentine's.

As we stood by the windows on the observation deck, we could see nothing but empty ocean, the murky depths a mile below the surface, the only things of interest the occasional fish that swam into the lights. Another aether image showed the black cliff of the continent off to port, rapidly falling away. I couldn't tell which way we were heading.

'We are all servants of Shadow,' Ukmadorian explained. 'The Domain associates us with evil, necromancy and the like, but we use the power that comes from absence of light. You won't find that we're more evil than the Domain – considerably less so, in fact. Shadow, I regret, is the least powerful of the Six Elements.'

'Are some of you mages, then?' I asked.

'Mages are few and far between, Shadow mages even rarer. It is an inborn talent, and most people simply don't have it, or only have a very small amount. There are about thirty Shadow mages. Most of them have only limited powers, equal to those of a lower-level Magus of the Domain. There are three truly powerful mages of Shadow, of whom Ravenna here is the best. I'm not one of them, although I have some measure of the talent.' I wondered why he'd admitted it.

'Are there more mages of the other elements, then?' Palatine asked.

'A few more, about fifty of each. But when you consider the Domain has a hundred very strong Fire-Magi and over three hundred merely good ones, as well as a thousand or more with some vestige of the talent, you'll appreciate how big a gap there is.'

He went on to tell us of the Citadel, and what we would learn and do there. Most of it I didn't remember because it was too much to take in all at once, only a few of his points, and the basics of what he'd said. And also that the Citadel was built on a fairly small island in a distant part of the western Archipelago that had been left untouched by the destruction of the Crusade. It was about four weeks' journey away.

I was not looking forward to the prospect of four weeks on a ship with only limited amusements; however, Ukmadorian informed us, our lessons would begin immediately. I gathered that we would learn not only the true history of Aquasilva, but once we were at the Citadel, a multitude of more active things.

In addition, there were six other recruits on the ship with whom we would study.

We met them later that day: six youths of my age, all from Equatoria. They didn't know each other any better than Palatine and I did, so for the first week or so of the voyage we made new friends – and enemies.

There were two people on board who I didn't get along with. One was Darius, the short but thickset son of a merchant from Uqtaal, the Gateway City that protected Taneth. He thought I was a jumped-up provincial; I thought he was an arrogant Equatorian with more brawn than brains. It didn't take long for us to realize that we didn't get on, but he didn't try to fight or intimidate me physically more than once. The one time he tried, I proved that all the time I'd spent swimming more than made up for his stronger, heavier frame. After that we politely ignored each other.

The other enemy was Ravenna, who attended some of the classes.

After a few more of her taunts I began to strike back, although I was nowhere near as good at it as she was. This only made it worse, and by the end of the week we were not even on speaking terms. Palatine remarked that she looked forward to the lessons because the cat-fighting provided great entertainment. I didn't think that remark was very funny.

What I found most interesting was the way Palatine managed to – for want of a better phrase – take over the group. Some of the men were rather suspicious at first, but she won them over very quickly, quite how I wasn't sure. Within a week she was the one whose suggestions we always followed, and I wondered how she managed it. She didn't dominate by being bossy like some of my female cousins back in Lepidor did, but there was something about her that made the rest of us defer to her.

Our friendship continued, though, even if I was at times a little envious of her abilities and the way everyone always listened to her. She'd been well taught, certainly, although she wasn't the cleverest of us. Among other subjects, we were taught leadership and how to command, but Palatine might as well not have gone to those lessons. She knew it all backwards, and all the knowledge survived the loss of her memory.

For four weeks we ploughed on through the great, endless blue ocean of Aquasilva, never once sighting another ship – why should we have, in such a vast ocean? It was rare enough to sight another ship in the Great Bay around Taneth, let alone in the open ocean – and only running into one underwater storm. It was a furious affair, which we watched while strapped into chairs in the observation room, but it was easily handled by the experienced sailors. The morning after, we resumed our previous course – I assumed – and continued our journey as if nothing had happened. Nor did we, as I'd hoped, run into any leviathans or kraken. They wouldn't attack a manta as big as this, and I'd always wanted to see one.

Equatoria, Taneth and Sarhaddon settled into my memory, forgotten for the time being amid the routine and companionship of shipboard life. I learned to play chess with Ghanthi, a quiet Tanethan, and although he consistently beat me, it was one contest at which I proved myself better than Palentine.

We did an hour and a half of weapons training in the exercise room every morning, under the watchful eye of the Archipelagan master at arms, who matched my father's skills with a blade and also taught us how to fire aether-controlled weapons. It didn't surprise me that Palatine was the best with the sword, followed by Darius, Ravenna and myself – so long as mine was light enough. Ghanthi was a good longbowman and crossbowman, as were some of the others, including one of the girls who was the best longbow shot of us all. It was rare for girls to be given weapons training, but the heretics had no prejudice against female warriors as the Domain had. One of the other boys proved, to his great distress, useless with most of the weapons until the sailing master tested him on dagger-fighting and -throwing, after which he enjoyed the weapons training as much as the rest of us.

In those weeks we weren't taught any of the central principals of the heretic movements, just details around the fringes. This whetted our appetite for more, which Ukmadorian promised when we arrived at the Citadel.

I had never served on a manta as big as this, so I coerced the sailing master into taking me on as a temporary apprentice during the voyage. He drummed into me – the hard way, often – the names of all the parts and components, and even how to steer the thing. Palatine and Ravenna occasionally joined me in this: it was very gratifying on the couple of occasions when Ravenna caught the sharp end of his tongue.

Three weeks and four days after setting out, we sighted the first of the islands of the Archipelago. Ukmadorian ordered the captain to surface the manta so we could watch it, and over the course of two hours we passed it quite close to starboard. I spent a lot of that time at the rail, entranced by a vision of what seemed like Paradise. There were no huge mountains with barren shores, or stunted trees. Instead, there were long, curving sandy beaches that sloped gently into a vivid blue lagoon. The shoreline behind them was covered in gently rolling green vegetation, with occasional hints of clearings.

That evening, I found Palatine staring into her cup of wine in the stern cabin, late, after everyone else had gone to the observation deck to see another island pass by. There was a stricken look on her face, a look I'd never seen before.

'What's wrong?' I said.

'It's been three months since I was picked up by Hamilcar, three months in which I've only remembered tiny little things about myself. Even then, there are no words, just the occasional floating images. These islands remind me of home, Cathan. I can't remember the name, or anything, but I lived on islands like these. I have hopes of finding a clue, and then I remember that there are tens of thousands of islands in the Archipelago. And all the people look like you and me. Are you sure you've never seen me before, or a relative who looks like me?'

'I'm not my father's real son,' I said. 'He found me in Tumarian, and I've no more idea who my real family were than you have about yours.'

'Did your father say anything back in Taneth?'

I was about to answer, but just then Ghanthi ran in and said, 'I thought you'd be in here. Come quick, there's a shooting star!'

Palatine's glum expression vanished, replaced by her customary cheerfulness, and we ran up on deck and watched the white streak cross the sky to the north-west. I remembered the old saying that a starfall such as that signified the death of a great man, and wondered who it would be.

Two days after the starfall, we arrived at the Citadel.

I couldn't have known it but, on the day the star fell, Prime Halezziah breathed his last in the primarchial apartments in the Holy City. It would be three months before news of his successor reached us in the distant Archipelago.

Chapter X

It was a larger island than any we'd passed so far – Ukmadorian said about ten miles across – and a small mountain rose up in the centre. Around its base was a jumbled mass of valleys, cliffs and ridges. It was on one of the ridges, stretching out into the sea like a peninsula, that the Citadel was built.

It didn't look at all like a building dedicated to the service of Shadow: it was either built of white stone or painted white, and it sprawled along the top of the ridge, almost down to the shoreline in some places. It looked the size of a small city, although I was sure that was an illusion.

All of us were crowded in the bow space, watching the island as it grew larger until we could see details, people walking along the sandy-white beaches. There were even people swimming in the sea, as we saw when the captain brought the *Shadowstar* round to head into the large inlet that formed the harbour, below the inland end of the Citadel. There didn't seem to be an undersea harbour here, which didn't surprise me. They were expensive constructions, and only necessary where there was cargo being moved.

'Can you actually swim in the sea here?' Ghanthi asked Ravenna, who seemed overjoyed to be home – if this was her home. She had called Ukmadorian 'Uncle', and he was a Halettite, though she herself was certainly Archipelagan.

'Yes. Any time you're free – even at night.'

I was glad of that, remembering Taneth where most of the water was too polluted even for fish to swim in; I couldn't imagine how I could have coped for a year without being able to swim. Ghanthi lived at the head of the Ardanes river, which would probably be muddy as well.

There were numerous small sailing boats in the harbour, along with a

couple of bigger thirty-foot cutters and a full-sized armed corvette. All of
the larger ones flew at their masthead a black flat with one large bright
silver star and six or so other, smaller ones in a pattern I didn't recognize.
The same flag flew above the Citadel itself.

The *Shadowstar* eventually docked along a quay that ran right underneath the cliff, presumably where the deeper water was. A reception
committee of about ten people stood on the quay. My luggage and
Palantine's – now that was strange, I thought, how had they known she'd
need it? – had been recovered from our respective rooms in Taneth
before we'd left. I'd deposited it on the decks beside all the others'
baggage when I came up this morning. I thanked the captain for his
instruction, thanks which he received with a wide grin and an
admonition not to forget it all, and followed the others down the ramp.

One of the people on the quay was Ukmadorian's wife, a lively-
looking Archipelagan whose hair was still black; another was greeted
warmly by Ravenna. The one who caught everyone's attention – simply
because of sheer size – was the Master of the House, an immensely fat
Archipelagan, who greeted Ukmadorian warmly and said, 'You've
brought more problems for me to deal with, I see.' He waved an arm
towards us, but his tone was friendly.

'Eight more. All but two are children of the Order.'

'That brings us up to a hundred and fifty-seven now, more than we've
had for a while. I'll see they're sorted out, introduced and all the rest.'

He led us through a wide door in the cliff face, up a broad set of spiral
stairs and into the heart of the Citadel.

It took the Master and his assistants the rest of the day to get us settled
in – at least as far as the basics were concerned. The Citadel was built on
a courtyard plan – it consisted of a number of open-air courtyards linked
by covered passages. A courtyard that had been unused for three years had
to be opened and cleaned out, and the furnishings checked; apparently
there were fifteen more novices – the official word for us – than at the
same time last year. We were shown the main parts of the Citadel, and
where we'd need to report the next day. It was a huge warren of rooms,
corridors and courtyards, and it had been built to accommodate far more
people than currently lived in it. The Citadel was run by Archipelagan
house staff and we were warned that, outside of lessons, it was not tactful
to mention the Crusade because most of them had lost family members

in that holocaust. We hadn't so far seen traces of it, but the Citadel and the islands we had travelled past were mostly uninhabited, and on the outermost edge of the Archipelago. Further in, towards the remnants of the former capital, Vararu, and the big island of Qalathar was where the Domain's legions had laid the islands waste.

The apartment I was allotted was made up of two rooms and a small wash cubicle. The floor was covered in a mosaic of blue tiles, and the whitewashed walls were enlivened by friezes, mostly of the sea. The furniture was simple but well made. I found it a refreshing change from the cloying luxury of Pharassa and Taneth. What was more, I had a view out over the island and the sea, from two large arched windows in each room.

Everybody ate supper at the same time, and it was then that we met the hundred and forty-nine other novices. The large dining hall was full of noise and laughter that was, for me, somewhat overwhelming after I'd had only ten or so people for company in the last few weeks. Some of the staff ate at the high table on the dais; Ukmadorian was there with his wife and a few others, though not Ravenna or her friend; I saw them at one of the other tables.

After we had finished the meal, a strange but not unpleasant spicy fish dish, Ukmadorian stood up and rapped his glass for silence.

'I hope you have enjoyed your meal,' he said. 'For those of you who have arrived since I left, I am Ukmadorian, Provost of the Citadel. I welcome all of you here. There are eight more novices joining you, who are a couple of weeks behind most of you in their studies; please help them to catch up.

'Now that everyone is here, your real education will begin. You are here to be trained in all the arts, subjects and disciplines required to become full members of the Order of Shadow and keep our resistance to the Domain alive. Many of you, and not just the Archipelagans, have lost family members or friends to the Domain. Here you will gain the skills to avenge them one day and here you will learn the secrets of this world that the Domain has tried to conceal, and also, so that you never forget why you are fighting, the greater crimes that they have committed. Your full programme of studies will begin tomorrow, and in a month's time we will test every single one of you for magical abilities. I can guarantee that there will be one or two of you with the power. But, even for the great majority of you who do not have it, I hope you will benefit from what we have to offer.'

As we left the hall, flooding out into the courtyards, I found it sobering that more than half of my fellow novices were Archipelagans and, while some of the others' faces showed indifference to Ukmadorian's words, not a single Archipelagan looked as if they didn't believe utterly in Ukmadorian and his cause. I was somewhat sceptical about a lot of this heretic business – I had seen none of the Domain's atrocities – and confused by what he'd said. But here in the Archipelago, the hatred of the Domain ran deep. Moritan had once said that the Crusade was not merely ineffective but counter-productive as well, and had turned nearly all the Archipelagans into heretics. Certainly those I knew at the Citadel never wavered in their allegiance. One of them – according to rumour – was the granddaughter of the last Pharaoh of Qalanthar, the Archipelago's overlord, who had valiantly resisted the Domain from the moment they torched the first island until his own death amid the ashes of Vararu.

We milled around the courtyard for a while, and I met a number of the other novices: some friendly, some less so.

Palatine was friendly to everyone, but I saw her looking around, assessing individuals, and wondered how she'd get on here, with so many more people, and others who liked to be in charge. I felt somewhat overshadowed as we moved through the crowd.

'He is far too full of himself,' she said, pointing to a tall Cambressian standing half a head above everyone else, surrounded by a group of his friends.

'How can you tell?' I said; I hadn't seen her talk to him.

'Listen,' I followed her through the crowd to where Ghanthi was standing, near the Cambressian.

'I'm beginning to wonder if Ukmadorian's ever going to *do* anything,' he was saying. 'So far, he's taught us a lot of things we already know, and gone on about the Crusade. I for one am here to become a member of the Order, not to play around winning sword fights.'

A moment later he noticed Palatine, and seemed to instantly switch to a different mode, one for talking to girls.

'Mikas Rufele,' he said, radiating confidence.

'Palatine Barca,' she said, with a neutral smile.

'Where are you from, then?'

'Taneth.'

'You don't look Tanethan.'

'That doesn't matter, and it is not for you to make comments.'

'Your cousin had better be careful,' someone beside me said. 'Mikas rules the roost here, and he arrived several weeks ago. He knows his way around.'

I turned round and saw a slender Archipelagan girl in a filmy green tunic. She gave a lopsided smile and introduced herself.

'Persea Candinal, of Clan Ilthys.'

'Cathan Tauro, of Clan Lepidor. By the way, she's no relation.'

'Really? You look far too alike to be unrelated. And where's Lepidor? I haven't heard of it before.'

'Oceanus.'

'I could have sworn you were Archipelagan. Her, as well.'

'As far as I know, she's no relative of mine. I think she can take care of herself.'

I turned back to where Palatine and Mikas were standing. They were talking, warily, and sparring, by the sound of it. Mikas had lost some of his confidence, which I thought was no bad thing. He was a little overbearing, perhaps, but I didn't see any reason to dislike him because of that.

'This could be an interesting year,' Persea said, beside me, 'with those two providing entertainment. I doubt the Citadel is big enough for both of them.'

'Where's Mikas from?' I asked, wondering what she meant. Palantine hadn't seemed very confrontational, although I didn't know her that well.

'Cambress. His father's an admiral, and his aunt's married to one of last year's Suffetes. Well connected, not that it counts for much here.'

'Have you enjoyed being here so far?'

'Yes, I have. It'll probably be even more fun now.'

The next morning I was sent to the Hall of Dreams, on the far side of the Citadel from my rooms. When I arrived, I found twenty-five or so of the others gathered there, walking around in small groups. Palatine was there, as was Persea, but no one else I knew. Nor was Mikas present, and I heaved a sigh of relief that this session, at least, did not contain both him and Palatine. Persea beckoned me over to where she was standing, and I crossed the floor to join her.

The Hall of Dreams didn't appear to have any connection with actual dreams: it was a large, high-ceilinged room, with an odd feature: there were more windows than wall. Door-windows led out on to a wide gallery overlooking the sea on the end of the headland. The walls there were painted sea blue, as were the roof timbers. 'Hall of the Sea' would have been a better name.

'What are we here for?' I asked Persea.

'To tell all you Continental sceptics about why we fight the Domain.'

'Sceptics?' I said indignantly, although, remembering some of the expressions on the faces of non-Archipelagans the night before, she was probably right.

'Come, Cathan, all of you who aren't Archipelagan-born are some-what sceptical – even derisive – about the Order and the whole business of heresy. Why shouldn't you be? You've all been brought up to believe in the Domain, and it'll take more than Ukmadorian's persuasion to change your minds.'

'But how can the history help? It tells us what they did, yes, but nobody's going to be converted by hearing of long-past atrocities, however terrible. The past is the past.'

'Not here, it isn't,' Persea said. 'Here in the Archipelago, the past is all we have left.' She hadn't even been born at the time of the Crusade.

The conversation was interrupted by the arrival of a tall, saturnine Archipelagan dressed entirely in black: black tunic, black trousers – trousers, in this heat? – black shoes, and a black wood staff. The noise in the hall died away.

'That's Chlamas,' Persea whispered quickly, 'one of the three mages.'

'Good morning,' Chlamas said, unsmiling. There was a tone of command in his voice, as well as an implied warning not to cross him. 'Those of you who are Archipelagan can leave. I'll require you to be back in an hour.'

The thirteen Archipelagans left, and Chlamas swept his gaze over the rest of us.

'All of you will have heard of the Archipelagan Crusade. Most of you consider it an irrelevance, a piece of past history. After all, it happened twenty-three years ago, and didn't affect any of you in your law-abiding

Continental cities. After all, why concern yourself with the massacre of two hundred thousand Archipelagans?'

Two hundred thousand? He had to be exaggerating. My father had told me that the Archipelago's population before the Crusade had been around two million – if both figures were correct then a tenth of the Archipelago's people had died.

Chlamas continued, his expression neutral. 'Perhaps some of you think we are too obsessed with this tragedy, that life can go on, or even that the Domain couldn't have killed that many people. I am going to show – not tell, show – you what happened twenty-three years ago, including the Domain's reasons for killing a tenth of all Archipelagans and destroying our cities. Remember, in what follows, you are not really present.'

He raised his staff, and there was a slight blurring of my vision.

Then I was standing, with all the rest of them, in a splendid hall, far more finely decorated than anything in the Citadel. It was unmistakably Archipelagan, and there were a number of people in the room, talking in small groups, as we had been. At one end of the hall was a chair, carved entirely out of blue marble, whose colours shimmered under the rays of the sun through clerestory windows. There was a man sitting in it, a noble-looking Archipelagan of about sixty wearing a long green robe. The smell in our nostrils was of the sea, of wet vegetation and fresh breezes. From one end of the hall, where a group of minstrels were sitting, came the sound of music.

The doors at one end of the hall burst open, and three crimson-robed figures marched in, straight up to the throne and its occupant. The others all turned to look at the newcomers, three Domain mages.

'Pharaoh Orethura, why are you obstructing the Domain's work?' one demanded.

'I will not allow you to burn any of my citizens,' Orethura said calmly. 'You have arrested five hundred of my people on spurious charges, charges that are unprovable in a court of law, and condemned them to death.'

'They are guilty of heresy!'

'Wrong. You have *accused* them of heresey, and tortured them to extract confessions.'

'They freely confessed to not burning their dead.'

'We have never cremated out dead here in the Archipelago or

Qalathar, and you know that. You are proposing to burn my people for refusing to pay the exorbitant tithes you have imposed on them.'

'It is their duty to Ranthas. You know the law.'

'It is not their duty to pay double. In my lands nobody will be burned, or punished, when they have done no wrong. They will be released.'

The scene switched, to the same hall again, only at a different time, and with more people. There were no Domain present.

'They have arrested and burned over two hundred people, at random,' a man in the front ranks of the courtiers thundered. 'They break our laws, they kill innocents, and we do not stop them?'

'I know they're doing wrong, but how do we stop them?' Orethura said. 'That would mean war, and we do not make war.'

'We have to protect ourselves.'

Two more shifts, each showing the throne room as the Domain intensified their terror. Finally the Pharaoh gave in, and ordered all Domain people within his lands to be arrested and expelled. They sailed away, vowing vengeance.

And returned with horror.

As the outer islands were put to the torch, Chlamas led us through the streets and houses of Vararu, showing us what it had been. I was to find that all humans have a darker side to them, but it can be tamed, and the Archipelagans had tamed it, Thetis only knows how. Their society had its problems, and we saw them, but the pre-Crusade Archipelago was closer to Paradise than anywhere before or since.

We saw the citizens of Vararu preparing hitherto unused weapons to resist the trained armies of Sacri and Crusader Knights who were coming against them, saw them erecting barricades around the harbour and the rest of the city, piling up walls of wood and sand. They could have fled, and some sent their children away, but many were simply not prepared to live anywhere else, after the existence they had known.

As the Domain's sails appeared on the horizon, against a sky black with smoke from the still-burning fires of the islands behind them, Pharaoh Orethura told all the heretic mages who had come to his aid to leave, and save as many Archipelagans as they could. It would be an automatic indictment if magic was used in their defence, and the rest of the world would feel justified in having destroyed them. He asked them only one favour, which they agreed they would do. Then they left, in three small boats, taking with them a pitiful few of Vararu's children.

And once they had gone, the true nightmare began. The Crusade had been four years before I was born, but through Chlamas's magic I was there to see it, every unimaginable horror. The Domain's fanatics and their allies swarmed ashore, the barricades and their desperate defenders only holding them off for a matter of minutes. All of those defenders, ordinary Archipelagan citizens wielding unfamiliar weapons, were cut down where they stood, even those few who tried to surrender. Then the Magi began setting the city on fire, their bolts turning people and trees into columns of living flame. Cold-eyed Sacri and blood-crazed Crusader Knights cut their way methodically across the city, destroying every house, killing every Archipelagan they encountered: fathers, their wives, daughters, sons, babies, old women, grandfathers. We saw all of it as if we had been standing there – the cries for mercy, the flashing blades, the dead and dying, and above it all the scent of the gardens of Paradise replaced by the stench of blood, death, and smoke.

They reached the Palace, drenched in blood, leaving us, ghostly presences on the sidelines, stunned and immobile. But Chlamas did not halt the terrifying vision. Within minutes the Palace and its hall had been turned into an inferno, its defenders burning, dying, without a chance to touch their enemies. The way the Domain killed.

And we saw Orethura, the last of a line of Pharaohs stretching back two thousand years, burn amid the ruins of Vararu. He was spared the destruction of the great city of Poseidonis on Qalathar itself, where he'd been born.

Chlamas showed us the aftermath, the Sacri butchering the wounded amid the smoking ruins, sowing the grounds with salt, levelling all the remaining buildings down to ground level, and then, in a last vindictive enormity, burning the jungle that covered the rest of Vararu Island, until the capital of the Archipelago was no more than a black, dead cinder floating in a sea of corpses. And then, as the last of them disembarked and headed east for the final round of island-purging, we saw the mages fulfil Orethura's last request, as the island itself broke apart and sank into the sea, taking its miasma and its pall of death with it. Then a huge whirlpool opened, sucking the wreckage down into the empty depths, the thousands of miles of abyssal ocean below, until no trace remained of Vararu.

Only then did Chlamas pull us back into our own time and place, away from the destruction and the corpses. It was a brutal way to convert us, but it worked.

I was able to close my eyes at last, but the horrors I'd seen were still there, burned into my brain. Chlamas had ensured that I would remember those images for the rest of my life, as vividly as if I had been there myself.

He curtly told the Archipelagans, who had returned quietly after their hour's absence, to move us out of the hall. Then he left the room.

I saw now why there were exactly the same number of Archipelagans as Continentals. I felt ghastly and ill, as did all the rest of us who'd seen it; some were retching.

Persea took my unresisting arm and led me out of the room, down a couple of corridors, and into the sun of another courtyard. We sat down on the rim of a fountain.

'Was it really that terrible?' I asked, hearing the tremble in my voice.

'What you saw was taken from the minds of some of the Crusader Knights who were captured after the end of the Crusade,' she said, 'and from the memories of the mages who saw it from a distance. That is exactly how it was, down to the smallest details, even the way the wind was blowing. And it was repeated all across the Archipelago, in all the cities and any islands they passed. But you have seen it. I shouldn't make it worse for you.'

Part of me still refused to believe that anybody, even a horde of barbarians, let alone civilized people, could have done what I'd seen. But I knew it was true, and I knew that it was evil – more than evil, there was simply not a word for it.

'Do you see, now, why we all hate them so much?'

I nodded, unable to speak.

We did nothing more that day: they left us to think over what they had shown us, the first day of thousands when we would remember those images. I did not eat until supper time, when a mind-mage came round all our rooms and alleviated the effects as best he could, removing much of the raw trauma but leaving the images very clearly.

At a silent supper that night, not a sceptic was left – all the rest of the Continentals had been through it, after us – and we all treated the Archipelagans with a new respect.

After supper, Palatine and I sat out in one of the courtyards, by one of the fountains.

'Did you know all that, about the Crusade? Before this morning, I mean,' she asked.

'Not much more than you, probably. I knew the bare facts about it, and that they caused a lot of destruction. My father always told me that it was evil, but never mentioned that it was on such a scale.'

'You father came here a few years before the Crusade, didn't he?'

'Yes, he did. He's never spoken about it to me, though. I didn't even know he was a heretic until Etlae gave me that message. Or that there was such a thing as heresy, until just before I set off for Taneth.'

'So you don't know any more than I do?'

'I've never met any of these brutal priests they mention, or even an Inquisitor. Before today I still believed in the Domain. Now I don't know what to believe in.'

It was true; now that the shock had faded, what I felt most keenly was a confusion, and an emptiness. My belief in the Domain was gone, and it had been replaced.

'I didn't believe in them before,' Palatine said. 'Wherever I come from, we don't respect them, which is a much better thing.'

'There aren't many such places on Aquasilva. I can't think of anywhere the Domain have no temples, or influence. At least, nowhere inhabited. There's the northern ice cap, but it's a barren wasteland and nothing could live there. And even there the Domain have their outposts. My father carried in supplies for them once, when the King asked him to.'

'What about this other island group, the one that nobody likes to mention?' She learned back over the water, putting her hands on the sides to steady herself.

'Ralentis?' I found myself instinctively making the Sign of Flame to ward off evil, and forced myself not to. 'Nobody knows about Ralentis. The Ralentians don't allow outsiders in and they only trade for the bare essentials. From what I hear, the whole place is perpetually covered in clouds.'

'I don't think I came from there,' Palatine said, with a frown. 'But I think that this heresy is worth following up. More than anything else I want to know who I am, but I can't spend all my time looking for that. Today . . . I remembered something.'

Her voice was very quiet.

'Remembered something clearly?'

'It was very like what the mage showed us; I thought I was just seeing it again. It was almost the same – these people in red destroying a city, on an island, in much the same way. I think I was experiencing it the same way, because it somehow seemed unreal. And I felt terribly sad.'

'So you saw a Domain army destroying a city like Vararu.'

'I think so. I don't know where it was. But somebody once showed me something like that, a terrible loss. I'm sure it wasn't just Chlamas's images being distorted. But whatever they did, it was wrong, and shouldn't have happened. The Domain – I've heard about in Taneth and here, and I don't like them. This heresy wants to sweep them away, and I want to be part of that. I've found something I believe in.'

Palatine was so sure of herself, confident that she was making the right choice in dedicating herself to help the heretics, who had hit us with those images to instil a lust for vengeance – even in my confused state I could tell that – that, again, I envied her.

I realized much later that even then she must have had other reasons, but from that moment on she believed utterly in the heretic cause. What they told us later would only serve to enhance that belief, and even restore a little more of her memory.

I took longer to come round to her way of thinking. At that moment, though, I had lost all trust and belief in the Domain, both as a civilized organization and as the representatives of God on Aquasilva – whichever God I believed in. But my own decision would be made for other reasons, and would be more absolute because although I lacked Palatine's certainty and convictions, as well as her desire to prove herself, she always had another agenda.

Chapter XI

My sleep that night was filled with nightmares, and I drifted uneasily in and out of consciousness. I had terrifying visions of the destruction of Lepidor, Pharassa . . . even Taneth, a city I hardly knew – the trees in the parks and avenues burning, finally the buildings themselves being consumed, terraces and gardens ablaze, then everything crumbling into ashes, and over it all the sound of maniacal laughter, and monstrous cowled priests. In the periods when I awoke, streaming with sweat, I cursed the heretics and the Domain equally. But even awake, it seemed I could see the slaughter going on.

After uncounted hours, with still no sign of light in the sky outside, I got up, dressed, and climbed out of the window. (I was on the ground floor; there were only two structures with more than one storey in the Citadel.) A silver half-moon gave enough light for me to pick my way down the rocky slope that led down to the shore, on the far side of the peninsula from the harbour. Ahead, the empty, glistening beach stretched perhaps half a mile along to the next promontory, while to my right, inland, the bulk of the mountain was a black shadow obscuring the stars.

The only sounds were the hiss of the surf and the occasional cries of nocturnal animals in the jungle, together with the soft noise of my footsteps in the sand. It was utterly peaceful, and the demons that had tormented me began to retreat.

I walked all the way along the beach, as far as the promontory at the other end. There I sat down on the sand and stared out to sea. The Domain taught that night, and darkness, were things of evil, and that only fire kept them at bay. And, living in a territory where to wander off any distance at night was tantamount to suicide, I had always believed them.

Here, though, it was different; here the night had beauty, of a different kind to the day, entirely more peaceful. After a while I felt myself growing drowsy, and moved away from the surf-line to lie down between some rocks.

I slept for two hours or so, on the beach, the dreams gone, and woke when the dawn sun lanced over the rocks and into my eyes. I dusted the sand off me, walked back to the Citadel, and was the first into breakfast.

Palatine and Persea joined me there, a few minutes later. Palatine was eating well – as usual, even though she never put on any weight – but she looked tired, and haggard.

'Did you have a good night?' Persea asked, seriously and without a trace of irony.

I didn't look anywhere near as tired as most of the others, though I hadn't had as much sleep as I'd wanted and could have done with some more.

'I got some real sleep,' I said.

'How on earth did you manage that?' Palatine asked hoarsely, waving a hand to take in the rest of the non-Archipelagans, who for the most part looked exhausted.

'It wouldn't work for you,' I said, preferring to keep the beach empty at night rather than have everyone else rushing out there looking for some relief from the dreams. Anyway, I doubted that what had calmed me would calm many others. I found it much easier to find respite from unpleasant things on my own, somewhere where I could forget that other people existed for a while.

'Your nightmares won't last long,' Persea said helpfully. 'Three nights, at the most. It's something to do with this island, and the fact that you know you weren't actually there. Even though it seemed real, your mind somehow knows that you were here all the time.'

Palatine shuddered dramatically at the thought of another two nights like the one she'd just been through.

There were no classes, training sessions, or anything by way of formal education for another two days; we were left to recover from the nightmares, and the newcomers to find their place and explore some of the island. I found solitude on the beach again the next night, but by the third I was able to sleep inside again, and most of us had recovered from the immediate effects of what Chlamas had shown us. The images were still their in our minds, though, and came to the surface whenever the Domain was mentioned.

On the third day, the training, both mental and physical, began. In the morning, there was weapons practice, generally on our best two weapons – in our case sword and crossbow. The Archipelagans, once a people who shunned war, trained along with the rest of us, many of them using large maces with polished, obsidian heads, spiked, that could crush a man's skull easily.

We practised in groups on a stretch of grass a hundred yards or so wide on the landward side of the Citadel. There wasn't much grass on the island; it didn't seem to grow naturally in those tropical forests.

'So,' said the swordmaster, 'let us see how well you newcomers can fight.'

He was fierce man of about fifty who originally came from Cambress, although he'd not lived there since before he came to the Citadel. What he'd done in between his first year here and becoming swordmaster again was something they didn't mention, but I guessed he'd been some sort of freedom fighter or assassin.

'What's your name?' he barked at me.

'Cathan.'

'Well, Cathan, let's see how you can fight. Uzakiah!'

A tall, slim boy stepped out of the crowd.

The swordmaster armed us both with practice swords, which were slightly heavier than real ones and had been left blunt, both along the blade edges and at the points. The moment I picked mine up I knew I wouldn't have a chance after a couple of minutes, and once again cursed that I was so sparingly built and lacked any kind of brute strength.

'Fight! Three touches!'

Uzakiah – an Equatorian name – dropped into a fighting crouch, holding the sword in his hand like he'd been born to it. He was nearly a head taller than me, which gave him a height advantage, and he looked better trained than Darius had been.

We circled each other warily for a few minutes, then he attacked. I saw his muscles tense, but even so I only just escaped his feint and lunge and had no time to launch a counter-attack, as he drew back quickly out of reach.

A moment later he tried again, and this time I managed to parry and riposte, but was blocked. He attacked again, with the same dazzling speed and grace. This time my counter-parry wasn't fast enough, and I conceded a touch.

I conceded the next one as well, my arm already beginning to ache, but then he became overconfident. On the third bout he lunged too high, and I hit his arm.

I lost three to one, but the swordmaster didn't say I was useless.

'I'll find you a lighter one for next time,' he said quietly. 'You'll have to work on building up your strength, though.'

Palatine, whose swordplay was far better than her longbow shooting, beat her opponent – an Archipelagan girl – with what seemed like a minimum of effort.

'Who trained you?' the swordmaster asked, after he'd finished.

Palatine paused for a terrible, awkward moment. Then she said, 'My father.'

'He was good, then.' I wondered if Palatine had made that up, or whether it was another fragment of returning memory.

Ravenna was the only other newcomer to the group, and the swordmaster evidently knew how well she could fight. When we'd fenced on the *Shadowstar*, we'd been fairly even. Apart from the insults, that was. She knew how to annoy me, and that was galling, because I could never distract her in the same way.

We spent an exhausting one and a half hours practising strokes against large wooden posts, then ran down to the beach for a swim, to cool down before lunch. The swordmaster had sent one of his assistants with me to the armoury to find a lighter sword, and after that I'd had much less trouble.

And then, after lunch, it was time for them to challenge another of our fundamental beliefs. Ukmadorian took the same group of us who'd been shown the images three days before to a room off the main library. We sat down on a variety of benches, tables and stools in the room, the walls of which were covered in copies of parchments in a language I couldn't decipher. Persea and Ravenna were both there, all the girls sitting in a group on and around one of the tables. Ravenna looked as if she knew what Ukmadorian would tell us but had come along for the company. Mikas and one of his henchmen were also present.

'What you were shown three days ago,' Ukmadorian said, 'is but the latest of the Domain's atrocities, and the one that has had the most impact on all of you. But there have been others, some committed in the name of the Domain by the Thetian Empire, and the worst of those took place two hundred and four years ago.'

Could anything be worse than the Archipelagan Crusade? I wondered. How many people had they killed then, to exceed those later two hundred thousand? And two hundred and four years ago – that was when Aetius IV had been killed.

Ukmadorian took us back through the last two hundred years, then and over the next few days, in the same room, telling us each time a little bit about each of the Domain's pogroms, and always stirring our hatred of them. After those images, we were prepared to believe almost anything about the Domain. But five days after we'd started those lessons, Ukmadorian came to something so unbelievable, and something that was so at odds with everything we'd been taught that it was far harder to accept.

'Do any of you know what happened in the year 2560?' he said.

'End of Aetius IV's reign of terror,' Mikas said.

'How?'

'Led an attack on one city too many and died in the fighting.'

'And what had Aetius done, in his reign of terror?'

'Butchered most of the world's population, devastated most of the Continents, unleashed the storms. Not very much, really,' one of the girls said.

'Quite right. Everyone knows what he did: he murdered his father and his uncle. Then he and his twin brother Carausius set out to conquer the world. They sent out huge armies, crushed anybody who opposed them, and drenched the world in blood. All right, where's the evidence?' Ukmadorian certainly didn't believe in beating about the bush, but what did he mean?

'Evidence?' Ghanthi said, looking puzzled.

'How do you know all this?'

'The *Book of Ranthas*, of course,' Mikas said, a touch of scorn in his voice. 'Everybody has to read it.'

'And the *Book of Ranthas* was written by who, exactly?'

'Temezzar, a prophet of Ranthas.'

'Who later became Prime. Now, have any of you ever considered that perhaps you might not be able to trust everything you read? Temezzar mentions Thetian armies half a million strong marching on Equatoria. Now, the population of the entire Archipelago, Aetius's original empire, is just over three and a half million, four million or so in those days. How could they possibly have had armies of half a million? You couldn't transport that lot across the sea in the entire Thetian fleet, let alone feed and clothe them for five years.'

'Temezzar was obviously exaggerating. After all, he was an Equatorian,' Persea said.

'And what's wrong with Equatorians?' Darius demanded.

'Nothing wrong with them, he'll just be inflating the figures to make his people's resistance seem more heroic,' said Persea, rather hotly.

'And you wouldn't do the same?'

'Of course we would.' The bickering went on.

Ukmadorian smiled faintly. 'If we could get back to what we were discussing?' He waited until the hubbub had died down. 'Temezzar also tells us that the first continent to be invaded was Borealis.'

'Where the hell's Borealis?' one of the less well educated Equatorians shouted out.

'Oceanus was called Borealis in those days, fool,' Ravenna said. 'Try waiting for people to explain things before you open your mouth.'

'All superior, aren't we,' the Equatorian said. 'Just because you've been sitting in a school in the Archipelago instead of fighting the Halettites.'

'That is enough,' Ukmadorian snapped. 'Be quiet.'

The Equatorian subsided with ill grace.

'To continue,' the Provost said loudly. 'Temezzar also mentions that the Thetians landed on the north coast of the continent. Doesn't it strike you as a little strange that the Thetians would land on the inhospitable northern coast, where it rains all the time and there isn't much food to be had, when there were richer provinces to the south that were less well defended?'

'Element of surprise,' Palatine suggested. 'They wouldn't be expecting an attack from there.'

'The other thing worth mentioning is that Aetius enlisted the help of a mysterious empire called the Tuonetar, who later realized how evil he was and turned against him.' Ukmadorian took a slim volume from the pile of books on the table next to him. 'This is a book of Thetian annals, stolen from the Imperial Archives in Selerian Alastre just after Valdur came to the throne. It covers the activities of the Thetian army in the years 2552–2555. I might add that all material relating to the years 2554–2562 is classified by order of the Emperor himself.'

He opened the book to a page he'd presumably already marked. 'For 2554, the year the invasion started, the annal concludes, "In this year five legions saw active service, of which two were in the Northern Islands, one in Liona, one in Kodalr and one in Tumarian. The total number of men and ships on foreign campaigns numbered at the Festival of Althana was nine thousand men, seventeen mantas of the Imperial fleet and one battle cruiser. These figures include the Third Elephant Cavalry." The Festival of Althana took place in mid-autumn, I remind you, and none of the countries mentioned are anywhere near Oceanus. These are official archives.'

I was puzzled, and looking round the room I saw the others were too. Nobody quite knew what to say. Surely if these were official archives then they must be telling the truth. But what about the army in the north?

'So . . . what is the real explanation?' I asked.

'I'll tell you in a minute. First, think about why the Empire would classify all its records for those years. Maybe to protect their own reputation, yes. But couldn't it also be because the material in the archives chronicles the real events? It's well known that the present Emperor, like his father before him, is completely under the thumb of the Exarch of Thetia.'

'Maybe somebody got the dating wrong.'

'The dating is quite right. But the real explanation is entirely different. You see, the Domain put the blame firmly on the Thetians for all the deaths during the 'Tuonetar War' as they call it. The actual truth is that the Tuonetar were no allies of the Thetians at all, no allies of anybody. They ruled Borealis, they ruled most of Equatoria, and they had total dominion over an empire on the northern ice cap, which we know as Thure. They also owned most of the northern Archipelago. And, quite simply, they wanted the rest of the world.

'The Thetians had been fighting the Tuonetar for centuries, and in Aetius's time they were quite definitely losing. They were being pushed

out of the Northern Archipelago island by island, and the Thetians had
very few allies left anywhere. In 2554, the Tuonetar launched a massive
offensive across the whole of the Archipelago, and in one of the first
defeats Aetius's father, the old Emperor Valentine III, lost his life. So did
Valentine's brother, the High Priest Titus V. The Thetian royal family
always had twins in it, and one twin would succeed to the throne while
the other became High Priest. The High Priest headed the Sanction
Order, which had all the Thetian mages. After the old Emperor's death
Aetius and Carausius took over, and for six years they struggled against
the Tuonetar.

'Aetius was a gifted commander, and Carausius a very powerful mage,
but there were simply too many Tuonetar troops for them to defeat. The
Tuonetar pushed further and further south in the Archipelago and on the
Continents, killing as they went. Hundreds of thousands were butchered,
and only the few skilled enough to make good slaves were kept alive.
Eventually they landed in Thetia itself, devastated the cities and occupied
Selerian Alastre.'

'If the Tuonetar were winning, how come we're all still here?'
someone else asked.

'Aetius realized he was about to lose his empire, so instead of using his
troops to fight a losing battle against the Tuonetar, he pulled together as
many cohorts as he could and sailed north to Thure. Somehow he
managed to cross the ice cap undetected and launch an attack on the
Tuonetar capital of Aran Cthun.'

Ukmadorian was certainly a good storyteller, and his voice was
compelling. As he paused for dramatic effect, I was on tenterhooks, eager
to hear what happened.

'The attack took the Tuonetar by surprise. Aetius and his men
managed to storm the city, and despite the Tuonetar defences they
managed to capture the citadel and kill their leaders. Aetius was killed in
the fighting for the citadel, at the moment of victory, while Carausius was
severely wounded. And then . . . the Tuonetar quite literally fell apart.
There was a massive earthquake that devastated Thure, while the
Tuonetar armies across the world simply melted away. Maybe they all
deserted, maybe they went to some other place. But the Thetians had
won.

'Aetius's army commander, Tanais, managed to rally the survivors from the army and get them back to the coast safely, taking Carausius with him. They returned to Thetia, but Aetius had no twin heirs and Carausius wasn't in a position to rule. They compromised, made Aetius's son Tiberius the Emperor, and Carausius's son Valdur the High Priest. Carausius himself retired to a remote island.

'Just a year afterwards, Valdur had Tiberius deposed and murdered, and then, with the support of the fire-mages who had fought on the Aquasilvan side in the War, turned on the water-mages Carausius had led. Every water-mage they could find was hunted down and killed, the Order's assets were seized and its troops exiled to the ends of the earth. Then the fire-mages founded the Domain and had Valdur declare theirs the only religion.'

There was total and utter silence. I was stunned.

'How . . . how do you know all this?' Palatine asked.

'We have three accounts of the war, along with a lot of Thetian records from the two or three water-mages who escaped.' Ukmadorian picked up a wooden casket from the small table behind him, and opened it reverently. The inside was lined with plush fabric, and within it rested a book.

Ukmadorian's explanation fitted all the facts. It was just so *incredible* that I found it almost impossible to accept, despite the evidence. They story of the Tuonetar War was something I'd accepted absolutely – as fundamental as the sun rising in the morning. Now that belief had not only been challenged, but totally demolished.

'This is Carausius's own account of the war. He was a wise and compassionate man who, as I told you, lost his brother and father to the Tuonetar. We also have an account written afterwards by an officer in one of the armies, and another chronicle, in a different language, that tells the same story from the point of view of one of the Emperor's subordinate nations, what we now know as Ilthys Province. We have several copies of each in the library for you to read, but you may if you wish look briefly at the original. It's had a spell of preservation laid on it, so you can't damage it.'

We wouldn't have dreamed of touching it, let alone damaging it. Still in a daze, I stood up and followed some of the others to the front. Mikas reached it just before me, and opened it. I craned over his shoulder – the animosity between us that came from his conflict with Palatine forgotten –

and peered at the pages as he turned them. The writing was neat and consistent, without the different-shaped letters and variations of a scribe. The pages were of higher quality, and the ink sharper, the lines thinner and more legible. It was much easier to read than anything I'd ever seen before.

Mikas let it fall open near the front, and read a passage out.

' "That year we paid a state visit to Azaca, as none of us had seen Tehuta for two years, and his wife had just given birth to an heir. We went with a great deal of pomp and ceremony, and Admiral Cidelis set aside his best ships for us. I can still remember him, full of pride at the new flagship he had designed, showing us around." '

Ukmadorian told him to move away, and I took his place in front of the casket. I touched the book almost reverently – it came from the library of an Emperor – and turned to a much later point. I read a passage out, like Mikas had, and I was amazed at the quality of the lettering and the thickness of the paper.

' "That day I lost another friend, and Aquasilva lost a staunch defender. I was leading the elephant cavalry along the Midworld coast, searching for the Tuonetar outpost that Berazoilos—" ' my tongue stumbled over the unfamiliar names ' "—had reported. Cinnirra got the message before I did, but I guessed what it said from her look before I even looked at it. There was an emptiness in me that has still not faded. He was one of the most *alive* people I ever knew, utterly tireless and always bounding with energy. Now my sister was a widow, her son an orphan, and Rhadamanthys was dead." '

Some of the others read passages out, going further towards the back of the book, with the war going steadily worse for the Thetian side. Palatine read a section on Aetius's hasty coronation, and then when all of us had looked at it, Ukmadorian himself turned to the final page, an addendum written by Carausius in retirement, the one that my Mother had copied out. He read what was there.

'And so it was that I stood by my brother's memorial, looking out over the empty ocean towards the continents that had once been green and were now shattered wastelands. I have often wondered if this would have happened if my father had lived, but then I remember the incessant wars between ourselves we went through before all this. We have lost a world, but now we have a chance for a lasting peace and a new beginning. I only hope that Aetius's shade can rest in peace, and that

we shall stay true to the vision so many have died for. I will never be able to fight or wield magic again, and even now I cannot walk up from the harbour without Cinnirra's help. Although I may recover some of my strength, it is my son and my nephew who lead Thetia now, and I hope that they will have the chance to forge a better world than I have ever lived in.
Hail and farewell,
Carausius Tar'Conantur.

'That was written about two months before his son betrayed him,' Ukmadorian said gravely. I wondered who the book had been intended for: it revealed a very human side to Carausius, a man who had fought for Aquasilva in the War, had lost his brother, most of his friends, and thousands of his men, and had ended up an exhausted wreck at only thirty-three, unable to walk a few hundred yards without his wife's help.

And everything he'd worked for had been ruined by his own son and the Domain, because they wanted more power.

Carausius's testimonial was far more poignant than Ukmadorian's account of the war, because it showed a personal sadness beyond the bland statistics and great affairs of the world.

'The Tar'Conantur line as we know it today is a shadow of the people who fought in that war. Valdur's son Valentine IV, as some of you may know, was feckless and irresponsible, while his descendants have hardly been a credit to the family. But the Tar'Conanturs were a great family once, no matter what you may see and read. And Thetia was a great country, too, an example to the world. What we today know as Thetia is nothing more than a shadow, a memory.

'Go now,' Ukmadorian said. 'That is all for today.'

We left, spilling out of the library rooms and out into the warm sunshine of the island.

'It seems almost impossible to believe,' Persea said. 'Carausius, the Tuonetar, that great war. And for the Domain to be founded like that, in treachery and blood . . .'

'The Domain was founded by twisted renegades, and it's still ruled by twisted renegades,' Palatine said fiercely. 'Have they ever done anything good, in their entire history? Or is that just what Ukmadorian wants us to believe?'

'They care for the homeless, and the poor,' I said, trying to think of anything else I knew about.

'I'm sure there were people who did that before. All they've done is to give themselves as much power as possible, so they can lie around enjoying themselves. And they trick everyone else into believing they're holy and benevolent. But their system is built on oppression. Of course, you can't really say the Tar'Conanturs were any better, because we don't know,' she added.

'There have been some genuinely holy Primes.'

'Why are you playing Devil's Advocate, Cathan?' Persea said with the fierceness that came over Archipelagans when they spoke of the Domain.

'There are two sides to any argument.'

'Yes, but in this particular argument they're very unbalanced.'

'They're still there. The Domain shouldn't be wiped off the face of the waters because of the actions of these past leaders. I know they were evil, I know they launched the Crusade, but that's no reason for us to commit our own mass slaughter.'

'We are not trying to destroy them, just break their power and give all the elements equal status.'

'Yes, but in order to do that we'll have to destroy all the Sacri, all the senior mages, all the senior priests. Not to mention contending with their allies the Halettites and any armies of Crusader Knights they raise.'

'Is he always such a pessimist?' Persea asked Palatine.

'He's far too gloomy for his own good,' Palatine said, with a broad grin. 'But, Cathan, I'm sure Persea doesn't want to argue with you.'

Persea pretended to glare at her. 'What she means is that I'm wasting my talents on arguing with you,' Persea said.

'Like Ravenna, you mean?' I said.

'Ah, but Ravenna doesn't do anything else,' Palatine said.

'The only way to deal with her,' Persea whispered to me, 'is to make her jealous.' She slipped her arm through mine, but Palatine just shrugged. I wasn't about to complain, either.

'He's my cousin, remember,' Palatine said.

'Obviously that's *not* the way to deal with her.' Persea didn't remove her arm, though.

'There is no way,' Palatine said. 'As the Domain will find out, to their cost.'

Chapter XII

'Have you any idea where we are?' I whispered.

All I knew was that we were somewhere in the jungle, standing by the trunk of a tree. Exactly where we were was another matter. A very faint bluish light from a thin crescent moon was the only illumination, and all we could see was shades of grey. My arms and legs were a patchwork of cuts and bruises – as, I suspected, were everybody else's.

'No, we are really lost this time. I can't even see the campfires,' Palatine said, a vague presence to my right.

'If you lot would trust my guiding skills, we wouldn't have this problem.'

'So far, Ravenna, your guiding skills have led us into three of Chlamas's clouds of shadow, one enemy patrol, and several trees,' I said, glad to be able to hit back at her for once.

'We ambushed the patrol, though. You, on the other hand, couldn't even lead us up the path.'

'Possibly because there were more patrols on it.'

'Will you two stop that! You'll give our position away!' Ghanthi hissed.

We were on exercise in the jungle, on a night with a sliver-thin moon to make things as hard as possible. We'd been divided into three columns, led respectively by Palatine, Mikas and an Archipelegan named Laeas, and sent out with the objective of reaching the watchtower on the top of the mountain and holding it until one of the Shadow-mages arrived. Everyone had – in the first week – been given bracelets, though Palatine and I already had them, and they were used to control the casualties. We'd been told that if they were touched by practice swords then we'd be temporarily paralysed. To complicate matters further, there was another force in the jungle. Ukmadorian, his staff and helpers, and all those who weren't novices were camped round the central hill. As far as the exercise was concerned, they were an army of occupation whose lines we had to break through to reach our goal.

Under Palatine's leadership, we had defeated one of Mikas's patrols, but now we were hopelessly lost. And Ravenna, our eyes-and-ears, was no help.

'Somebody climb one of these trees and look around,' Palatine said impatiently to Ghanthi, who passed the message back. A moment later there were rustlings, and the canopy above shook as one of the Archipelagans made his way up.

'We're about halfway up the mountain, on the north side,' he reported a few moments later. 'There are campfires in a line just above us.'

'Which way is above?' Palatine said, waving her hands around.

The scout pointed, and Palatine nodded.

'We must be at their picket line, then, but there are far too many plants here to see anything. How far apart?'

'Can't see that well, but looks like about a hundred yards. We're in a valley, by the way, and there's a fire right in our path.'

'Thank you,' she said. 'Pass the word back: prepare to attack.'

'What will we be doing?' Ravenna asked.

Palatine gave out a stream of orders. 'I want thirty people spread out across the valley, you tell them which directions to go in. Sithas in charge of the right, Uzakiah the left. I'll stay here with the rest. Cathan, you're our best scout. Tell me how many people there are around that fire and what they're doing.'

I nodded, handed the end of my scout-reel to Palatine and, with the other end attached to my belt, set off through the forest. I was wearing black, like all the others, with three white chevrons on my shoulders indicating which column I was in.

Moving through the forest, even in this kind of darkness, was becoming second nature: following patches of clearer ground so as not to make the undergrowth rustle too much, keeping the twine that would guide me back reeling out straight behind me. I kept to the shadows, avoiding the pools of light where there were gaps in the canopy. It was far too hot and everything was streaming with moisture – I couldn't even lean against a tree without getting my shirt soaked. Still, I thought, there was a vibrancy in the jungle that the forests at home lacked. Maybe it was because there were far more creatures in the jungle – not all of them friendly.

I hadn't gone far before I saw the yellow glow ahead of me and slowed down to a snail's pace. There weren't likely to be many people around this fire: there was a lot of jungle and not many people to cover it, even with Chlamas and his fellows spreading their confusion.

I inched forward, crouching down in the undergrowth – soaking myself again in the process – until I reached a small gap in the vegetation through which I could see. There were two men and a woman by the fire, all sitting looking into the jungle. They'd be dazzled by the firelight, and would not detect movements as easily as one of us would. There were no signs of any more.

I gave three sharp tugs on the rope, then, after a pause, two more. It was a code worked out beforehand, indicating to Palatine that there were three people, and that they were watchful, not half-asleep.

After a moment's delay, four tugs came back. *Go on further.*

I moved back away from the campfire. I crept around to their right, passing my thread around a tree, and went a little way further on up the valley. A few yards up I stepped on a twig, or something, that snapped with a crack which seemed very loud. For a moment I thought I'd been heard and didn't move a muscle, but there were no sounds of people approaching and I heaved a sigh of relief. I was lucky, I suppose, that everything was so wet after the day's storm – far milder than any I'd seen back home. On the other hand, my clothes were almost soaked through with all the water dripping from the canopy, and it wasn't very comfortable.

The valley was narrowing, and the ground on either side began sloping up, slightly steeper, as I started moving again. I was reaching the reel's limit, and Palatine had made it clear in no uncertain terms before we left that I was to go no further than the end of it.

Something moved, ahead of me. Instinctively I dropped and froze. After a moment, I heard the low, indistinct sound of voices and a rustling noise.

I gave a series of sharp tugs on the string and made my way back to Palatine, moving as quickly as was safe and avoiding the campfire.

'What is it?' she asked.

I reported what I'd seen.

'Do you know who they were?'

'No. I don't think they were Mikas's or Laeas's people.'

'It could be Ukmadorian's patrol force,' Ghanthi suggested.

Palatine only took a second to decide.

'Ghanthi, recall every third person from the patrol, and take Uzakiah's place. I'll take thirty up and around the end of the valley, and we'll see how good these people are when we come up behind them. Cathan, Ravenna, follow me. Uzakiah can stay in charge here.'

We waited until Uzakiah appeared, then Palatine said, 'Move forward, and take up station within sight of the campfires. Count to three hundred, then attack, and move on when you're finished. And count slowly, like I said earlier.' She was very brisk and businesslike when she gave instructions.

'Will do.'

Palatine gathered the rest of us together and, with Ravenna and me guiding, we swung out around our line and up the sides of the valley, with what seemed like agonizing slowness. I was convinced that any moment Uzakiah would launch the charge and we wouldn't be in position. But the night stayed silent.

'You're going the wrong way!' Ravenna whispered at one point.

'I'm not, I'm following the lie of the ground.'

'That's all very well, but the ground isn't following the contours of the valley. We're in a dip here, trust me.'

'Why should I?' I said, but I knew she was probably right. She could see in the dark almost as clearly as in daylight, as she'd demonstrated on the *Shadowstar*. I could follow the lie of the ground, but not small changes like that.

'Imbecile.'

I bridled at the insult but didn't say anything.

We adjusted our course and quickly reached the level ground at the far end of the valley. There was no one to be seen, so we inched down a little and formed a battle line.

I'd barely got myself into a position where I could leap up and attack when I heard the noise of a charge, and fighting in the forest below.

'Wait!' Palatine hissed to us, as we gathered around and behind her. The sound of clashing swords rang out, followed by the noise of people running through undergrowth.

'Now!' Palatine paused a second, but I leaped to my feet and jogged down the hill, dodging tree roots as I went. There was a lot of noise in the jungle in front of us, and shapes reared up a few yards ahead.

As one turned, sword raised, I attacked, taking advantage of the moment of confusion to hit out at their other hand, past the sword guard. His – her? – sword dropped from nerveless fingers and they sank down to the floor: I'd hit the bracelet. It was one of the staff, not any of the others: they wore no chevrons.

Other shapes appeared, but as I began fighting two at once Ravenna appeared beside me, then someone else. And then more people crashed through the jungle on the far side, trapping the would-be ambushers between our two forces. Palatine's plan had worked.

There were more of us than of them, and we made short work of Ukmadorian and his guard. Ravenna disarmed Ukmadorian himself, and then it was over.

'Well done, Palatine,' he said, pulling off his helmet. His men were slowly recovering, but they weren't a threat, being officially dead. 'Now, go and defeat the others as well.' He and his men turned, walked through Uzakiah's lines, and vanished into the jungle.

Palatine said 'Well done,' then snapped at us to form skirmishing order: we'd be marching up the slope, towards the watchtower itself. The top of the mountain was ringed by a series of cliffs, with only two ways up them: a narrow, curving ravine, and a ramp where some long-ago landslide had toppled part of the rock face.

'The ravine's easy to defend,' Palatine said, going over our plan as we advanced slowly, 'so there's going to be someone there, Mikas, Laeas or the Order. If they've got any sense, they'll have most of their people over by the ramp, but if it's attacked they won't rush to support it, they can't leave the ramp open. We won't be going up either. There's a place near the ravine where Cathan and Ravenna think the cliff can be climbed. Once they've climbed it, they'll lower a rope down and we'll haul about twenty of you up, then attack the ravine from both sides at once.'

We crept up through the jungle on uneven, sloping ground, careful to advance in two lines so that we'd appear to be only half-strength to any enemy scout. I could hear the noise of animals all about us, probably disturbed by all the creeping around, but any scout worth their salt could tell the difference between chittering monkeys and creeping humans. At least, that was the theory.

We reached the edge of the cliff, where the trees grew right up against it. Somewhere to our right was the ravine, leading directly up to the watchtower, but so narrow and confined it could be defended by three toddlers with toy swords. I slipped on a patch of mud and cursed softly; up here conditions were, if anything, even worse, and the insects around these cliffs seemed to have a particular grudge against me. Some of them were far too big for my liking.

'Is this the place?' Palatine whispered. There were no noises from above us, and it was impossible to tell whether the Order, Mikas or Laeas were in command of the ravine.

'Not quite.' I'd left a marker, which I hoped hadn't been detected. Were we too far to the left? The cliff curved outwards towards the entrance of the ravine, but I couldn't tell exactly where we were.

At last I spotted the marker, and Ravenna and I hurried forward to the cliff. We had no way of knowing if someone on the heights had already seized the watchtower, up there on its forested plateau. Ukmadorian could already be on his way up there. Palatine had deliberately chosen a long way round, so that we would – we hoped – reach the top *after* the other two. It was risky, because if we were too late then the exercise would already have been won. On the other hand, Palatine hoped that the other two sides would have done a good job of eliminating each other, while we'd still have most of our people.

'Can you climb it, Oceanian?' Ravenna said. 'Or is it too much for you?'

'Perhaps you should stay at the bottom. That's about your limit.' Without waiting for her reply, I reached up for the first handhold, checking that the coil of rope I carried was secure, and began the ascent.

The cliff was no more than a few yards high, but it was nearly vertical, and made damp and slippery by a stream running down inside it. Climbing rock was easier in some ways than climbing wood, because there were more handholds, but the stone cut into hands and feet more, especially the sharp granite of this island. I was glad I'd decided to wear shoes, even though they squelched with water and mud at every step.

My world shrank to the immediate area of the cliff face: searching for hand- and footholds, testing them, gradually working my way up with excruciating slowness. Once, when I grasped for a knob of rock, it moved, and for a terrible moment I thought I was going to fall. But it didn't detach and I clung to the wall for a moment, ignoring an impatient hiss from Ravenna.

Then, suddenly, there was no more cliff in front of me and I scrambled up onto the earthy lip. There was a fair-sized palm tree a few feet away, and I looped and tied up one end of the rope around that, then hurled the rest of it down to the bottom.

'Your aim is as bad as your tracking,' Ravenna said, pulling herself over the lip, clutching at a root for support. I didn't reach down to help her.

The rope went taut as the first person began pulling themselves up. I told Ravenna to wait and, without waiting for her retort, slipped off into the jungle to make sure we were in the right place.

Sure enough, the ravine was there, a few yards away, but as I peered down from the shelter of the trees I couldn't see any defenders. No defenders? The ravine wouldn't have been left unguarded: even if Laeas's or Mikas's people had dispatched Ukmadorian's sentinels, they would have placed their own men here.

I made my way slowly along the ravine, moving back into the jungle when it began to rise and I could be seen from its base. Where were the defenders?

There had to be another trap here, I could feel it. I inched along, trying to detect any sounds of defenders or our own side climbing the ropes.

Then I stopped dead, heart hammering. About ten yards ahead of me was a tree with two people in its shadow, single chevrons gleaming on their arms, absolutely still. There were more, further on, and as I began looking for them, I saw some on the other side.

Laeas had laid a trap. We were almost certainly surrounded.

I went back to the cliff's edge as fast as I dared; already ten of our people were up there, including Palatine. I told her what I'd seen, and what I suspected.

'Laeas is cleverer than I thought,' she said. 'But if he's got all these men up here, he'll have fewer at the ramp. Cathan, I'm leaving you with Ravenna and these ten. Uzakiah and I will go down and along, to attack the men at the ramp.'

'You're leaving us here to get eliminated by Laeas's men?'

'If we all start leaving now, Laeas's men will think you're escaping and close in. After I go down, I'll send a couple more up, and they'll think you're still pulling people in. Attack the moment I leave, and try and break through their line and head for the ramp. You can do it.'

The next man pulled himself over the cliff, and then Palatine took hold of the rope, nodded to me and stepped backwards off the edge.

Ravenna seemed surprised; evidently she couldn't abseil. But by the time I looked over, Palatine was already at the bottom. I untied the rope and tossed it down, then she waved and led the column off into the jungle, leaving me with eleven people and what was tantamount to a suicide mission. I hoped she wouldn't do this kind of thing if we ever ended up on a real battlefield.

And then, as I wavered, doing nothing at all to help us win, help came from where I least expected it.

She wouldn't have given you this task if she wasn't confident you could do it,' Ravenna said, in a tone entirely free of scorn, then, 'So are we just going to sit here?' Her old self was back again.

She was right: Palatine didn't delegate unless she could be sure things would get done. And I wasn't going to let her down. This was the biggest exercise we'd done so far, and I was determined to win it, to prove to Mikas that he wasn't the best general and his Cambressian mafia weren't the best subordinates.

I motioned for my group to wait, and scouted out along the cliff face, seeing how many of Laeas's silent sentinels were blocking our path. I counted four, closing off every route of escape, all looking towards us, swords drawn. One of them was Persea, I was sure of it; she'd ended up on Laeas's side. I decided we'd attack the one on the extreme edge, the one furthest from her comrades' help. Persea was two trees along.

We attacked in a single rush, sparking off chaos and confusion in the jungle as we all attacked one point. I'd told them all to keep running, that we wouldn't stop for anyone, and try to avoid fighting.

The sentry was taken by surprise, but managed to shout and strike out at Ravenna before we reached her. Ravenna parried the blow, then two more of us engaged the sentry and, a moment later, hit the bracelet on her wrist. The silent jungle erupted with shouts and running feet, as figures began racing towards us.

'Go!' I shouted, sprinting for the shelter of the trees beyond, hearing the rest of them respond, as Laeas's troops raced to cut us off.

Someone reared out of a bush directly in my path, sword drawn, too late for me to stop. I ran straight into him – or her, as I soon realized – and we fell down in a heap in the undergrowth. She shrieked, and I heard footsteps close by. My sword had fallen from my hand and I reached out for it, my fingers scrabbling desperately, but all I could find was earth.

'Capture him!'

A moment later I felt fingers grabbing my arms, and I was hauled away from my ambusher, who sat up, dusting herself off.

'Prisoner!' one of my attackers called. I tried to escape – being taken captive was infinitely worse than being 'killed' – but to no avail.

'Don't celebrate too soon!'

One of my captors stiffened, and dropped to the floor, then the other, a second later. I wrenched myself free and kicked the ambush girl's feet out from under her. A moment later my rescuer's sword put her out of action as well.

'Take a sword!'

I picked up the nearest one and we sprinted off into the jungle.

'Thank you,' I said to Ravenna, when we stopped at last, gasping for breath. My shirt was soaked through with mud and sweat, and there was a large rip down one side.

We arrived at the ramp, nine of us left from my group of eleven, to find a battle already in progress. Laeas's men were being driven back up by a concerted attack but were still holding the slope.

I glanced down, saw the triple chevrons of the attackers, and ran into the thick of the fray, striking at the defenders' backs.

I eliminated one before he even had a chance to turn round, and saw Laeas's thinned line, his position, clogged by the inert bodies of the 'dead', waver and break. Then Palatine's people were through. I saw Laeas, resigned to defeat, join one of the knots of his men that were being pushed back on themselves, and called out a challenge.

'With pleasure, Cathan, since you seem to be my nemesis tonight!'

Over a head taller than me, broader and stronger, he leaped towards me, swinging his sword in a hammer blow that would have knocked me off my feet if it had connected. I parried and riposted, testing the speed of his reactions. He was fresher than I, and seemed not to have blundered into so many sharp bushes in the early stage of the ascent – his skin wasn't covered in scratches. This was the Archipelago, after all, his home territory, and he was much more experienced in this hellish jungle.

As I parried – barely – his next attack, there was a roar, and suddenly Mikas's army appeared out of the jungle, thirsting for blood, running up to cut down Palatine's and Laeas's men alike.

'You've lost, Laeas, but do you want to change sides?' I asked, panting, as I thrust back.

'It's against the rules.'

'There are no rules in war.'

He grinned madly, then yelled, 'Laeas for Palatine! Laeas for Palatine! Attack Mikas! Attack Mikas!'

Mikas's advance halted, his troops pulling up in dismay as Laeas's voice cut across the battlefield and fights in progress paused.

Then Palatine lifted up her sword, grinning maniacally, and shouted, 'All of you, get them! *Move!*'

Laeas and I turned, standing side by side, and then, brandishing our swords, charged down towards Mikas's front line.

I felt a shock as we hit Mikas's line, our swords hammering down on theirs, helped by the height advantage. For a moment we were alone, then, all around, were other members of Palatine's and Laeas's columns, hacking down at Mikas. Only ten or so of Laeas's troops were left, but that remnant, coupled with the shock of our joining, turned the tide against Mikas. He was pushed back down the ramp.

'Surrender and we'll spare you!'

Palatine's voice, laughing, rose above the line as she headed remorselessly towards Mikas himself, standing with Darius and his staff, the surly Cambressians, terrible anger showing on his face.

'Surrender!' I called. 'Surrender!'

The call was taken up by the rest of the line, even though I was lost in the heat of battle, my blood almost singing with exhilaration.

And then Mikas's men threw down their weapons, and Laeas gripped my arm, grinning like a demented demon.

Only Mikas and his bodyguard still had weapons in their hands, with Palatine barely three paces away and others of us beside her.

'You can lay down your arms, too, Mikas,' she called as she halted. 'You've done all you can.'

Mikas paused for a minute, then shrugged and threw his sword to the jungle floor.

'Why not?' he said. 'There's always another time.'

It was over, then Laeas shouted, '*Palatine! Palatine! Palatine!*' and then Ravenna joined in, followed by the rest of us, standing there on the ramp in the aftermath of battle, and the noise echoed out into the jungle. I had never felt so alive, so elated, as I did then, and for the first time realized what a victory felt like. This one was bloodless; others I would one day fight would end with heaps of dead piled across the battlefield, but even then, for a while, after the end of combat there was always elation. This time, there was no sobering aftermath of slaughter to temper it, and the cheering went on and on, even Mikas joining in, giving Palatine a hug. I could see, even from several yards away, how pleased she was.

Ukmadorian and his staff, standing at the bottom, waiting until the cheering had finally died down.

'I pronounced Palatine's column the victors', the Provost said. 'As if it isn't obvious enough.'

We made our way down the hill again, picking up the people who'd been left by the wayside from the last few fights, to the grassy sward outside the Citadel building. A bonfire had been lit in the centre, and torches fixed to the trees around the edge. Wine had been brought up, and a party was now in progress.

I was drinking Thetian blue wine in a small group that included all of the leaders from the exercise tonight, as well as Persea, Ghanthi and a few others.

Palatine lifted her glass. 'To Cathan,' she said, 'and his silver tongue.'

I went red, but Laeas slapped me on the back, nearly knocking my glass out of my hand, and told me to drink up my wine before he stole it all.

'Don't protest, my friend,' he said. 'You persuaded me to change sides.'

'Remind me to put in bribes for the right people next time,' Mikas said; he seemed to have taken his defeat with good grace, at least since the party began. 'Palatine, your luck is suspicious.'

'Ah, but I'm not as good at planning as you,' Palatine conceded. 'I only won because of Cathan, but you deserved the victory.'

'No plan survives first contact with the enemy. I was too clever.' It was the first time I'd ever heard Mikas admit that he hadn't done something right.

We heard what Mikas's plan had been, and then Palatine and Laeas revealed theirs. While they were talking Persea moved over to stand beside me, slipping her arm through mine. 'I nearly got you in the jungle,' she whispered, 'But with enemies like Ravenna, I doubt if you need any friends.'

'I was as surprised as you were.'

'I don't know. I don't think she hates you as much as you hate her.'

'Possibly because she always comes out on top.'

I'd been at the Citadel for just over a month now, and the images of the Archipelagan Crusade were just a sharp memory, still painful, though, so I wouldn't forget them. We had learned more about the heretics, their aims, structure, organization . . . and history. I had read all three of the accounts of the Tuonetar War from cover to cover. Carausius's had been better reading then the other two, but some of the things I had read preyed constantly on my mind, only forgotten at times like the tumult of tonight's exercise.

What had happened to Carausius, in the end? Had he lived on to a peaceful old age with his beloved Cinnirra, or perished in the purges? The custom that the Domain had initiated, of having the younger son of each pair of royal twins bring up the two boys: the Hierarch ruler of the Water-Mages had always been the Emperor's twin brother. Thetis only knew how each generation managed to produce twins.

Outside the reading rooms, my swordsmanship had advanced in leaps and bounds. I was now the equal of Uzakiah with the sword, and nearly as good as Ghanthi with the crossbow. I'd begun learning the intricacies of command and warfare at sea, on some of the Order's fleet of small ships and on the corvette. We had fought two land exercises already, one of which Palatine had won – the other she'd narrowly lost. The Order was training us in all kinds of warfare, as well as the arts of spying, scouting and undercover operations, depending on our skills. I'd proved remarkably good at slipping around in the shadows, though not so good on the open field.

Persea and I had taken a while to get together. I liked her and enjoyed her company, but our friendship wasn't particularly deep. She had taught me what the Archipelagans called 'the arts of the night' – a poetic people, the Archipelagans, for whom love was an art form – which I had known little about before, or how enjoyable they were. Palatine seemed totally uninterested in all of that, and I'd wondered whether she was bound by some religious obligation. That didn't seem likely, because surely she'd have had to remember things in order to recall something as significant as that?

The night after the exercise, I slept alone; Persea was sleeping off her glasses of blue wine, as were most of the rest of the Citadel. I'd only had one glass, careful not to over-indulge; I enjoyed wine but the nightmare I went through if I drank much more than that simply wasn't worth it. The others complained about hangovers; they had no idea what one of mine was like, and I hadn't even had the pleasure of being properly drunk the night before.

It must have been four or five o'clock when someone shook me roughly. I opened my eyes sleepily to see a shadowy figure in robes standing over the bed. For a moment I panicked, and tried to move away. Had the Domain arrived . . .

'Mage-testing,' the figure said, and my unfounded terror subsided. Why did they have to do it at that time of the morning? There was only a slight lightening of the sky.

I pulled on a tunic and followed the figure – who wasn't really wearing robes, just a tunic that my sleep-fuddled eyes had mistaken for an Inquisitor's gown – up to the lower watchtower, on the ridge above the Citadel. There was a narrow path leading up through the trees, but the undergrowth was trying to creep out on to the path and within a few dozen yards I was soaked again. I didn't mind being wet; I just objected to the clinging wetness of the jungle, especially at this time of morning when it was quite cold.

The watchtower was a squat, two-storey building of creeper-covered grey stone. Two torches burned in sconces at either side of the door, and one of the staff waved me through and told me to go downstairs.

Inside was a round room that had been furnished as a guardroom, with a chair and a few tables, but nobody was in it. A spiral staircase led down from one corner into the darkness. Feeling a slight trembling of anticipation overlaying my excitement and the elation I still felt from our victory, I went down the stairs and found myself at the end of a long, dim hallway that stretched away under the jungle. Why were there such big cellars here?

'To the right, please,' someone called. I took the first door I could see on the right. It opened into an even darker room lit only by a silvery globe floating in mid-air, above a black circle of stone set into the floor. Ravenna was standing in it, barefoot, with an assistant to her left. Her expression was neutral, as if there was no connection between us.

'Take off your shoes and stand on the circle,' she said.

I pulled off my sandals. The floor was ice-cold and damp, and the circle smooth, dry and even colder. There seemed to be no markings on it at all, not even scratches.

Ravenna caught my gaze and held it. Then, without warning, there was a great rushing noise inside my head, as though a river was flowing through it.

Followed by a jolt, and a feeling as if every nerve in my body was on fire. My muscles spasmed and went stiff, and Ravenna's eyes were suddenly very round and astonished. Her skin seemed to dance with silvery light as I stood there, transfixed, unable even to scream. I had never felt such pain in my life. Then, abruptly, it was all gone. But my muscles slackened and I collapsed to the floor like the victims of the previous evening's combat.

Ravenna slumped down beside me, managing to sit upright, and said, in an astonished voice. 'Cathan, who *are* you?'

Chapter XIII

The assistant stepped forward to help us up, but Ravenna said, 'Could you bring Ukmadorian here, please? Immediately.'

The man nodded and left. I felt as if every muscle in my body was exhausted and trying to go to sleep; I could barely move, because every time I tried my limbs felt overwhelmingly tired. For some reason, the room seemed much brighter than before, but I couldn't be bothered to try and move my head to see where the light was coming from.

'Are you all right?' Ravenna asked, and I could see genuine concern on her face.

'Very . . . tired.' It was frustrating, hardly being able to speak.

'It must be some kind of reaction to the magic,' she said. 'Do you know if your father is a mage?'

'Don't know . . . who he is.'

She pulled me out of the awkward angle I was lying at and propped me up against the wall. I felt the tiredness beginning to fade, but didn't try to move yet. Being helped by Ravenna was getting to become a habit.

'You mean your father isn't Elnibal?'

'No. Am I a mage, then?' I found it hard to believe, but my head was still spinning. I even wondered if this was really happening or whether I was still fast asleep.

'Yes. And a very powerful one. You've got magic running in your blood; it's not just that you have the inborn talent for magic, it's as if you *are* partly magic. I don't know how to explain.'

A moment later, Ukmadorian appeared in the doorway. 'Elements, what happened?'

'Cathan isn't who he seems to be,' Ravenna said, looking up at him; she was still sitting on the floor, apparently unconcerned by the cold.

'He's got magic running through his whole body, in a way I've never seen.'

'Do you mind if I see for myself?' he asked me.

'No.'

He picked up one of my almost nerveless hands. I felt a smaller version of the jolt I'd felt when Ravenna tested me, but this time there was no pain.

'Incredible,' he said a moment later.

Then I had to tell Ukmadorian, too, that Elnibal wasn't my father, and let him know what Elnibal had told me about my true origins.

'It's the same thing with you as with Palatine. She doesn't have any magic talent, but she does have a trace of the same thing that's in your blood. I would guess that either you've had a line of powerful mages for immediate ancestors, or else you're part elemental.'

'But only the Thetian Emperors ever married elementals,' Ravenna said.

'That's what worries me – there's a very strong trace of Water in your blood, which points to that idea. Magic talent normally isn't specific – you can learn to work with any element if you've actually got the ability.'

'Can we discuss this some other time, Uncle?' Ravenna said. 'He's been almost burned out by the testing, and this really isn't a very healthy room.'

'Can you walk?' he asked me.

I was recovering from the tiredness, and, while still physically exhausted, I felt I could probably summon enough energy to stand up.

'Lean on me,' Ravenna said, and for the second time she helped me to my feet. Why was she so agreeable now? Was it because she had the advantage, and I was in no position to respond?

'Go to one of the upper rooms,' Ukmadorian said, 'or outside if you want. I'll see both of your before lunch tomorrow.'

We met Laeas in the room upstairs, looking very bleary-eyed, but before he could stop to talk the assistant motioned him downstairs. They would have to work faster, I supposed, now that Ravenna wasn't helping. But why had she stopped?

We sat down on one of the benches in the room on the first floor, which was brightly lit and where the wine had obviously been stored, judging by the stray scraps of packing that littered the floor.

'Do you really not know who your parents were or what they did, only where they lived?'

'No. All I know is what I told you and Ukmadorian, what my father told me.'

'I would have said you were pure Archipelagan – Thetian, even. If you know what you're looking for, you can tell the difference.'

'Where are you from? You've got different-coloured skin from the rest of the Archipelagans.'

'I'm not allowed to say where I'm from, on Ukmadorian's orders. I doubt it's the same place as you came from, though – it's not somewhere Elnibal would have been.'

'You're Archipelagan, though,' I said. 'Not Continental, at least.'

'How very perceptive of you.'

There was silence for a few moments, then I asked, 'Will I be training as a mage now?'

'Yes,' she said. 'With me.'

'Does that mean you'll still use me to practise your wit on?'

'Don't you enjoy it?' she said, with an impish smile. It was the first genuine smile I'd seen from her.

There was no sword practice the next morning, and we all slept in several hours past dawn, catching up on the sleep missed while we'd been stalking each other around the forest. In the afternoon, there would be a post-mortem in the Great Hall on the exercise, with everyone present, followed by more sessions involving the command groups and the rank-and-file separately.

But first, Ravenna and I had been summoned to see Ukmadorian.

When I arrived in his light, airy study on the seaward side of the promontory, Ravenna was already there, her usual unsmiling self, but at least she didn't greet me with an insult. That was encouraging, I felt. I'd lain awake for a while wondering at her behaviour the previous night, still unable to explain it. And, despite the taunts I'd endured since I met her, I wasn't sure I hated her any more. What I found most frustrating was that I could fathom her, or even work out what I thought of her.

Ukmadorian was leaning back in his padded chair as he had done on the ship. I'd never been in his study before, and was surprised at the small number of furnishings: there was only a desk, a couple of chairs, some painted bookcases and a drinks table. The walls were a plain light blue, and there were a few plants in one corner. Beyond the large windows that ran down one wall was a small balcony, sticking out over the cliff, with more plants on it. Beyond that was the dazzling blue of the Ocean.

'Good morning, Cathan,' Ukmadorian said. 'Do sit down.'

I sat down on one of the hard chairs, across the desk from him. Ukmadorian was very keen on formality, and always insisted that we call him 'Provost.'

'From what happened in the tower last night, it's clear that you're a mage of a kind we've never seen before. Your talent's for Water, but you should be able to learn to master any of the elements. Some people can learn more than one, anyway; Ravenna's one of them.'

'So I can be trained in Shadow, Wind, Water . . . any of them?' I asked. It was confusing, given what they'd told me a month ago, when they'd implied that mages only use one element each.

'Any of them, except you'd be strongest at Water. However, it would be a waste to transfer to the Citadel of Water now. With a talent like that in your blood, you should be able to learn it on your own, if you've already been taught the principles in one of the other elements – Shadow, for instance.'

I still found in hard to believe what he was telling me. It seemed like part of a childhood fantasy, something everybody had probably dreamed of at some time in their lives – to be suddenly gifted with awesome powers. But in my case – would my father really have happened on somebody with my kind of power in an obscure village in Tumarian? If I had magic in my blood, then what had happened to my real parents, with whatever strange powers they'd had? How had they come to lose me?

'Cathan, do you want to be trained as a mage?' Ukmadorian said. I opened my mouth to answer, but he held up a warning hand. 'If you are, you will have to become a full member of the Order and devote yourself to the heretic cause. You won't be able to succeed your father as Count of Lepidor. A mage is too valuable to waste in some corner of the world where the Domain aren't a serious threat.'

I was thunderstruck, yet again. I had no idea that becoming a mage would lead to such a commitment, although, I suppose, I could have foreseen it. They would have to be sure of my loyalty.

'I won't have to spend all the time on this island, will I?' I asked. I loved being here, but the thought of spending years and years on such a small island, with only a small variety of people for company, was unnerving.

'Not if you don't want to. I'm not asking you to decide quickly, but it's up to you. You have the potential to be one of the most powerful mages we've ever had, just as Thetian is one of the best leaders I've ever seen. You'll have a chance to strike at the Domain, far more than you would otherwise. If not . . . you'll stay out the year like all the rest and then go home, but we'll have to ensure that you can never use your powers against us.'

I recognized the implications in this last sentence, and shivered. They weren't really offering me a choice, were they? Join us – or lose your powers and go home. I suppose it wasn't really surprising, given how few of them there were.

The problem was, what would I *do* as a mage? What did Chlamas and his fellows do when they weren't teaching on the island? I had no desire to teach anyone; I wanted to see the rest of Aquasilva and live life to the full.

'Can I think it over?'

'Don't take too long. If you are to be trained, we'll need to start as soon as possible. You may go. Ravenna, please stay.'

I left the room, mind churning, and went to find Palatine. She was down on the beach with Persea and Laeas.

'Cathan!' she shouted when I was some distance away, waving me over. 'Where were you last night? We didn't see you at all after you went up to the tower.'

'They've asked me whether I want to train as a mage or not,' I said, keeping my face impassive. 'How about some friendly advice?'

'Are you serious?' Persea said.

'Of course. Why wouldn't I be? I could be the most powerful mage they've had in decades.'

'You're inventing it,' Palatine said suspiciously.

'I'm not! Ravenna's even stopped making comments because she's afraid she'll have to train with me.'

Only then did they believe me. Persea embraced me very tightly indeed, and then Laeas slapped me on the back yet again – I was getting used to this huge, mad Archipelagan and his enthusiasm.

'Why do you need to ask us about the training?' Palatine said, after the initial euphoria had died down.

I told them what Ukmadorian had said, and the choices I had now.

'How much do you want to be Count?' Laeas said.

'I'd like to succeed Elnibal,' I said, 'but it isn't always hereditary; my father could choose someone else from my house. I think he'd be hurt if it came to that, he's spent years trying to train me to succeed him. But it isn't that so much as the prospect of being based on this island, and having to spend months at a time out here, training or whatever. And I don't want to be another pawn from Ukmadorian and the Elemental Council to push around as they see fit. It seems to me that the best mages are always at the beck and call of the Council, never having any freedom of choice.'

'They're afraid of losing the few good mages they have,' Persea said, 'so they protect them, and they never get used for anything.'

'I don't want to be protected,' I said.

'Nor does Ravenna,' Persea said. 'She argues with Ukmadorian all the time, and she's argued with the Council once or twice. I gather that she's had a rather restricted life for some reason, and she wants to be allowed out. They don't want to lose her, so they won't let her go.'

I'd never seen Ravenna even disagree with Ukmadorian, or any signs of tension between them. She'd always seemed to be the dutiful servant of the Council and her 'uncle' – though I knew now that he wasn't – the Provost.

'How do you know?' asked Palatine.

'I'm a friend – of sorts. She isn't at all like what you see on the outside, any of you. She's got a temper like a volcano, and she's very hot-blooded. But she can't see any way to escape Ukmadorian's clutches, because she's so valuable to them.'

Ravenna? Was Persea talking about the same person? I was astounded – how could Ravenna have two sides like that, one of which I'd never even got a hint of? It didn't bode well for me, either, if she was having such trouble with them.

Then Palatine said, 'Cathan, would you do something for me, on trust?'

'What favour, exactly?'

'Take the mage-training. Learn everything you can, and more. Become the most powerful Mage of Shadow they've ever seen, or whatever they let you do in a year. I'll make sure they don't keep you here at the end, and if they do I'll stay as well.'

'Are you going to tell him now?' Laeas asked, lying down on the sand with a contented expression on his face.

Palatine shrugged. 'I might as well, it can't do any harm. I was thinking about this after they showed us all those books. What have the heretics done since then? They kill a few Exarchs, a Prime even, and they make sure people remember all this.' She waved a hand, talking in the Citadel, the island and the flags floating on top of the buildings. 'Perhaps they also manage to influence people here and there, keep some of the lunatics out of the way. But they're not getting any bigger, are they? Ukmadorian won't tell us how many heretics there are; I don't think there are very many.'

She sketched a rough map of the world in the sand with her forefinger. 'Here we are, somewhere in the Archipelago.' She stabbed her finger down a few times to give the impression of scattered islands, then drew a ring in the centre. 'And Thetia. In the Archipelago, most of the population are heretics. A million people or so, plus the ones in Qalathar. Thetia – who knows? They're all crazy there if you believe Ukmadorian. Then the rest of the world. Equatoria, Huasa, New Hyperian, Oceanus. Nine million people or so, and how many of them are heretics? A few tens of thousands, not many more.'

Palatine sat back again, and looked around at us. 'Where does it get us, if we kill the Domain leaders? Nobody will care, maybe they'll even get annoyed. And the Inquisitors will rush round, burn a few people. Most of the world don't know any other gods, and how are we supposed to convert them? Show them all Chlamas's little theatre? She sounded scornful. 'Not very useful.'

Laeas interrupted her during that brief pause.

'Palatine, what you've said is all true, and that's exactly why we cannot win, because the Domain are so much bigger.'

'Why can the Domain launch these crusades to kill people they don't like?'

'Because they use the Haletties, and troops belonging to their victims' enemies,' Persea said.

'Yes, because everybody else is always fighting.' She banged her hand down on the sand. 'The Halettites fight the Tanethans. Cambress fights Mons Ferranis. Taneth fights Cambress, and helps the Mons Ferratans.

Oceanus sits in the north and sulks. The Thetians spend all their time in bed with each other's wives, and as for the Archipelago – "Look, here's a treasure-chest".'

We all said nothing, held by her magnetism, waiting for her point. She was a very good speaker, where she was trying to convince us that her ideas were right or telling a joke at the supper table.

'So what happens if everyone else joins together? Then they wouldn't help the Domain against their neighbours, because whoever was in charge wouldn't let them. We can't hope for the Halettites to get involved, because they think they're God's gift to Aquasilva. But everyone else – they'd control the seas. Not even Lachazzar and his hair-shirt brigade can travel any other way.'

'The Domain would crush any state or leader who threatened to grow too powerful,' Laeas said. 'That was what the Fourth Crusade was.'

'And how would you unite everyone in the first place?' I objected.

'The Halettites,' Palatine said, shifting position to sit cross-legged on the sand. She never kept still; even when she wasn't moving around, she was fiddling with something. 'Soon the Domain won't be able to control them. They've conquered everything they can, and now that Eshar is back their King will want more. And where else can he go but Taneth? There's no other place he can get hold of mantas.' She leaned forward and made a hole in the sand in the middle of the squiggle that was Equatoria.

'You think he'll attack Taneth?' Laeas said.

'What do you think?' Palatine said. 'Where else is there to go? He brings up Eshar, a hundred thousand men, and whoosh! The end of Taneth.' She flicked sand over the hole she'd just made. 'The Domain don't want that, of course, but what can they do?' Another shrug. 'The Halettites have all the troops, so all the Domain can do is try and delay them. If they help the Tanethans, the Halettites won't like them any more. Once Taneth falls, everybody else realizes that they can be invaded as well, so they all declare war on Haleth.'

'But you're counting on Taneth falling in order for your plan to work,' Persea said, horrified. 'Your own city, and you're prepared to give it up?'

'This is only a theory, and anyway I wasn't born in Taneth. And Hamilcar always said that.' She looked challengingly at Persea. 'How do we stop them? The Council of Ten control the city, and they're all fat merchants who don't care about anything except their own purses,' she said vehemently. 'I'm not a Lord, what can I do to stop them? Hamilcar tried, and did he get anywhere? No.'

'Why not try and take control of Haleth?' Laeas asked, unexpectedly. 'It's a single state, and could probably destroy the Domain with a single blow.'

'Something I think about, but then I realize how much they hate foreigners. Besides which, they are the enemy. Even if we use them, all the Exarchs who survive declare a crusade and we have yet another war, with too many people dying, and then the Halettites lose and where are we? Back at the beginning again.' Palentine's voice carried a note of finality; she definitely felt that was out of the question.

'I think I understand your plan,' Persea said, 'and I agree with it, in principle. But who would everybody follow? The Kings all distrust each other, there's no Pharaoh, and the Thetian Emperor's a violent megalomaniac who enjoys watching people suffer. Nobody in their right mind would follow him.'

'I've thought of that as well. It's complicated, and there's too much to explain now.' Palatine grinned. 'Actually, I haven't quite decided yet. But I will have, soon.' She folded her hands in her lap and looked at me. 'So, Cathan, will you go through with the training?'

I thought of what Palatine was proposing, and compared it with the alternatives. Despite the far-fetched aspect of what she was putting forward, I believed in her, and I believed she might eventually have a chance of success. Her plans always seemed to work; last night's had been unusual, and even that had gone right in the end. Did I want to let her and the others down, to spend the rest of my life in Lepidor? That had been all I'd hoped for before I arrived here, but now there were other chances, other things I could do, and my life no longer seemed so set in its future path. The only thing I worried about was my father. He'd tried so hard to make me into a ruler, and I didn't want to let him down . . . But Palatine had promised she'd be able to get me out of here, and I could worry about the future in eleven months' time.

'I'll do it,' I said.

'Then I promise that you'll be able to go where you want when we leave. Witnessed – Laeas, Persea?'

'Witnessed,' the two of them said together.

'I'll go and tell Ukmadorian later this afternoon,' I said. 'Not now, because it'll seem suspiciously hasty.'

'You should get to know Ravenna better,' Persea said. 'She doesn't hate you, and she needs an ally in this. Chlamas is Archipelagan, and of course he loves it here. He's obsessed with getting into the Council, and the other mage is getting on a little. She can help you.'

'I didn't insult her for no particular reason the first time I met her,' I protested, feeling that Persea was shifting the blame on to me.

'I think she does have a reason for all of this, Cathan, which I hope you learn sometime.'

The sound of the bell on the cliff top, ringing to signify that lunch was ready, interrupted any further discussion.

'Race you back to the Citadel?' Laeas said.

'Go!' Laeas set off, leaving the rest of us to catch up. When the three of us caught up with him at the top he was lying in the grass, pretending he'd been there for ages.

Later that afternoon, after the end of the post-mortems on the battle exercise, I went along to Ukmadorian's study again.

'Come in,' he said, when I knocked, 'Ah, Cathan. You were quick.'

'How much of a choice was it?' I said, the only reply I was likely to make to his veiled threat of earlier that morning. Then, more formally, 'I would like to be trained as a mage.'

'Excellent,' he said, smiling broadly and, I felt, with far too much satisfaction. 'Of Shadow?'

I'd have loved to be able to throw his smugness back in his teeth and tell him I wanted to join my natural element, Water. But it was something I'd never really considered – I had friends here, and I knew the place. I didn't want to swap it all for a strange and much bigger place.

'You'll be taking lessons alongside Ravenna every morning, after the rest have gone to bed. It'll be tiring at first, but you'll find after a few days that Shadow-mages need very little sleep.'

He was genuinely pleased and friendly again, all trace of the pressure he'd put me under vanishing. But I would not forget it so fast, nor what Persea had told me about his near-oppression of Ravenna.

'How long does the mage-training take?' I asked, outwardly matching his mood. 'Or, more to the point, how does magic work?'

'Essentially, you train your mind to use its power to influence things outside your body. Most of the spells are based on Shadow, although there are some things that mages of any element can do. Naturally, Shadow-magic is limited in the daytime and far stronger at night, unlike the others that don't depend on the light or darkness.'

'And how long does it take?'

'A few weeks to learn how to do it, then years to hone your skills, learn all the commands for the more intricate aptitudes – you have to learn how to think in a different way – and actually gain experience by using them. By the end of this first year, while all your friends are here, you'll know all the techniques, only you'll be very inexperienced and not much good yet at manipulating them and regulating yourself. Because you're using your mind as a channel, there are restrictions on how much you can handle. The more powerful your techniques are, the more you can handle before the channelling exhausts you.'

'Was that why I was so exhausted after the test last night?'

Ukmadorian nodded.

'Ravenna had to see if you could channel, so she pulled a large amount up through you from the stone in the floor, which is a kind of magic-storage device. If you'd had no magical abilities, it would simply have gone through you, into her and back down into the stone. As it was, you instinctively channelled it and, because you were so unused to handling it, you burned out. We'll talk more about this tomorrow evening. Now you need to rest and recover from last night.'

He had dismissed me, so I turned and left the room. I realized I was terribly eager to try the magic out. Perhaps it was the prospect of so much power at my fingertips, or the fact that whoever I really was, I would become one of the most powerful – in the physical sense – people on Aquasilva. Maybe not as much as the long-dead Carausius, whose powers had been extraordinary, but still a powerful mage. And if the first stage of Palatine's mysterious plan worked, and I was able to decide where I went, I wouldn't be cooped up on this island running the Elemental Council's errands, but roaming the whole of Aquasilva, helping to build up the strategy that would break the Domain's power once and for all.

I had barely reached the end of the passageway and started down the next one when Ravenna appeared, literally out of the shadows.

'Follow me!' she said, and I did, down that corridor, through the

Citadel's main ante-room, down the steps and out onto the quays of the deserted harbour.

'Did you accept?' she asked when I was standing, out of breath and once again confused, on the shady stone of the quay.

'Yes, I did,' I said.

'Yes!' A faint smile lit up her serious face. 'Cathan, you're a saviour. Did anyone tell you what I feel about that old goat and his Council of bleating sheep?' She was hotly dismissive of them now, all the deference I'd seen before vanished. For the first time I heard her 'real' voice; she wasn't speaking in that flat, clipped tone she normally used.

'Persea has, and I like your way of putting it.'

'Good! It is better than they deserve – they couldn't even run a temple, let alone a heresy. No wonder we haven't won yet. Now listen. We'll have several months together learning the ways of magic, because he's taught me almost nothing so far. Chlamas and Jashua – Jashua was the older mage – will be teaching us most of the time. Chlamas reports everything directly to Ukmadorian and the Council, Jashua is harmless and rather nice. Occasionally we'll have the chief goat himself, but later on we will have to do things on our own, because there is only so much that can be taught.'

She paused for a moment, seemingly unsure of what to say. 'Listen, I'm sorry if I'm hurting you with these comments. I don't know whether I like you or not, but that isn't the point. Neither of us want to stay here, so we might as well work together. I'll try not to be quite so harsh later on, but they mustn't know we're cooperating, so we have to let things go on as they are. I know you don't like me, but will you help me?'

'I will,' I said a moment later, rather confused.

'Try and forget what we said, lay your plans with the others, and at the end of this year we can escape their clutches.'

'Fine.'

Ravenna walked quickly away, back into the Citadel. I wondered whether I could put up with her taunts for a whole year, but I was puzzled by what she'd said. And it never occurred to me to question what I got out of the agreement. I walked back to the beach the long way, wondering why, when everybody had explained to me what was going on, it all seemed as clear as mud.

Chapter XIV

I crept along the corridor, crossbow hidden under my cloak, swathed in a cloud of shadow. There were mage-guards just ahead, guarding the door of the room where my target was holding a council.

I had no intention of entering through the door, though. Now I knew which room he was in, I retraced my steps back along the corridor and into the courtyard. It, and the rooms leading off it, were deserted. I had unlocked one of them earlier; now it opened when I turned the handle the wrong way, and I slipped into the room, an unused bedroom or something similar.

The large window on the far wall was shuttered, but in the dark I could see the fastenings easily and I unlatched it. It showed a black square of the sky dotted with stars and given colour by the interstellar dust-clouds. There was no moon tonight, which was why I was making this attempt now; my getaway would be much easier.

Beyond the window the cliff dropped down sheer to the sea, rocky and treacherous at the bottom, lethal to anyone who fell too near.

I uncoiled the rope and fixed the clamp at its end to the window-sill, then pulled on my black gloves, checked my equipment and jumped up on to the wide ledge, careful to keep my balance. I twisted the rope around my hands, sat down with my legs hanging out, and then, careful to keep my grip on the rope, manoeuvred myself until I was dangling from the window by the rope. I kept my nervousness at bay, hanging there above the killing sea, and calmly went on with what I had to do. I was glad once again of Ukmadorian's special training that he'd given to the elite few of us who were the nimblest and the quietest. A lot of it had been rather unpleasant, especially the escape training, but in the last few days it had paid off.

I lowered myself down the rope until my feet touched the tiny verge between the base of the wall and the edge of the cliff. Then, still held up by the rope, I pulled out from a pouch at my waist two resin-coated pads, which I slipped over my gloves.

The resin had the quality of a very strong and fairly quick-drying glue. It would allow me to hold the walls as I moved along the ledge, but I had to move quickly. Not only would it stick fast to the wall if I held it too long, but would also be drying out as I went.

I put my hand on the wall to my left, feeling the pad stick, then moved my feet and my other arm along, moving crabwise. I was below the level of the windows and so wouldn't be illuminated by the light coming from most of them, and because it was so dark there was no risk of being seen by the single bored sentry on the balcony until I was very close.

As I got closer to the target, I felt the resin beginning to dry, and quickened my steps as much as I dared.

I heard a step above, to the left, and froze. But there was no call of alarm, no arrow, so after a moment I looked up. The sentry had sat down with his back to the house, facing out to sea; that much I could see through the balustrade.

Now came the most difficult part of the operation: getting over the wooden-railed balustrade without alarming the sentry. Fortunately, I had brought along a blowpipe and a small pouch of treated darts – always very useful. It was the work of a moment to pull it out, slip one of the tiny darts inside, and blow it at the sentry's bare arm.

He slapped at the spot in annoyance, brushing the dart away as he did. 'Damned insects,' he muttered.

I held myself in place, growing ever more anxious about the resin, until the sentry's head dropped and he nodded off, dead to the world for several more hours.

I pulled at the pads, but by now they were stuck. I swore under my breath. I had to pull my hands out, breaking the fastenings in the process, and grab hold of the railing to stop myself falling.

After that, it was the matter of a minute to haul myself up and over the balcony and crouch next to the door, open to let in air. I risked a quick look around the frame – even here, the mage guards would spot my use of shadowsight.

There were six or seven people around the table, some with their backs towards me, some facing me, but all poring over something that was laid out on it. I had to look again before I identified my target.

Then, as quietly as I could, I untied the rope around my waist and slipped it off, unhitched my crossbow from where it hung at my belt, and loaded it with the arrow made of compacted leaves – the best non-lethal replica of a real one.

I leaned around the doorpost, sighted, and fired.

In the split second before I leaped to my feet, I saw the arrow hit its target and relished the expressions of dismay on the others' faces. Then all hell erupted. I dashed to the balustrade, jumped up onto its broad top, and, as the quickest guards reached the door, dived as far out and away from the cliff as I could.

The water was warm but dark, and the moment I hit it I angled myself so as not to hit the bottom. I'd landed away from the rocks, but the water was only twenty feet deep here. Then, having left behind crossbow, rope and other implements, I swam as fast as I could away from the Citadel and along to the far end of the beach. I could breathe underwater; it was something I'd always been able to do – as had Palatine. That news hadn't really surprised me.

'There you are!' Ghanthi said, when I broke the surface. 'Hurry, they've gone absolutely wild. Did you get him?'

'Yes!'

As we sprinted off into the forest to Palatine's camp, Ghanthi was grinning broadly. Victory was now almost certain.

'Well done, all of you!' Ukmadorian was beaming.

The Great Hall was packed to capacity with every single novice of the Order of Shadow and many of the staff and helpers of the Citadel standing around the edges. In the front row of seats the Shadow Command were sitting, all very pleased with ourselves: Palatine, Mikas, Laeas, Ravenna, Ghanthi, Darius, Uzakiah, Telelea, Kuamo, Moastra, Jiudan and I. For the first time in three years one of the orders had won every single exercise in the 'war' fought between the novices of the heretic orders. We had defeated Earth, Wind, then, in the last battle, Water.

It had been on of the most enjoyable things I'd ever done. But now Water, their occupation of the Citadel over, had gone back to their own island, and the congratulations had been handed out all round.

Ukmadorian dismissed us, and we all spilled out into the afternoon sunshine, the last great event of our time at the Citadel now over. There were a little under ten days remaining before the day when we would all depart, after a ceremony in which we would be confirmed as members of the Order of Shadow, our novitiate over. Then we would board the *Shadowstar* for the long journey home, no longer callow adolescents but fully trained and indoctrinated heretics.

Those departing would include Ravenna and me, with any luck.

'Coming for a walk, anybody?' Palatine said, 'Along to the second beach?'

Laeas, Mikas and Ghanthi agreed and we walked along the edge of the forest to the beach beyond the first headland, where there would be few people and no chance of anybody unhelpful listening in. Mikas was a firm convert to Palatine's cause, and had been since the first, brilliant victory over the Order of Earth five weeks ago. He knew some of Palatine's plan, although not as much as I did. Palatine treated him as an equal, despite the fact that she was clearly a better leader than Mikas. But then, Palatine never treated anyone as an inferior during the exercises, only as a subordinate.

'One thing Cathan's taught us is how vulnerable we could be to assassination,' Mikas said. 'After we killed off the entire Earth leadership, that Water commander had more guards than the Prime himself. But Cathan took him out, and won the war for us.'

'It was a long shot,' I reminded him. Since the operation I had discovered a thousand little things that could have gone wrong but had somehow held together, a thousand things that would need to be corrected if I was called upon to do that again.

'You still did it,' Mikas reminded me. 'And the Domain will have an inexhaustible supply of assassins.'

'Hardly inexhaustible,' Laeas said. 'Many willing, but few good enough.'

'*Few* and *many* are relative terms when dealing with the Domain.'

'Set a thief to catch a thief,' Ghanthi said, grinning. 'By the time the Domain get sufficiently worried to notice us, Cathan will have a whole corps of assassin-mages.'

'Aren't you being a little optimistic? There are hardly enough mages to hold a dinner party, let alone a corps of assassins. Besides, I don't intend to be an assassin.'

'You certainly enjoy it.'

'It is enjoyable, but I don't think I'll feel the same when it's a real bolt I'm sighting.'

'Think of the Crusade,' Laeas said.

Think of the Crusade. He was right: when I imagined I was assassinating Domain leaders as vengeance for the Crusade, it cleared my mind and made my missions frighteningly easy.

'Being a mage is far more of a help, though,' Ghanthi said. 'Two mages – well, the world is at our feet, with your help.'

I had the feeling she was being sarcastic. But I didn't respond in kind.

'If they can stand each other for any period of time,' I said, remembering the frequent arguments Ravenna and I had had over the year.

'You and Ravenna?' Palatine said, incredulously, 'You don't need to pretend with us.'

'What's that supposed to mean?' I asked, as we began climbing over the ridge that separated the two beaches.

'Pah! Obviously you spend too much time using your magic powers instead of your brain. Surely you know how much you enjoy her company?'

'I enjoy her company?' I said. 'I argue with her nearly every time I see her.'

'Look, surely you know how much you like arguing with her?'

'Are you sure?' Ghanthi said, puzzled. Obviously he was saner.

Persea and I had gone our separate ways a few weeks before, but Palatine had been there when she'd told us about Ravenna's other side. But I'd never had any particular feeling for her, other than hate when we'd first arrived. Then there'd been the violent disagreements we'd had over the finer points of Ukmadorian's teaching.

'Isn't she a little cold?' Laeas said. 'When she isn't in a temper, I mean?'

Palatine hadn't told them, I realized, and I opened my mouth to say something. It was left unsaid, though.

We had reached the top, and were walking down the narrow path along the slope of the cliff towards the beach. Laeas was ahead, then Palatine and Mikas, then Ghanthi and I. Palatine must have stepped on a tussock and been thrown off balance.

I saw her stumble and lose her footing, leaning dangerously over to one side. My sight, enhanced by Shadow during the day as well as at night, meant that I realized she would fall before any of the others did. But even my lightning reflexes weren't enough. I reached out with what seemed like painful slowness, trying desperately to catch her and urging Mikas to move faster. But it was too late.

Palatine toppled over the cliff and fell with a sickening thump onto the sand twenty feet below.

'Oh, Althana, no!' Mikas said, leaning over. Laeas, who'd begun turning a second before, saw what had happened and stopped, horror-struck.

I pushed past both of them, careful not to knock them over, and ran on down the path until it was only a couple of yards above the sand. I jumped down and sprinted along, reaching Palatine's inert body before any of the others had even left the path.

She was lying limply on her back, eyes glazed and staring off into the sky. The sand had cushioned her fall somewhat, and she was still breathing. I thanked some divine power that she was still alive, and called up to Ghanthi, who was the fastest runner of us, 'Go for help, get a professional healer!'

He halted and began running back up the path, just as the others joined me.

'She's still alive,' Mikas said.

'I'm going to examine her,' I said. 'I don't think we've got time to wait.' We'd all been trained in basic medical skills, but I wasn't proposing to use those. I grasped one of Palatine's hands, closed my eyes, and emptied my mind of all extraneous thought. It had taken weeks and weeks of exercises before I could do it at will, and even now it was still hard.

Then, as Ukmadorian had done, I sent my consciousness along the link between us, filling her body with magic that had no outlet, and allowing me to 'see' it in another way. I probed her skeleton, seeing it as a silver outline in her body, floating in the utter blackness of my mind. There were no broken bones, thank Thetis, and I gave a mental sigh of relief as I wondered what was going on. Her neck should have been broken, but I couldn't even detect a fracture anywhere.

I went to another layer, seeing her tissue and blood, and for the first time seeing what Ukmadorian and Ravenna had reported: the *alien* overlay, the residue of generations of magic in her ancestors' bodies. The muscles along the back of her body had been damaged by the impact, but there appeared to be no serious damage there either. What was Palatine made of? She hadn't been ill once during the year – almost all of the rest of us had contracted one mild illness or another – and now she fell off a cliff and was unharmed.

Now I went one layer deeper, into the realm of the mind, the realm that only mind-mages could influence. I could explore it, but not do anything. Here I didn't have a separate form, only a *being* that encompassed the whole indefinable space. It was not only dangerous but intrusive to enter this realm, but somehow I had to see if it had been damaged.

There was something that shouldn't have been there, like a wall across part of her. But since I was there I could sense it had been very severely weakened, that traces of her memory could slip through.

There was another realm beyond that, the realm of the soul, but that was a place where no one could go, or had a right to go.

I slipped back up again through the layers until I was alone again, then breached the barrier that held my own mind back and allowed it to flood in. My eyes opened and I slumped forward slightly, releasing her hand.

'Cathan!' Laeas said, as if from far away. I pulled myself together and looked down at Palatine's comatose form.

'How is she?' Mikas asked, concern and fear etched on his normally inscrutable face.

'She's all right,' I said. 'Unbelievable.'

They both gave deep sighs of relief, and I sat back, propping myself against a rock, to wait for the healers who would move her.

Mikas, Laeas and I stayed at Palatine's bedside in a small room off the Infirmary until she woke up. Ghanthi stayed outside, calming everybody else down and looking in on her at frequent intervals. But he didn't let anybody else in except Ravenna, who came to see Palatine twice, looking worn and tired as she had for the past few days.

It was well past nightfall, after we had had supper delivered to us, before she came out of the coma. Her eyes opened and she stared at us with a strange expression, but it was a couple of minutes before she was able to speak.

'Orosius,' she said weakly.

We looked at each other in alarm. I was sure she hadn't had another memory loss, because there'd been no sign of anything seriously wrong. So why that name?

'It's us, Palatine,' Laeas said. 'Cathan and Mikas and me.'

Palatine turned her head to look at me.

'You look like him,' she said. 'So similar, I wonder how I missed it.'
What was she talking about? Did she think the Emperor was here, or did she know another Orosius?

'Palatine, where are you?' Mikas asked.

'The Citadel . . . but which Citadel?' She pushed herself upwards slightly, leaning on her elbows, and shook her head. She still looked very dazed.

'The Citadel of Shadows, Palatine,' I said. 'What other one is there?'

'I was born in the Citadel. My mother lives there.'

Mikas rose to find a healer, but Palatine croaked out an order in a weak voice, stopping him in his tracks.

'Stay! I'm not mad!' she said, a faint note of protest in her voice.

'Then what are you talking about?'

'It's what I can remember, as clear as I can see you three here: Cathan to my left, Laeas to my right, and Mikas on my right near the door.'

'Who were your parents?' I asked, dreading the answer.

'My father was Rheinhardt Canteni, president of Clan Canteni. My mother is . . .' She paused a minute, and put a hand to her head. 'Neptunia Tar'Conantur, sister of the old Emperor Perseus. I was born on the fifteenth day of summer in the year 2752, in the Imperial Palace in Selerian Alastre.'

'Do I understand you right?' Ravenna said. 'Palatine's claiming to be the Thetian republican leader who was murdered last year.'

We were in one of the unused quarters I'd passed two nights before; Ravenna had accosted me as I left Palatine's room to get some rest. It was pitch dark in the room, but I could see her clearly in shades of grey, as if through a filter.

'Ravenna, the mind-mage has done another mind-search on her. She believes in it totally.'

'There's still the little problem that Palatine Canteni was buried with

full honours eighteen months ago. Ukmadorian made some discreet
inquiries in the Citadel of Water, and apparently the body they buried
was definitely that of Palatine Canteni.'

There weren't any Thetians at the Citadel of Shadow; they still hated
the Tuonetar too much.

'How coherent is she?' asked Ravenna.

'Not very. She can remember who she was, and a few other details
scattered here and there. She's lost nothing from the present.'

'Anything about how she ended up floating off Equatoria? Hamilcar
picked our Palatine up near Taneth only a week after Palatine Canteni
was murdered in Thetia. No manta that ever existed could take her that
far in a single week. Which means that either she flew, or she's just
making it up.'

Halfway round the world in a week . . . no, not even the Thetians
could go that fast. But what else could she be? A pure-blood Thetian,
trained to lead, to command, and with a perfect grasp of the Thetian
language – something that she'd used to good advantage during the mock
battles with the other Citadels.

More importantly, as far as I was concerned, she was my cousin. The
only link I had to my real family. That was something that couldn't be
denied, not by anyone who'd seen us together.

'What do you think she is, then? A Domain spy who's spent the last
five years training to be someone else to be infiltrated into House Barca?'

'Of course not House Barca. Us! They're quite capable of doing that.'

'Are you saying she's a plant?' I demanded.

'No, I'm not. I'm saying that we've trusted her, we've let her lead, all
without ever knowing who she really is. Better safe than sorry.'

'What are your proposing to do about it? Take her to the Emperor and
ask if he can confirm whether or not he knows her?'

'Of course not, you fool. No point in bringing more Thetians in on
this than we have to.'

'What is it with you and Thetians, anyway?' I demanded.
'Ukmadorian likes pointing out that we have nothing to do with the
Tuonetar, but he never misses an opportunity to run the Thetians down,
and nor do you.'

'He's a Halettite, and they don't like Thetians. Is that too much for
your brain to stand?'

'Will you stop ridiculing my intelligence! It's not as if you're on a higher plane of existence, is it?'

'You seem to be displaying a total lack of thought this evening.'

'My cousin fell off a cliff earlier today, I *do* apologize for my lack of concentration.'

'Your cousin is claiming to be related to the Emperor. Not only that, but she's a Thetian martyr come through a rift to save us from the Domain.'

'It's called vengeance. The Domain hates the Thetian republicans almost as much as the Emperor does, and they didn't have any scruples about killing her father.'

'Funny how she was already plotting against them *before* her memory returned. Are you sure she's lost her memory? Or is she a very clever actor who's been playing the lot of us for fools?'

'Does everything have to have an ulterior motive?' I said.

'I'm somehow very suspicious of a resurrected Thetian republican with a mission to save us all from the Domain. I mean, a Thetian, of all people. All they do is drink and hold orgies.'

'Is that why you don't like them? Are your people paragons of virtue, who never drink, never have affairs, never pass up the chance to criticize?' I paused a moment. 'For Thetis's sake, I don't even know where you're from. Not Worldsend, by any chance, is it?'

'My people were living in cities when you ancestors hadn't got further than huts, so you had to come along and destroy it all,' she replied hotly, then stopped, as we both realized how silly this sounded. And that she'd just given something away that she hadn't intended to.

'Destroy it all?' I said, breaking the heavy, uneasy silence that followed. 'I didn't know you were that close to the Tuonetar.'

'The Tuonetar aren't the only ones who are older than the Thetians.' She seemed to have entirely forgotten that I wasn't Thetian by anything except blood.

Qalathar's history stretched back more than two thousand years; it was the only place I could think of that was older than the Tuonetar. But she wasn't Qalathari, at least not entirely. Too pale-skinned, too fine-boned.

'Where, then?' I asked her, hoping she wouldn't clam up on me again.

'You call it Upper Qalathar, but we call it Tehama.'

Chapter XV

I was more bewildered than anything else; I didn't seem to be very quick off the mark today. Was it really surprising, though, given what people had been telling me?

More to the point, were any of my friends normal human beings? I could just about take Palatine claiming to be the cousin of Emperor Orosius, although I wasn't sure how much I believed her. Ravenna had suggested that Palatine might be who she claimed to be, but it was unlikely.

I'd heard the name Tehama before, of course. They'd sided, inexplicably, with the Tuonetar during the War, and after it was over the Thetians had responded by isolating them, destroying all means of contact with the outside world. Almost totally cut off on their plateau high above Qalathar, yet still here two hundred years later?

'Not your day, is it, Cathan?' Ravenna said with sympathy, one thing I'd never have expected from her. It was something that I'd find she showed only occasionally.

'How do you expect me to believe this?' I asked, bewildered again. Why? Why were all my friends lunatics? 'In two hundred years almost nothing's been heard of them.'

'Are you surprised? No one can trade with us, so they all ignore us. This is the Archipelago, remember – trade is everything. We forgot the Tuonetar long ago, but because it's so hard getting in or out, we keep to ourselves. That way the Domain don't bother with us.'

But I was hardly in the mood for another discussion, and I was tired of standing there, in the dark, arguing with her. I had simply had enough impossibilities for one day. Nevertheless, I was unable to break away and tell her I was going to bed.

'Why keep apart? Surely if it's that difficult to get in or out, you don't have to worry about the Domain?'

'Haven't you learned anything over the past year, Cathan? They never give up. Do you think for a moment that if they knew Tehama was more than a few pathetic villages they'd leave us alone?'

Why was she putting me on the defensive again? 'Elements' sake, Ravenna, calm down! It was a stupid thing to say, and I'm sorry.'

But I'd had enough. I turned away and walked the couple of paces to the doorway, disturbing the dust on the floor as I went.

'Cathan, please! I didn't mean to upset you.'

'What was the point of telling me about this, anyway?' I demanded. Without waiting for a reply I opened the door and left, running as fast as I could away from her, along the deserted corridors, until I found my room and closed the door behind me.

I was angry at her for leading me on that wild-goose chase, but I was angry at myself as well, and I couldn't think why. My hands were shaking as I got a glass of water, and I didn't try to go to sleep. Instead I went back to the library, purloined one of the copies of Carausius's *History*, and read through some parts of it over and over again, trying to find any reference that would help.

I didn't find any such thing and it was past three before I put the book away, dissolved the cold silver shadowlight I'd been reading by, and lay down to get some sleep.

Even then, I had no rest. My dreams were all nightmares: I was being tortured by the Domain, only the torturers all had Ravenna's face; Palatine fell off the cliff, but when I reached her body it wasn't her any more, but the grey, dead-eyed corpse of Aetius IV, marked by terrible wounds.

There was no respite until somebody shook me awake.

I almost lashed out at them, thinking it was another part of the nightmare, but then I realized it wasn't. I looked around and saw it was still dark. Ravenna was kneeling by the bed, and I hastily straightened the sheet.

'What now?' I asked, my head still thick with sleep, once again, not surprisingly, feeling at a disadvantage.

'You father's the only person who can help us. He must know who you are, maybe he can even help Palatine. Do you want to go home?'

'How?' I said groggily.

'There will be a way, I promise you. It'll be easier for you to leave then me.'

'What about Palatine? She's the one who really needs to agree.'

'She can come, too. I saw her above five minutes ago, and she agrees.'

'You've been busy tonight. Oh, well, if there's a way I'll take it.'

I wasn't really in any condition to decide, in the middle of the night with a head still full of nightmares. But after what Palatine had said today, I desperately wanted to know who I really was, and if the Seer had the answers – which we weren't sure of – then going all that way to see him would be worth it.

'Good,' Ravenna said. 'Don't under any circumstances, mention Tehama to anyone except Palatine or me. Even the Archipelagans could be dangerous.

'I won't,' I promised sleepily.

She stood up and left by the window she'd come in through, a trace of her scent lingering after her.

When I woke up, that was all that reminded me it had been real.

Ukmadorian summoned Ravenna and me to his office the night before the *Shadowstar* left. The room was illuminated by six or seven candelabra and a pungent oil lamp, which cast odd shadows on the walls. For some reason, he disliked aether lighting; maybe it smacked of too much innovation.

'It has come to my attention that you're planning to leave tomorrow, Cathan,' he said, harsh and unsmiling.

'Yes, I am,' I said, keeping my face expressionless.

'You volunteered to be mage-trained, which means you are a permanent member of the Order of Shadow, and under my jurisdiction. Your training hasn't finished yet.'

'My training now consists of two hours of practice every night,' I said. 'There is nothing more I can do here.'

'The Council will decide that.'

'The Council is incapable of deciding anything,' Ravenna said. 'It can't even agree when to adjourn.'

Ukmadorian snapped, 'Silence, Ravenna! I'm talking to Cathan here.'

She didn't reply, and he continued, talking to me again, 'I warned you nine months ago that you wouldn't be able to return with the others. You didn't object then.'

'You didn't warn me. You hinted at it. I never had any intention of staying here longer than everybody else. I set out from home intending to be back within three months. I've now been away a year and a quarter. Also, there is nobody in the Archipelago who can tell me who I am, so I'm going back home, then on to find somebody who can.'

'We cannot risk you in the outside world!'

'I'm perfectly capable of taking care of myself in the outside world. I have no intention of remaining on this island for the rest of my life while your Council dithers. I have a life to lead, and it doesn't belong to you.'

'Rudeness will get you nowhere, Cathan,' he said coldly, every trace of his usual affability now vanished. 'I can simply forbid you to go. I have ways of enforcing it, too.'

'Ukmadorian, he isn't a hermit, and neither am I,' Ravenna snapped. 'You have no intention of ever letting me go outside your reach, either, not even to go back home.'

'*You?* You have even less right than Cathan, Ravenna. You cannot endanger yourself and your people like that. Listen, both of you. This nonsense will stop. The Domain have people who can detect either of you across half a city. The moment you set foot in any major centre of population you'll be seized.'

'That's nonsense,' Ravenna said hotly. 'Worthy of you, and your stinking Council. Weave your web of lies, and see what good it does you. I was eighteen a year and a half ago, so your wardship's officially ended. I'm not living my life on this island wearing your collar. I'm going with Cathan and Palatine. Maybe one day I'll even get to go home.'

She was in full flow now, and I thought I saw Ukmadorian flinch. She lifted her left hand, the one with the bracelet on it, and I saw the bracelet shiver apart as if it had been made of ice.

I did the same, a moment later, breaking the bond that held us to the Order of Shadow. I was amazed how calm I felt: a year ago I'd never have been able to stand up to Ukmadorian when he was in a mood like this. Now, despite the fact that we were still bound by Citadel regulations, I felt no fear of what he could do, or of what he might say. I wondered whether the change in me was entirely due to my own development or whether Ravenna had something to do with it.

After I broke my bracelet and its fragments had fallen to the floor, there was absolute silence, during which Ukmadorian looked from one to the other of us as we stood side by side in front of his desk. For a moment a stunned expression flickered over his face, but he masked it, and his rage intensified.

'Both of you? Cheats and deceivers already?'

'If I choose to cooperate with Cathan, that's my own business, and something else that is none of your concern!'

'You're disgraces to the Order of Shadow.'

He had lost, but he didn't realize it. After what he'd said, there was no possible way he could convince us to stay. And if he tried to force us . . .

'No,' I said, as fervently as Ravenna had. 'We just want to live real lives, instead of sitting on this island playing at heresy.' The 'we' slipped in without my even thinking about it; I was so angry at the way he'd been trying to stop us that I plunged on, 'In two hundred years you've achieved nothing by sitting on this island and keeping your mages safe, in case the Domain could get them. You can't win that way!'

'Would you rather burn at the stake?' Ukmadorian demanded. 'You know what happens to heretics who are caught by the Domain.'

'We aren't going to get burned at the stake,' Ravenna said. 'That would only happen if we didn't know how to conceal ourselves, and not to use magic.'

Ukmadorian sat back and took in both of us with a cold glance.

'If you leave, it will be without your magic. You aren't leaving the island unless you surrender every last bit of it.'

'You fool!' Ravenna was laughing, a laugh without any mirth in it at all. 'Do you really imagine you can do anything that you've threatened? Drain the magic from Cathan? You'd kill him. Only you wouldn't because I'd kill you first, *Uncle.*' Her eyes were flashing with fury, and I could see a magic field crackling as she moved.

'Are you threatening me, Ravenna? I can call upon the entire staff of the Citadel to subdue the two of you, which I will if you won't apologize, back down or submit.'

Then she attacked him again, heedless of any consequences.

'Do you really think you can do that? Out in the world, we can be of some use in the heresy. But that goes against your precious plans, so if you can't use us, nobody will. Are the heirs of Carausius nothing but petty old men now? Hoarding what they have, and too cautious to do anything other than play at Domain power politics? If Cathan is related to the Emperor, will that make any difference to you? We have lives to lead, Ukmadorian, and they aren't going to be spent here. We are leaving on the *Shadowstar* tomorrow, powers intact, and you aren't going to stop us.'

Ukmadorian opened his mouth to say something, half out of his chair, red-faced with rage and seemingly on the verge of attacking us physically.

And then, quite suddenly, his fire died and he slumped back into his chair. He looked haggard and defeated, and ten years older. All he said, in a low, malevolent tone, was, 'Go.'

We turned round, without looking at him any more, and walked out. As we did Ravenna put her arm around my shoulders, quite deliberately, but I never saw Ukmadorian's face.

We shut the door and walked away down the corridor. Round the corner Ravenna motioned for me to wait and darted back. She returned a moment later.

'Hasn't moved,' she said, with some satisfaction.

'Why did he collapse like that?' I headed in the direction of the front gates. Outside, on the grass exercise ground, there was a bonfire and the last-night party was being held.

'He lost the will to stand up to us any more,' she said. 'It's happened several times before: that's how I come to be on the ship that attacked you. He didn't want me to go, but I argued and in the end he just gave up.'

'Will he try and stop us?'

'No,' she said, confidently. 'And if he does, we'll be waiting for him.'

'What about Chlamas, and the others?'

'They won't protest if he doesn't. And now, shall we go and enjoy the evening? I've been on this island for nearly two years, and this is my last night.'

'I hear they've brought out some of the better wine.'

'I hope so. They did last year.'

We stopped in the hallway, and she looked at me with her very serious, unfathomable expression, he head titled slightly to one side.

'Thank you, Cathan. I've been horrible to you, and for that I'm sorry. But you seemed to enjoy arguing with me once you got the hang of it.'

That sentence had been all the apology I was going to get. Still, I didn't feel any rancour now, and I realized that she and Palatine had been right. I *had* enjoyed matching wits with her over the past few months – and I no longer hated her.

The party was already in full swing, and an Archipelagan minstrel group was playing, hired from one of the nearby – heretic – islands. There were torches fixed in all the trees around the edge, and lanterns hung from posts and the walls of the Citadel. The dancing space was a large area to the right of the bonfire, and the table with the wine was on the other side.

We headed for the bar, and then went to look for Palatine.

It wasn't hard to find her: even in the flickering torchlight, we could see the huge form of Laeas from the other side of the bonfire. And, generally, where Laeas was Palatine, Mikas and Ghanthi would also be. Most of Palatine's friends were male, although none of us were ever anything more than friends to her.

They saw us coming, and – somewhat to my embarrassment – cheered. I wasn't sure if it was for having outwitted Ukmadorian – although of course they couldn't know yet – or because for once we weren't arguing.

'Did you do it?' Palatine asked, stepping forward with a wide grin.

'We're leaving tomorrow!'

Ghanthi punched the air with his fist, and Laeas grinned madly. Mikas lifted his glass.

'A toast, to Cathan and Ravenna!'

They toasted us loudly and cheerfully amid the merriment of the party, and then we forgot about the formalities, and the Domain, and everything else, and started to enjoy ourselves. Palatine was in fine form, and there wasn't the slightest hint that she'd fallen over a cliff the week before, or that she claimed to be the girl who'd been Thetia's bright hope until a few months before. Laeas spent an hour helping Ghanthi summon up the courage to ask one particular girl to dance, and himself danced with nearly as many partners as Palatine. Since that was in her case virtually every man present, he managed to chalk up an impressive total. I was unadventurous by comparison, although I was blissfully happy spending this last evening in my friends' company – Laeas, Mikas and Persea would leave on a different ship, bound for the Archipelago's capital in Qalathar and then on, for Mikas, to Cambress. Under normal circumstances it would have been years, if ever, before we saw them again, but Palatine's refusal to accept Domain control demanded otherwise. With luck, within a couple of years I would see most of them again.

I danced with Persea and several other girls I knew, as well as with Ravenna. She could dance much better than I: for all my quickness of foot, I was a fairly hopeless dancer. But she was more than good enough that I could follow her and not notice my own clumsiness, and the end of the dance was cause for regret.

The evening passed amid a general haze of goodwill: Darius and I, who'd never got along that well, toasted each other, and promised to forget any animosity. I spent a lot of time talking with Palatine and the others, mostly about the things we'd done during the past year. Like the time I'd gone in the wrong window by mistake, and ended up in some girl's dressing room instead of in the headquarters of the enemy, or when Mikas had mistaken a lump of rock for Laeas and attacked it with a practice sword, breaking the weapon in the process. Laeas didn't seem to mind being compared to a lump of rock, and he was more than happy with Ghanthi finally danced with the girl.

The wine was consumed in large quantities, although not by me – no magic had been able to improve my poor head for drink. Towards the end, Laeas picked up one of the empty wine barrels, a huge wooden thing, lifted it above his head and threw it onto the bonfire, where it landed with a spectacular shower of sparks and a roar of approval from the crowd.

All good things had to come to an end, though, and eventually the party did. It must have been about two in the morning, when even the strongest heads were beginning to feel the effects of wine, that the staff set off a fireworks display. For a few short minutes, galaxies of sparks in all colours filled the sky, and the sound of banshee rockets rang in our ears, concluding with a final, seven-tiered silver starburst that bloomed, for a moment, like a silver sun, bathing us all in its radiance.

And then we were back in the light of the bonfire, and the time for talking was over.

For most.

I hadn't quite been sure where I was going to spend this last night, but it came as a total surprise to me when Ravenna came across as I was talking to Palatine and looked at me inquiringly.

I said goodnight to Palatine, Laeas and the others – those I could find, anyway, as the novices had scattered across the Citadel and cross the island – and then, with Ravenna, walked away along the edge of the forest, parallel to the beach. Gradually the firelight and the sound of revelry faded behind us, and the quiet of the night took over.

We walked in silence, and after the first promontory, the one where Palatine had fallen, moved down onto the beach, took our sandals off and walked barefoot through the surf.

It was an utterly peaceful night now, and a beautiful one, very much like that first night after we'd been shown the Crusade, when I fled to avoid the nightmares. One of the moons was full, hanging in the clear, star-studded sky above and illuminating the white beach, the dark grey sea lit by patches of blue phosphorescence. The other was a slim, perfect crescent, low on the horizon with only stars behind it, away from the brilliant blues and reds of the interstellar dust clouds that covered great portions of the sky. On some nights, the rings would have been visible as a thin silver line arcing across the cosmos, but tonight there were none, only the moons.

We stopped a while later, after crossing a sandbar that marked the edge of a lagoon, palm trees along its low-lying edges. Here there were only gentle waves lapping on the curving beach in the centre, and it was even calmer than before. The water was very clear, and in the moonlight we could see right down to the bottom, the waves making ripple patterns on the sand.

'I told you swimming at night was an experience,' Ravenna said. 'Have you ever done it?'

'A few times,' I said.

'It's not the same on your own.'

'Shall we, then?'

I slipped out of my clothes and swam out until it was deep enough to submerge, feeling nothing except an incredible calm and peacefulness.

Afterwards, we sat on the sand, neither of us wanting to disturb the intense feeling of peace and well-being. I could truly appreciate why this place had been compared to Paradise: it had a rare and precious quality in that there were very few places like this where you could find solitude and near-absolute silence, without any of the worries of sounds of the continental storms.

'I promised I'd tell you sometime why I behaved like that at first,' Ravenna said, her voice quiet. She'd used some strange Shadow spell to keep her hair dry, and it hung loose, almost the first time I'd seen it like that, tumbling around her shoulders and down her back in a wavy mass, framing her face and her smile.

'Why did you, then?'

'I was very certain of everything about myself, until I met you the first time. For some reason I couldn't fix on, even the thought of you disturbed me, and I thought it was because I didn't trust you, you were on the side of the Domain. That second time, I still wasn't sure, so I kept on lashing out at you. I didn't even realize why until the night of that exercise and the mage-testing. I didn't hurt you too much, did I?'

'I was afraid of you, if you must know,' I said. 'You behaved as if you were on a higher plane than me, and the idea got fixed in my mind. I could never work out why you had to keep insulting me, though.'

She laughed. 'So we unnerved each other equally. Oh well, at least it wasn't just one of us imagining the other was out to get them.'

Again, there was a pause. A zephyr of breeze chilled my skin for a moment, making me shiver slightly, then passed, hardly moving the leaves of the jungle canopy. Was there something magical about this island, I wondered? Or was it that I felt calmer at night-time now I was a Shadow-mage?

'We've been so anxious to leave this island,' Ravenna said finally, 'and I don't regret it. But there are some things I'll miss. These beaches, and the swimming, and the freedom to go anywhere on the island without having to worry about storms or tribesmen. Once we leave here, there's nowhere like this, nowhere peaceful. Tehama, I suppose, but it's always cloudy there, like a constant pall over everything.'

'I'll miss the sense of space,' I said dreamily. 'Here there's open ocean on all sides, and whichever way we look there's open sky, even beyond the mountain.'

'Do you think we'll ever come somewhere like this again?' she said, wistfully. 'Ever feel this peaceful? Once we leave the Archipelago, we're back to the outside world and the constant danger of being found out. Then we have however many years it'll be when we're never able to come back here in case Ukmadorian won't let us leave again.'

'I will miss it,' I said regretfully, 'but too much peace can be boring.'

'Too much peace can never be boring. The Archipelago was Paradise once, when it was still peaceful. War is something we should always hate.' She closed her eyes. 'Still, I suppose this war will serve some purpose.'

'You, not wanting conflict?'

She opened her eyes again. 'Conflict, not war. Still, let's promise that we'll come back to the Archipelago sometime, when it's all over, perhaps. It can't do any harm.'

'Promise. I wish I could sit like this one day by the shores of Thetia, Thetia as it was. Why do the Domain have to destroy everything they touch?'

'They were founded in treachery, they survive by treachery. But, Cathan, remember what you've learned. The Tuonetar tried to destroy this world. They came with the hand of peace, and with blood. They killed millions of people, but they didn't win. We're still here, the world is still here. The Domain are only a shadow of the Tuonetar, and in the end, they won't win.'

'Right now, I have to confess I'd far rather know who I really am.'

'It's strange: these last few days you've found the first clue to who you are, and I've been reminded of who I am and there's nothing I'd like more than to forget it.'

I was too entranced to say anything, but some part of me wondered why Ravenna always had all the answers. And why I always followed her.

We talked for a while longer, and for the first time we didn't argue about anything. It must have been an hour or so later than we finally stopped, more through tiredness than because we'd run out of things to say. I could tell that this was all she'd wanted, and I still wasn't sure what to make of her. We lay down beside each other, behind some rocks at the top of the beach that would keep the sun off us in the morning.

'There must be so much more up there than there is on this world,' she said dreamily, staring up at the panorama of the skies. 'Things beyond the Domain and our other concerns, maybe some answers . . .'

'Answers to what?'

'So many questions. Every question must have an answer, or where would we be?'

As I looked up with her, my eyes beginning to close, I almost missed the tiny, twinkling speck of light that was moving faster than any star.

'What's that, do you think?' I showed her what I was looking at.

'Part of history? Or perhaps the future? Who knows? She shifted position slightly.

I followed the strange speck on its course across the sky, until I stopped wondering and went to sleep with her head on my shoulder.

Part Three: The Clan

Chapter XVI

We met the pirates less than thirty miles from Pharassa, after a long and otherwise uneventful journey.

I was playing cards with Palatine, Ravenna and another Oceanian acolyte in Palatine's quarters, one of the largest apartments on the upper accommodation deck of the *Shadowstar*. There were so few people left on board now that we had virtually a free choice of rooms, and had appropriated the suites that would once have been set aside for the admiral and his staff, back in the *Shadowstar*'s fighting days.

The alarm sounded: a strident wail that cut across our conversation and made me jump. Ravenna, who was dealing, dropped the pack on to the floor, and cursed.

'What is it now? A school of dolphins?' she said, bending down to pick up the scattered cards.

'Let's go and see.' Palatine pushed her chair back, rose, and headed towards the door. 'Forget the cards for now.'

We followed her out of the room and down the corridor. The screech of the alarms echoed down it, and the red warning panels in the roof flashed. Other doors opened, and two or three acolytes emerged.

The deck began to tilt slightly as we reached the forward stairwell, and I had to catch at the rail to steady myself. I could see seamen rushing across the base of the stairwell two levels below us, and could hear shouted orders coming from the bridge.

The first thing I looked at when we reached the bridge and wedged ourselves behind the railings at the back, out of the crew's way, was the scene on the aether table. For weeks, every time I'd come in here, it had showed only the *Shadowstar* cruising through empty ocean. Now there were three more mantas visible.

One looked like a merchantman, but I couldn't see the colourings on the horns to find which House it belonged to because the arm of someone's chair was in the way. The other two were small, sleek corsairs, compact and heavily armed. The first of them was still pursuing the merchantman, which was veering round in a desperate effort to escape the blue streaks of pulse-cannon fire; I hoped that when it turned, I'd be able to see the House insignia. The other had broken off and was heading towards the *Shadowstar*. Why were they so confident, I wondered? Even a demilitarized battle cruiser should be a match for them.

'Open fire!' the captain ordered, and I saw the *Shadowstar*'s armaments coming to life: more streaks of pulse fire, this time heading towards the pirates, followed by flame lances and a couple of torpedoes from the lower launchers.

'I've identified the pirates, sir!' said one of the seamen, who'd been crouched over an information console behind us. 'According to the library, they're frigates stolen from the Cambressian Navy two years ago, now thought to be part of a corsair group operating out of northern Equatoria. They're double-reactor ships!'

'Elements!' the captain said, a sudden look of worry on his face. 'Increase shield strength as much as you can, and launch the pressure charges!'

I grabbed hold of the rail as the first of the pirate's shots thudded into the *Shadowstar*, the shields directing it harmlessly across the surface of the hull. The captain looked worried, as well he might. I'd never seen a double-reactor ship before, but the *Shadowstar*'s master had told me about them on the way to the Citadel, and I knew that two reactors instead of one increased fourfold the ship's available firepower and defensive strength.

'Sir, pressure charges are illegal, and the House manta might report us!'

'The House will keep its mouth shut if it knows what's good for it. Launch those charges!'

'Aye, aye, sir.'

Two black voids sped out of a weapons port in the *Shadowstar*'s belly, and headed on different paths: one above and one below the pirate ship. I wondered exactly what a pressure charge did; at a guess I'd have said it was some way of getting round the problem of the aether shields.

I found out a moment later, when the two ovoids exploded directly in

line with the ship, the one above the vessel slightly further away from it.
A moment later the pirate was slammed upwards as if pushed by a giant
hand, and then pushed downwards again with equal force. Its weapon-
fire stopped. Immediately the other pirate broke off its attack on the
manta and sped over to its damaged fellow.

'Keep on firing until they turn away,' the captain ordered. There was
a hushed silence in the room as we waited, the only movement the
flickers of light on the aether table.

Then the first pirate vessel's wings began to beat, and as the
Shadowstar's weapons shut down they both glided off into the oceanic
murk. The captain looked satisfied.

'Before I open a channel to that House manta, can you tell me who it
is?'

'Colours are midnight blue and silver; I don't recognize . . .'

'House Barca,' Palatine said instantly. 'They're friends.'

'Oh, they're your House, aren't they?' the captain said. 'I forgot that.
Hail them, Comm. Bridge projection.'

A moment later the aetherized image of the other manta's bridge
appeared on the *Shadowstar*'s forward screen, obscuring the view out to
sea. I could see the bridge crew, and while I'd never seen the other
vessel's captain before in my life, there was one face there that I definitely
knew.

Hamilcar Barca.

I watched Hamilcar and his captain thank the *Shadowstar*'s captain and
crew gratefully, then relate what had happened. The pirates had no doubt
been hired by Hamilcar's enemies House Foryth to dispose of him and
his House at one stroke. They'd attacked a few miles back, and the
Barcans had tried to outrun them, without success. We'd arrived at
exactly the right time, because their shields were about to fail.

It wasn't until Hamilcar had finished his account that Palatine stepped
forward.

'Palatine!' Hamilcar said, his solemn face breaking into a smile. He
looked just as careworn as the last time we'd seen him, but seemed
somehow happier. 'Where in Ranthas's name have you been for the
past year? All Elnibal would tell me was that you'd been accidentally
kidnapped by some friends of his, and might not be back for a year or
so.'

'I can't explain, really – at least, not yet,' Palatine said. 'Where are you going?'

'Lepidor, to pick up the first full iron cargo.'

That *was* a stroke of luck, because it would save us time waiting in Pharassa.

'In which case, could you take us?' I asked

'Of course,' Hamilcar said. 'Who's *we*?'

'Palatine, another friend, and me.'

Hamilcar eyed Ravenna with some suspicion when she emerged from the hatchway, and his greeting wasn't the warmest I'd even heard. Ravenna seemed equally reserved, and I wondered why Hamilcar seemed to dislike her when she hadn't even said anything. I was in two minds about her still, even after that last night in the Citadel, but I didn't see what his problem was. The *Shadowstar* stayed docked to Hamilcar's manta, the *Fenicia*, and helped to patch up some of the damage. In case the pirates attacked again, the captain also transferred some extra weaponry, including two of the pulse charges, reminding the *Fenicia*'s commander that they were only to be used in extreme circumstances. After the transfers and repairs were complete, we said goodbye to the *Shadowstar*, her captain, and the remaining acolytes, and the two ships parted courses: the *Shadowstar* to head for Pharassa to unload the last of the acolytes and pick up the Oceanians who would be the next year's students, and the *Fenicia* to go north, up to Lepidor.

That night the three of us – for Hamilcar could hardly exclude Ravenna – dined in Hamilcar's quarters. Our host and Ravenna exchanged a few words in chilly tones, but mostly ignored each other.

'What have you been doing for the past eighteen months?' Hamilcar asked, when the servant had brought the first course and left. It was a Tanethan salad dish which I liked, but after a year of Archipelagan food it tasted unusual, and I ate slowly.

'I can't tell you that,' Palatine said. 'We had to swear not to.'

'Was it something involving the Domain? I have no more love for them than your father does, Cathan.'

'Palatine, remember what we agreed,' Ravenna snapped before she could say anything. 'Cathan and I are in far more danger than you.'

Palatine was quick to respond. 'Ravenna, if Hamilcar tells the Domain anything he will get arrested as well as us. In any case, I trust him.'

'Never trust a Tanethan,' Hamilcar said, gently reproving.

'My mother told me never to trust anyone if they could gain by betraying me.' Palatine shrugged. 'You betray us and that would ruin Lepidor too, so why would you want to? And you saved my life instead of throwing me back in the sea like a too-small fish.'

'That was a gift from the sea,' Hamilcar said. 'I'm never ungrateful.' He looked puzzled. 'You mentioned your mother. Can you remember who she is now?'

'She's called Neptunia, she's Thetian. My father's dead, he was Rheinhardt Canteni.'

'President Rheinhardt? The Thetian reformer?'

'Who else?'

'I can see the resemblance,' Hamilcar said, looking at her. 'I met him once.'

'Are we getting anywhere?' Ravenna asked irritably. (Why did she have to keep interrupting? This was a reunion, for heaven's sake.) 'Are you going to tell him everything, even though he's a friend? He's still not one of us.'

Palatine glared at her, then paused, seemingly lost in thought. Hamilcar took a few more mouthfuls, his gaze never leaving Palatine's face.

'It's important for the plan that we have a Great House helping,' Palatine said, staring off into the black distance outside the manta's windows. After another moment's thought, she looked back at Hamilcar.

'You live for profit, don't you, Hamilcar? The more, the better.'

'Yes.' Hamilcar didn't seem worried by Palatine's roundabout approach and the discussions that excluded him. Was he being too patient, I wondered, and could Hamilcar gain something by betraying us?

Did Tanethans have any moral code at all? Maybe that brief friendship with Palatine hadn't stood the test of a year's separation.

'How far would you go for profit?'

Ravenna had closed her eyes and was sitting back in the chair; I sensed she was using shadowsight to check for someone standing outside the door. Moritan would have been more thorough, or course. He'd have sealed off the entire corridor and scanned the whole room for spy devices but we didn't have the expertise. Ravenna would detect any obvious ones, but there was nothing I could do to improve on that. I wondered how the little assassin was doing, how his clan was faring. How was Lepidor, more to the point? I'd have to ask Hamilcar that later. I'd hardly thought about the place during my time at the Citadel, but often during the voyage back I'd longed to be home and see those familiar faces again.

'It depends how big a profit,' Hamilcar answered. 'And it would have to be fairly immediate, not a vague promise of profit ten years in the future.'

'Would you put your purse before Ranthas?'

'You mean, would I do anything that could get me burned at the stake as a heretic?'

Ravenna looked daggers at her, but Palatine continued. 'Would you deal with heretics?'

This time it was Hamilcar's turn to pause. 'There'd have to be a big profit, even to help friends like you. But I have no feelings for the Domain either way. None of my family were particularly religious; my mother was a heretic, and she drummed out of me all the Domain ideas my tutors taught me. After she died I found her room was full of heretical books.'

'Then would you help a heretic rebellion? Sell it arms, give it the occasional loan . . .'

'It'd have to have a chance of succeeding,' Hamilcar said.

'It will,' Palatine promised. 'You won't even know it's a heresy until the very last minute.'

'So that's where you've been for the past year,' Hamilcar said. 'Learning how to be heretics somewhere in the Archipelago.'

'What's wrong with the Archipelago?' Ravenna asked belligerently.

'What is it to you?' Hamilcar said. I thought his urbane calm was showing signs of strain. 'You're not an Archipelagan.'

'I've lived there long enough to know it's a lot better than Taneth.'

'Excuse me,' Palatine said hastily, as I sunk back further into my thinly upholstered chair to escape the argument. 'Hamilcar, will you or won't you?'

'I'd like to know a little more about your plan before I decided anything,' he said. 'I'm fond of grilled food, but not when I'm the guest of honour. Oh, and Palatine?'

'Yes?'

'You're supposed to have been murdered eighteen months ago.'

'Ah,' said Palatine. 'You don't believe in magic, do you? This could be hard to explain.'

I don't think Hamilcar believed us, but he didn't disagree too violently or ridicule outright any of the wild ideas we'd formed about how she'd got here. Ravenna watched our efforts in amused silence, ignoring Hamilcar totally. We didn't mention Tehama.

Eventually Hamilcar held up a hand and said, 'I'll accept what you say, whether I believe it or not. But even if you *are* Thetians, Tar'Conanturs or just pretending to be, you're still going to be a major threat to the Domain – and also a focus of resistance.'

'For those who believe in Thetian supremacy,' Ravenna said.

'More people than you realize, actually,' Hamilcar said. 'The heads of the Great Houses hate Thetia, but they'll all have read the Histories. I can remember a Qalathari official who came on an embassy two or three years ago – Ramunou or something like that. He said that there were a lot of people in Qalathar who'd welcome a Thetian restoration, because they're fed up with being exploited by the Continents.'

'We Qalatharis have our own Pharaoh,' Ravenna said indignantly. 'We would not welcome foreign control.'

I looked at her in surprise; I'd thought the non-Tehaman half of her ancestry was from one of the islands, not Qalathar itself. Still, I should have guessed. They had a reputation for fierceness.

'You're Qalathari?' Hamilcar said.

'Yes.' I thought Ravenna looked as if she was daring him to comment.

'Interesting. But, Cathan, before you think of starting rebellions I'd suggest you look closer to home.'

I started. 'What do you mean?'

'The pirate attack today was the second since you've been gone. One of my ships was attacked off the Cape of Storms on its way back to Taneth with the sample cargo. Fortunately, just for once the captain was awake and they beat off the pirates.'

'You think someone's trying to destroy you?'

'I know they are: it's our old friend Lijah Foryth, who's once again on the Council of Ten. He regards the Oceanian metal trade as something of a personal preserve, and he's angry that he wasn't approached.'

'I wonder if he knows he offended us before we even had a chance to offer it to him,' I said, remembering the incident in the ante-room of the Saleva Palace, when only Courtières's timely intervention had saved Sarhaddon and me from being thrown in the dungeons. How was Sarhaddon getting on in the Holy City, I wondered? I'd almost forgotten my travelling companion during my time in the Archipelago.

But now I was a heretic, and he was probably firmly ensconced in the Domain hierarchy. I hoped he hadn't fallen foul of Lachazzar's fanatics.

'Foryth wouldn't care about a petty thing like that, even if you would. My point is that he's bent on ruining me so that you'll have no choice but to offer him the contract instead. Even two lost cargoes would break the agreement, and Foryth has enough influence here to ensure that nobody else would sign a deal.'

'What are Foryth's House colours?' Ravenna asked abruptly, as if she'd just remembered something.

'Yellow and orange. Why do you ask?'

'Palatine and Cathan were kidnapped in Taneth – not by us. We rescued them a little while later, but we did find that the men who'd done it were Houses employees. When we searched them one was carrying a pass with orange and yellow colours.'

'So Foryth were already working against us back then,' Hamilcar said. 'You don't know who they were after, Cathan or Palatine?'

'Nothing more than what I've just told you. If you think about it, though—' her tone was very condescending, as if she was talking to a child '—Palatine would have no value to them as a hostage; you hardly knew her. They'd have been after Cathan.'

Hamilcar didn't reply, and I thought he showed remarkable control by completely ignoring her. He turned back to me.

'I should think your father will need your help at home for a while. So, if you were planning to go off again shortly, could you change your plans?'

Why did Hamilcar want me to help? Surely that was his affair, and Lepidor's business could be handled by my father and First Adviser Atek? I wondered whether something was wrong – but if there was, it seemed unlikely that Hamilcar wouldn't have mentioned it.

Although I wanted to return home, I didn't want to stay there. If we were going to start a movement against the Domain, Lepidor would be no place to start – it was too isolated and on the fringe.

'I don't need to go home yet,' said Ravenna.

'This is a strange way to be going to Qalathar from the Archipelago,' Hamilcar said.

'The route I take to go home is none of your business,' she said.

'I could have guessed,' he said. But Ravenna ignored the jibe.

My quarters on the *Fenicia* were plain and functional, another sign of Hamilcar's lack of money. He'd told us that the iron profits so far had paid off all of his House's creditors, and he was hoping to make more profit from this voyage. But he was still in dire straits financially, and it would be a couple of years before he'd have money to spare for jobs like upgrading his mantas – the *Fenicia* sailed like an ungainly slug – or undertaking new ventures. The loss of a manta to pirates would almost certainly ruin him, simply because he wouldn't then have enough operational capacity to do the iron run.

I couldn't see what possible use I could be in fending off Lord Foryth's corsairs – I wasn't a qualified captain or a brilliant strategist. Palatine might be able to help – in fact, she'd be more use than I would.

Having unpacked as much as I needed to, I pulled my copy of the *History* out of the bottom of my bag and sat down in what passed for a comfortable chair. I'd paid for the Citadel library to have another copy made for me, and while it wasn't as legible as the magically written original, it was in a fair hand and had the necessary text.

I opened the *History* to one of the later passages, looking for some more reference to what had happened in Qalathar after the War, more information on the mysterious highland people who had allied themselves with the Tueonetar. It was on the four hundredth page or thereabouts.

Something fell out of the book onto my lap, and I picked it up. It was a scrap of parchment torn off from a larger sheet, with a couple of sentences scrawled on it in Ukmadorian's spidery handwriting.

Cathan, it read,

I may have been a little harsh on you, but I bear you no ill will for what happened. You have chosen to ally yourself with Ravenna, and I wish you good luck in this. However, I warn you that she is not who she seems to be, and that you put yourself in danger by being as close as you are. Even if she does not want to harm you, some of those connected with her may. They are people way beyond your and your father's league, and I do not want to see your talents go to waste.

He didn't sign it.

I stared at the note for a moment, then ripped it apart savagely. Thousands of miles beyond the Citadel, Ukmadorian was still trying to control me and poison my mind. I was free of the old fool now, and I planned to stay that way.

Chapter XVII

We reached Lepidor three days later; battered though *Fenicia* was, she still made the passage from Pharassa twice as fast as the *Parasur*. I found *Fenicia* more comfortable, too, if a little dull. Staring at the empty ocean wasn't quite as interesting as looking at the continents.

I was very glad to be coming home again at last, even though I didn't intend to stay. It was all very well spending eighteen months away, and for the most part I'd enjoyed it. But it just wasn't the same as home, and I was looking forward to a time of being Escount of Lepidor again, rather than a trainee heretic mage. The mage-training and being taught how to skulk around were considerably more exciting – sometimes a little too exciting, being taught how to escape from ropes, cells etc. came to mind – but it would be good to see the familiar faces of Lepidor again. For a while. There had been a time when I wouldn't have minded spending a lot of my life in Lepidor as Count or an oceanographer, but now . . .

I was standing on the bridge again as *Fenicia* approached Lepidor's undersea harbour. It seemed so small after Pharassa and Taneth, just the four gantries in a spiral round the hub. Only – it wasn't four any more. There was a construction bubble over the lower levels, and the skeleton of a fifth gantry. I spotted another loading warehouse, too just behind it, and wondered what was going on. I'd never seen such a major construction effort in Lepidor. It must be the iron profits, I thought, watching the hub; as we came closer, I could make out figures in the reception lobby.

We docked at the fourth gantry, and I noticed more new additions – an extra lift running down the side of the central core, which until now had been concealed behind the bulk of the main structure. The gantry was larger, too, I saw: the cargo loading platform had been widened, and a linking tunnel ran from that to the top end of the new warehouse.

'I forgot to tell you about this, Cathan,' Hamilcar said, smiling. 'You'll hardly recognize Lepidor; it's changed hugely in the last year. Your father's been ploughing all his profits back into the city.'

I wasn't sure how I'd feel about huge changes in my home city but thank Thetis that the decline we'd all be so worried about had been reversed. From being a city that couldn't afford to pay for forest clearing, now we were building new harbour gantries – an expensive improvement, and certainly one my father wouldn't have undertaken lightly.

The docking clamps latched onto the *Fenicia*'s hull, and after the moment's pause while the water drained out, the hatches opened. We thanked the captain, and Hamilcar gestured for me to go first out into the well – only two storeys: the *Fenicia* was just over half the size of the *Shadowstar* – and along the corridor and the gantry. I picked up my bag, the same one I'd set out with except it now contained a mage's staff instead of the iron samples, and the others stepped back to let me through.

My father was standing in the carpeted gallery of the core, at the end of the gantry. I saw an incredulous look come onto his face as he saw me – he'd obviously been expecting only Hamilcar – then I hardly had time to drop my bag before being crushed in his vicelike hug.

'Cathan!' he said, and I could see the pleasure in his face. 'Where've you been all this time? You've grown!'

'I'm still half a head shorter than you,' I reminded him.

'Not that way, fool. You came through the door as if you owned it, rather than sidling through the way you used to. It's good to have you back – although I doubt you'll recognize anything.' He caught sight of Palatine, Ravenna and Hamilcar coming through the gantry a little way behind. 'Palatine as well; welcome to Lepidor!'

'And Ravenna, from the Citadel,' I said.

My father didn't have any of Hamilcar's coldness to Ravenna; he gave her another smile and welcomed her as an honoured guest. She, for her part, responded with charming grace and none of the stiffness she'd shown towards the Tanethan. I was glad about that; my father could be quite sharp with people he didn't like. A year ago, I wouldn't have minded, but now I didn't want her to have a bad time in Lepidor.

My father welcomed Hamilcar, then swept us off up the central staircase and out into the sunlight beyond the gates of the harbour.

I stopped dead, at first dazzled by the sunlight. Then I looked round, astonished, at the changes. And Hamilcar had said they'd only sprung up in the last few months.

There were construction scaffolds all over the place, and the streets echoed with the sounds of building and the calls of workmen. They'd renovated the row of slightly seedy dockside taverns and chandlers along the quay, for a start. A previously rather dingy row of buildings now had an immaculately gleaming façade and its roofs were covered in luscious greenery. There were changes at ground level, too; some of the old taverns had been replaced by smarter bars.

It wasn't just the harbour district that had benefited, as I saw a moment later. Storeys had been added to some of the buildings, while new towers and even the odd dome had altered the skyline. Then I looked over towards the inland side, and almost gasped as I realized that the land beyond the Eastgate had become a fourth district of the city, its scaffoldings dominated by the unmistakable shape of a foundry. And as for those huge pavilions in the marketplace . . .

I looked at my father, speechless with amazement. This was far beyond what I could ever had imagined – but at the same time I was wondering, *how*? Surely this couldn't all have been funded by the mine profits?

'How come?' I asked, almost in a daze.

'We called in a mining survey team after Istiq left. He'd barely scratched the surface; there was far more there than the iron deposits. The whole mountain's full of minerals, and there's another gem seam over on the far side. So, when we got the results, we decided we might as well produce weapons here too. There's far more profit in them – and more need, at the moment, than for raw iron.'

'And the rest of the continent rushed to make sure they weren't left out,' Hamilcar said. 'Are all the guest houses still full?'

'We had to build four more hostels just to keep up with the influx.'

I said the first thing that came into my head, which was, 'What about the danger from pirates?'

'That's being taken care of. I'll tell you more when we're back in the Palace, and you've surprised your mother as you did me.'

'What about Moritan and Courtières?' I asked as we set off up the main street, my father having waved an elephant drover – an elephant, for personal transport? – aside because there wasn't room on his beast for all of us.

'Moritan and Courtières are doing very well out of this,' Elnibal said. 'Clever of you to have thought of them. They're contributing the lion's share of the investment, as well as a lot of the trained craftsmen. Moritan's taken a part-share in the mines; after all, he's got all those trained miners of his own, and Courtières has paid for the foundry.'

So our allies were doing well out of Lepidor's new prosperity. *Good*, I thought. I knew from my studies at the Citadel, and from the *History*, that discontented allies were often more of a threat than lifelong enemies.

It took us ages to get up to the Palace – although I couldn't see it yet because the walls of the Harbour Quarter and the buildings beyond them blocked my view. We kept on stopping as people greeted my father – and, on several occasions, me – warmly, and overseers wandered out of the sites with friendly smiles on their faces. There were more outsiders than there had been, and somehow the atmosphere was very different. I could sense that the small town I'd left was no more, the iron discovery had changed things so much.

As we entered the market square, coughing in the dust from stone drills and having to wait while an important roofing beam was hoisted into place, we met Shihap, the cloth merchant who I'd last seen while galloping along the other main street to tell my mother of the discovery, eighteen months ago. He'd been the first person in the city to know, and, to my surprise, he remembered.

'Greetings, Cathan!' he called, emerging from his purple-and-white-striped stall with banners fluttering on the top. 'Are you glad to be back? Could you even have dreamed of all this, when you told me about a little iron deposit in the hills?'

'*You* certainly did, Shihap,' my father said, looking at the fat merchant's crimson robes trimmed with silver thread. I could smell the costly oils in his beard from several feet away.

'I merely took advantage of the situation when it arose, for which I have a good business sense.'

'And a few outstanding loans.'

Shihap shrugged deprecatingly, and said to Ravenna and Palatine, 'You haven't been here before, ladies. Come to my stall sometime, and I'm sure I'll be able to interest you in some top-quality goods . . .'

We moved on, through a market that was more busy on this, a normal day, than I had ever seen it before, almost as busy as when the Great Northern Fair had been held here, six years ago. There were a lot of traders I didn't recognize, people new to Lepidor, and the ones I knew had changed as well: their clothes were finer, their bearing haughtier, their stalls more opulent.

The last great surprise was the Palace. I didn't see it properly until we were level with the last stalls, and even then I didn't recognize it.

The quiet, slightly run-down courtyard was run-down no more. The stonework had been repaired and newly painted; the tiles on the gallery and staircase roof were new, unbroken and more expensive.

And to the left of the central building, where the royal stables and the end of the gardens had been, was an entirely new structure, in the same unassuming colonial style as the old, but now boasting a blue dome that I guessed was over a hundred feet in diameter. My father had built a proper Council and Throne Hall.

'Wherever did you find the money for that?' I asked my father, and my face must have shown my surprise. Ravenna looked a little amused, but Palatine's face was solemn and a little sad.

'The next cargo will refill the treasury,' he said proudly. 'Do you like it?'

'Like it? It's amazing!' Some of the other changes had been a little unsettling, but seeing the dome I felt a surge of immense pride that my clan was now rich enough to afford such a symbol of its power. Domed halls were the ultimate expression of grandeur, I knew, and on my way to Taneth eighteen months ago I'd envied the domes in other cities. Now we had our own, and it was far grander than any other north of Pharassa.

I could see why Lijah Foryth wanted to get his hands on Hamilcar's contract. How big were Hamilcar's debts, then? He was getting a fifth of the profits – surely that should have been more than enough to pay off any creditors.

The two guards – in new uniforms, I noticed, and more alert – at the gate waved us into the courtyard, which now boasted a fountain carved in the shape of a tigress. My mother was standing at the bottom of the steps, with First Adviser Atek and a small reception party of officials and servants. She was no less surprised than my father had been, but her welcome was more reserved. She hadn't changed, except that her clothes were finer and the pin that fastened back her braid was gold, not silver.

'You promised you'd only be away for three months,' she said.

'I never was very good at arithmetic.'

She smiled warmly. 'Your brother will want to know where you've been. He's grown so much you'll hardly recognize him.'

'He's seven now, isn't he?' I said, suddenly finding that I couldn't remember when Jerian's birthday was.

'Last month. Courtières gave him a practice sword, and he hasn't stopped waving it around since.'

I introduced Palatine and Ravenna to her, and greeted First Adviser Atek. His clothes were still as crumpled as ever, but his waistline had expanded somewhat. Then we went up the steps to the Reception Hall where a welcome had been prepared for Hamilcar. The Reception Hall was a large, high-roofed room that had been regilded since I'd left; one side of it opened onto the south-side colonnade, looking over the sea. Servants stood by with small glasses of blue wine – their livery, too, I noted, was new. (Wouldn't it be simpler to count the things that were the same?) Lepidor had been so run-down, I realized, that anything would have been an improvement, yet somehow I missed the old, worn liveries with the patches where the thread had come out and the stylized seal, Lepidor's emblem, was missing its flipper or tail.

I talked to my parents and Atek for a while about what had happened – discussion of events at the Citadel would be in secret, and later – and then looked around for Palatine, remembering the forlorn look on her face as we'd approached the Palace.

I found her at the end of the balcony, staring out over Palace gardens towards the sea, empty wine glass in hand. Over to the left the banner of the Domain flapped from the roof of the temple, a storey higher than it had been.

'What's bothering you?' I asked, without preamble, as I stood next to her.

Palatine didn't turn round. 'The dome – and everything else. It's envy, I suppose. Your dome looks like the one we had in Cantenar, maybe a little smaller. But that's not really what I mean. I envy you, Cathan. Here you have the life and the security that I lost eleven years ago. A home, parents who love you, even though they aren't your blood parents, a brother.

'My father died eleven years ago – my mother always said he was poisoned. Even before that, I saw so little of him. He never liked my mother's family, so I always ended up in Canteni territory, while he was in Selerian Alastre. And my mother, she's always so busy. She was always in the capital too, looking after the Emperor and all his people. It wasn't much fun, even when I did go there, because it's not a very nice city. Always I had tutors, swordmasters, companions . . . but never any parents.'

There wasn't a trace of self-pity in Palatine's voice, only a soft sadness.

'When Perseus died, it seemed things were going to change. There was so much to do, so many opportunities. Orosius could have been so brilliant, so great, one last chance for the Tar'Conanturs to show they're worth the effort we gave them. And instead he joins up with the Domain, and now I hear he sends people he doesn't like off to a great prison castle, and they're never seen again. The Domain destroy everything they touch, they are like a plague, a blight. And now I come here, to this peaceful place where you live, and I see their people are at work here as well.' I was stunned by the sheer hatred in her voice, a hatred I hadn't noticed before.

'We're going to stop them,' I said, unsure.

'Yes, but we find a threat here and we haven't even started. That's what House Foryth are. The Domain attacks in places you can't see, they're insidious. If only we had even a few legions of Aetius the Great, things would be so different. But look out there: would even they survive here?'

As if the very planet was listening to her, I saw cloud formations beginning to build up to the east, piling higher and higher as I watched. Another storm. The Domain's legacy. Palatine was right; I only had to look out of the window to see why I should hate them.

We went back inside and I mentioned the storm formations to my father.

He asked, 'From the east?'

I nodded.

'Most of the big storms have been coming from the east in the last few weeks. They were coming from the west for a while, against the prevailing winds, and we were getting worried. At least now they seem to be getting back to normal.' He told one of the servants to open a line to the watching post, and gave instructions for them to call a storm alert in ten minutes. Meanwhile, I turned my attention again to the reception, spending a few moments talking to Atek about Taneth – for all his knowledge about trading systems and the like, he'd never been there. My father had obviously told him not to ask about where I'd been, at least not in public; I didn't know whether Atek was a heretic as well. He was my mother's cousin, though, and he'd been brought up with her. I thought it unlikely that he wouldn't be.

Exactly ten minutes after I'd told my father about the clouds, the familiar lilting wail of the storm siren rang out across the city.

I finally got the chance to talk to my parents in private late that evening, after everybody else had gone to bed. I went along to the reception room attached to my parents' private suite, well lit by warm shaded aether lamps and a few torches. Rich hangings on the walls and over the windows kept it soundproofed and also cut out the howling of the storm. It was only a faint background noise inside the Palace's walls, but it wasn't nearly at full intensity yet.

I sank down in one of the soft Pharassan armchairs. Oceanian furniture, strangely enough, was another thing I'd missed. The Archipelagans believed in cushions rather than chairs, and even the copies of Oceanian furniture installed in my father's lodgings in Taneth had been designed by somebody who'd never seen the real article.

'How was your time at the Citadel?' my father asked, as I sipped a fruit cocktail; I'd nearly drunk too much at the reception earlier – two glasses seemed about my limit, as usual.

'I enjoyed it.' I briefly sketched out what had happened and what it had been like, omitting any reference to Palatine or Ravenna, or to our last argument with Ukmadorian. Other than his evil note, there'd been no more protest from the Provost about our departure.

'So you're a mage,' Elnibal said when I had finished. I'd expected him to be surprised, but he wasn't. I felt curiously disappointed.

'Did you expect that?' I asked, trying to find out why he hadn't seemed more impressed by my news.

'I knew,' he said. 'I always knew.'

'Ravenna's one as well, isn't she?' my mother said.

'How can you tell?' I said.

'She uses shadowsight. One of my friends when I was at the Citadel had some magical talent, and I can still tell when someone's using shadowsight. How powerful is she?'

'More powerful than me,' I said. 'I think.'

There was a pause, and my parents looked at each other, awkwardly.

'Father,' I said, 'was what you told me about finding me in the ruins of a village true? You've got to tell me now.'

'No, it wasn't,' he said, bluntly. 'But the truth is so strange, I couldn't risk telling you until you'd been to the Citadel.'

'Palatine claims to be the cousin of the Emperor, someone I thought was murdered last year.'

'Palatine looks a little like you, and she may well be right. What I tell you now you mustn't ever repeat to anyone, not even your real relatives.' Elnibal fidgeted with a stray thread on the end of the armchair, looking, for once, slightly uneasy.

'Twenty years ago, when I was fighting as a mercenary in Tumarian – it's a clan in the eastern Archipelago – I was on a few days' leave in Ral Tumar with Moritan and Courtières. We were trying to sample the wine of all the bars in the city in four days.'

I tried to imagine the three of them drinking and carousing, but failed.

'One evening we stayed very late, I can't remember why, and came out at about two in the morning, in the middle of a storm. On our way home, we ran into a fight.'

I stopped him there, and, when he nodded his approval, used a method Ukmadorian had taught me, of how to imprint someone's memories on to one's own mind.

Then I was there, in that street in Ral Tumar eighteen years ago.

The three of them skidded to a halt as they saw three exhausted men in white uniforms facing four hooded figures in red robes. The street was slippery with gore, and two more whites lay on the stones in pools of blood.

One of the whites shouted for help, in a desperate voice, and Elinbal, Courtières and Moritan drew their swords. They rushed at the red figures – somewhat unsteadily: they were all drunk. Another white – the one who'd shouted – fell a second later, but the arrival of three more fighters turned the tide. Two of the red figures were dispatched, and another, holding a bundle close to his chest, took flight.

My father, who was the fastest runner, went after the fleeing one, while Moritan and Courtières stayed to finish off the last of the reds.

My father nearly slipped in the blinding rain, but after a few dozen feet he caught up with the runner and swung an unsteady blade at his ribs. The man groaned and toppled over, landing on his back. Then the bundle wailed, and I realized I was looking at me as I had been twenty years ago; wrapped in some coarse blanket, from inside which the ends of a green silk wrap could be seen. It was a shock to realize that this little bundle had been me once.

'Stealing babies, are you?' my father said savagely. But there was no answer.

He cut me loose from the dead man and, sheathing his sword, carried me back to the others. The last of the white-clad men had fallen, a dagger protruding from his stomach; around him lay the bodies of three reds and four whites. I thought that I could just make out a silver dolphin emblem on the dying man's chest, but the only lights were from the aether lamps, and his surcoat was soaked in blood.

'Who is this baby?' my father asked urgently; I could see the man was dying. 'Who are you?'

'I'm Baethelen . . . of Clan Salassa. This baby . . .' He gasped, coughing up blood, and Moritan shook his hands helplessly. But the man somehow clung to life. 'Who are *you*?' he asked, his voice dreadfully hoarse. There was a bubbling in his throat.

'Elnibal, Escount of Lepidor.'

'Lepidor . . . where's that?'

'Oceanus. What is it you want?'

The white-clad man reached down with a shaking hand and drew a medallion on a thong out of his shirt. As he held it up, his face was grey with pain and he was losing blood faster than Moritan could staunch it with one of the dead men's cloaks.

'Do you recognize this?'

I didn't, but my father did.

'It's a Justiciar's medallion – Thetian.'

'I was once Chancellor of Thetia. Please . . . swear to me that you'll bring him up, and never tell the Domain of this.'

Courtières's eyes were wide, but my father grasped the medallion and said, 'I so swear.'

Another dreadful paroxysm shook the dying man; his back arched and he tried to scream, but only a gout of blood came out of his mouth. He collapsed back onto the stones.

'Cathan . . .' His limbs spasmed one more time, and he died. My father and his friends were left alone with the baby in the rain.

'Better get away from here,' Moritan said. 'There will be patrols along in the morning, wanting to know what happened and whose baby this is.'

'He never told us,' my father said.

The scene faded from my mind as I sank back into the warm comfort of the room in Lepidor.

'That is as it happened,' my father said. 'How we got away, and all that, is irrelevant.'

'Are Moritan and Courtières heretics as well?' I asked.

'Yes, they are. Courtières never went to the Citadel – his tutor was a Cambressian Earth follower. Moritan went to the Citadel, but he's turned into an atheist; he'd never support the Domain, but he doesn't care much for the Archipelago either.'

'Your friend, Palatine,' my mother said. 'An unusual name – I'm sure I've heard it recently.'

'You have,' I said. 'The rising star of the republican party in Thetia was a twenty-one-year-old woman called Palatine Canteni. She was supposed to have been murdered about a year and a half ago.'

'You think that's who she is?'

'I don't know,' I said, as much to myself as to them. 'She's my cousin, apparently.'

'You're certainly Thetian, but for the rest I can't help you,' my father said, rising. 'We can talk more about the Citadel, and other things, tomorrow evening.'

I said goodnight to my parents and went back to my old room, in the corner tower a floor above the reception room. My luggage had been left there, and I'd unpacked it earlier; now I sat in my chair staring out at the storm, thinking of what my father had seen twenty years ago.

I hadn't recognized the Justiciar's medallion, but I knew what it meant. They were the symbols of supreme legal authority in the Empire, and they were made specifically for each individual. They couldn't be copied or stolen . . . so why had the Chancellor of Thetia given up his life in any alleyway in Tumar to protect a baby? Who was I, that I had to be safeguarded from the Domain like that?

I was Palatine's cousin, but not even my father knew who I really was . . . which meant there wasn't anybody who could tell me. It seemed unlikely I'd find the answer in any archives, because if it had been written down, someone would surely have come after me by now.

I felt unbelievably desolate and disappointed; finding Palatine had raised my hopes, and now they'd been dashed again. I was sure I could find out who I was eventually, because Palatine could only have a limited number of first cousins . . . but it could take years.

CHAPTER XVIII

The storm was still raging the next morning, and since each of the previous two had lasted for three days, this one probably would as well. Even though the Domain forbade study of the storms, it was common knowledge that storms came in cycles, often with several storms of about the same strength and duration following fast on one another.

My father summoned a Council meeting, taking advantage of the only time none of the councillors would be busy with their new construction projects. It was an open meeting, so I asked Ravenna and Palatine to come and watch, to see how Lepidor worked. I myself was now a non-voting Council member; able to attend the meetings and have a say, although I couldn't decide anything.

The Council Hall – as opposed to the Council Chamber, where secret meetings were held – had hardly changed, unlike the rest of the city. It was a large room on the second storey, with a vaulted roof and tapestries covering the walls. The floor was still covered in the same dark blue matting; I was glad my father hadn't had that replaced, it was a lovely colour. No less elegant were the oval Council table and chairs – made of ancient polished whitewood.

My father was seated at one end of the table, with his back to the high windows at the end of the hall, the curtains now drawn to shut out the storm. Atek was on his left, and the head of the Council, Osman Tailiennus, on his right. Osman had been head of the Council for years, and I'd never quite been sure why, because he seemed incapable of making decisions.

I was next to Atek, and I knew that was so he and my father could keep a rein on what I was doing. My father said I would take my own seat once I became a proper member, and I dreaded having to tell him I wasn't planning to stay.

With me there were now fourteen councillors, who included the Harbour Master, Janus Tortelen; the Avarch, Gaius Siana, Shihap and Rear-Admiral Dalriadis, commander of Lepidor's navy and marine contingents. Rear-Admiral was his rank in the Imperial Navy, but since they were only a name out here he had all the powers of a full admiral.

All of the councillors except Siana and Dalriadis were in their seats by the time we arrived, and the gallery, at the opposite end of the room from my father's seat, was about half full. I could see my mother in the place reserved for her, as well as Ravenna and Palatine a few places along. I looked up and caught their gazes; Palatine grinned and Ravenna gave one of her slight half-smiles. Seeing them helped keep down the butterflies. I wondered why it was that I hadn't been afraid clambering along a wall above sharp rocks but was nervous attending my first peacetime council meeting in my home town with people I knew.

Dalriadis swept in a moment later, depositing his hooded blue raincape with a servant and taking his place next to me. His thin mouth twitched upwards at the corners when he saw me – his welcome to the Council. I knew Dalriadis quite well, and liked him despite the hard training he'd given me during my lessons in seamanship on board Lepidor's manta, the *Marduk*. Would we be getting a new manta as well, I wondered, with the next iron profits? Their price was rising as the seawood supply slowly dwindled, but a second one would make all the difference if we were attacked by a large number of pirates.

My father rapped his gavel on the table and said, 'Where is Avarch Siana?' It seemed oddly out of place, the gavel, I thought, made of worn mahogany in contrast to the spotless brightness of the table and chairs.

As the talk in the gallery died, Tortelen said, 'I saw him an hour ago, and he said he was coming then.'

My father was about to say something else, but the doors to the chamber swung open again to admit Siana, leaning on his stick. The last grey hairs in his beard had changed to white, but otherwise he was the same as when I'd seen him accompany Sarhaddon down to the docking gantry eighteen months ago. How old was he now – seventy-three?

'My apologies for being late,' the old man said, hobbling up to his chair and lowering himself into it. 'A *consigno* arrived from the Holy City.'

A *consigno*, Sarhaddon had told me, was a high-priority letter from the

Primarchy, usually containing urgent orders.

'Are we allowed to know what was in it?' my father asked.

'I have to tell the Council officially.'

My father nodded, and called the Council into session. 'Avarch, your announcement is first on the agenda.'

'Gentlemen, forgive me if I don't stand,' Siana said apologetically. Then he continued, 'The *consigno* contained orders for my replacement. The Prime Lachazzar has decided my long and valuable services to Lepidor warrant a promotion to the vacant post of Chancellor to the ziggurat at Pharassa. My successor, Avarch Midian, will be arriving shortly to take over the post.'

There was silence for a moment, then my father started clapping, sparking off a wave of applause and congratulations. But – Siana was *leaving*? He'd been Avarch for over twenty-five years, since my grandfather's time, and we hadn't been expecting a replacement for another few months at least. So why was he being promoted and moved now, to take up the prestigious but empty post of ziggurat Chancellor?

And this successor didn't bode well either. Midian was a Halettite name. Oceanus was supposed to have native Avarchs, not foreigners. Was Midian some wild-eyed fanatic?

I couldn't voice my doubts in open Council, so I kept quiet; later on would be the time to discuss those things. I wondered if it would be worth asking Siana what, if anything, he knew of Midian.

'We are sad you're leaving, and wish you well in your new post,' my father said.

Then there were a few more minutes of confused babble before he restored order again, and asked Siana, 'When will your successor be arriving?'

'His transport left Taneth four days ago, so he'll be here in less than a fortnight.'

'We shall hold a banquet in your honour early next week, then, as soon as we can arrange it. A small enough reward, I'm afraid, for twenty-seven years as Avarch, but your superiors have moved too quickly for us to prepare a fitting send-off.'

We moved on to the first listed item, which concerned harbour tariffs, but I found my mind wandering. I supposed I should have seen this coming: Siana was a pleasant old man, not particularly gifted, but just right for the sleepy, declining outpost Lepidor had been. But for a city that was rapidly growing into the largest one north of Pharassa, the Prime would need someone more charismatic – and probably more zealous. Possibly even a careerist, one who saw an Avarchate as merely a step up to the Exarchate, and from there to the Primacy.

And if, as I feared, Midian was a protégé of Lachazzar, that put us all in grave danger, Ravenna and me in particular. But for the first time I found that I was more worried about Ravenna.

We went quickly through most of the agenda. Atek had told me before the meeting that the last item was the most important. It was a proposal by one of the Council factions to demand annulment of Hamilcar's contract if only a single cargo was lost. It seemed they were an anti-Barca group, who were displeased with my father's choice of House – what did they know, the fools – and wanted to secure an alliance with a bigger house as soon as possible. Foryth money was already at work, then, as Palatine had said.

Mezentus was their spokesman, a hawk-faced merchant who ran Lepidor's spice trade; his seconder was Haaluk, the mine manager. Surely he should have gone back to his homeland by now?

'House Barca have already suffered two piratical attacks, Sire, the second one only averted by blind chance. With so much hanging on each new cargo, do we want to risk ruin? Lepidor will go into debt if one fails to get through, but a second capture after that would ruin us as well as House Barca.'

'The pirate attacks are designed to force us to do just that,' my father said. 'With the money from the cargoes, House Barca will be able to upgrade their defences and maybe even buy new ships. We gain more by establishing a long-term relationship based on trust than by switching Houses at the first sign of trouble.'

'Trust won't help us if we go bankrupt,' Haaluk said belligerently.

'The *Marduk* will stop us going bankrupt in the first place,' Dalriadis said. 'The *Fenicia* will be escorted on her next voyages.'

'Now we're having to strip Lepidor's defences to help protect our cargoes,' Mezentus protested. 'This isn't the way to go on.'

'Lepidor's defences are perfectly adequate,' the admiral said dryly. 'Unlike the people they're defending.'

Elnibal reprimanded him for the comment, though I felt it more for form than because he meant it, and Mezentus glowered.

'I'm not casting aspersions on anyone else,' said Dalriadis innocently, spreading his heads wide to include the rest of the hall.

'Good,' Shihap said. 'Anyway, who says those defences are there to protect the people? Forget the people, and think of all this poor defenceless money in the city. We can protect ourselves . . .'

'How, Shihap?' Dalriadis interrupted. 'By rolling over the pirates?'

Shihap grinned good-naturedly – I knew he wasn't in the least bit concerned about his weight and didn't mind people joking about it – and continued, '. . . But what can the coins do?'

'Stay salted away in your strongbox, supported by more fortifications than the Holy City.'

'Gentleman, this is a serious Council meeting,' my father said reprovingly, but the others were smiling. Had Dalriadis and Shihap, both – according to Atek – staunch supporters of Hamilcar, planned this beforehand?

Mezentus was fuming, seeing how everyone's attention had been diverted away from his item. 'I demand a vote,' he said. I wondered if that was wise of him: did he risk exposing the limits of his support too early?

As it turned out, he had more than I thought: the motion was rejected by eight votes to five. I wondered if Foryth was intervening – or were there other agendas at work here that I had no idea of? Siana's replacement was an unknown factor: if an issue like this came up again, who would he side with? Mezentus only needed to win over two more for a majority.

Still, my father could veto any decision passed with less than ten votes, so we were safe.

After Mezentus's item, my father declared the meeting dissolved; I hadn't said a word, mostly because I didn't have a clue about most of the topics. I didn't even know the names of some of the streets and businesses that had been mentioned. In a way, I felt as though this wasn't my home any more. I'd known everything that was going on before I left, but now there seemed to be so much more in which I wasn't involved.

The audience got up and left, chattering among themselves, and Palatine and Ravenna came down; I met them on the floor of the hall, away from the councillors leaving in groups, Mezentus looked daggers at

Dalriadis as the admiral made a particularly witty comment and several people laughed.

'Very educational,' was Palatine's verdict. 'Your admiral is very good at distracting people.'

'Do you ever get anything done?' Ravenna asked, 'Or do those two sabotage any proposal they don't like and turn all the Council meetings into comedies?'

'I can remember them doing it before,' I said, 'I've had to watch every public meeting from the gallery since I was fifteen, so I'd know what was going on. But before, it didn't matter quite so much. They used to argue incessantly about tiny changes in tariffs, and Mezentus joined in. Today it wasn't the same . . . it's as if he believes in it now.' Mezentus's behaviour had left me feeling uneasy. He and Shihap had always been friendly rivals, but their disputes hadn't gone outside the Council chamber or the accounts. But now Mezentus had his own little faction, and from the look in his eyes he wouldn't be drinking with Shihap in the bar any more.

'It's all changed, hasn't it?' said Ravenna, showing her uncanny ability to fasten on my exact thoughts. She always came out with some helpful advice, but I bitterly resented the way she always seemed to *know*, both what I was feeling and thinking. How did she get this perception – was she reading my mind? 'You've come back, and it's not the same, or as friendly, as it used to be.'

Palatine interrupted just as I was about to say the first thing that came into my head, which wasn't very pleasant.

'They haven't turned against your father at all, Cathan,' she said, 'or Lepidor. Mezentus and his cronies still want the best for your city and your family – not even Foryth want to change that. It's Hamilcar who they don't like.'

'But that's something else that's changed,' I protested. 'They all welcomed him with open arms when he came to collect the first cargo, apparently. Now they want to break the contract at the earliest possible opportunity. Mezentus always prided himself on being a man of his word; now he wants to dishonour his whole city.'

'Only so it can gain more. He's just misguided,' Palatine said. 'However much this city has changed, the Council is still united behind your father. The iron hasn't changed that.'

'But will it? If Mezentus has changed so much this far, how much more can he change?'

I saw some people hanging round unconvincingly a few yards away, and took the others out of the Council chamber via the door that connected it with the courtyard of the Palace, heading them towards one of the rooms on the upper west level that I'd had fitted out as a private retreat, somewhere to go aside from my own room. It was quite small and fairly dark even in sunlight, but its great advantage was the open fireplace, a leftover that my quarters, in a newer wing and with the benefits of wall-heating, lacked. It was primitive, but during storms it made all the difference in warmth and comfort.

It was grey-dark in the room, but I knew it inside out. It took me a few seconds with a tinderbox to set light to the desiccated seawood kelp logs that lay there, while Palatine turned on the other lights, shaded to be warm and welcoming.

'You've got an eye for home comforts here,' Palatine said, sprawling down on one of the rug-covered sofas facing the fire. I'd hung more tapestries over the otherwise bleak whitewashed stone walls; before that the room had been less welcoming than the Tanethan desk clerk. Ravenna and I sat on the other couch, facing Palatine.

'I think this is all rather suspicious,' Palatine said musingly, a moment later, staring into the dancing flames in what seemed like fascination. I wondered if she'd seen an open fire before in a building; surely Thetia was too hot for that? Not that we had that much wood to burn here; my firewood was what was left from the *Marduk*'s engine core after it had last been cleaned out, because no one was rich enough to burn fresh seawood.

'In what way?' Ravenna asked, unknotting her hair-band and freeing her hair with a shake of her head. It hung strangely, I thought, as if it wanted to be curly rather than straight. Watching her reminded me of the other side of the argument, why I felt so guilty about distrusting her, and why I resented Palatine and Hamilcar's attitude.

'There are two lots of people involved here. House Foryth want the iron contract, so they try to buy the Council and sabotage Hamilcar. That's obvious, we can see why they're doing it. But the Domain – what are they doing?' She leaned forward, using her hands to emphasize her words as usual. 'They replace the Avarch, even though he was going to retire soon, and give him this empty post in Pharassa. Why do they do that? They could have waited, given him a less valuable post. Lachazzar doesn't give out honours for no reason.'

'Maybe they want more control over us?' I suggested.

'Then why not wait a few months, sent this Midian person up as deputy until then? Why do they sent him out now in such a hurry?'

Ravenna flicked a stray lock of hair away from her face and stared intently into the distance. 'Maybe it's more infighting, nothing to do with Lepidor at all? Perhaps Lachazzar wants to promote Midian very quickly, and needs to give him a year or so as Avarch before raising him to the Exarchate? Perhaps he's being sent here to get him out of the way. I'm sorry I can't help you more, but we haven't heard from Etlae.'

'Surely there must be other good Avarchates coming up anyway?'

'It's no loss to them, giving Siana that Chancellor's post,' I said. 'They've plenty of empty honours to go around, and I can remember Sarhaddon telling me they even invent new ones if they need to.'

'But even if it doesn't cost them anything,' Palatine said, 'why not wait? There are three hundred Avarchates or so. There'll be another free one in a month or two. This isn't just a shuffle – they must be up to something. I'm sure of it.'

'I'll ask Siana what he knows about Midian,' I said. 'He was one of my tutors, so I know him quite well, and I'm going to see him anyway. I think it may be better if I leave you two behind; he's never talked to either of you, and it would probably make things more difficult.'

That evening I wrapped myself in a heavy storm-cloak and made my way through the windy, rain-drenched streets to the Shrine, a little way away from the Palace. I wasn't doing anything suspicious, although that wouldn't be any help to me if the reason for my visit was known. I told the amiable priest on duty that I was there to pay my respects after such a long absence, and he showed me up the familiar flight of steps in the building and into Siana's office.

The Avarch had never been inclined to asceticism, and as he became progressively more crippled by rheumatism and arthritis, his office had grown more and more heavily furnished. There were cushions on every seat, and a fire blazing all the time the sun wasn't shining. I'd often wondered where the Domain got the money for extravagances like that. The carpet was very soft underfoot.

There was a shelf running along one wall, covered with antique carvings; I knew every feature of every one from long hours spent staring at them during Siana's theology lessons. I'd never been interested enough in metaphysics to concentrate on his words for long.

'Come in, Cathan,' a voice said from an ornately carved chair facing the fire.

My feet sank into the rugs as I crossed the floor to where Siana was sitting. I knelt before the chair for his blessing, wondering as I did whether that meant anything any more.

'Sit down,' he said when he'd given it, pointing to a slightly less ornate chair with fewer cushions opposite.

'You've changed, Cathan, changed a lot. I haven't spoken two words to you since you came back, but I can see you're not the same person I used to teach.' He was sitting with his gnarled hands on the arms of the chair, deep-sunk eyes fixed on my face. He looked even frailer than he had earlier, and I wondered if he was ill.

'I've been to Taneth, and the Archipelago,' I said. 'That's enough to change anybody.' I was choosing my words with care, and I was afraid of sounding too long-winded. However well I knew this man, he was still an Avarch, in the hierarchy of the Domain. The enemy. I still found it hard to think of Siana and Lachazzar as linked in any way.

'Did Sarhaddon show you safely to Taneth?'

'Yes, he did, and he was a very good travelling companion.'

Siana smiled faintly. 'I haven't heard anything from or about him since he left here. I hope he found a powerful enough patron to get his foot on the first rung of the ladder.'

'He didn't seem all that interested in climbing up the hierarchy. Not seriously.'

'He wasn't, but I think once he got to the Holy City he'd have changed his mind. The Holy City offers many opportunities for those clever enough to see them, and Sarhaddon is very clever indeed. Who knows, maybe when you rule here, he may return as Avarch. Lepidor will be an important posting within a few years.'

This was as good a time to ask as any, I reckoned. 'Could you tell me about this Midian person they're sending out? Is he a careerist?'

I thought I saw Siana's face darken for a moment, but I couldn't be sure in the flickering, uneven firelight.

'Midian,' the Avarch said heavily, 'is a protégé of Lachazzar. He is from one of the oldest Halettite families; his eldest brother is one of Reglath Eshar's generals, and another brother is a senior Avarch. And he's a Sacrus. Sarhaddon will have told you about Domain politics, and how unstable anybody's position is, but the way Midian's career is advancing he'll wear an Exarch's robes before he's forty.'

My heart sank, and I tried desperately to keep my shock from showing. We couldn't have done worse if Lachazzar himself had come as Avarch. Palatine had been right: they were clearing Siana out to make room for a fanatical, dyed-in-the-wool religious maniac.

Siana sighed, gave a wry smile. 'I can see you don't like the idea, and I don't blame you. Midian is one of those people who believes in the absolute power of the Domain. Spiritual ascendancy, they call it. For him the Domain has a divine mission to rule – not just souls, but states as well. If your father knows of any heretics in the city to whom he's turning a blind eye, he would do well to tell them to leave before Midian arrives. There will be vultures above the square before long.'

I must have gone absolutely white, and I felt sick all of a sudden. It wasn't just Lepidor in danger now, but my own life, my parents' lives, Palatine's and Ravenna's. Within the space of a few heartbeats, heresy had gone from being an idea, something that we played at on a safe island thousands of miles from anywhere, to something that could kill me within the year.

'Are you all right, Cathan?' Siana asked.

I pulled myself together as best I could and tried to look unconcerned. 'Yes, I'm fine. Listen, I never found out how Lachazzar got elected Prime,' I said, trying to divert his attention. 'Sarhaddon said he was regarded as part of the lunatic fringe, something of an outcast in the Holy City, and that whichever moderate was elected the next Prime was certain to pack him off with a hundred Sacri and tell him to convert the Ralentians. He wasn't even an Under-Prime, so how did he get elected?'

Siana gave me a shrewd glance. He saw right through the diversion and, as I wondered whether he could possibly have guessed, he answered the question.

'Don't spread what I tell you around, as this is inside information. This isn't something I should be telling anyone. But it is fair to tell you, because your clanspeople are having Midian inflicted on them while I end my days in Pharassa.

'Almost until the very end, a few days before Halezziah's death and the election, the obvious successor was the Second Prime, Kareshurban. He's a little more conservative than Halezziah, perhaps, but just the person to rule for a few years, keep things going nicely, and not introduce any radical reforms. He's sixty-eight, so in a few years he would have died and it would have been someone else's turn.

'About a fortnight before Halezziah died, the Sacri uncovered a nest of heretics hiding in the Palace of one of the more liberal resident Avarchs, with a cache of weapons and some revolutionary plan. Lachazzar immediately took charge of the clean-up, and proceeded to arrest the Avarch and anyone in the City who looked remotely suspicious. It looked as if the heretics had nearly succeeded in bringing the Domain down, and so Lachazzar came out looking like a hero. He then used the large numbers of troops in the city to "persuade" the Exarch Council to vote for him.'

'You mean he coerced the hierarchy into voting for him?'

'He did,' Siana said, sounding very tired. He seemed to shrink a little as he pulled his robe tighter around him. 'Many senior people have gone, replaced by Sacri and fanatics. The Domain isn't the same as it was five years ago. There are fundamentalists everywhere, and even the most pious have had their faith questioned.'

I remembered Etlae and her plotting, the attacks on Domain figures and Sacri, the conversation Sarhaddon and I had heard in the ziggurat of Pharassa. She'd been trying to bring Lachazzar to the Primacy. Why? What possible benefit could it bring to elevate someone whose contribution to Aquasilva would be to start purging left, right and centre and probably kill thousands of innocent people in the process?

'How long do you think Midian will stay here?' I asked.

'It depends. Whether Midian remains in favour, whether Lachazzar stays alive. But if Lachazzar lives, Midian should be promoted to a Sacri generalship or an Exarchate within two years.'

Two years. For as long as two years we would have this ravening wolf eating at Lepidor's heart; for two years my father would have to watch his every move. And Jerian – what if Midian insisted on taking over his education, as was his right? Would my adopted brother be corrupted by Midian's influence?

Siana switched the conversation to less contentious matters – such as what I'd done in my eighteen months away. I was telling anyone who asked that I'd been doing the sort of training everyone of my position did, learning how to fight, sail a manta, getting combat experience, only not at the Citadel. The Avarch also asked me what I'd thought of Taneth. He hadn't been there for years, and his memory of it was fading, so he wanted me to tell him what it was like now.

It was about half an hour later when he said that he was going to bed, and that it was time for me to leave.

'Wait a moment, Cathan,' he said, commandingly, as I began to get up. What was he going to say now, I wondered? I sat back down again.

'I saw the look on your face when I told you about Midian, and I'm not going to ask you why you were so afraid of him. But I will say this.

'The Domain are the agents of Ranthas on Aquasilva. We act as mediators between Him and humanity, and we protect humanity from the worst of the storms that cover our world. Most of what we do, the basic work of the Domain, has nothing to do with the Holy City, the Hierarchy, or anything like that. Whether you believe in souls or not, most people do, and we are the only people who can look after matters of the soul.

'I want you to remember that Midian and his butchers are not the true face of the Domain, that this ruthless hunting-down of those who do not conform is not what we are really about. The heresies arose because our founders gave no room for compromise. I'm sure you have read the *History* – it would be unusual if you hadn't, because most clan leaders do. What the Domain stands for is unity. No more religious warfare, no confessional disputes, and a guiding force that watches over the world, despite its flaws. Midian will die, Lachazzar will die, and in a decade or two this extremist movement will be forgotten. You have grown up here seeing what a shrine's keepers should do. Do not let yourself forget, whatever Midian does.

'Goodnight, Cathan.' He leaned back in his chair and closed his eyes, and I quietly stood up and made my way out of the room.

I collected my cape and went straight back to the Palace, to ask my father if we could leave on the next boat.

CHAPTER XIX

'No,' my father said, again.

I stared at him in disbelief as he sat behind his desk in the Count's Office, papers spread out in front of him. He was tired and had been about to go to bed when I'd burst in with Siana's news about Midian.

'If you leave after only two days, Midian is going to start asking questions when he arrives. The Domain feel that everything is their business, and we can't give them any reason to start investigating Lepidor. Or would you rather half the population was burned at the stake?'

'What are we supposed to do, then?' I protested. 'Wait until Midian's inquisitors start probing around? For all we know, he could be a mage as well.'

'That's unlikely in the extreme.' He sat back in the chair, rubbing his eyes. 'Cathan, I have to stay here anyway, so I'm in as much danger as you are. Secondly, Midian is *not* going to assume we're heretics. He'll start hunting heretics, but not inside the Palace. The Domain have to have cast-iron proof before they can even arrest one of us, and they believe that the aristocracy are their most fervent supporters – it's the lowest orders, especially merchants, that they're worried about.' Mainly, I knew the aristocracy tended to like the Domain just because they helped the clan leaders keep everyone else in line. More fools the nobility.

'How am I going to explain it to him when I do go, then?' I asked.

'Where is this place you keep alluding to? It sounds as if you've been planning to leave anyway,' he said, a little angrily. 'What else haven't you told me?'

I cursed silently; I hadn't been intending to tell him yet.

'We have to confirm Palatine's story, because if she's right, I may find out who I am as well.'

My father's anger died. He got up from the desk, and beckoned me to follow him into the sitting room and close the door.

'Sit down, Cathan, and tell me exactly what happened at the Citadel.'

'It's a long story,' I said.

'Just the bits about magic.'

I told him almost everything about the magic and Palatine's heritage, from the mage-testing at the end of the first month to the argument on the last night. Everything, that was, apart from my feelings – and misgivings – about Ravenna. My father listened in silence, only interrupting once or twice to clarify things. I found it strangely nerve-racking.

When I'd finished, he said, 'So you think – or Palatine thinks, at any rate – that you're both related to the Tar'Conanturs.'

I nodded in agreement.

'How much do you know of what's been happening in Thetia in the last few years?'

'Not much, just some things about Orosius and his father.'

'Emperor Perseus II, who died about three years ago, was a weak man who should never have become Emperor. His elder brother was killed in a shipwreck and their father dropped dead in shock, so Perseus ended up on the throne. He wasn't a very good ruler – he was weak and easily led. Very artistic, but that's hardly an advantage in an Emperor.'

Whatever his point was, Elnibal was coming at it in a very leisurely way. I began to say something, but he held up a hand to tell me to stay quiet.

'Under Perseus, the Empire lost control over everything outside Thetia itself except a few islands. The Exarch was virtually running the country, treating the Emperor as little more than a puppet. I'm told some quite phenomenal sums of money vanished from the exchequer. The Exarch even arranged a marriage for Perseus, to a girl from one of the fundamentalist clans. But about a fortnight before the wedding, the Emperor met a woman called Aurelia. By all accounts, he fell in love with her at first sight.

'For once in his life he managed to assert his authority as Emperor, and ordered his personal chaplain to marry the two of them. When it became known there was a public outcry, because no one knew where Aurelia had come from, which clan she was, or who her parents were. The Exarch was furious; he threatened to excommunicate Perseus but the Emperor held his ground, and eventually the Domain gave up.

'The main reason the Emperor was able to assert his authority was because of a man called Reinhardt Canteni, who'd just made himself President of Canteni. He marshalled the few clans who were really interested in reform to support the Emperor, and his support carried the day. He also grew attached to Perseus's sister, Neptunia, and in gratitude Perseus gave the two of them a state wedding.

'Both couples had children; Reinhardt a daughter, Palatine, and Leo a son, Orosius. At the time of Orosius's birth, an alleged plot was discovered to oust the Emperor and bring in a republic. The Imperial Chancellor was implicated, and supposedly executed. I told you last night why that can't be true, but I'm afraid I don't know what was behind it.'

I got the impression he was holding something back here, but I wasn't sure. I didn't want to say anything, still unsure of where he was leading.

'With Perseus's patronage, the reformists grew stronger. They managed to introduce some new measures in the Thetian Assembly to try and encourage the clans to stop holding drunken parties and start trading again. For a while, it looked as if Thetia might be going to break out of its rut.

'Then Reinhardt died, almost certainly poisoned. The Domain know all about poisons, as well as every other way to kill somebody discreetly. Other leading reformers were discredited or blackmailed into silence at the same time, and the reform movement came to an end.

When Perseus died a few years later, his wife was pushed into exile by the Domain. Their son Orosius had some brilliant qualities, and he was respected by almost the whole of Thetia. It seemed as if he was going to provide the leadership they'd missed for so long.

'It didn't work out that way; Orosius felt ill, and when he recovered he was firmly in the Domain's hands – he'd also gone mad. Reinhardt's daughter Palatine began speaking out for more reforms, and managed to get control of her father's clan. Then – so we think – she was murdered, on the eve of proposing a measure in the Assembly that would have been the first step towards making Thetia a republic. Since then the reformers have been cowed, Orosius is showing how truly evil the Tar'Conanturs can be, and the entire Archipelago is firmly under Domain control.

'The Domain has ruled Aquasilva for two hundred years by keeping the continents and cities at each others' throats, making the merchants distrust the aristocracy, and vice versa. Now the hatreds go too deep for one continent ever to aspire to an imperial throne, because the others would divert all their efforts into sabotaging such an effort. Thetia's an exception because they've been so insulated.

'At the moment most of the aristocracy support the Domain. True, they find the tithes oppressive, but the Domain helps them keep the lower orders in line. If that situation were to change for any reason, and the Domain lost their standing among the aristocracy – or, for that matter, the merchant classes – the Thetians would be the only people everyone would follow. Everyone would have their own agenda, but none of them would feel they were submitting to a hated enemy.

'That isn't going to happen while Orosius is Emperor, but if what Palatine claims is true, the two of you would be a rallying point not just for Thetia, but the rest of the world as well.'

'But surely Midian will connect the two Palatines,' I said.

'As far as the world's concerned, Palatine Canteni is dead. If Midian's a Halettite, he'll despise all Thetians anyway and he won't be interested. To make sure, we'll invent a background for her. As for other precautions, you must bring any items that could conceivably connect you with the Citadel to me; I'll hide them somewhere Midian's searchers couldn't find if they tore the city apart. As for her name – well, it's unusual but not unheard of.'

'And Ravenna?' I asked, doubting that we could manage it – but somehow, my father always managed to solve these problems. It was a pity Moritan wasn't here, I thought, the master of disguise.

'Ravenna's Archipelagan, like you. I could pass them both off as distant relatives, actually.' He tapped his fingers absently on his cheekbone, a gesture I knew indicated he was thinking. 'Yes . . . it might just work, as well.' He grinned at me. 'Better be distant relatives, because Midian would have to be blind not to see the way you look at her.'

I ignored the comment entirely, wishing that people wouldn't take such pleasure in telling me. Surely it couldn't be that obvious – in any case, I wasn't sure myself what I felt for her. It was my business alone – and hers – but not anybody else's.

'Listen,' my father said, serious again. 'It'll only be for a few months, then I can let you go off without suspicion, wherever you want to go. I don't mind you going to Selerian Alastre even, although personally I'd rather you didn't. But for now I need you here, to help me run the city and fend off this lunatic.'

'And what if he does find out?' I asked, still unsure.

'If we plan properly he won't. And, without the Sacri, there's no way he can arrest any of us here.'

I wished I felt as confident as my father sounded.

We held the farewell banquet for Avarch Gaius Siana a week later, the day before Midian was due to arrive. Siana would leave that same day, returning on the ship that had brought Midian. There could only be one Avarch resident in a city, so by Domain custom Siana had to leave on the same day as his successor took up the post.

It was formal occasion, the city's farewell to its old Avarch, so formal dress was required, as it would be for Midian's arrival the next day. I had found out only three days before that Palatine had no formal dress – why should she have, when she'd never needed it before? My father told me to take her down to Lepidor's tailor-cum-dressmaker immediately, with an official order that Palatine was to be given the highest priority.

The tailor had groaned, glaring crossly at us and muttering dark imprecations about dissatisfied customers and loss of business. But he grudgingly took Palatine into his fitting room to measure her up. This was followed by another outburst that he couldn't possibly make a dress in only three days, as he didn't have patterns, and what were his wife and four children to do if he let his other customers down – he'd be ruined.

It took a ten per cent rise in price to get him to agree – even though I knew the fat, moon-faced tailor lived with only his old mother, and had no children at all. Most of his earnings were spent on drink. At least he hadn't changed much from his old ways, although his shop had expanded.

Palatine chose a green fabric – which, she told me, was the colour of Clan Canteni – and the tailor had promised to finish it in time for the banquet.

Palatine had been doubtful that he could keep the promise, but by the night of the banquet the dress was complete – even if we'd had to dash down for the final fitting ten minutes before the formalities started, with the tailor's fitter exclaiming over the buttons.

The banquet, and the reception before it, were held in the new wing of the Palace, the paint on the walls still unnaturally new and bright, a faint residue of its smell in the air. As we arrived, I gave a quick thanks to the Lady of the Wind, Althana, for giving us fine weather. It was going to be hot inside with so many guests, and in a storm, with the doors and windows closed, it would have been stifling.

The doorman, one of the Palace servants, let us pass through the wide, square doorway from the outer courtyard and into the teeming, well-lit corridors inside. There were two large reception rooms, the floor covered in the same blue carpet as the Council chamber, and a glass clerestory running down the centre of the roofs, to let in more sunlight than the three large windows on the western sides.

My parents had already arrived, along with, to my surprise, Jerian. I wondered why my parents were trusting him to behave at a gathering like this.

The first person we met was Dalriadis, standing with the first lieutenant of the *Marduk*. Both were in naval dress uniform, dark blue with silver braid.

'Evening, Palatine, Cathan,' he said, smiling slightly. 'A splendid dress, Palatine; I'm amazed the tailor managed to tear himself away from his ale long enough to make it.'

'It wasn't wasted,' the first lieutenant, a tall, stooped man with a curled beard, said. 'Haaluk drank it all instead.'

'Drowning his sorrows,' Dalriadis said. 'Lord Foryth's money being put to good use.'

'The world would be a better place if someone would drown Lord Foryth,' I said.

'I'm inclined to agree. But of course, you met him, didn't you?'

'I don't think "met" is the right word.'

We set off through the throng, in their bright formal dress – mostly shades of red, blue or darker green – to look for Ravenna. I spotted her by one of the windows, just finishing talking to Harbour Master Tortelen. Her hair was bound up the same way as it had been when I first met her, on board the *Paklé*, and she was wearing a dark sea-green dress.

'You managed it, I see,' she said, gravely. 'Cathan, I like your dress suit. And Palatine, you found some family colours.'

'Not something we should tell everyone,' Palatine said.

'You could proclaim yourself Emperor in here, and the only reaction you'd get would be a Council member asking you to drop a quiet line to somebody or other.' Her eyes flicked over to where Tortelen was standing, his back to us, engaged in an intense conversation with Dalriadis's lieutenant.

'What was he after?' I asked.

'He wanted me to use my "influence" with you to find out what you really think of Hamilcar.'

'They're even jockeying for power here?' I said, angry at the way politics was intruding into events like this. In the outside world, perhaps, all the business was done at gatherings like this. Lepidor had always been different − a social occasion was a social occasion. Until now.

'I remember,' Palatine said suddenly, her head tilted slightly to one side, 'at a memorial service, I heard a general and a minister talking. Not about the person who died or how sorry they were, but about who would succeed him. During the service, it was, while the Exarch was saying a prayer. I know we don't like the Domain, but that was a service, not a meeting. I was angry about it.'

I looked at her in astonishment, but she just shrugged, a very disturbing movement in the figure-hugging dress she was wearing.

'I can remember the odd thing, here and there,' she said.

'What about specific people?'

'Only from the little fragments. The only one I can remember clearly is my war tutor, because he was very tall. Anyway, now isn't the time to talk about it. Shall we enjoy the party?'

'You mean go and ask everybody whose side they're on,' I said, and was surprised at my own bitterness. What sort of a homecoming was this? Everything possible seemed to have gone wrong.

Ravenna looked at me again, but the trace of sympathy in her eyes died a moment later − she must have seen my gesture the previous day. It didn't make me feel any better, though, just lonely.

We headed over towards my father and Siana, to show them we'd arrived. Palatine somehow managed to waylay a butler and get us drinks, even though I couldn't see a servant anywhere nearby.

'Good evening,' Siana said as he saw us. The old priest was dressed in his gold-trimmed red Avarch's robes, his ceremonial best. The braiding was supposed to be only a pattern, not representing any non-religious objects or symbols, but he'd shown me a long time ago the seals worked into the design. Lepidor's emblem. 'You look wonderful,' he said to Ravenna, his seamed face cracked by a smile.

'Thank you,' she said. I think I was the only one who realized the effect the Avarch's simple courtesy had on her. Too few people paid her genuine compliments.

'As do you, my dear,' he said to Palatine, and I saw him studying her. For a second there was a look of puzzlement . . . or was it recognition? I couldn't tell. But he shook his head very slightly, and the expression was gone.

To me he said, 'Try and eat something for a change, Cathan. You're as thin as a skeleton still, and you're obviously starved after eighteen months away from Zephehat's excellent cooking.' Zephehat was the clan's best chef, and a better cook than many I'd encountered in the Palaces and ziggurats during my journey. The light-hearted comment was typical of Siana, his way of dealing with momentous events in his life. Lepidor would be a worse place after he'd gone, and Midian sounded as if he didn't even know what a joke was.

We moved away to let the next arrivals greet my father and the Avarch. I sipped my drink and looked round the hall. Near the doorway to the banqueting hall, Mezentus was engaged in an intense conversation with a group of House heads.

I drew Palatine's attention to him.

'Shall we go and tell him how pleased we are to see him?' I suggested.

Palatine grinned. 'We don't want to be too friendly with those House heads, do we? He can't canvass them and talk to us at the same time.'

We went over to the small group. Mezentus had his back to us, but I saw one of the others nod, and Mezentus quickly turned with an insincere smile on his face.

'Good evening, Escount.'

'Good evening, Mezentus,' I said. 'Allow me to introduce my distant cousins, Ravenna and Palatine.' Fortunately, one of my father's cousins had married out into an Archipelagan House, so I did actually have Archipelagan cousins. Mezentus wasn't to know that I'd never set eyes on them. I was glad I hadn't, actually; they lived in the Worldsend Islands, which according to Persea, were the bleakest places north of Silvernia.

We managed to interrupt Mezentus's conversation and break up his group. It wasn't as if they were plotting or anything, but there were rarely this many House heads gathered together and Mezentus would be sounding them out for their opinions on Hamilcar.

Speaking of which, where *was* Hamilcar? It wasn't like him to be late.

I made polite conversation with the head of House Setris for a few moments, until Mezentus was trapped by Dalriadis – who presumably wanted to hone his insults. Then I excused myself and went to look for Hamilcar.

I couldn't find him at all, and it wasn't until ten minutes or so later that I glanced over towards my father and saw Hamilcar's unmistakable silhouette looming above the crowd. He was wearing a green suit that seemed a bit shabby even for everyday wear. Why wasn't he wearing formal dress?

'An accident in my apartment,' he said; I though he looked rather angry. 'A water flue burst and soaked most of my clothes; I had to borrow this one from your House wardrobe and it took some seamstress a while to adjust the size.'

I sympathized with him. That was bad luck, no decent clothes to wear at a party. The suit, I realized, must have been my great-uncle's – he had been the tallest in my father's family by a long way.

'You might want to talk to the head of House Setris', I said, still angry at the way a farewell party was turning into a political masque. 'The fat man in yellow, Mezentus, was at him earlier and he's not sure that you're the right Merchant Lord for the iron route.'

'Thank you,' Hamilcar said, then, 'You know, I get tired of the way these things always end up with people trying to convince their fellow guests to support their plots. I don't know whether you're used to it, but in Taneth you can never relax for a moment. No one ever drinks at parties, because they're afraid of revealing House secrets while they're drunk.'

'This is no better,' I said, looking glumly round at the knots of people. And the banquet hadn't even begun.

'It is in one way,' Hamilcar said.

'Really?'

'Your clanspeople don't knife each other in the back. You have to have an escort after big parties in Taneth, because thugs like Lijah Foryth send gangs of their private hoods to attack people on their way home.'

I drifted around the two rooms for the next half-hour or so, trying to enjoy the party as I would have done before we discovered the iron. That had changed the atmosphere in the clan for the worse, I reflected. Before, when everything had been so uncertain, everybody had made up for it by letting their hair down, holding parties and trying to disguise the decline in a cloak of gaiety. Now that our future was assured, they were all serious again and jockeying for position. Was it like this in the outlying Houses I wondered? Or was it just in Lepidor itself?

When the banquet began I found myself seated between Siana and Ravenna. Ravenna wouldn't normally have been of high enough rank to sit on the high table, but the two women of our House who would usually have sat up there were absent – one very close to childbirth and another in Kula's hospital, recovering from a fall.

To my left, beyond Siana, were my father, my mother, Hamilcar, and three House dignitaries; the Pharassan ambassador, representative of the King, was to Ravenna's right. Mezentus and his cadre had been split up, and I guessed my father had 'helped' with the seating plan – Haaluk was opposite Dalriadis, at the top of one of the lower tables, while the ancient, craggy master oceanographer was next to Mezentus. I could see Palatine a few places along from Dalriadis on the middle table.

The starters were brought in, and then the first course: fried flamefish.

'There's a story about a Prime and a flamefish,' Siana said to me as the plates were put in front of us. 'It was a few hundred years ago, and the Domain had just elected a new Prime, a man from Equatoria who'd never seen the sea. At his enthronement banquet, the servants brought a huge flamefish in on a platter and put it in front of him. He decreed that, because of its colour, flamefish could now only be eaten by him and his Exarchs.

'The rest of the priests weren't happy about this, so they thought up a plot. They ordered tons and tons of flamefish – out of the Prime's own coffers – and ordered the kitchens to feed it to the Prime every day. Eventually, he got sick of the taste, but there was still the problem of his edict – he didn't want to lose face. So the priests suggested he should burn all the rest, sacrificing it to Ranthas. They piled all the kitchen scraps up and then covered them with a layer of flamefish, so the Prime thought they'd all be burned. The moment his back was turned all the priests held flamefish feasts at his expense. The next Prime reversed the edict, of course.'

Siana's story gave a human side to the Domain for me; the image of the priests tricking their Prime somehow didn't fit with Lachazzar and his Sacri.

'Don't pass it on.' Siana whispered. 'The powers that be don't like jokes about Primes.'

That sounded more familiar, but as I ate the flamefish I wondered how long it would have taken the Prime to grow tired of it. It certainly was my favourite fish, and I could have eaten a lot more of it if it hadn't been so rare.

Ravenna had hardly had time to get a word in edgeways around the Pharassan Ambassador's monologue. But at one point when he stopped talking to finish up the flamefish before the plates were taken away, she said to me in her usual cold voice, 'Is everyone usually this quiet?'

The noise didn't seem any different from the usual banquet chatter.

'Not that I've noticed,' I said.

'The table with Mezentus at it is making very little noise, and the one with Haaluk is very boisterous.'

'Is that significant?'

'It was just an observation,' she said, turning away again and asking the Ambassador something about Pharassan wines.

'She's right, you know.' Siana's leathery voice said, by my left ear. 'They're being very quiet over there.'

'Most of the people there aren't Mezentus's cronies, though,' I pointed out.

'No, but they have to be polite and talk at the same volume he does. And Mezentus is drinking rather a lot, yet not getting any noisier.'

'Maybe Lord Foryth paid him to shut up this time,' I said.

The waiters took away the first course and brought the main one. It was roast selka, and very well cooked, but I wasn't really concentrating on it. I didn't touch my second glass of wine.

It happened at the end of the feast, after a consort of lutenists had left the minstrels' gallery to a round of applause. I heard Hamilcar say something to my mother, but he was interrupted by Mezentus, who lurched up from his seat.

'Enjoyed that, did you?' he asked Hamilcar loudly. 'Soothed your soul, did it?'

Siana pushed himself out of his chair and faced Mezentus. 'I won't have you insulting a guest in this hall, Mezentus.'

'Not insulting him, Avar— Ava – arch. But his soul needs soothing, doesn't it? It's tormenmemted by his uncle's shade.'

'Mezentus!' my father snapped. 'Leave this hall.'

'What about the murd— murdered . . . murderer sitting at your table, Count? Wolf in sheep's clothing, murder you as well if you're not careful. Tanethan killed his uncle, he did.'

There was a shocked silence in the hall, then Siana turned to one of the waiters. The old man was almost shaking with rage; I'd never seen him this angry.

'Take this man to the Temple and lock him in a penitent's cell.'

'But what about the murderer?' Haaluk asked.

'Only guttersnipes in Taneth pass that rumour on,' Hamilcar said angrily, and he looked altogether cold and unforgiving, every inch the Tanethan aristocrat. 'You would do well not to associate with them.'

CHAPTER XX

The people grouped around me in the reception lounge of Lepidor's undersea harbour seemed uneasy. I saw Dalriadis glance quickly at the clock, and even Siana, dressed in simple priest's robes and leaning on his stick, seemed to be fretting.

I shifted my weight from one foot to the other again, wondering why Midian's manta was taking so long to dock. What was the man doing – blessing the door to remove heretics?

I looked out of the huge windows towards the end of the gantry, where the manta was already docked, but I wasn't quite far enough over to see if they'd connected the airlock yet. They'd moored nearly ten minutes ago, but since then we hadn't seen anything of the manta.

An echoing creak and then a bang reverberated along the gantry, and I saw my father and the other councillors stiffen, their gazes flicking back towards it.

Another bang as the doors swung open, and then the sound of voices, very briefly. Then I heard footsteps advancing along the gantry. I pulled my sleeves down, and then fixed my stare on its entrance.

As the footsteps got nearer, I found myself wondering how many steps it would take Midian to walk along the gantry. But my calculations were halted abruptly when Avarch Midian strode out of the gantry's end door and I got my first look at our new high priest and heretic-burner.

My first thought was that he didn't seem like an evil fanatic at all. A broad-shouldered man with the traditional Halettite curled beard and moustache, his face was open and cheerful. His Avarch's robes were far more splendid than Siana's had ever been, adorned with copious amounts of gold thread – but no images that I could see, unlike the stylized seal on

Siana's sleeves. As custom required, Siana stepped forward, holding his staff of office out in both hands.

'Be welcome in the name of Ranthas, Avarch Midian of Clan Lepidor. To you I surrender this charge and the care of these souls.'

Midian bowed to him, then reached out his hands and received the staff from Siana. '*Domine* Siana, I accept this charge which you have laid upon me. May Ranthas guide your path from here in peace.'

Siana stepped back as Midian held his staff up. As I kneeled, following the rest of the people in the room, pain shot through my head and I nearly had to put out my hand to hold my balance. It was gone as soon as it had come, but when I looked up I caught Midian's glance for a moment and realized he'd seen it.

'In Ranthas's name, blessings on all of you, and may you be for ever protected by His flames.'

There was a brief pause, and then my father stood up again. 'Welcome to Clan Lepidor, Avarch,' he said.

'It is an honour to be here.'

My father, with the two Avarchs, old and new, then walked back through the crowd to the lift. They'd now hold a private meeting in the temple on the religious state of the clan, after which Siana would leave on board the same manta that had brought Midian.

Once the lift had risen out of sight, the councillors headed for the stairs, anxious to get out of the stuffy atmosphere in the small reception room. My job was to take care of Midian's personal entourage, the priests and their families who would be replacing some of Siana's people. Several of the posts at each temple were filled by dependants or protégés of the Avarch, and three or four of Lepidor's priests and acolytes would be accompanying Siana to Pharassa.

By the time I heard the voices of the others in the gantry corridor, only two junior acolytes – the only ones not needed to receive Midian at the temple – were still in the room. Both were about my age; one shaven-headed and aloof, the other, who'd known Sarhaddon, with brown curly hair and a ready smile.

'Have you any idea how many he's bringing?' the second one whispered.

I shrugged. 'Not a clue. He's a Halettite, and they don't travel light.'

A moment later, Midian's entourage appeared. As I advanced to greet their leader, a distinguished-looking man in his forties, I counted three full priests – including the leader – two acolytes, four women, and one child. As well as two others.

One was Elassel, the girl I'd met in the Pharassa ziggurat, now out of her Domain robes but looking no less wild and rebellious. The second was a journeyman mind-mage.

'Why? Why did he bring one?' Palatine said, stalking around my sitting room. 'What possible help can a mind-mage be out here? Do you think he suspects there are mages here?'

'How could he?' Ravenna said. 'The orders must have gone out before we arrived, and there's no reason to suspect us anyway.'

'What if there's another mage in the city?' Palatine slumped down in a chair.

'It's possible, I suppose,' I said, trying to conceal the fact that I was scared. Even if the Domain didn't generally persecute clan leaders, if that mind-mage detected the tiniest trace of magic from either me or Ravenna we'd be exposed. Even if he simply picked up the presence of sorcery and couldn't actually find us, they'd bring in someone who could . . . and that would be it.

'If you don't use any magic at all – *then* can he find you?' Palatine asked.

'There's a chance,' Ravanna said, sitting in the chair by the desk. Her face was even more serious than usual, and she was staring down at the rug. 'If he used any kind of magic while he was within a few feet of one of us he'd realize what was going on. There are a few other ways he could find out entirely by accident. And, of course, if they start scrying for mages, we're in trouble.'

'Can you do anything to shield yourselves?'

'Shield ourselves? That'd just . . .'

'I don't mean to protect yourselves. Something to make it less likely that he'll detect you.'

I racked my brains, trying to remember if there was anything in Chlamas and Jashua's lessons that could be any help. They'd taught us a couple of ways to camouflage ourselves from Domain mages. But most of those only worked when there was one of you. There were two of us in Lepidor, and, for some reason, that made us individually far easier to detect.

And there was nothing we could do against mind-mages.

'I don't think there is a way,' I began, but Ravenna cut me off.

'There *is* a possibility,' she said. 'But it's not one I like, and actually doing it in the first place is very dangerous with a mind-mage around.'

She looked from the rug to me for a second, then to Palatine. I wondered what she was proposing – Chlamas, Jashua and all the old books had been very insistent that the only way to avoid detection by a mind-mage was to lie low and hope for the best. Fortunately, they were rare.

'Cathan, do you remember when Palatine fell off the cliff, what you did then?' she asked, looking at me again; was that doubt I saw in her face?

'I used magic to check if she'd been injured at all.'

'How deep did you go?'

'Realm of the mind.' I looked at her suspiciously – she seemed hesitant, and that was so unlike her that it didn't bode well.

'I think it could be possible for us to . . . contain . . . our magic by sending it into the soul-realm. It would keep us safe unless the mind-mage actually touched us while he was using his magic.' Her voice trailed off.

'But?' Palatine prompted.

'But we can't do it to ourselves. We'd have to do it to each other.'

I stared at her in near-shock, but she refused to meet my look.

'No wonder it's said to be impossible.'

'And undoing it would be almost as difficult as doing it,' Ravenna finished.

'We can talk this over later,' I said, getting up and going to the door. 'I'm going to look for someone.'

I hadn't had a chance to talk to Elassel earlier, because the priests might have taken offence, but just before I'd left to go back to the Palace she'd whispered to me to come and find her when I could. She'd intrigued me at our first brief meeting fifteen months ago, and I felt I wanted to know her better.

On a more prosaic level, she might know why Midian had brought the mind-mage. And I wanted to get away from Ravenna.

My mind was still in turmoil as I walked through the streets. The afternoon heat was heavy and oppressive, which meant there'd be another storm soon. Was Ravenna's proposal really serious, I wondered? I knew it would work, at least in theory, but was the price too high? The thought of having anyone in my mind was frightening, as it would be to anyone. I'd used it after Palatine had fallen off the cliff but only because it had been an emergency. I'd told her when she'd come round, and she'd said it was fine, the right thing to do.

But what Ravenna was proposing, even if it was on equal terms, was something else. Actually sealing our magic away in a place where no mage yet born could go without consent was all very well. But once it was there, the only person who could retrieve it would be whoever had put it there in the first place. We'd have to be in the same place and undetectable in order to unseal the magic as well – until then, neither of us would have any more supernatural power than a normal person. Namely, none.

Not that it was necessarily a bad thing – we could hardly have used any magic with Midian's cohorts swanning around. Elassel's parents were part of his entourage, and I wondered what their connection was with him.

Tomorrow would be Midian's enthronement service, and all was chaos when I arrived at the Temple, as acolytes and temple servants carried baggage and robes here and there. Only a handful of people were worshipping at the altar in the outer courtyard, and they left very quickly, presumably to avoid being run over by any more priests carrying chests in from the harbour.

I went inside the tall main door and into the echoing, sepia-panelled ante-room. Two of Lepidor's remaining old priests – Siana and his entourage had left an hour ago – were talking to one of the new arrivals, the one I'd guessed was Elassel's father.

I didn't want to interrupt their conversation, though, so I stopped a passing acolyte, the curly-haired one from the harbour, and asked him where Elassel was.

'The girl?'

I nodded.

'Probably in the gardens. Be careful, she's a wild one.'

'You mean she didn't appreciate you trying to chat her up.' I slipped

out of the ante-room by a side door and went along the servants' corridor
to the gardens.

I loved the Temple gardens; they were overgrown and bursting with
plants, the trees growing so thickly that they were almost a maze. It was
a maze that I knew, from escaping here when Siana was late for my
lessons and wandering off into it when Temple lessons grew too boring.
Now that Midian was here, I was glad that I didn't have to have those
lessons any more; Siana might have been boring, but at least he hadn't
been a fanatic.

I found Elassel sitting by a moss-covered fountain towards the back of
the gardens, in a grotto whose entrances had long ago been overgrown
by creepers. I pushed my way through them. She looked up in alarm,
then relaxed somewhat.

'Cathan,' she said. 'I was afraid it was one of those old goats, come to
put me to work. Who told you I was here?'

'One of the acolytes.'

'You can't trust acolytes, they're a nosy bunch. I like your city, by the
way. The luthier is friendly.'

Obviously Elassel had the same homing instincts as me, except in her
case it was to the musical instrument makers instead of the
oceanographers.

'Why have you ended up out here with Midian?' I asked. 'I thought
your parents were missionaries.'

'Not full-time,' she said. 'That was just a tour of duty. My stepfather's
a recorder and treasury clerk; they needed one at the mission, so they sent
him out here. I've no idea why that creep Midian wanted them.'

'Why has he brought a mind-mage?' I asked. 'They're hardly the sort
of people Avarchs drag around with them.'

Her expression suddenly turned wary.

'Why are you asking me?'

'This is my father's clan, Elassel. Midian's supposed to be a heretic-
hunter, and if he's brought a mind-mage with him that means trouble.' I
kept my voice down, but I wasn't sure this was the best place to talk. 'I
don't want him to go round burning clansmen.'

'Fine,' she said, 'Midian's brought a mind-mage for exactly that
reason: to root out heretics. Does that satisfy you?'

'I'm not an inquisitor,' I said.

She smiled, and absently pulled a leaf out of her hair – she looked slightly older, but still as untidy and challenging as when I'd met her in the ziggurat at Pharassa more than a year ago. 'You're the only person here I know even slightly,' she said. 'This temple's not going to be a good place, not with Midian running around breathing fire down everyone's neck and retiring with his concubines when he gets bored.'

'Concubines?'

'Those two dusky beauties – well, you could call them that – you saw earlier, when you brought us up here. Midian's a high-born Halettite, and they still believe in slavery there. Horrible place, really. But he believes in one law for him and another for the rest of us.'

'Is he into heretic-burning?' I looked round anxiously, in case someone could be listening in the bushes.

'Are there better places to talk?' Elassel said, noticing my nervousness.

'Are you free to come and go?'

'What do you think?' she said scornfully. 'Anybody who tries to stop me deserves what they get. The novice master in Pharassa, that snake Boreth, tried to lock me up. Hah! I got out and then poured acid into all his keyholes. He had to pay for the repairs out of his own pocket.'

I wondered where she'd learned to deal with locks, as I showed her the way to climb over the garden wall and into the narrow street that ran almost round the edge of the district. I took her through the side door of the Palace gardens; I wasn't going to bring her inside the Palace itself until I knew her better, and had introduced her to Palatine and Ravenna. I very much doubted she was working for the Domain – or, for that matter, House Foryth – but I wanted to be absolutely sure.

Elassel confirmed what Siana had said, that Midian was a confirmed heretic-hunter. She also said he was friendly and agreeable to those not on his target list. In other words, anybody in high authority. I didn't get time to ask her anything else, though, because just then the Palace bell rang, summoning me, and the councillors, to the banquet that was being held in Midian's honour. Banquets were becoming rather frequent all of a sudden.

I agreed to meet Elassel in the street outside the garden the next day, then hurried in to get out of my briar-torn tunic and into my formal suit again. I hadn't been down to the oceanographers since I'd arrived; tomorrow, I promised myself, I'd go.

★

Mezentus was allowed to attend this banquet despite his insulting behaviour last time; Palatine had also persuaded Hamilcar to come, against the Tanethan's better judgement.

The charge Mezentus had levelled against Hamilcar was an old one, apparently, which the merchant had tried hard to disprove, considering it a stain on his honour. In Taneth he'd told us how he'd wrested control of House Barca from his corrupt uncle, Komal. Apparently Komal had died of a stroke less than a week later, and this had given other merchant lords ammunition to use against Hamilcar. From what I'd heard of Taneth, corporate murder was fairly common, but usually more subtle.

Dalriadis, who had Great House relatives, had said this morning that Hamilcar's story was almost certainly true. Komal had been heading for a breakdown of some kind anyway, what with his heavy drinking and use of exotic substances. And, he'd added, no Great House merchant would have arranged a murder like that, because it was too obvious.

Midian's arrival banquet was little more enjoyable than Siana's farewell, the night before, although for different reasons. I felt that everybody was on edge, uncertain about the new Avarch. Word of his reputation had spread, apparently, and the House heads were all uneasy, fearing that Midian would pick on their House or even – Ranthas forbid – them!

If his intention was heretic-hunting, it seemed so pointless and destructive. We'd had hardly any heretics in Lepidor for as long as I could remember. There had been two or three cases of denunciation by some overzealous priest, but Siana had dismissed all of them through lack of evidence. It seemed to me that Midian's attitude was going to be based on an assumption that there were a lot of heretics, and thus he would be determined to root them out regardless of how much hard evidence there was.

Midian was friendly and jovial at the banquet; he joked, he told stories (though never about past Primes or the Domain) and waxed lyrical about my father's wine cellar. I remembered what Elassel had said, and to me his cheerfulness didn't ring true. I wondered whether he'd have been half as polite if it had been Exarch's robes he'd been wearing.

This time there was no jockeying for support at the reception, either. But there was one awkward moment.

It was at the beginning, when my father introduced Palatine, Ravenna

and me to the new Avarch. Midian complimented Ravenna as Siana had
done, but where Siana's words had been spoken with an old man's
affectionate courtesy, Midian almost leered. Ravenna's smile disappeared,
and she stared icily at Midian. For a moment, as his friendly manner
melted away, I saw what I thought was the real Avarch, the heretic-
hunter. His expression didn't bode well for Ravenna.

Then the moment passed, and Midian smiled again, albeit tightly and
passed on to the next guest. He didn't try the same thing with Palatine,
though.

We saw the mind-mage as well; his expression reminded me of a
puzzled dog's. He seemed slightly absent-minded, but I wasn't about to
treat him as if he was harmless. It was probably a deliberate act, to throw
people off the scent and make them forget his all-black robes and the
hammer hanging by his side.

He was the first mind-mage I'd ever seen, actually, but his distinctly
unmenacing air came as rather an anti-climax. Most of what I knew about
them – aside from Jashua's confused teachings – came from the *History*.
There had been mind-mages involved in the War – the Emperor's sister
had married one, a man who'd served Aetius faithfully to the end and had
died in the ruins of Aran Cthun. Another man the Domain had betrayed.

I met Palatine and Ravenna again after the banquet, in my sitting room.
Most of the Palace's population was going to bed, and the only people
still up were the servants, helping to clear away downstairs.

Ravenna was still fuming.

'Foul man!' she said, almost spitting out the words. 'Aren't his personal
playthings enough to satisfy him?'

'Are all Halettites like him?' Palatine asked. 'The only one I've known
was Ukmadorian, and he wasn't bad.'

'Ukmadorian left Haleth so long ago to moulder on his desert island
that he couldn't even tell you what colour the grass there is any more.
And I don't know any more about Halettites than you do, so why ask
me?'

'Sorry I spoke,' Palatine said, looking offended.

'And now the creature's going to start arresting people he doesn't like
the look of. What will it be, I wonder – personal interrogations for the
women? Maybe that's why he does it.'

I hadn't thought of that, but surely he wouldn't get away with it?

'You can't assume that after meeting him just once, Ravenna,' I protested. 'Maybe he is a lecher, but that doesn't stop him being a genuine fanatic.'

'No, of course not,' she said, voice heavy with sarcasm. 'Where outside Haleth can he find women who aren't free to protest? If I was your father I'd post marines in the Temple to keep an eye on the man. Concern for clan welfare and all that. I'm quite sure Midian doesn't have their spiritual well being in mind.'

'Ravenna, you're really exaggerating here,' Palatine said, tossing a pebble from one hand to the other. 'Maybe he did look at you the wrong way. But you are very pretty when you're not arguing with somebody. Just because he leered at you, it doesn't mean he wants to start up a harem of heretics.'

Ravenna glared at her. 'Very pretty, am I? Compared with you, even?'

Palatine held up her hand. 'I'm sorry. I'll remember not to pay you any compliments in future.'

'Don't,' Ravenna said curtly, then turned to me. 'Cathan, have you made up your mind yet?'

I'd been hoping she wouldn't ask until she'd calmed down.

'No, I haven't.'

'Why not? That mind-mage was drinking like a fish at the banquet. Tonight he'll be out like a light – this may be the only chance we'll get.'

'Are you sure he was actually drinking it all? Surely he'd think that now would be the time to be on alert, in case any mages in the city were going to hide themselves.' It was a pathetic excuse, and she saw straight through it.

'He's a mind-mage. As far as he's concerned, we're defenceless against his magic, so he'd be expecting us to lie low rather than try anything.'

'Ravenna, I don't like the idea,' I said, annoyed at the way she was putting pressure on me.

'I don't like it either, Cathan. I don't want you in my mind any more than you want me in yours. But would you rather wait until it's too late and they're tying you to the stake? It isn't a decision you can make on your own, because if one of us is caught we're both caught. I've spent the whole evening thinking about it, and I'd rather go through with this and live with the consequences than lose my life – or yours – if that thought-twister realizes what we are.'

We were standing facing each other in the middle of the floor, but this time I couldn't meet her eyes. I said to Palatine, 'Could you wait outside, please, until we've finished?'

I had been worried that I'd offend her, but she nodded cheerfully and left. Neither of us said anything until the door had closed behind her.

I stepped away from Ravenna, refusing to look at her, and went over to stare into the fireplace. She didn't move.

Ravenna was right, I realized: this wasn't something I could decide on my own. But the idea of somebody seeing into my mind, into my soul, terrified me. The terrible dreams I'd had when I was younger; the terrors and the fits of rage one of my father's friends, the Visitor, had taught me to keep under control. Would this bring them to the surface again?

We both stood, unmoving, for a few seconds, then I turned back to her. There was only one choice I could make, however much it frightened me. To do otherwise would be unfair to Ravenna.

'I'll do it,' I said, meeting her gaze again.

'Thank you,' she said, with a slight smile.

'How?' I asked.

'Come here and I'll show you.'

I went back to where I'd been standing a minute ago. She took my hands and held them.

'Join your consciousness with me the same way you did with Palatine. That's all you'll need to do on your own; from there we'll be together.'

I took me several seconds and a lot of effort to empty my mind the way I'd been taught. Then I sent my mind along the link between us. In the nothingness I saw our forms, silvery against the darkness, and descended through the layers into the realm of the mind.

And then we reached out and drew in the magic from both of us, leaving only the innate magic that was part of my blood. And hers, I realized, wondering where it came from.

As we gathered it in, I felt a joy and completeness I'd never known before. But, more importantly, I experienced peace, free from the constraints of thought.

Then, as our minds directed the magic through a gate of nothingness into the soul-realm, the chaos surged around us again. I broke the link, retreating in horror, and as the last of my magic was sealed away I spiralled back up through layers and out into the room again, utterly disorientated. I swayed and crumpled to the floor, and as I struggled to regain my bearings I saw Ravenna fall across me as if clubbed, limp and unconscious. Something inside my head was drumming and attacking my skull with an axe. I cried out with the pain, but then it subsided.

When my head cleared I looked down at Ravenna and, to my relief, saw that she was still breathing. Then the door opened and Palatine came in.

CHAPTER XXI

I replaced the cover on the last ocean-probe and bolted it down again, careful not to drop any of the nuts. Then, after swimming round to check that everything was secure, I swam back to the searay, a dark shadow like that of a cloud on the bright ocean surface. I came up beside the port wing, my lungs automatically adjusting to air-breathing again, and pulled myself onto the smooth surface.

The ray's side door was open, a hatch so small that even I had to bend down to go through. I pulled off my flippers and left them on the wing, then took my sample belt inside to transfer the water specimens I'd gathered to the safe.

The searay was minuscule – an eighteen-yard wingspan and two tiny rooms inside, the largest of which I could barely sit down in. It had seen better days, too, but if it was old it was at least reliable. And it was mine.

I'd persuaded my father to requisition it after the oceanographers had bought a newer, bigger one four years ago. He'd grudgingly agreed, fearing – quite rightly – that it would encourage me to take even more time off the business of learning how to rule the clan, and that I could get caught in a storm out in it. But he'd saved it from the scrapyard, and a friendly engineer had repaired it for me. I'd called it *Walrus* because the engine sounded like a walrus barking whenever I went at a decent speed.

Once I'd stacked the samples, I left the belt behind in the cabin and went back out again, this time just for a swim. I was over a reef near the shore a few miles down the coast from Lepidor – a good place, and a quiet one: there was no town on this bay.

And quiet was just what I needed. I'd been planning to come out anyway, although I didn't really need to. The oceanographers would have looked after my probes as well as everyone else's during my absence –

they'd even replaced two that had been destroyed by a storm. But I needed somewhere I could think without being interrupted.

Somewhere where I could wonder what had gone wrong the night before last.

I hadn't told Palatine exactly what had happened, just that something had gone wrong at the very end of the link. I had wanted to check if Ravenna was all right, but my magic had been shut away, so I couldn't. All of a sudden I'd felt very lonely, with the power that had been part of me for the last year gone somewhere I couldn't reach. And the memory of that brief second of joining had stayed with me, even though it had been too fleeting for me to remember properly.

Palatine felt Ravenna's pulse and said that she couldn't find anything wrong. But it wasn't Ravenna's body I was worried about, it was her mind. There was no way we could summon a healer, not after what we'd done, and in any case I doubted a healer could have helped. Whatever had happened, it was my fault.

Palatine carried Ravenna back to her room, because I was too exhausted and drained. I went with them, and Palatine and I had disagreed over whether I should sleep in the room next door, in case something happened to Ravenna. In the end Palatine won, pointing out that without magic I had no way of helping, and it would so mortally offend Ravenna's dignity that she'd never speak to me again. Palatine stayed to get Ravenna out of the formal dress and put her into the bed.

Then I spent a long, tormented night wondering how Ravenna was. Even when I did, finally get to sleep the old dreams came back to haunt me, the wild, formless nightmares I'd endured for years without telling anyone.

I met Ravenna, seeming unharmed and unchanged, at breakfast. It was too public place to talk about anything, but at least I could assure myself that whatever had happened hadn't injured her. Nor did we get any chance to discuss it for the rest of that day, what with Midian's enthronement and my father insisting that I attend the justice session in the hall during the afternoon.

Now, the next day, I still didn't know why she'd collapsed, or why the link had gone wrong. What had that darkness at the end been, and whose mind had it come from? I felt Chlamas, Jashua and Ukmadorian hadn't taught us enough about the body and its realms, concentrating too much on how to actually work the magic and use it as a weapon.

The trouble was, there was nobody in Lepidor who knew about magic – nobody I could remotely trust, apart from Ravenna. At least on the Citadel one of the mages would have been able to help. Or would they? Had their teachings skipped over the structure of the body because they didn't know much about it either?

Suddenly it struck me that all their teachings had been like that, in a way – they had taught us how, but not why. I'd been shown how to work Shadow in every standard way possible, and I'd worked out some Water for myself. But *why* using those techniques had those effects, or the relation between Water and Shadow, or the layers of the body, had been something nobody had taught me. It wasn't the way the oceanographers taught – I'd been made to understand the theory before they'd even begun to teach me the forms.

Did they omit all the *why* because there was none, no reason behind it all, I wondered? Magic was something many people could use, but surely, even if the way it worked couldn't be explained, the relationships between its elements could?

As I swam along the sun-rippled sandy bottom, a little bit above the spiky urchins and flatfish cruising along the seabed, I remembered what the master oceanographer had drummed into me almost from the first lesson. *The ocean is more than the sum of its parts, Cathan. Everything that happens is related to everything else. If the eddy current in Lepidor Bay changes direction, it causes whirlpools off Huasa. If the water's too cold around Selerian Alastre, Cambressian fishermen go hungry. Never forget that we aren't just studying this small stretch of Oceanus coast, but the whole of the plant.*

How much did mind-magic have to do with the other elements? Only mind-mages could influence thoughts, whereas if I entered someone's mind I could only look around – enough of an intrusion anyway. But we'd done something in the mind-realm that affected the body and the soul-realms as well. Was there any precedent for that?

I kicked out hard in bitter frustration and almost swam into a rock. Carausius would have had people who knew about these things, even if only the individual aspects of them. I was floundering around looking for answers to questions that it seemed nobody had asked before. Or, most probably, they had, but the answers had been lost with the mages and their libraries. Even if the mages had survived the Domain holocaust, I couldn't believe that anybody outside the Orders had managed to keep their knowledge alive down the centuries. And even the Orders had lost so much of it.

I thought of something suddenly, stopped, and then had to pull myself down again as I began floating up, scattering a shoal of tiny silvery-blue coral fish. What about The Visitor? He'd shown me how to block out the dreams, and he was the one who knew the secret of my birth. He wasn't a mage, but perhaps he would know something about it or, if not, he might know somebody who did.

But The Visitor hadn't come to Lepidor for years, and my father wasn't even sure if he was still alive.

I still hadn't found any answers by the time I pulled up from a final series of loops through the rock pillars under the cliff and swam back up to the searay. The black wing was hot under the sun, and I had to put a reed mat over it so that I could lie down and stretch out to dry before I went back into the city.

How much did Ravenna know? Maybe she held the answers I was looking for. It was an extraordinary idea she'd come up with in the first place. How much had they taught her before she came to the Citadel of Shadow? She was a mage of Wind as well as Shadow – had her Ralentian people, whom she so despised, taught her things beyond the normal scope of magic?

I was still unsure as I changed back into dry-land clothes, closed the searay's door, and headed the *Walrus* underwater, back towards Lepidor.

After I'd moored the *Walrus* to one of the searay gantries below the oceanographers' building, I went up to give them my samples and copies of the probe readings. The master oceanographer was in the sample store-room, checking that everything was in order. He was a fierce old man with flowing white hair and a thick moustache, older than Siana but as strong as he had ever been, unlike the arthritic Avarch. *Ex-Avarch*, I reminded myself.

'Oh, it's you back,' he said 'You missed a bit of a fuss.'

'Oh?' I began slotting the thin tubes into their racks inside the cabinet.

'The Avarch announced he'd be setting up a tribunal of the Faith. Everyone in the clan to be questioned about their knowledge of the basic

principles. Those who don't measure up,' and here the old man turned
with a ghoulish expression on his face, 'to be given *further instruction*.'

I remembered what Ravenna had accused Midian of, and began to
wonder.

'When does this start?' I asked.

'Today.'

I put the last sample tube in and closed the cabinet again.

'These are from all the southern probes. There's more silt than usual
around Taraway Point; other than that, nothing unusual.'

'Did you take a sample of the Point?'

I nodded. 'It's in there with the others.'

'Good to see you haven't forgotten your training.'

I went next door to the filing room and left my written data there
before going back to the Palace. Palatine met me at the gates.

'Where have you been, Cathan? Midian's summoned us for the first
round of questioning and you're already a half-hour late.'

'I've been out,' I said. 'If Midian disapproves, he can jump off a
cliff.'

'And you say you don't want to be noticed,' she said, as we set off
towards the Temple.

'I'm a member of the Oceanographic Guild,' I said, 'and I've been on
Guild business. He can't complain; if he wants to set up tribunals he'll
have to work around everybody else.'

'Have it your way.' She shrugged.

'Where's Ravenna?' I asked.

'She's already been. You remember what she said about Midian the
other night?' Palatine went on without waiting for me to reply. 'I didn't
believe her then, but now, with this tribunal business, who can tell? She
could be right. And remember, Midian doesn't like her. You saw him at
the reception, the way he leered at her. She's Archipelagan, she has no
rights as far as swine like him are concerned.'

'What's the point of all this, Palatine?' She didn't usually go into details
unless she wanted to convince me of something.

'Um . . . perhaps if you and Ravenna try to act as if you're in love. No
that you are,' she added hastily, then grinned. 'At least, not that you'll
admit to. But Midian can't offend you, you're too important, and that
would protect her.'

'Have you asked Ravenna?'

'I asked her first; she's touchier than you. She agrees, and she said it was probably a good thing if we didn't want Midian to end up with a knife in him.'

'If she's agreed, I'll play along,' I said.

'Oh, and Hamilcar's gone. He wanted me to say goodbye for him, and he said he'll be back soon, for the next cargo. Your admiral's gone with him, to escort him part of the way.'

I hoped that would be enough, remembering the pirate ships we'd met off Pharassa on our way here. The *Shadowstar* was a battle cruiser and had been easily able to deal with them, but what about the *Marduk*? Lepidor's manta wasn't nearly so powerful.

We reached the Temple to find a small crowd of people waiting in the courtyard, and one of Midian's new priests standing by the inner door. When he saw us, he beckoned us over.

'The Avarch is busy now, and will see you at eight o'clock this evening.'

'We can't come then,' I said, without thinking. 'We dine at eight.'

'The Avarch does not shift his schedule around for other concerns. If you had come when you were requested earlier, this problem wouldn't have happened.'

I stared the gaunt priest in the eye, suddenly angry. 'If Midian had summoned me more than five minutes in advance, I might have been able to make it. As it is, I have no intention of neglecting my duties to hang around at his pleasure. With all respect, of course, *Domine*.'

I turned away and stalked out of the courtyard, Palatine close behind.

'For Ranthas's sake, Cathan, what are you doing?'

'I'm not letting Midian order me around in my own city. If he wants to call me before his tribunal, he can at least be polite about it.'

'Don't annoy him. Please, for Ravenna's sake if not yours or mine, be a little bit subtler.'

'When Midian learns to be polite I'll be a bit subtler. This isn't Haleth, however much he may think it is, and he has no authority outside religious matters. Certainly not to summon me from the Palace at any hour of the day or night.'

'But if you offend him he'll start trying to get back at you. Cathan, you know how dangerous he is. Please don't ignore me.'

'What Midian's trying to do, Palatine, is beyond his authority. This isn't a heresy trial, just an education tribunal, and I'm perfectly within my rights to ignore him. Now, are you coming to lunch? I'm expected back at the Guild in half an hour.'

In the end, Midian did cave in, and eventually sent a messenger to ask me when I wanted to come. It was three days since his tribunal had begun, and they'd questioned over a hundred people. I was able to prove to him that I knew more than enough of the principles of the Faith; even if I didn't believe in them, I'd been taught them at the Citadel on the principle of 'know your enemy'.

However, when a new crisis hit Lepidor, I wondered whether my refusal was to blame. Exactly a week after he'd arrived, Midian seized a group of tribal traders who'd arrived in the city.

We had no official links with the tribesmen, or with anybody in the interior, but there was an understanding between us and one of the friendlier tribes. Once every couple of months, they brought a small caravan through the north pass and down into the city to trade furs for fish and other objects that weren't found in the valleys. As long as we left them alone, they didn't cause us any trouble.

Of course, that didn't matter to Midian. He had his priests haul the merchants before the tribunal to find out how much knowledge they had of the Faith.

The answer, of course, was none. He order their possessions seized and the tribesmen themselves confined to the penitents' cells, where Mezentus had been a short time before. My father tried to intervene and persuade Midian to let them go, but Elnibal was on shaky ground: relations with the barbarians were against Domain custom, and it seemed Midian was going to be as inflexible as he could and follow Domain law to the letter.

It didn't help that he looked on the skin-clad, bearded tribesmen with utter contempt. I'd had few dealings with any of them – I could hardly even understand their dialect of Archipelagan – but I knew they were a proud and independent people, who treated each other – and their womenfolk – a lot better than the Halettites did.

That afternoon a storm blew up, giving us a welcome breathing space, because the tribesmen could hardly have left anyway in such weather. My father invited Midian to the Palace to try and persuade him once again to release the tribesmen; he told me to be there as well.

We met him in the secret Council chamber. Midian was all smiles as he came through the door, but the moment my father mentioned the natives his cheeriness vanished.

'I thought we had already discussed this, Count. They are heathens, worshippers of false gods, and it is against the law of Ranthas to even let them into the city.'

'That is as may be, Avarch. But if those tribesmen don't return to their valley once the storm is over, there'll be a raid, and some of my people may die. Out here on the frontier, we can't afford to offend the tribes.'

'Your marines can deal with the tribes any day.'

'Of course they can. But if we make enemies of the tribe, they'll begin to raid our outposts, our passes, steal out belongings and food, and kill people. I will *not* have my clansmen killed because you couldn't honour an agreement. I swore an oath to protect my clan and I will hold to it.'

'Count, this is a matter entirely within Domain jurisdiction. It is heresy to worship any other god than Ranthas, and these men are guilty of it.'

My father leaned over the table and stared at Midian down its length. 'Then why don't the Domain have missionary posts here to show them the true path? Then you could bring them peacefully into your fold.'

'We have tried, haven't we? They don't listen to reason, only brute force.'

'Exactly. You don't have missionary posts up here because it's too dangerous. You don't want to endanger your people. *And nor do I.*'

'I am warning you to keep out of this, Count,' Midian said. 'You have your authority, and I have mine. Now, I have business to attend to.' He walked out, not bothering to bow.

My father slammed his fist down on the table. 'Damn him to hell's furnace! He'd see us all dead before he drops his damned principles.'

'Is there anything we can do?' I asked.

Elnibal looked at me as if noticing my presence for the first time; I'd sat next to him through the whole discussion without saying a word.

'No, there isn't. Not now; if I interfere he'll call down the wrath of his fanatic friends on us. The only thing I can do is write to the King, tell him what's happened, and see if he can talk to the Exarch.'

I wondered if by then it would be too late.

★

The storm cleared after two days, but Midian still didn't release the imprisoned traders. The next day, he announced that they would be tried for heresy.

'He's mad,' Palatine said, 'or stupid.'

'Both,' Ravenna said. 'Maybe he gets paid by the number of heretics burnt, and he's worried that they'll cut his stipend if he doesn't produce some trials.' It was an unusual thing to hear from her, almost a joke, and I wondered whether it was part of the act.

'I hope not.'

The morning after Midian announced the trials, my father summoned me to his office. He was sitting behind his desk, which was covered with a mound of official paperwork and files.

'We've had no word from any of the native tribes,' he said. 'I want you to go up to the mine and the pass and inspect the defences. Take Palatine if you want, but not Ravenna. Midian might make trouble, and I don't think she can defend herself as well as Palatine can. Midian sent a priest up to the pass earlier this morning to take care of the guards' souls; you may meet him coming back.'

'Do I have to have an escort?' I asked.

'I've assigned you eight marines. They'll be waiting for you at the city gate in a quarter of an hour.'

'I'll go and find Palatine.'

'I put her to work in the armoury; she's got to have something to do apart from hanging around,' my father said.

I left his office, went back to my room to change my light trousers for riding ones and put on a warmer tunic – the pass wasn't far from the sea, but it was quite high up and decidedly cold. I also belted on my sword.

The armoury was in a vaulted cellar under the main barracks, on the other side of the main square. The marine guards on the gates didn't bother to stop me, and the armoury clerk merely asked me to leave my sword by the door and write down my name in the record book.

There was very little going on in the series of stone rooms and passageways that made up the armoury, but the echoes off the high roof magnified every little scrape with an eerie, cacophonous effect. I heard Palatine's voice several rooms away, and Ravenna's too.

They were in a long, narrow room, almost a corridor, along with a few marines inspecting the swords further down. Palatine was checking the mechanisms of the crossbows that hung like instruments of torture on the room's walls. She was calling out their condition to Ravenna, who held a ledger in one hand, a tiny stick of graphite in the other and was busy ticking off figures on a list. I hoped Midian hadn't seen the boots and clothes they were wearing; I was sure they'd break one of the petty restrictions the Domain had added on to the laws of Ranthas.

Ravenna and Palatine both turned from their work as I approached. I was trying to be as quiet as possible, but the rasp of my boot soles against the stone flags was painfully loud.

'Ah, there you are,' Palatine whispered. 'We were wondering when you'd escape from your state papers.' She mouthed something and jerked her head towards Ravenna; I'd forgotten about the masque we were putting on for Midian's sake; it had to be maintained even out of his sight. I took her hand, wondering as I did why I found it so difficult.

'My father wants you and me to inspect the mine and the pass defences,' I said to Palatine.

'What about me?' Ravenna asked.

To reply without creating an echo I had to whisper in her ear, 'My father won't let you go. It's too dangerous if we run into any raiding parties and someone sees you fighting.'

'Wretched Domain,' she whispered back.

Palatine got someone else to take over from her and went with me up to the surface; I collected my rapier on the way. Ravenna stayed behind to help the others; even the younger marines wouldn't give her any trouble – her supposed relationship with me would ensure that.

We were already late, I realized, and we had to run across to the stables to get horses. I had a horse of my own, although I didn't take him out very often and shared him unofficially with one of my House cousins. He was a bronze-maned gelding, sedate enough to compensate for my lack of riding skills. Palatine, who had memories of riding all sorts of strange creatures, including Silvernian elephantines, was given a more spirited gold-maned stallion.

The eight marines who made up our escort were waiting at the gates when we arrived, a couple of minutes late. They were wearing armour,

I noticed, rather than the usual light cuirasses; overlapping light metal strips on a silk jacket, with wide padded side skirts to protect their legs and helmets with neck-plates. I cursed Midian for his stubbornness – this wasn't necessary, and it wouldn't have happened if Siana had still been here.

We rode out along the inland road, heading through the fields and up, into the valley of the cedars that lay below the mine. I hadn't been up here since the day the iron was discovered, eighteen months or more ago, and the area up here, like the rest of the city, had changed. The road that had been so full of potholes and loose stones had been repaired and, so one of the marines told me, would in time be paved.

We didn't turn right up to the mine, though; we were going up to the North Pass first, because it was further away and a worse place to get stuck if a storm hit. Besides which, the Pass's defences were more important than the mine's.

Once we reached the end of the valley, the marines spread out and moved into formation: four ahead of us, four behind, with two lengths between each pair of horses. We were still in forest country, but to either side of us the slopes of the hills rose steeply away, the vegetation thinning and breaking off. Ahead and beyond rose the grey shapes of the mountains, colossal and awe-inspiring. I always shivered when I saw those remote inland summits: seeing them, with the snow on their peaks, seemed to make it feel colder even down here.

'You know,' Palatine said after a few moments' silence, as we trotted up the stony path, 'anybody else in your place, or Ravenna's, would have welcomed my suggestion, and enjoyed playing the part. They wouldn't have needed telling! Just what is it with you two? I thought I understood, but it seems I don't.'

'I would tell you if I knew,' I said, reluctant to reveal any of my confused thoughts, even to her. 'Why do you trust her now, when you didn't used to?'

'We're in your home city now, not following where she wanted us to go. Don't change the subject. Do you think I believe you don't know what's going on?'

'No, I don't,' I said. 'She obviously isn't interested. Now can we talk about something else?' Her questioning was beginning to irritate me, even though I knew it was only friendly concern.

'We can't,' Palatine said firmly. 'You don't really believe that she isn't interested?'

'Palatine, I don't know what to believe. This isn't something I want to discuss, not with you, not with anyone.'

'Fine, I'll drop it,' she said. 'But before I do, please don't think that she has no feelings for you. Perhaps you haven't noticed, but you're the only person Ravenna's allowed to touch her in all the time I've known her.'

Palatine said nothing for the rest of the ride, and soon we rode up the high path at the end of the upper valley, where the trees were little more than scrub bushes. Ahead of us loomed the two-hundred-yard-long wall with its three towers and single gate that blocked off the only pass into the interior of Oceanus for dozens of miles on either side. The only way into the towers or onto the wall was through a gate at the side of the central tower; that was to prevent isolated raiding parties who sneaked along tiny mountain paths from surprising the garrison and opening the gates.

As soon as we got close, though, we saw that something was wrong. There was no guard on the side door, where there should have been, and I couldn't see the heads of any patrolling sentries above the parapet.

'Quickly,' I said, the annoyance caused by Palatine's intrusion swamped by rising fear. We broke into a gallop and swept up the last hundred yards of the pass at top speed. At the top, the marine commander ordered us to wait.

'If you hear any fighting, ride away immediately,' he said. With the leading three marines, he dismounted, drew his sword and advanced into the central tower.

For long moments I watched the tower where it stood silhouetted against the peaks and the dazzling blue sky. Nobody moved, although the horses fretted nervously.

Then the commander ran back out of the door.

'Escount, we've been betrayed. The garrison are all lying inside in a stupor, and the gates are unlocked. I reckon they've been like this for at least three hours.'

The tribes had broken through our defences, and they were loose inside our territory.

CHAPTER XXII

'Where will they be heading?' Palatine said, swinging her horse round so she could look down over the valley.

'The mine, probably,' the commander said. 'The city and the towns are too well defended for a native raiding party.'

'We don't know how many of them there are,' I said. 'This could be one tribe or several working together.'

'They still won't be able to get through the towns' aether shields.'

'What if there are traitors in the towns as well?' Palatine said. 'If there was one here, there could be others.'

'We're wasting time hanging around up here.' I said. 'I don't suppose the emergency transmitter still works?'

'They've smashed all the equipment, including the signal flares. There's no way of warning anybody.' The commander's face was grim, and he was looking uneasily down the valley.

'What's the best thing to do, then?' I asked him.

'We could stay here, try and catch them on the way out, or we could ride back to warn the mine or the city.' As he spoke, two of the other three marines emerged on the battlements and ran along towards the other towers.

'No point in staying here,' Palatine said to me. I saw her fidgeting with the reins; she wasn't as calm as she looked. 'There's nothing ten of us can do against an army. We have to ride back and warn them!'

I looked at her, then at the marine commander. I was supposed to be in charge, but I was the least experienced. How could I decide? Go back and risk an ambush? Surely it would be useless to stay here. I dithered for a second.

'Summon your men, Captain,' I said. 'We'll go back.'

'Good idea, sir. We'll close the gates again before we go; that'll delay them when they return.' He ran back towards the gates, shouting to the men on the battlements to come down. A moment later I heard the grinding noise as the bar was pushed across. It seemed to echo off the grey hills, and I was sure the tribes must have heard it.

They seemed to take an eternity, even though it was only a couple of minutes, and I sat and fretted on the horse. Then the marines ran out from the gatehouse and mounted their horses. They moved into close formation ahead and behind us – only half a length's distance – and we rode back down the path. The commander spurred on his horse when the path levelled out and became somewhat straighter.

The woods to either side of us suddenly seemed dark and menacing despite the dappled sunlight on the forest floor. Every time a branch rustled or a bird warbled I jumped. I saw tribesmen behind every bush. The sides of the mountains were grey and bare, with clouds behind them, but even there I saw shadows crouched behind boulders on the scree. But there were no tribesmen in wait, just a silent, tense ride down to the junction with the mine road. The noise of the horses' hooves on the track filled my ears; none of us said anything. We slowed again as we reached the end of the upper valley. Nobody wanted to ride straight into a trap. I was felling more and more apprehensive the further we went.

What would the tribesmen have done? They'd surprised us with the traitor in the tower, a trick they could only use once. Now that they were inside our defences, what were they going to do? I wondered if the mine was an important enough target. And how many of them were there?

I'd been taught some tracking at the Citadel, so I tried to work the last question out myself, from the tell-tale signs on the road. I cursed myself for not having been more alert on the way up. The natives had concealed their tracks well, but I should have been able to pick them up if I hadn't been talking to Palatine.

The marine commander reined in his horse just above the fork in the road and held up his hand for the rest of us to stop.

'Do you hear it?' he said.

'Hear what?' I strained my ears, but couldn't hear anything beyond rustling leaves and the occasional screech of a gull or cry of a falcon. Nothing out of the ordinary.

'Exactly,' he said, grim-faced. 'The machinery's stopped. You haven't been up to the mine since we discovered the iron, I know, but you can always hear the hum of the machines and the clank of rocks even from here.'

'What are the defences like? Have they been improved?' I asked.

'There are stone walls now, and a proper gate, with a flamewood cannon. But if the tribesmen managed to creep up on the mine's guards, they mightn't have been able to close the gates in time.'

'What do we do?'

'We leave two men behind to scout out what's happening, and I'll escort you and Palatine back to Lepidor. We're heavily outnumbered, and this is no place for you to be without protection.'

'Do we know how many there are, though?' Palatine said. 'If they captured the mine they could be blocking the road further down. We don't want to ride into a trap.'

'Do you have a better idea?' the marine snapped. He seemed ill at ease with Palatine, and irritated that she was contradicting him.

'We move into the forest, send scouts up to the mine. Then we can find out how many there are, what they're doing.'

'But what if they're not in position yet? We might have a chance to get through.'

'We're wasting time arguing about it,' Palatine said. 'Cathan, you're in charge.' All of them looked at me, and I realized with a sinking feeling that they expected me to decide. I cursed myself for having skipped all those lessons to go out with the oceanographers. For all my training at sea, I was at a loss here. What should I do? The marine was experienced and knew the ground, but I'd seen Palatine's military genius in action several times in the Citadel. Would she be as good in real action, though? Yet again I dithered.

'Quickly, sir!' the marine said, with ill-concealed impatience.

'We'll—' I never got the chance to finish, because at that point there were sudden yells and tribesmen appeared from the woods on both sides, brandishing their spears. My gelding reared in alarm as a spear thunked into the ground in front of him, and I had to hold on to his neck to stop myself falling off.

'Ride!' the marine commander shouted. I spurred my horse on as the marines drew their swords and the horses milled around in confusion. 'Try to break through!'

'Cathan!' I heard Palatine's voice from just behind me as I turned my horse down the road. 'Watch out!'

I saw the tripwires just in time and managed to avoid both of them; someone else did too, but one of the marines, from the sound of it, wasn't so lucky. I drew my sword and urged my horse to a full gallop, hoping to escape any traps further down.

I didn't make it. Less than thirty yards ahead, a double line of natives with throwing spears ran out of the trees and barred my way. I thought for a moment of trying to run them down, but then realized I'd be virtually a sitting target for their spears.

I reined the horse in and looked back. All but one of the marines had been pulled off their horses, and one lay in a heap on the verge. It was Palatine who'd made it over the tripwires, and she'd stopped too. Her face was twisted with disappointment, and she looked angry.

'Dismount and throw your swords down, or we will kill you,' someone shouted from behind us.

'Do as he says,' Palatine said, letting her sword drop to the ground. A moment later I did the same, then slipped off the horse. I looked down at my sword lying in the dust of the road, and couldn't bear to meet Palatine's gaze.

A couple of moments later, I was seized by a pair of wiry tribesmen who tied my hands behind me and prodded me towards the mine with their spears.

I saw the marine commander had been right as we were marched up the well-kept road that led to the mine's gates. It had been taken – the gates were open, and a few natives with ferocious expressions were guarding them. Even now I couldn't help noticing how much the mine had grown since I'd left. The compound had been expanded, its crude palisade had been replaced by a proper wall, and several new buildings loomed up inside. A water-filled ditch ran around the outside where the ground was flat; at the gates this moat was crossed by a drawbridge. As we were pushed inside the gates, I saw a vastly expanded entrance with rails and a huge wheel by it, next to a building that I guessed housed the flamewood reactor.

There was no sign of activity except for a large number of natives standing over by the mine's entrance, which had been blocked with crates. I wondered what was going on over there.

Our captors took us to the centre of the courtyard and told us to turn and face the gates. My hands were beginning to go numb; the thongs used to bind them were cutting off the blood supply.

The warriors who'd ambushed us – I estimated over fifty in number – filed through the gates and stood in an expectant crowd, while some of their comrades took seven bound marines – one sagging in his captor's grip, face bloodied – into one of the buildings. Who were they waiting for? I wished they'd hurry up; whatever they had in store for us, it was preferable to standing tied up in the middle of the compound with sixty or seventy natives staring at me.

A moment later, I saw a short, thin figure in leather armour walking out of a building, accompanied by two hefty bodyguards. He sauntered over to us and made a gesture to our guards, who forced us to our knees. The tribal chief was no taller than me, I realized. He was small and dark, with sharp features and brown eyes. It was hard to tell how old he was, but I guessed about forty.

'So,' he said in only slight accented Archipelagan, 'we have caught a bigger fish. Escount, I am Gythyn of the Weidiro.'

I stared defiantly up at him, shame gnawing at me.

'Perhaps you could tell us why you broke the sacred agreement, Escount, and are holding some of my people,' he said, after a brief pause.

'My father didn't break it, our priest did. He's new to the city and intent on punishing heresy.'

'*Heresy*? Our faith is heresy?' the man said, dangerously quietly.

'It is not the faith of Ranthas,' I said. 'To him, that is anathema.'

'Your Count is responsible for the actions of his priest.'

'My father has no authority over him!' I protested. 'If he stepped in to release the prisoners, he'd be arrested as well.'

'Nevertheless, your priest represents your clan, and your clan has broken its word of honour.'

I had enough experience of the barbarians to know that they considered a man's word to be his bond. They would never break a contract without giving warning and getting agreement from the other side. For the first time since we were captured, I was really afraid.

'Is there any way we can atone for it?' Palatine said.

'Atone for breaking your sacred word? You and the rest will atone in blood.' He turned away.

I shouted, 'Wait.'

'Do you wish to plead for your life?'

Though I was rigid with fear, I still bridled at this. 'No, I don't,' I said. 'But if one of your people betrayed you against your wishes, would you think it right for the whole tribe to suffer?'

'Do you have a better idea?'

'Can I ask my adviser?'

He looked annoyed, but said, 'Very well. Be quick.'

'Is there anything we can do?' I whispered to Palatine.

'Yes.' She outlined a plan, very briefly. I didn't get time to ask her about it, though, because the chief interrupted.

'You've had enough time. What do you have to say?'

'Would you consider an atonement that would leave you and your people in peace afterwards, without the revenge that my father would exact on you if you killed me?'

'Our laws demand a blood price for breaking a bond.'

'If we return your tribesmen with the goods you need, what else would you ask?'

'If you can return them, why haven't you done it already? Did you think we were too weak to take revenge?'

'I'd break them out without our priest's consent, and so that my father can't be blamed.'

'That will be acceptable, as long as you also give us a ship.'

My heart sank and I looked away again. Surely he knew that was impossible? 'If I gave you that I'd be executed by my own people,' I said. 'Could we give you gold instead?'

'I'm not interested,' he said. Then he spoke to the men behind us. 'Lock them up somewhere and tell the other chiefs it's time we moved on to the next stage.'

We were pushed unceremoniously across the compound and into the blessed shade of one of the new buildings. A lean tribesman inside the door said something in their fluting dialect to one of our captors. After a brief conversation, they took us upstairs and locked us in what I guessed had been somebody's office.

'Turn your back to me,' I said to Palatine.

'Why?'

'So that I can untie you, idiot,' I snapped, then said, 'Sorry, I shouldn't be calling anyone an idiot.'

I studied the rough leather thongs for a minute, then turned my back to her so that I could use my hands. It took me five minutes to loosen her bonds enough for her to slip out of them; I'd been confident that I could do it, but I almost messed it up because my fingers kept shaking.

After that, she untied me. I looked around at the room. One wall was covered by bookshelves holding accounts ledgers, while those on another wall were empty; I wonder what had been on them. There was a desk – clear of any objects – and a chair. Because we were on the outer wall of the compound, the window was narrow and several feet above the ground.

I'd dreaded what Palatine was going to say now that we were able to talk freely but she didn't say anything I'd been expecting.

'It wasn't your fault, Cathan. We were trapped the moment we rode into the upper valley. We couldn't have done anything against them, even if your decisions had been quicker.'

I said nothing, just stared miserably down at the floor. It *was* my fault, for not seeing the tracks on the way up, and for being so indecisive at the crucial moments. Not to mention that I'd turned to flee at the first sign of trouble. What would happen now? I'd heard the chief mention other tribes. Were they massing for an attack on Lepidor? There'd be no warning, not with us taken prisoner.

'Cathan, you can't blame yourself . . .'

'Stop trying to make me feel better, Palatine. Because of me we weren't ready when they hit us. And I should have seen the trap in the first place. It was stupid to go along the road.'

'Feel guilty if you want. When you've wallowed in it enough I'll tell you how we get of here.'

I stopped whining, shamed into silence.

'No more of that, all right?' she said.

'How do we get out?' I said sullenly.

'Can you get through that window?'

I went over and pressed my face against the glass, trying to see to the bottom of the wall to judge the distance.

'The ditch is about fifteen feet below, but it's only six feet deep; I'd have to be careful where I landed. Anyway,' I said, glad to find a flaw in her plan, 'there are natives on the walls. I wouldn't get ten yards across the killing ground.'

'You would in a storm. It rains so hard up here nobody can even see out in it. And the wind – how are they supposed to fire at you in that?'

'It's a lovely day out there – for everyone apart from us.'

'Didn't you notice the clouds over the mountains? Or were you too busy being ashamed? There'll be a storm very soon.'

I was astonished that, my feeling of shame momentarily lifted.

'You want me to go out in a storm?'

'Why not? You've done more difficult things before.'

'Palatine, I've got to cross the open ground out there, and it isn't walled in like the crop fields. The wind literally picks you up and throws you about, and I'm not big enough to stand it. Maybe you Thethians know how to cope with that, but I don't.'

'Please, listen to me just once. The stream in that ditch goes all the way down to the city, doesn't it? It comes out just along the shore.'

I was nonplussed; what did this have to do with anything?

'When it starts raining over the mountains, that stream will become a flood. You can ride it all the way down to the harbour, and you won't need to worry about the wind at all. Maybe the odd flying branch, but you can avoid those.'

I thought about the stream's path; down alongside the road in the main valley, through a deep channel in the middle of the crop fields, round a couple of bends and out through a small circle of rocks between the city beach and the shoreline beach. I hardly dared contemplate the prospect, but Palatine was right.

Overriding my protests, she sketched out the rest of her idea: I'd get into the city, warn my father, and arrange for the prisoners to break out and come back up the road.

'And what will you be doing?' I asked her.

She grinned. 'I'm going to rescue the miners who're cooped up inside the mine.'

Palatine explained that she'd smash the door-lock during the storm, when nobody would hear, and then run across the courtyard and into the mine. I pointed out that there'd be guards in the corridor, downstairs and at the mine entrance, and that she seemed to have forgotten that they were armed and she wasn't.

'The ones over the entrance will have run inside like rabbits. And I can deal with the rest. Once I recapture the mine, I'll come and help you.'

Outside, the blue sky was fast disappearing when we heard a clamour from the courtyard, and then the sounds of armed men going through the gate.

'Where are they going?' I asked Palatine.

'Why should I know? Maybe they'll hide in the woods and attack the city after the storm, catch everyone by surprise.'

'Palatine, your plan's crazy,' I said. 'It depends on everything going exactly right – me making it to the city, you managing to get past the guards – and that's not going to happen.'

'Are you always so pessimistic, or have you just given up?' she retorted, arms crossed. 'How do you think we're going to escape otherwise? You have to prove to yourself that you aren't a failure.'

'Maybe I can swim down a torrent in spate, but it doesn't excuse my getting us into this situation in the first place.'

'Cathan, this is all Midian's fault. He started it in the first place, and he's the Avarch. What could we have done about it? Now, will you do it or not?'

'Are you sure you can carry out your part?'

'Yes, I am. But you're more important – we have to warn your father or nothing will work.'

'I'll do it,' I said, offering a silent prayer to Thetis and Althana that nobody would come up and move us before the storm hit.

Someone came into our makeshift cell an hour or so later, but all he did was open the door, look around to check we were still there, and leave again. We had looped the loosened thongs round our wrists again to make it seem as if we were still tied, and the man didn't seem suspicious.

A few minutes later, as the aether lights were switched on, the rain began to fall.

The first drops spattered against the window, and I could see them trickling down the outside. Soon, though, there were no more trickles, just sheets of water that made the window look more like a waterfall than a sheet of glass. Thankfully the wind wasn't blowing straight in. I looked round the room, which was at least dry, light and warm, one last time. The noise of the water on the roof and in the stream below was deafening, and the wind howled like a thousand lost souls. The sky was dark royal blue, and getting gloomier; there was no light on the horizon.

'Are you ready?' Palatine asked.

I shuddered at the thought of what lay ahead. But then I remembered how I'd felt on the road, and at the sight of the tribal chieftain strutting around in our mine compound.

'Yes, I am,' I said. I pulled off my boots, left them in a corner and picked up one of the twisted thongs. I wrapped it around my right wrist; it would protect my arm, and could possibly come in handy for something else.

I opened the window and sat up on the wide sill, trying to look calm, and nodded to Palatine. Out of the corner of my eye I could see that the water was at least six feet higher than it had been, a raging white torrent of waves and flotsam almost up to the lip of the ditch. The window was barely wide enough to fit me, and I had to shuffle round until I was in a position where my clothes wouldn't catch on the lip. Within seconds my clothes were soaked from the rain driving along the walls and just inside the room.

I pushed my legs out and almost fell, so strong was the force of the wind. Then I breathed a quick prayer to Thetis that Her waters would carry me safely. And jumped.

CHAPTER XXIII

Ranthas, it was freezing! Icy water like a thousand needles splashed over my feet, legs and torso, and even before my head went under the current was dragging me downstream. I plunged beneath the surface with my eyes tightly shut, and was spun round and round by a torrent moving at an incredible speed. If I hadn't been a water-breather I'd have died in those first minutes as I was hurled along, held remorselessly under the surface.

I had no idea where I was, and in the dark of the storm channel there was no up or down. There was a little light but I was so dazed from the impact that I couldn't see where it was coming from. I couldn't tell how far I'd come, and I didn't dare raise my head above the water in case I hit the drawbridge.

The stream changed direction and I was flung against the stone wall of the channel, bruising my arm. My world shrunk to a confused maelstrom of eddies and waves as I was carried helplessly along, fumbling about in the dark and gripped by the terrible chill. I'd never been so cold, and there seemed to be no end to it, no way out. I was shivering uncontrollably, but there was nothing I could do to keep myself warm.

Something crashed past me, missing my shoulder by a few inches, and then I was spun around completely as the stream twisted again. Panic-stricken and confused, I couldn't think, couldn't pray to the powers above for this to end, couldn't do anything except keep my hands out in front of me to shield my head.

Abruptly, my head broke the surface and I gasped, still breathing water. But before I could do anything more than realize I'd surfaced, an undertow tugged at my feet and pulled me down again. I spun head over heels as the current flipped me over.

I managed to right myself and kicked out against the current, trying to bring myself to the surface, when suddenly I felt as if the world had fallen away from under me, and I left my stomach behind as I plunged down into blackness, falling . . . falling . . .

And then, as the fall ended and my feet almost scraped the bottom, I bobbed up again, into the foaming pool at the bottom of a waterfall.

I looked round wildly, suddenly even colder as the wind blew on my drenched hair, plastered against my head and my face. Where was I? How far down the stream? Had I reached the city yet – surely not? There was a tremendous swishing sound filling the air, like the rustling of a thousand trees; then I realized that was what it was.

The rain drove at my face, and I had to turn my head before I cold open my eyes again, but I could see the indistinct line of the forest to one side, and a bank on the other – what was up there? Above me the clouds echoed with rumbles of thunder and pulses of lightning, illuminating parts of the landscape here and there. As a white flash lit up the sky, I looked up into a swirling cauldron of clouds, layer upon layer, deck upon deck, rising into the atmosphere, as the lower belt momentarily split open.

Then it was dark again, and I realized that I was next to the road, being carried through the Valley of the Cedars. In the forest beside me the native chief and his army might be waiting for a signal to attack. At least in this tempest they wouldn't be able to stop me.

There was an almighty crack, not thunder but something else, behind me, and a moment later a splash, as the upper branch of a cedar broke off and fell into the pool. I was seized by fresh panic – what if one of those were to hit me next time?

I was briefly sucked under again and dragged down, my shirt ripping on the rough floor of the channel. Then I came back up and when I opened my eyes I could make out the shape of a branch beside me. I grabbed at it, and though it was slippery I managed to cling on desperately with both hands. There were more branches all around me, some of them the size of small trees. I pulled myself closer to the branch, inching my left hand further up to get a better grip. If I could just hold on to it, I'd be able to stay on the surface and see where the branches were falling in time to avoid them.

The current swept my branch along, and as I gripped it, I suddenly felt a wild feeling of exhilaration, of joy as I followed the current around its twists and turns. I'd never travelled this fast before – not without being inside a manta or a searay – and I hadn't realized what it felt like. The rain was driving into the back of my head, and my body had stopped being cold and was beginning to feel almost pleasantly numb, but I felt more *alive* than I ever had before despite this warning sign.

I kicked my legs to try and restore my circulation as the stream carried me out from under the forest and onto the foreshore, between the road and the stone wall at the edge of the fields. There were no branches falling here, at least, because there were no trees. But there was also less shelter from the wind, which howled over the empty landscape.

I looked ahead and saw the lights of Lepidor, glowing under the soft blue hemisphere of the aether shield above the city, the walls getting nearer and nearer. My arms were frozen, and despite the impossible exhilaration I was worried. The cold was draining my energy, and I didn't have Laeas's or even Palatine's physique to withstand it for long.

Then I was next to the towering walls of the new quarter. The fields to my left ended, replaced by scrub and then, almost as quickly, by beach.

Then I was out of the cold current and into the warmer waters of the ocean that had been heated all day by the sun. I felt some of my energy return and let go of my branch. It had served me well, but now it was time to swim. I knew that the current along the walls of the new quarter would carry me all the way to the undersea harbour, and so I kicked out with all the fading energy I had.

My muscles felt leaden, but I managed to push myself out of the still water by the stream's mouth to where the current ran along the beach. The surface of the sea was dimpled by rain and waves were dashing themselves against the wall to my right. The harbour suddenly seemed a ver long way away. I was already exhausted; how was I going to swim all the way along there?

Lepidor, I kept telling myself. *You're the only person who can save it . . . save it . . . save it. Yours is the most important part, Cathan. Without you anything anyone else does is pointless.* But I was so cold, and so tired; I'd let my father down, and I didn't want to face him.

But you don't want to let him down now, I told myself. *Only you can warn him.*

I was still swimming, but my strokes were slower and slower, and even the relative warmth of the ocean hadn't helped as the waves carried me up and down. Trying to swim along the line of the waves was almost worse than going down the stream.

Then an eerie sound off to my left almost startled me out of my wits. A moment later I relaxed, as one of the seals surfaced and roared at the storm before disappearing into the depths. He'd been close enough that his bark hadn't been drowned out by the noise of the storm. A moment later there was another, further ahead.

They can't do it, why can't you? But I didn't have layers and layers of blubber, only a soaked shirt and a pair of trousers. *Swim.*

And somehow I swam, along the breakers, past the line of the walls, as my thoughts seemed to slow down and I became unsure where I was. I felt a hard blow to my right forearm, the one with wet thongs around it, and looked round in slow indignation for whatever had done it. A moment later, I saw a whiskery head emerge and heard a deafening bark a few inches from my ear. The seals weren't wary of me; I doubted I looked very threatening.

Then I was at the point where the new quarter gave way to the harbour quarter. Just a couple of dozen yards to the right and below me the warning lights of the undersea harbour gleamed dully.

I looked around one last time, for what, I reflected absently, could be my last ever sight of the sky and the city – *No, it won't be, or you won't be forgiven* – kicked my tired legs, and dived.

Beneath the surface, in the strange reddish-white light of the lamps, I saw the seals, arching and twisting in a silent dance, drifting lazily beneath the surface in clouds of plankton, illuminated by the light. It was almost balletic, a world away from the fury of the storm.

I don't want to die, not here, not now, with so many things unfinished. One day I would like to see this again, when I can truly appreciate it.

Below me the uppermost gantry projected out into the gloom, and I saw the lights of the hub. Less than twenty yards away from me, a few feet under the surface, was the cliff face and an overhanging ledge that was the entrance to the southernmost of the harbour's moon pools, where the repairmen dived from. I kicked out towards it, swimming through the graceful dance of the seals, my limbs somehow responding again. I saw the white glow of the aether lights, always left on in case someone was stuck outside, and dived under the sharp knife of rock, up and into the moon pool, where I was almost dazzled by the brightness of the aether lights.

My feet fumbled for the ladder, and even when I found it they were so cold I almost couldn't feel the rungs. I hauled myself up and collapsed in a dripping heap on the wood of the platform, feeling utterly spent.

I had no idea how long I lay there, in a half-daze – something was digging into my thigh, but I didn't move. I was ready to collapse, but I realized I couldn't. I pulled myself upright and activated one of the drying chambers, a niche in the wall with hot air vents at the top and sides. I couldn't remember whether it was dangerous or not, but I had to get my circulation going again, or I wouldn't even be able to climb the steps that led up to the cabin above me, against the city wall.

I sat there in the hot-air stream against the wall for several minutes before my clothes began to dry and I felt able to move again. There was no time to be lost – I didn't know how long the storm would go on for. It could be hours or days, and if it didn't last long I'd have to move fast. I'd got this far; I didn't want to fail here just to feel more comfortable.

My clothes were almost dry. I switched off the air stream and walked unsteadily towards the ladder. I couldn't feel or move my legs very well, and it was agony pulling myself up when my legs wanted to give way at every point.

I came up into the dark interior of the diving cabin. The door was locked, but I didn't have time to look for the key; I turned the light on, looked for a large blunt instrument among the pieces of equipment, and broke the lock with a few heavy, inaccurate blows that did almost as much damage to the wood of the door as to the lock.

I was on the far side of the harbour quarter, near the oceanographers' building. I headed along the deserted streets through the rain, much less fierce inside the walls and the shield than it was outside. My half-dried clothes were soon soaked, and I was cold again. I cut my foot on a sharp stone, and a stabbing pain lanced up my leg with every other step I took from then on; I could feel sticky blood on my foot, but couldn't stop to do anything about it.

I hobbled painfully through the streets to the gate into the Palace quarter. No one stopped me; of course, the guards would be in the gate-house gambling and drinking. The main street was deserted, as anyone with any sense was indoors at this hour on a storm day, but lights burned behind blinds in most of the windows, warm and welcoming.

I had to keep my return a secret, especially from the priests. Midian undoubtedly had something to do with this predicament, and the less he knew the better. I took the first side street on the left and followed the smaller roads towards the postern gate at the back of the Palace. As I went past the back of the Temple the bell tolled: the ninth hour. It was earlier than it felt; there'd still be people awake in the Palace.

Thankfully the guards hadn't yet locked the postern, because I didn't have the key with me. I winced as the door creaked shut behind me, but then I was safe in the rain-swept garden of the Palace. I stepped onto the grass, softer on my painful feet.

How could I get into the Palace without being seen? It only needed one person to tell Midian, I was sure, and the plan would be revealed. I looked up at the windows. I could just see my parents' rooms on the town side, but no light shone from them. Nor from Atek's. But there was a light in Ravenna's, thank heavens.

I stubbed my toe and involuntarily fell to my knees. I hardly had the energy left to stand, so I crawled across the lawn to the path below Ravenna's window. I moved to the edge of it, picked up a handful of small stones, and pushed myself unsteadily to my feet again. I flung the stones, but they went hopelessly astray and hit the rose trellis covering the wall two windows along. My second, third and fourth attempts also missed, but thankfully nobody poked their head out.

On the fifth try, I hit Ravenna's window with the shower of little pebbles. I waited, but nothing happened. Wasn't she in? I tried twice more, missing the first time.

Then I heaved a sigh of relief as the window opened and her face peered out.

'Is anybody there?' she said; I was in shadow at the wall's base.

'Ravenna!' I called, but it came out as a croak. I tried again. 'Ravenna! It's Cathan!'

'I can't hear you,' she said. 'Who is it?'

I almost cried in frustration. 'It's Cathan!'

'I can't hear you still, whoever you are,' she said. 'Wait a moment, and I'll be down.'

I sank back onto the grass, heedless of the rain and the mud on my clothes, waiting for her to come. For what seemed an eternity there was no sign of her, then one of the doors opened and I heard footsteps. Light flooded out onto the grass. This time Ravenna saw me immediately and hurried out towards me.

'Who . . . Thetis's name! Cathan, what's happened to you?'

'Tribesmen,' I croaked. 'Escaped. Have to get me inside . . . without anyone seeing . . . message from Palatine.'

'I'm not strong enough to carry you,' she said. 'Could you lean on me?'

I struggled to get to my feet, but I couldn't.

'You've cut your foot as well.' She moved round to the other side of me and pulled me upright. I put an arm across her shoulders and got unsteadily to my feet, leaning on her. With painful slowness, we made our way inside, and I leaned against a wall while she shut the door. Then, with agony jabbing through my foot with every step, we went up two flights of spiral stairs and into Ravenna's room. She lowered me gently onto the blankets of the bed, and I sank into them in exhaustion.

I didn't say anything while she wrapped a cloth around my foot to soak up the blood, but then I realized I still hadn't finished.

'Go . . . please, could you bring my father here . . . I have to give him a message . . . no one else must know.'

'Are you sure you'll be all right?'

I managed a weak nod, and she hurried away.

As I lay there on Ravenna's bed, every one of my bruises throbbing, I did nothing but stare up at the ceiling. The blankets grew uncomfortably hot, but I couldn't, and didn't, move.

It must have been only a couple of minutes later that my father burst into the room, with Ravenna close behind him. Nobody else was with them.

'Heavens, Cathan, what happened to you?' my father said, crossing the room in two strides, horror on his face. 'We heard you'd been captured by the tribesmen. One of our woodsmen saw them taking you into the mine and managed to get away to tell us.'

'I escaped,' I said weakly. 'Came down the stream, but that's not important.' I told him what Palatine had said to pass on, word for word as I remembered it. Only once did he ask me to confirm something.

'It's the only way out we've got,' my father said, 'and as far as I can see it's a good one. But how do we release the prisoners without my being involved?'

'There's a girl, at the Temple – Elassel. I know her slightly. She's the daughter of some of the priests, but she hates Midian and the Domain. She's something of an escape artist, I believe, she should be able to help you.'

'What does she look like?' Ravenna asked.

'Curly brown hair, wild expression.'

'I know the one you mean,' my father said. 'But who'll contact her?'

'I will,' Ravenna said. 'If she'll help me, I'll let the prisoners out. Is there anyone else we can trust? I don't think two will be enough.'

'I'll go and find someone. But I'll get the healer first.'

'Please, father,' I said. 'Get the healer, but don't wait around.'

'I won't.' He leaned over me and held my shoulders for a second, then went out again.

The world started to swim around me; I saw Ravenna's concerned frown.

'I'll find her and free them, I promise,' she said.

I felt an overwhelming urge to sleep come over me, and my eyes closed. I felt her hold my hand and tried to say something else. But the words didn't come and I slipped away into sleep.

I heard the rest of what happened that night from my father, Palatine and Elassel, when I woke up again.

My father had been talking to Atek, and when he left my room again he hurried back to his office. He didn't tell the First Adviser about the plan to free the prisoners – the fewer people who knew about that, the better. But he ordered Atek to muster the marines as quietly as possible and to send the captain of the guards, a veteran who was an old comrade of his, to the Palace. Then he sent two of my House cousins out, one to ask Elassel to come from the Temple, the other to summon Tetricus.

When the messenger came, Elassel had just thrown her green coat on the floor and pulled out her lute case from under the bed. There was hardly enough room to practise in the tiny cubicle that was her room here, and no music stand, but she'd manage. She propped the music up on the small table and had taken the lute out of its case when somebody knocked on the door. She hurriedly pushed the lute back under the bed and moved the music, just in case this was Midian or one of his henchmen, and answered the knock.

It wasn't the priest at all, but a young man with tousled brown hair and an uncertain expression.

'What do you want?' Elassel demanded, irritated at having her practice interrupted. She hadn't been able to do it outside, earlier, because of the storm and then all that terrible fuss about the tribal attack. She was very worried about Cathan; her parents had told dreadful tales of what the natives did to prisoners even in the more peaceful areas where they'd worked.

'Are you Elassel?'

'Who else could I be?'

He winced, and Elassel decided to be nicer to him – after all, he wasn't Domain.

He looked up and down the passageway nervously, then lowered his voice to say, 'Count Elnibal requests your presence at the Palace; he'd like your help with something.'

'He wants me? Are you sure?'

'Quite. Be quick, please. I don't want somebody to find us here.'

Elassel put her lute away and pulled her green coat on again. Then she led the messenger through the servants' quarters to the tradesmen's door; no priest would be likely to concern himself with the servants at this time of night.

They ran through the darkened streets in the pouring rain, and the messenger took her through the postern gate of the Palace and up the same flight of stairs Ravenna had helped me up earlier. She saw the dried blood on the steps, and asked whose it was. The messenger only shrugged.

He led her along a plush, carpeted upper corridor and into a large study, warmly lit with tinted aether lamps. There was a man sitting behind the desk, who she knew was the Count, although he looked very careworn tonight, and a serious-looking dark-haired girl in a chair next to the bookshelves that covered one wall.

The Count rose and inclined his head slightly. Elassel bowed with a flourish; she'd never cared for curtsies.

'You must be Elassel,' the Count said. 'I am Count Elnibal; this is Ravenna.'

The girl in the chair nodded slightly in acknowledgement. She seemed rather cold and aloof.

'What can I do for you?' Elassel asked.

'Before we start, will you swear an oath not to reveal anything that either I or Ravenna say now, in case you decide not to help us?'

What were they up to, Elassel wondered, and what was going on? Why all the secrecy? And what possible use could she be? Anyway, it sounded interesting, so she swore an oath by Ranthas.

'Good,' the Count said, when she'd sworn. 'Now, how much do you know about what happened today?'

'There was a tribal attack, and Cathan was captured; I heard they're in control of the mine and the pass.'

'News travels fast,' Ravenna said.

'What nobody outside this room knows yet is that Cathan escaped from the mine by swimming down the stream, and managed to get back here.'

Cathan escaped . . . Ranthas! By swimming down the stream, during a storm? There was more to him than met the eye – she wouldn't have imagined someone so thin and frail-looking could have done that.

'Before he collapsed – he'll be all right, by the way – he said that you might be able to help us with something, part of a plan to foil the natives, who are probably massing to attack the city. There may be a traitor inside the walls.'

'So what do you want me to do?'

'Help us free the natives Midian's captured and get them to the gates. So long as you pull it off nobody will ever know who did it, if you're worried about that.'

Elassel thought about it for a moment. If she was caught, it could mean serious trouble, and she didn't want to be locked up again – even though Midian's penitents' cells were paradise compared to the prisons of Haleth. And she was a musician, not an agent. On the other hand, why not? It would be one in the eye for that lecherous, hypocritical bastard Midian, and she'd meet some more people as well.

'I'll help you,' she said. 'Is anybody else doing this part?'

'Ravenna's in charge, and there's an oceanographer called Tetricus who's an old friend of Cathan's; he's been summoned as well. You're the only one who knows the inside of the Temple and what goes on, though.' The Count walked around his desk and went to the door. 'I've got to muster my soldiers now; Ravenna's in charge of this. Is that clear?'

Elassel didn't protest.

'My captain of the guard will be along in a few minutes, to give you some help, and so that you'll recognize him when you see him at the gatehouse. Good luck, both of you.'

A moment after the Count had left, before Ravenna could say anything, there was another knock on the door.

'Come in,' Ravenna said.

The newcomer, Elassel guessed, must be Tetricus. He was about the same height as Cathan, she guessed, but what a difference. Tetricus was as broad-shouldered and squat as Cathan was slender. He had coarse black hair, a broad, rough-cut face and huge hands.

'Tetricus, good evening,' Ravenna said. Elassel noticed for the first time that her voice was completely flat, never varying from its emotionless, clipped tone.

Ravenna introduced Elassel and swore Tetricus to secrecy as well before telling him what they'd told Elassel. They seemed to have taken his cooperation for granted, and Tetricus didn't pause before committing himself.

'How are we going to do it?' he asked. 'And when?'

'It has to be before the storm starts to blow itself out,' Ravenna said, 'but we've no idea when that'll be. Elassel, what's the security inside the Temple like, and when will fewest people be awake?'

'He's holding the prisoners in the penitents' cells, which are all off a short corridor with only one way in – or out. An armed servant guards them at all times, but I think Midian or one of his cronies actually has the keys; that won't be a problem. Most people will be in bed by eleven o'clock, and everyone by midnight, apart from a night watchman who makes his rounds. The whole Temple's surrounded by a flamewood shield, but I can turn that off from inside once I've deal with the watchman.'

'How near are the penitents' cells to the sleeping quarters?' Tetricus asked.

'They're below them, on the cellar level with the storehouses. There's only one way down, from the main antechamber.'

'It would seem to be a case of knocking out the watchman and the servant guard, and then opening the doors,' Tetricus said. 'Fairly simple, if we use blowpipes with soporific on their darts. The tribes use them, so it'll make things look convincing, like a tribal rescue.'

'But we have to get you into the Temple in the first place, and once we've unlocked the cells, we then have to get the prisoners out and through the town without waking everyone up. We can't open the main gate without rousing everyone, so we can't use it on the way in.'

'Do you have any ideas, Elassel?' Ravenna said.

'You'll have to go over the wall, I think,' she said, after a moment's pause. 'We'll need padded grappling hooks, if you've got any.'

'No tribesmen would have those.'

'Come on, nobody'll believe there were natives inside the city,' Elassel said scornfully. 'Everybody will assume it was just more traitors.'

'Can we unlock the main gates before we leave?' Tetricus asked.

'They're barred. It should be easy enough to slide the bar along, but it'll make the devil of a noise.'

Nothing seemed so easy to Elassel later on, as she crouched in the darkness behind a pillar, waiting for the night watchman to come past. Her legs were cramped and she wasn't sure she'd be able to spring up quickly enough when the time came. Where was he, for Ranthas's sake? She stared at the shielded aether lamp on the opposite wall, the only light in this part of the Temple. That, and the paintings on the wall beyond it, were the only thing she could clearly see.

At last, she heard footsteps coming down the corridor. She pulled one of the tiny darts out of the quiver, careful not to let the sharp end anywhere near her skin, and fitted it into the blowpipe. She could remember using one before, but the guard captain had given all three of them a quick lesson, warning them that the range wouldn't be more than a few yards.

Elassel raised the blowpipe to her lips, aimed it at roughly where the watchman's waist – largest target – would be, and waited. A moment later he appeared around the edge of the pillar, a short, dour figure in rough trousers and jerkin, holding a shuttered lantern. She wondered, in the second before she fired, whether the dart would go through the layers of coarse cloth.

She needn't have worried. A second later, there was a muffled curse from the watchman and he swatted at his side. He looked around, stared directly at her, and moved a step towards her. Elassel shrank backwards in fear, even though her face was almost completely covered and she was in darkness.

Then, as the man crossed the few yards towards her, his legs gave way and he fell to the floor, a puzzled grimace on his face. By the time Elassel had extricated herself from her cranny, he was sound asleep.

After that, it was child's play to take the keys from his belt and make her way to his tiny office in the yard, where the aether-shield controls were. They were locked behind a protective panel, but she guessed the right key from the five or six on the chain first time, opened the panel and pushed her hand onto the cold glowing pad on the other side, focusing her mind on deactivating the shield. Lucky that nobody had come up with a way to secure aether pads yet, really. Anyone could use the things.

The faint whining noise died away. The shield was now switched off.

Elassel went back out into the yard, in time to see Tetricus climb over the top of the wall and jump down to join Ravenna in the courtyard.

'Good work,' Tetricus whispered; Ravenna said nothing.

'This way,' Elassel realized she was enjoying herself as they crept through the darkened inner doorway and into the antechamber. The black hole of the stairway gaped off to their left, with a small light flickering at the bottom.

'Ready?' Ravenna signalled. The other two nodded.

She pulled a child's ball from a belt pouch, a soft thing made of bound-up twine, and rolled it down the stairs.

A moment later the servant appeared and bent over the ball where it had rolled against a wall. The two of them fired their darts before ducking back out of sight. Elassel heard a cry of surprise and pain, and a couple of footsteps before the servant, too, collapsed.

The corridor was darkened, and the only noise was the faint sound of deep breathing. Ravenna nodded to Tetricus, who went up to the nearest cell and called softly through the bars.

There was no answer, and for long, agonizing seconds, Elassel fretted and wondered why they weren't responding. Then a tribesman, suspicion apparent in his scowling gaze, appeared at the doorway and said 'What?' far too loudly.

'Ssh!' Tetricus said. 'We're here to rescue you.'

'Rescue?' the trader said blearily. 'Why?'

'We are enemies of the priest who captured you, and your tribe is waiting. Will you help us wake up your fellows and come quietly? We have to get you to the gates, or there's no way you can get out.'

'Wait a second.' The man disappeared into the cell; a moment later Elassel heard the sound of voices conferring. Then he reappeared. 'Yes, we'll come.'

Elassel set to work on the locks, pouring acid from a phial she'd kept in her pack onto them, and very shortly there were eight dazed barbarian traders standing with them in the corridor. They almost reached the courtyard before they met anyone. A figure emerged from one of the side corridors, and Tetricus turned and fired one of his darts. There was a cry, and Elassel recognized her stepmother's voice. She tried to run back, but Tetricus barred her way.

'What are you doing?' he hissed.

'She's my stepmother,' Elassel said frantically.

'She'll be all right. Now run!'

They led the barbarians out into the yard, and Tetricus and Ravenna moved aside the bar on the gate. As Elassel had predicted, it squealed like an animal in pain as they slid it back.

All she remembered after that was a confused flight through the rain-drenched streets, as shouts rang out from the Temple behind them. Someone had thoughtfully left the gate between the districts open, but they didn't see anybody at all until they reached the landward gate of the new quarter. Winded, Elassel staggered into its shelter, almost hitting a wall, but someone put an arm out to stop her, and she looked up into the guard captain's seamed face.

'It'll be all right now,' he said. 'I've got everything under control.'

At that moment there was a *whoosh!* from somewhere above her, and a moment later the town was covered in an eerie blue glow as the twin explosions of starshells sounded.

Somebody else came and started to help Elassel into the gatehouse. She heard the clopping of hooves, and a moment later saw the barbarians' shaggy ponies being brought round, piled high with goods.

'Tell your chiefs,' she heard the guard captain saying, 'that—'

The guards bundled her and the others inside and out of the wet, and took them upstairs to dry out in front of the fire in the guardroom. She watched from the window and saw the traders moving along the causeway in a tight huddle through the storm. A moment later, presumably as a warning, two flamewood shells exploded over the very edge of the wood where the tribal armies lay in wait. Then in answer she saw a flare burst above the valley, a bright flash that was quenched almost immediately by the sheets of rain.

'They did it,' the guard captain said, with satisfaction. 'That's from the mine.'

So Palatine had succeeded as well. That would teach Midian.

CHAPTER XXIV

I woke up in my own room, with sunlight filtering in through gaps in the curtains. There were too many covers on the bed, and I was swelteringly hot. I rubbed my eyes and squinted at the aether clock on the opposite wall – the circle was a fraction more than half lit. About the sixth hour of the morning, from the sun.

But of which day? I could remember collapsing onto Ravenna's bed, giving my father Palatine's message, then nothing. Surely that hadn't been only ten hours ago? But otherwise it would have been nearly two days ago, and in that case I'd been asleep for a *very* long time. As it was, I certainly felt as if I'd been starved for that long.

Healing sleep might explain it; I knew that it was one of the best ways to heal somebody, to put them into a very long sleep.

I got out of bed, stood up, and cursed as pain shot through my leg. I'd forgotten about that cut on my heel; I looked down to see if it was healing, but there was a bandage on it. I pulled a robe on and limped along to the washroom for a shower. There was nobody else to be seen, nor, when I'd dressed and gone downstairs, was anybody up. The servants were usually up at six-thirty, and my father at seven; he'd always been an early riser.

I went into the kitchen, its fires damped down, and grabbed what I could from the breakfast larder. The day's fruit and bread wouldn't be delivered for another half-hour or so.

I still had no idea how things had turned out, but from the air of quiet and stillness, I gathered that the barbarians weren't an immediate threat. Lepidor didn't have the feel of a city under siege; I remembered Lexan's attack when I was seven, the Palace constantly guarded and exhausted marines sleeping in the corridors.

There were still no servants around when I let myself out of the postern gate and made my way along the main street. The streets were dry, but the grass in the garden had been glistening wet, and not from dew, so I knew it must have been raining during the last couple of hours.

The Temple's gates were open, I saw as I went past, but I didn't see any signs of life. I wondered if the hostages had been rescued, but it wouldn't have been very tactful to ask anyone there, even if there had been someone up and about.

I found the answers when I got to the gate into the Land Quarter. There were two soldiers on duty on the walls above, and I knocked on the door of their guardroom, next to the archway. A moment later it was opened by a blond soldier in his forties, his armour jacket hanging loose round his shoulders.

'Master Cathan,' he said with a grin and a look of respect on his face which had never been there before. 'Good to see you up again. What can we do for you?'

'I thought you might know what day it is, and be able to tell me what happened.'

'What day it is, Escount? Are you joking?'

'I've been in a healing sleep for a while, but nobody's up and I don't know what's been going on.'

'Well, it's market day today, so you've been asleep for a day and two nights. Don't you remember what you did?'

'I can remember what I did, but only until I arrived in the Palace.'

'Well, you'd get the best story from the decurion, or someone up at the Palace, but I'd be glad to tell you. Come up.' He took me up to the battlements, introduced himself and his comrade, a recruit from one of the town Houses a few years older than me, and told me the full story.

'We were playing cards in the barracks when the centurion runs in and tells us all to get our kit on and assemble in the courtyard. Course, he didn't tell us why until everyone was there and we'd all got wet. Then he say's there's a tribal army in the wood, waiting to make an attack on the city at dawn. It sounded fishy – I mean, not even the tribes are stupid enough to attack during a storm. Perhaps they thought someone was going to let them in.

'In any case, the tribune comes in and leads us out of the barracks, but we hadn't got more than a few yards when another decurion comes running up the street, saying there's been an attack on the Temple and the prisoners have escaped. Then the tribune tells us to go back into the courtyard and wait, while he goes down to the gates. Of course, he had a proper cloak on – the rest of us were soaked.

'Anyway, while we were standing there someone started firing pulse cannon over by the walls, but I couldn't see who they were aiming at. Then a few moments later the tribune comes back, dry as a bone, and dismisses us, says the tribes are on the run.'

'They just ran away?' Cathan asked.

'Turns out somebody sent the prisoners back to tell them they hadn't got a hope, we knew all about their nasty little plan. Your friend had taken back the mine, too, so there wasn't anything else for them to do except go back to their huts. Haven't had sound nor sight of them since, and it's all thanks to you. Can't say I'd have like to go down that stream on a raft in midsummer, let alone swim down during a storm.'

'Did you really go all the way down the stream, out to the bay?' the other one asked.

'Yes, I did.' I chatted with them a few moments longer and then set off back to the Palace along the circuit of the walls. Below me, the town was beginning to wake up, but I didn't want to go through the streets. The guards were talking as if I was some kind of hero. I was no hero. I didn't deserve it. I might have enjoyed it, but I still couldn't forgive myself for being captured on my first command, or forget the shame of kneeling in the dust of the mine compound.

The back of the Palace gardens were directly below the seaward section of the walls, although they were screened from the guards by trees. There was a place where I'd attached a rope ladder just below the parapet on the garden side, so that I had another route out of the garden. I went down the rope ladder and back into the Palace, to find the servants up.

I heard the full story from my father as we ate breakfast in the almost-deserted dining hall. He confirmed that the tribes *had* retreated back across the pass, and that the fortifications there were repaired and manned again.

'What about the traitor?' I asked.

My father's face darkened. 'One of the soldiers up at the tower had been bribed by House Foryth. We didn't find out why; he escaped with the tribes when they went. I've proclaimed him a renegade, but there's nothing else we can do, really. It seems the tribal chiefs had been paid as well, so they'll protect him.'

'Foryth bribed the chiefs?' I said. Even getting to talk to the chiefs was difficult unless they'd known you for a long time, were sure of your intentions. Perhaps Foryth had agents among the missionaries. 'How did you find out?'

'They overreacted. Usually they'd send an envoy to ask for their people back, not mass an army and attack us. Even then, they should have accepted the blood money you offered them in the mine.' He must have caught my expression, because he said, 'That was the right thing to do, offer to pay them. Always try and bargain. Going down that stream was a very brave thing to do, and you certainly saved us because of it. But you can't always do that, so try and come to terms first. Except with House Foryth.'

Despite my father's reassurance, I still couldn't forgive myself, although I didn't tell him. He'd just say the same as Palatine had, and I didn't believe either of them, however much I wanted to.

After breakfast, he told me he was going down the coast to visit Gesraden and Ygarit, the two clan towns to the south of the city within easy distance, and that he was leaving me in charge until he got back the next day. I saw him, my mother and their entourage off an hour or so later, then went back inside to ask Atek if there was anything official I'd have to do.

I went up to my father's office, unlocked the door and sat down at his desk. There was a note in his precise handwriting telling me everything that needed attention while he was away. There weren't that many things, and I didn't think it would take long to deal with them. At the end was a single line – *I dealt with Midian. He won't be a problem* – that reassured me greatly: I'd been worried about what the Avarch would do. And I was still curious to find out who'd freed the prisoners, and how my father had explained that to Midian.

There was a knock at the door as I settled down to read some papers, hoping to get as much as I could out of the way early on.

'Come in,' I said.

It was Ravenna.

'Good to see you awake again,' she said as I put down the papers and stood up; I wasn't going to talk to her sitting behind a desk.

She swept round the desk and hugged me fiercely, to my astonishment, and for once she didn't feel like a pillar of ice. 'Don't get captured again, please,' she whispered. 'I was so worried.'

I said nothing, touched by her sudden warmth; it was only the second time I'd heard her speak without that cold, clipped tone. The moment was brief, though, and a few seconds later she stepped away again, still smiling her faint smile.

'What you did was very brave, Cathan, even if it was Palatine's idea,' she said, moving over to stand by a window.

'Not really.' I went over and stood beside her, looking out over the town and the harbour quarter, the sails of a few small boats visible out on the bay. 'I had no idea it would be so bad. I've never met any water, however fast-flowing or dangerous, that I couldn't handle. Until then. I thought my main problem would be getting past the woods without being caught, but I didn't even see any tribesmen. As it was, I barely got to the harbour alive.'

I remembered the dance of the seals in the silent world below the waves. That was something I would keep to myself, something never to share.

'But you did, and you kept going. And because of that, the tribes had to withdraw with hardly a drop of blood shed, and House Foryth have wasted a lot of money.'

'But there must have been someone inside the city to open the gates. Nobody could have attacked the walls in a storm.'

'If there is, we'll find him,' she said, looking over at me. 'Taking Foryth money and supporting them, like Mezentus, is one thing. But I can't believe they found a second traitor to let the tribes in. One of Midian's henchmen, perhaps.'

'That only means we can't get him.'

'I'm sure we could find a way.'

Neither of us said anything for a few moments, as we looked out over the waking city.

Then the peace was interrupted by a message alarm from the aether communicator on my father's desk. I went over and pressed the button to receive: the glowing blue image of Harbour Master Tortelen, sitting in front of an aether console, appeared on the floor in front of the desk.

'Where's the Count?' he demanded.

'The Count's away.'

'I think you'd better come down here, Escount. Our farsweep picked up a damaged manta heading this way a few minutes ago. We sent out a searay to make contact, and they requested a berth; they've been badly damaged.'

'Whose manta is it?'

'It's Archipelagan – an Archipelagan trade delegation on its way to Thure. But the man in charge is a Cambressian, Admiral Karao.'

I heard a rustle of cloth behind me, but I didn't turn round.

'How long until they arrive, Janus?'

'Less than half an hour. They won't be able to dock, so we'll have to bring them along the quay of the surface harbour.'

'I'll be down there soon.' I closed the connection with Janus and switched over to the Palace calling system, something my father used occasionally. 'First Adviser Atek to the Count's office, please, urgent.'

I turned back to Ravenna, and saw her smile had gone.

'Do you know this Admiral Karao?' I asked her.

'He's an Archipelagan clan noble as well as a Cambressian admiral. He has great influence in both countries, pulls a lot of strings.'

'And?' There was something else unsaid, hanging in the air.

'He's a heretic.'

A few minutes later, having consulted with Atek and sent a messenger after my father, I stood on the mole along the south harbour, watching as the dark blue shape of a manta was towed across the water towards us. The surface docking gantry, an unwieldy wooden construction, had been wheeled out of its shed by the harbour workers and stood out from the mole, ready to be connected as soon as the Archipelagan manta, the *Emerald*, was within range.

I was glad that it was a warm sunny day, and not the stormy nightmare it had been two days ago. Tortelen had explained that the *Emerald* had been caught in the undersea part of the storm that had hit us – it'd been far bigger than we suspected, and only the edge of it had struck Lepidor. They were in a terrible state, apparently, and the Admiral hadn't even been sure they'd make it as far as Lepidor.

There were only a few people with me – the town council hadn't considered this an important enough event to abandon business for, especially without my father there to insist. I suspected that it was because we didn't trade with Cambress or the Archipelago. Dalriadis, Tortelen, Atek, Palatine and Ravenna, as well as a couple of House cousins to act as runners or guides, were the only people there with me.

After a painfully slow approach, its wing dragging along the quay, the *Emerald* finally grated to a stop with its door alongside the gantry. The shiny polyp surface of the manta was covered with abrasions, and I wondered what had caused them in a storm far out at sea, where there were no rocks or branches being thrown around.

The hatch was opened and a man in a rather tattered Cambressian uniform stepped out and walked quickly along the gantry. Then people started coming out of the manta's hatch, and I noticed wisps of smoke or stream drifting out from inside.

The man in front, I guessed, was Admiral Karao: there were two stars – and an empty patch for a third – on the collar of his indigo uniform, which was torn in several places and disfigured with burn masks. He looked to me like a Thetian – which was what the Cambressians had once been – with a slightly flattened Southern Archipelagan face and brown skin.

'Welcome to Lepidor, Admiral Karao,' I said. 'I'm Escount Cathan.'

'My thanks,' Karao said. 'I'm afraid we're not looking our best; most of our luggage has been fried.' He stepped aside to let some of the mass of people on the gangplank on to the quay. Some of them were Archipelagan or Cambressian sailors, in the remnants of blue or green uniforms, while others were Archipelagan civilians. The Archipelagans were an odd crowd, I thought, for a trade delegation – there were a few older men and women but almost as many my age or even less.

'Allow me to introduce the Archipelagan delegation to Thure,' Karao said, and introduced a few of the civilians and sailors. Why Thure, I wondered?

I in turn introduced the people with me, all of whom the Admiral greeted cordially. One of them, he already knew – Ravenna.

'You again,' he said with a smile that didn't reach his eyes. 'So good to see you.'

'And you, Admiral. Congratulations on your promotion – you were only a Commodore the last time we had the pleasure of meeting. I trust you remember what I said.'

'How could I forget? You were fairly direct.'

'Have your replaced me yet?'

'I could never replace you, Ravenna. I've got another ward, but she's a successor not a replacement.'

'I hope she's better off as your ward than I was.'

'She doesn't have your spirited debating style.'

'If you'll follow me,' I said, obliged to break up this fascinating banter, 'we could find you somewhere to clean up.'

I took Karao and the delegation to the Palace, where the staff had been warned to expect battered survivors and had been preparing rooms for them. A minion took the sailors to the marine barracks. On the way up, the Admiral explained that the *Emerald* had been caught on the edge of an abyss vortex and severely shaken about, flipped right over, in fact. Luckily they'd been able to pull away from the vortex itself or they'd have been sucked down with it to a gruesome death. All vortices were dangerous, I knew from my oceanographic training, but abyss vortices were by far the largest – although some had speculated that there might be even worse terrors, ring vortices, that could turn thousands of square miles of ocean literally upside down. Abyss vortices could form central funnels several miles wide and hundreds or thousands of miles deep. The *Emerald* was lucky to have escaped at all.

The Admiral , who asked me to call him by his first name, Sagantha, was good company and talked most of the way up to the Palace. Just as we entered the gates, though, and I saw servants and House people waiting to help the *Emerald*'s crew – who were in a sorry state – Palatine tapped me on the shoulder and said, 'There's someone in the delegation from the Citadel.'

'Who is it?' I asked.

'Persea.'

The Archipelagans, cleaned up and wearing a variety of borrowed clothes, joined me for lunch in the Great Hall. Persea had seemed delighted to see me and the others, but I hadn't had time to talk to her yet. I'd asked Ravenna how she knew the Admiral, though.

'I was his ward for a while, three or four years ago,' she said. 'When he was Cambressian consul in Xianar. One of his . . . business partners . . . wanted to marry me, or rather my fortune, so I told him I wasn't staying. Eventually I ended up at the Citadel, and I haven't seen him since. Until now, of course.'

I wondered how Ravenna had been able to leave Sagantha's protection. Wards couldn't change guardians without royal permission – and there was no Archipelagan monarch. And how come, since she was Tehaman, she'd been Sagantha's ward? Why had she left? 'Tehama wasn't safe,' was all she said when I asked her. 'The High Priest, who's in charge, had complete control over me there. My mother was very rich in her own right, but all her brothers died and I ended up inheriting all their money too. Her family didn't want the Tehamans to get their hands on it, so they made me Karao's ward.'

I wondered where her wealth had come from – the Tehamans weren't known for their commercial activities, and why would any rich Archipelagan family have allowed an heiress to marry a Tehaman?

While I sat at lunch with Sagantha and the others, Tortelen and Dalriadis inspected the *Emerald* for damage.

'Three weeks, four at the outside,' was their verdict, when I called them up from my father's office.

'Do you want us to take you to Pharassa, to try and find another ship?' I asked Sagantha, who'd been looking out over the city from where Ravenna and I had been standing a few hours earlier.

He considered my suggestion for a moment, then shook his head. 'No one sails from Pharassa to Ralentis, and there's no way the Imperial Navy would lend me a ship. Could you possibly put us up until the *Emerald*'s repaired? I know it'll be a nuisance, but I can't see any other way.'

'You're welcome to stay in Lepidor, Admiral,' I said. 'We won't be able to put you all up in the Palace, but there'll be enough beds somewhere.'

'My grateful thanks, Escount,' he said, smiling warmly.

There was something else I had to say, and I wasn't sure how he would react.

'There is one other thing.'

'Which is?'

I took a deep breath. 'We've just had a new Avarch arrive. He's a Halettite and rather a fanatic; he's already started a war with the natives by arresting some traders for heresy. If you could warn your people to be careful what they say here . . .'

'I understand,' Sagantha said. 'Tensions are running high in the Archipelago just at the moment. What's your Avarch's name, by the way?'

'Midian – I don't know what his family name is, though.'

Karao sighed. 'Perhaps the *Emerald* was more comfortable than it seemed. You've got the worst of the lot. If it's any consolation, he'll be wearing an Exarch's tiara in four or five years, and you'll be rid of him.'

Four or five years? Could we survive that long?

I sent messengers south to call my father back; Karao was an important guest, and my father wouldn't want to ignore him. My father arrived back around mid-afternoon; he hadn't even got as far as Gesraden, so he decided to postpone his visit. He assigned me the job of organizing accommodation for the Archipelagans, and I spent a couple of hours finding enough rooms for them all, in the Palace and neighbouring Houses. I politely declined Midian's offer to put some of them up in the Temple – we had enough trouble as it was.

Once I'd got everybody settled and had the satisfaction of sending my cousins on numerous small errands, I was able to slip away and talk to Persea.

She, with Palatine, Ravenna, and several of the younger Archipelagans was sitting on the grass of the lawn, passing round a flask of some Archipelagan liquor. Persea introduced me to the rest of them, two men and four women. Only two of them were actually from the islands; the other four were Qalathari.

As I sat down one of them looked around at the bushes as if he was expecting somebody to be spying on him, then said, 'You're the one who knocked Hiroa out, aren't you?'

'You were at the Citadel?' I asked, amazed that he was so open about it. Hiroa had been the leader of the Water forces in the intra-Citadel mock war – he'd been the one I 'assassinated' by creeping along the wall.

'I was at Water,' he said. 'You really picked your moment – he was about to explain the winning strategy.'

'Are you all heretics, then?'

'All of us,' said one of the girls, wearing a shapeless hat of some kind. 'That's why we're here; it was too dangerous back in Qalathar.'

'How bad are things in the Archipelago at the moment?' Ravenna asked.

'Not good,' another girl said. 'The Domain's sent out preachers to try and persuade heretics to recant – they're not hiding any more. The people who aren't heretics don't want the Domain interfering, and there was a riot when the Exarch tried to arrest someone.'

'We've heard that Lachazzar's thinking of launching another crusade,' Persea said. 'Whatever the Domain does, it doesn't work in the Archipelago. We had to be shipped out because we were calling for the Elders to build more ships and restore the Pharaoh.'

'Why?' Ravenna demanded. 'That's senseless. Even if you could find her, it would only lead to disaster. Either you set her up as a figurehead and Lachazzar declares another crusade, or the Domain get wind of it, kidnap her and use her as a puppet ruler.'

'The Pharaoh's the only person that everyone would follow, the only way that we could get all the clans to fight together.'

'Forgive me for asking,' Palatine said, a frown on her face, 'but how do you know the Pharaoh exists, that she's not just a figment of the imagination? No one's ever seen her.'

Several of the Archipelagans suddenly looked angry, and one scrambled to his feet. 'How dare you suggest such a thing! No one's ever seen her because if they had, the Domain would know where and who she was.'

'Tekraea, sit down!' the girl with the hat said. 'She didn't mean to insult us.' She turned to Palatine. 'Never cast a slur on the Pharaoh's name. Her grandfather founded the Archipelago and she is the symbol of what we are.'

'A few people do know who she is,' Persea said. 'Sagantha's one of them, but he's under oath to her not to reveal her name.'

'It makes it easier to hide her, and because nobody's ever seen her the Domain don't have a description to work on.'

'So the Pharaoh is disguised as an ordinary citizen,' said Palatine.

'Exactly,' Persea said. 'There was a rumour that she was at the Citadel when we were, but I think that was just somebody with an overactive imagination.'

'Do the Elders know where the Pharaoh is?' I asked.

'No, they don't.'

So who did?

★

That night, Elassel came to find me in the Palace. While she'd been cutting off Midian's water system in revenge for something he'd done, she'd overheard him talking to the mind-mage. Apparently Midian believed that the Pharaoh of Qalathar and the Archipelago was currently a ward of Sagantha Karao.

In which case, she could be one of the *Emerald*'s delegation.

Chapter XXV

'I won't have it!' my father said. 'House Foryth's behaviour is unforgivable. Their dispute is with House Barca, not with my clan.' He looked down at the Tanethan Ambassador with cold fury. 'You will tell Lord Foryth that if there is one more act of sabotage I won't hesitate to use force.'

Atek looked at me uneasily. I was afraid that my father might have gone too far over the sabotage attempt on the harbour two days ago, Foryth's latest attack on us. It was because my brother Jerian had almost been caught in it, I knew. And we'd just had the funeral service for the three workers who had died. It was thanks to the quick thinking of one of them that we still had a working harbour. That, and the incompetence of the Foryth agent. I couldn't believe that a man as ruthless as Lord Foryth would employ somebody so stupid for a task like that. Using only one charge, all he'd done was to knock the upper gantry askew. With two, he'd have put the harbour out of action for weeks or months.

'Count Elnibal,' the Tanethan began, looking rather nervous. I thought he had a right to; after all, he was a fairly junior official, all we merited on the Tanethan scale of things.

My father interrupted him. 'And remind Foryth that he rules a Great House, not a clan. However much power he may wield in Taneth, however many trading ships he may own, I am a Count of the Thetian Empire. Remind him that clans have destroyed Great Houses before this.'

'My lord, Lijah Foryth is a powerful man. Do you want me to tell him in these words?'

'If House Foryth wants to behave as if it were a clan, I will treat it as one.' He thought of something else. 'And tell him, *in these words*, that if he had behaved like a civilized man instead of a loutish barbarian at the Conference then he might have got the contract he so wants. You are dismissed.'

The Tanethan did not dare say anything else, but bowed and walked out of the hall amid a heavy silence. The doors were closed behind him with a reluctant creak.

My father told a few of us to follow him as he dismissed the Council, and we went upstairs to the secret Council room.

'Atek, have a message packet ready,' he said when we'd closed the door behind us and sat down. 'I'll write to the King telling him about what's going on here. His Tanethan connections are mostly with House Canadrath, and they're no friends of Foryth.'

'My lord, surely you're overreacting,' Atek said, looking round for support at the others sitting around the table – Dalriadis, Shihap and me. 'That could put us in even more danger.'

'You're like a flock of sheep today, all of you,' he said, grim-faced. *'Don't do anything, it'll only make things worse.* My son Jerian is nearly killed by Foryth agents and you tell me it's too dangerous to take any action? Who else do you think would want to damage the harbour? If we do nothing Foryth will think we're weak and try even harder.'

Atek tried again. 'But what if the letter doesn't reach the King?' he said. 'If it falls into the hands of one of Foryth's supporters inside Clan Pharassa? It could provoke him into trying something more drastic – he might even be able to turn the King against you.'

'Foryth doesn't have enough money for that. If he spends much more it'll amount to years of profit from an iron contract. Besides, there's always the Imperial Viceroy to restrain him.'

That part, at least, was true. The Viceroy, Arcadius Tar'Conantur, a cousin of the Emperor, hated the Houses of Taneth, as most Thetians did. Unlike most of his fellow countrymen from the Empire's heartland, though, he took an active interest in the Empire – how else could he have become Viceroy? From what I'd heard, most of them, including the old Emperor, directed their energy into orgies and drunken parties. Arcadius must have done at least some hard work to merit his appointment, even though he had less actual power than my father did.

After Atek had tried again to dissuade him from writing the letter, my father dismissed all of us and sat down to draft it without Atek's help.

'What do we do now?' Shihap asked when we were safely down the corridor and out of earshot.

'Damage limitation,' Atek snapped, as irritable as my father had been. 'You go back to your shop, I'm going to find out how things are in Pharassa at the moment. Cathan, that friend of yours used to live in Taneth. See if she knows anything that can help us – especially anything more she has on that bastard Foryth.'

'I told you most of what I know about Foryth,' Palatine said, when I asked her later that day, in my upper sitting room. The fire was burning and I'd closed the curtains though it was only mid-afternoon. Another storm had blown up; the weather had been atrocious for the last five days and showed no sign of letting up. The oceanographers reckoned it was a super-storm, one not confined to the Haeden storm band. It had been almost impossible to sleep, with almost constant electrical storms and the noise of thunder like a huge artillery battle in the sky.

'How's he likely to react to this?'

'I don't know that much. Hamilcar would be better, he's known Foryth for longer than I have. I know nobody threatens him. They're all too scared. And he's on the Council of Ten as often as he's allowed to be. They have a strange system there: you're only a Councillor for a month and you can't serve twice in four months. He has a lot of people in the Senate to support him as well. But what your father's doing – maybe he'll get furious, or perhaps he'll just ignore it.'

'But he's more likely to fly into a rage.'

'Yes.' Palatine leaned back on the sofa and stared into the fire. 'So we have to ask what he does next, and if we can predict it.'

The room was suddenly lit up by a white flash, and there was a deafening series of cracks from outside, dying away into faint murmurings again. I was glad it hadn't been like this nine days ago when I'd gone down the stream.

'So far there've been two pirate attacks, the tribes' attack and now this sabotage. And he's throwing money around at people like Mezentus,' I said.

'But you can see he likes using force, he's not that subtle. You wouldn't put up with this from another clan, you'd be preparing invasion fleets, declaring war. He thinks he's different because he's a Tanethan

House. But he wants to do a lot of damage.' She leaned forward, resting her chin on her hand. 'What does he get out of it?'

'The iron contract, of course.'

'In that case, what good does it do if the tribesmen conquer the city? Or if the harbour's destroyed? *Why does he concentrate on Lepidor rather than House Barca?* It doesn't make sense. For half what he must have paid those tribesmen he could have hired a fleet of pirate ships. Then he could blow anything out of the water, even your manta, and bankrupt Hamilcar.'

'I wonder if he'll go on the same way. We've been lucky twice, but I can't see our luck holding.'

Palatine thought hard for a moment. 'You're right. We have to try and anticipate his next move.'

'How are we supposed to do that? There are hundreds of ways he could strike at us, and we can't read his mind.'

'Or we could attack him first. I think that's what your father's trying to do, get the King to move against him. Even if he wanted to invade, he can't. He won't have enough armed men to defeat your marines, and his men aren't allowed out of Taneth.' Palatine paused, a look of intense concentration on her face. 'What about an alliance with another house, another clan? Has anyone ever done that?'

'Not that I can remember.' I tried to recall my history lessons. 'There've been nine wars between Great Houses and clans since Taneth was founded. As far as I know most of them ended with the destruction of the House. I think. Anyway, unless he allies with another Oceanian clan, say Lexan's, the Empire would come down on him. He can't bring other Houses into this, even the Thetians might stir themselves then. And if Lexan launched a direct assault on us, Moritan and Courtières would join in, Lexan would call up his allies, and we'd have a civil war.'

'So we've got the same forces on each side and he won't try a direct assault.'

'No.' Another burst of thunder crashed across the sky outside. I'd got used to it in the past three days or so. I wondered where the Archipelagans were – they'd been terrified when the first huge rumblings started. There were never storms this size in Qalathar or the smaller islands – some of them hadn't seen a super-storm in their whole lives.

'Well, if not that . . .' Palatine threw up her hands in despair. 'We can't sit here trying to out-think him. I told you all I know, but you need to find out more. Why not see if you can get in touch with somebody who has a spy in House Foryth? Hamilcar might know.'

'By then it may be too late.'

'It might also be a good idea—' she hesitated, then plunged on '—for you to pay off anything you owe to contractors or guilds, as soon as you can. Don't spend any more money until we can deal with Foryth. Then if he does manage to blow something up, you won't owe anything or have to worry about creditors.'

She was telling me to prepare for the worst.

'I'll pass it on,' I said. 'I'm not sure that he'll agree.'

There was an uneasy pause before she spoke again.

'Do you remember that conversation we had with the Archipelagans – on the lawn, the day they arrived?'

'Yes.'

'They said the reason they were sent with Sagantha was that they were becoming too outspoken in support of the heresy and the Pharaoh. Don't you think it's a little odd that they're put on a ship heading for Thure?'

I couldn't see what the significance was. True, I'd thought it was strange; the few Tuonetar survivors who lived on the frozen northern continent had very little to exchange, and generally weren't interested in contact. Except to buy the items they needed to survive.

'Thure may be a peculiar place, but they still need to trade. And there are no Domain there.'

'Ral Tumar, in the Archipelago, is the only place they trade with normally. But it's still wrong. Thure has an agreement with the Domain, and they don't like the heretics any more than the Domain do. Why would heretics go there?'

'The Domain can't actually arrest them in Thure.'

'The Thurians can, and they're just as unpleasant as the Domain. So either they *are* going to Thure, and there's something important there, or they're going somewhere totally different.'

I thought Palatine was blowing this out of proportion. After all, the Thurians would know that the Archipelagans were heretics, and what would they gain by arresting the *Emerald*'s delegation? Maybe the Archipelago didn't have much clout, but from what I'd heard of him Sagantha Karao certainly did. Had the threat of Foryth and the Domain convinced her everyone had a hidden agenda? Still, she'd been right so often I wasn't going to dismiss her idea out of hand.

'What do you think they're really doing, then?' I said, not hiding my scepticism.

'It's got something to do with this mysterious Pharaoh of theirs, I'm sure. Elassel said that the Domain think the Pharaoh is on board the *Emerald*, in which case they weren't going to Thure, but maybe somewhere else. If they were passing the northern tip of this island – north rather than south – where would that take them?'

I went over to the large globe my father kept in the corner. Palatine got up and came over to stand beside me. The aether torches kept flickering in time with the lightning flashes, which made it hard to read.

I traced a course round the top of Haeden and westwards into the Ocean. Thure, Tumarian, Liona, the Northern Islands, Mons Ferranis. The last one seemed unlikely – it was only a few thousand miles north-east of Qalathar, so what would be the point of going this way round? Thure we'd already discussed. Tumarian? Not by the route they were taking. Liona and the Northern Islands? Also Archipelagan provinces of little note. There was nothing that suggested itself from looking at the map. Except that, without a doubt, they were going to Thure by the longest route possible.

'I'm sure you're exaggerating,' I said, although I wasn't really quite so certain.

There were other people who shared Palatine's views, though. The next day, with the storm still raging, there was a knock on the door of the office. I was sitting at the desk and I tensed and looked up, wondering if it was one of Midian's priests, come to badger me on some point of protocol. I'd already had two visits from the Temple today, both of them on some trivial matter that Midian seemed to think was important. My father had gone away on his visit the day before the storm hit, and I didn't expect him to be back for a while. I was in charge, once more heavily dependent on my mother and Atek. I wasn't looking forward to the weekly assizes tomorrow – it would be the first time I'd ever done it on my own.

'Come in,' I said, looking up from a tedious revenue document, actually glad of the interruption, even if it did turn out to be a priest.

The door opened and Ravenna came in, dripping wet. Was the

storm that bad, I wondered? Or had she come from the other end of the city?

'I thought I'd find you here,' she said, moving over to the fire, leaving a wet trail on the floor. 'It's horrible out there. I haven't come far, only from the barracks, and I'm sodden despite this cloak. Is it like this a lot of the time?'

'We get storms this bad about once a month in spring and autumn. Count yourself lucky you're not here in winter; it's like this continuously for weeks or months.'

'It doesn't get this bad in Qalathar even in winter.' She untied her hair, and fat drops of water fell onto my father's carpet.

'Was it something urgent you came over for?' I asked.

'Midian was on the prowl, and the armoury master didn't want more trouble. Of course, I'm trouble, Palatine isn't. What the goat's doing visiting the armoury anyway I don't know, let alone at a time like this. But I have no desire to be in the same building with him unless I have to, so I came over here. Enjoying your work?'

'It's fascinating. You don't know what you're missing.'

'I've had to do this sort of thing as well.'

'When was that?' I asked, curious.

'With Sagantha. I had to earn my keep.' A moment later she said, 'Palatine thinks the *Emerald*'s not heading for Thure. You don't agree with her, do you?'

So she hadn't come here for want of anything better to do. 'She seems to be rather paranoid, seeing plots in every corner,' I said. 'Maybe there are, but they're mostly Lord Foryth's.'

'In this case she isn't,' Ravenna said, turning away from the fire and sitting down in a chair nearby. She fixed me with her cold stare. 'This voyage has nothing to do with trade. The Domain has somehow got a lead on the Pharaoh, and it's desperate to get hold of her. Sagantha, I think, has orders to protect her any way he can, and he wouldn't achieve that by going to Thure. They'd keep her to use as a pawn, or sell her to Lachazzar.'

'You mean the Pharaoh is on the ship?'

'It's a fair guess. But before you ask me, I have no idea who it is, and I'm unlikely to find out. No one on the ship has guessed yet, either.'

'Then how do you know?'

'Has all this state business atrophied your brain? I leaned on Sagantha – he still has some obligations to me, and I know how to put pressure on him.'

'Do you know where they're going, then?'

'No, I don't. He wouldn't tell me that. But if one of the girls from the *Emerald* is the Pharaoh, she's in serious danger. Midian's been trying to call them in for questioning by his tribunal ever since they arrived. If he manages it he'll arrest them, and then what can we do? He can send them off to Pharassa, out of our reach. I'm sure the Inquisitors there could find out which one's the Pharaoh.'

I was still doubtful about this whole business of the Pharaoh; it sounded very far-fetched. But if Sagantha had confirmed it . . .

'What's your point?' I said.

'Palatine thinks the Domain will try to keep the Archipelagans here as long as possible, maybe long enough for some Inquisitors to arrive. I'm asking you if you could try to help them, make sure they finish their repairs and get away as soon as possible. You may not understand, but to us the Pharaoh is almost a god. You saw how Tekraea reacted when Palatine suggested she didn't exist. She's the last link we have to the old Archipelago and the time before the Crusade. And she's the only ruler in the world the Domain have no influence over. Outside Thure, of course, but Thure doesn't matter any more.'

She was speaking very fast and urgently by the end, as if she wasn't sure of saying everything in time. I couldn't remember her being so impassioned about anything before. And she was quite right – if the Domain were on to the Pharaoh's trail it was imperative that we got her away from Lepidor as fast as possible. I still wondered where they were going, though.

I switched on the aether comms unit on the desk and opened a channel to Admiral Dalriadis's office. He wasn't there, but his secretary knew where he was and diverted the line through to a unit in the harbour hub.

'Dalriadis here,' he said, his image appearing in front of the desk. 'Ah, Cathan, what can I do for you?'

'It's been suggested that certain people might wish to delay the *Emerald*'s departure. From now on, nobody is to be allowed on the ship or in that section except the Archipelagans, the crew and your repair teams; I also want a round-the-clock armed guard on the hatch. If any

Domain types come round, tell them there's a conduit leak or something.'

Dalriadis looked a bit surprised, but he didn't disagree. 'Very well, I'll see to it,' he said, then added with a touch of his normal sarcasm, 'Are you sure you don't want the *Walrus* guarded as well? After all, there might be Tanethan spies after your oceanography kit.'

'Since you're so concerned about it, that can be your job.'

'Of course. But in that case, only naval personnel will be allowed near it.' He grinned and cut off the link.

'Does that satisfy you?' I asked Ravenna.

'It's a good start.'

'And what else am I supposed to do, except in due course admire your wisdom and perception in forecasting another sabotage attempt?'

'You can do that when the *Emerald* is safely on its way again.'

I wondered if Ravenna had any sense of humour at all; I'd certainly seen few traces of one in the year or more that I'd known her. Did she always have to be so serious?

The room flickered as another barrage of lightning swept through the clouds. The curtains were open, not that it made any difference. But it was only morning, and it was depressing to keep them shut all day. I pushed the chair back and went to look out of the wide windows, only glass between me and the fury of the storm. Much better than nothing at all.

It wasn't raining at the moment, so I could see a long way out through the aether shield. The sky was covered by dark clouds in all directions, from horizon to horizon, a vast blue-grey river flowing westwards at dizzying speeds. The cloud cover wasn't continuous but broken up here and there, to give glimpses of higher cloud decks, layer upon layer upon layer of them. Above the seething cauldron of the lowest levels, white lightning flickering across the clouds, I saw more formations boiling up, expanding at a rate of thousands of feet every second, whipped along by the titanic winds of the atmosphere. Midian and his priests had erected the second shield early on the second day of this storm, after they decided it'd be here to last, and I was glad of the protection.

Two hundred years ago there simply weren't any storms like this, and there was no such thing as a global winter. A Tuonetar legacy, but the Domain had blamed it on Hierarch Carausius, who was the only man who'd foreseen the damage early in the War and tried to stop it.

'It's terrifying, isn't it?' Ravenna said. I hadn't noticed her approaching, and she stood next to me. 'Our ancestors commanded all the power of the oceans, but they couldn't stop these storms. We know nothing about the storms, or how they work, and we can't do anything to control them.'

'Not all due to the power of nature. Without the Domain we could have done something.'

'Nobody has ever been able to control storms and weather, not even the most powerful wind-mages. I don't think we can blame that on the Domain.'

'To control something you have to understand it. That's what the Domain won't let us do. No storm probes, no SkyEyes, no wind-magic – how could we possibly do anything?'

'You could be right, I suppose,' she said, her eyes following a cloud vortex across the sky. 'But these storms are a combination of so many elements – Wind and Water and Shadow – that no one can ever work with them. You'd have to have mages of three different elements linked together in a way we can't even begin to understand.'

'One can always hope.'

'Even if you could control the storms, what good would it do? Surely the atmosphere is like the ocean: it's a single system. You can no more stop the storms than the ocean currents. We might be able to use them as weapons. But as it is, we have to make do with small winds from our wind-magic.'

Again, she was right – it was infuriating. But I hadn't realized before to what extent the Domain's control depended on the storms. They were the only people who could protect the cities from the storms' worst effects, and the only people who knew the weather patterns. And because of that, nobody could conduct a campaign or wage war unless the Domain were helping them. Without Domain help you'd be at the mercy of the storms. It all depended on those SkyEyes, the probes that circled Aquasilva far above the atmosphere and could see everything that was going on.

'Ravenna, do you know where the Domain control their SkyEyes from?'

'Presumably the same place Aetius used,' she said. 'They're far older than the Empire, he didn't actually put them up there. I think there was a control centre in the Ramada Valley, west of Mons Ferranis, in some ancient fort.'

'The perfect place, then. Only one way in and out, and hundreds of Sacri guarding it.'

'They must have had another control centre earlier on, though,' she said, looking over at the globe again. 'Aetius was using them even before he took Mons Ferranis from the Tuonetar, so there must have been somewhere else . . .'

I tried to remember any references in the *History*. It was the only insight we had into Aetius's technology, but the author hadn't been much interested in that side of things. To him the SkyEyes were useful tools; he hadn't been interested in how they worked or where they came from. I found his lack of interest irritating, because there was so much he could have told us but didn't. Especially about the mantas they used . . . that was it!

'*Aeon*! That was where the SkyEye controls were, on a huge submarine called the *Aeon*.'

'Out of luck there, again,' Ravenna said, not sounding disturbed. She shrugged. 'The *Aeon* was destroyed on Valdur's orders because it had some kind of connection with Carausius's mage-city, Sanction.'

It had been a nice idea, I reflected, even if no more than that. Valdur had an awful lot to answer for. Not least blind stupidity. The *Aeon* had been the biggest ship in the world, with enormous potential. Doubtless the Domain had put him up to it.

What a waste.

My father arrived back five days later, four days after the storm had blown itself out. Things were fine in the towns, he told me, apart from the usual niggling complaints and a protest by one that not enough of the money from the iron profits had been spent there. My father had promised to rectify the situation, but agreed to postpone it for now when I told him of Palatine's warning.

'I'll make sure the debts are paid off, then. I don't want to jump at shadows, but your friend's been right before.'

Supper that night in the Great Hall was a merry occasion. All the Archipelagans were there, more relaxed since the storm had gone, and

Sagantha was entertaining everybody with his dry wit. Midian hadn't been invited.

'Another week and our repairs will be complete,' Persea said to me. 'I'll be sorry to leave here, even though you have got that awful priest hunting the Pharaoh.'

'I'm glad you like it here. How much longer have you got on board ship?'

'I'm not sure. Three weeks or so, I think. Far too long, and there isn't enough space, and nothing to do. Very boring.'

'Be thankful Laeas isn't with you. There'd be even less space.'

She smiled, and I wondered how the giant Archipelagan was getting on.

Palatine had earlier passed on to Persea some instructions for the others, to convey to them when she returned to the Archipelago. Three weeks' journey was a long time, though, and I wondered where they were going. That was certainly longer than it would take to reach Tumarian, Thure or Liona. Was Persea telling me the truth, though? I expected Sagantha had told them not to give any clues. It wasn't anything I could really go on.

We had just finished the main course when the doors of the hall opened and a man in the royal blue of the Imperial Thetian Navy walked in. I saw the insignia of a captain on his collar and wondered what an Imperial captain was doing in Lepidor.

He walked slowly up to the dais, very formally, and something in his look made my stomach clench in apprehension.

'Count Elnibal, a word with you in private. You and any other members of your family who are here.'

What were they doing? Was this some kind of trick?

My father stood up, motioning for me and the naval officer to follow him out of the side door and into the antechamber. He shut the door behind us.

The captain turned to face my father. 'Count Elnibal, it is with the deepest regret that I summon you to Pharassa for an Oceanian Congress. The King is dead.'

Chapter XXVI

I threw my travel bag across the floor and sank down on the bed, glad to be home again. The Congress had been a disaster, an unmitigated catastrophe from start to finish.

Captain Jerezius, who'd brought us the news, his beard cut short as a sign of mourning, had orders to move as quickly as possible. He'd got us to Pharassa in a night and a day, too, which must have been a record. We arrived to find the city in mourning, black flags hanging from every mast, and a funereal pall of smoke over the ziggurat. The city was under martial law, and military checkpoints were everywhere. Viceroy Arcadius was in charge, and he wasn't taking any chances. The mood in the upper city and the Palace was sombre and shocked, the clan leaders unable to believe that such a thing had happened in their city.

As the manta sped south, braving undersea storms and reefs, Jerezius had told us what he knew. The King wasn't just dead, and he wasn't alone in being not just dead. He had been assassinated.

It had happened at a late-night Council session; the King had been meeting with two of his sons and three other clan leaders. It had been a routine meeting, although it was unusual for so many clan leaders to be in Pharassa at once. According to the survivors, six black-clad assassins, each armed with a pair of short swords, had broken in through the windows. Most of the people in the meeting had been unarmed, and they hadn't stood a chance. Jerezius had been in the Palace that night, and he'd seen the carnage: blood dripping from the walls and lying in pools on the floor, mangled bodies and broken glass everywhere.

The King, his eldest son, two aides and the Count of Clan Carvulo had died in the mêlée. Two more aides and another Count had died later of their wounds, while the King's second son and three others had got away with minor injuries. A third Count hovered between life and death.

That third Count was Moritan. I'd gone to see him in the hospital, but he'd been unconscious and pale as death. He'd fought off two of the assassins with only a dagger, severely wounding one of them, but had been stabbed in his side and shoulder. I remembered him in Taneth, full of life and deeply cynical. I wanted to tear those assassins apart – but nobody knew who they were.

They'd attacked the Viceroy, rushed him in a hallway a few minutes later, but Arcadius was a Tar'Conantur and they were notoriously difficult to kill. He'd run away from them, grabbed a pike from a wall display and charged back at them. When the guards came running, the assassins had decided discretion was the better part of valour and vanished into the night. They made their way to the harbour, stole a searay and made a getaway out to sea, where a rescue ship was doubtless waiting for them.

Everyone was stunned. Nothing like this had happened for years. It went far beyond the boundaries of accepted clan feuds, a massacre like this, especially with a King among the victims.

'The Emperor will be apoplectic,' the manta captain said. 'And the Halettites will probably get the blame. Serves them right, it's the sort of thing they do.'

As Palatine pointed out, though, that was too obvious a lead. And what had the Halettites to gain from the King's death? Nothing that we could think of.

The clan chiefs who weren't already present, and the heirs of the ones who'd died, arrived within a few hours of us. And the morning after, Arcadius presided over an emergency Congress that named the King's second son as his successor.

There was no other choice, really. The eldest son, who would have made a good King, was dead, and the youngest a wastrel with no ability whatsoever. The second son possessed most of his father's abilities, and if he wasn't quite as intelligent as his father had been, he was still competent and able to think. Arcadius, an aristocratic man in his early fifties with an imperial air of command, obviously approved of him, and delivered a stirring eulogy of him to the Congress. Although any new clan leader, including the King, technically had to be approved by the Viceroy, he wouldn't have had the power to object. But Arcadius threw his weight firmly behind the second son, and since he had the necessary ability, the Congress confirmed him as the new King.

For us, it was a disaster. He was a religious fanatic who had surrounded himself with Domain advisers and was keen to ensure that all Oceanus was strong in its faith and obedient to the Domain. Which meant that now we had no allies in high places – the new King would encourage Midian and give him wholehearted support, while the Viceroy wouldn't care about anything that didn't threaten his or the Emperor's position.

Not realizing there were worse things to come, we stood reluctantly to hail the new King, who stood in the centre of the Council hall flanked by the Exarch and the Viceroy. After the funeral, we were summoned for another meeting, to resolve various urgent matters. One of them was Moritan's regent.

The Palace physicians had gloomily said that Moritan would be convalescing for months, if he survived at all, so a decision had to be made about who was to look after Clan Delfai's affairs in the meantime. Moritan had no male heir and there was nobody in his House with enough experience to rule in his stead. There was, I knew, a very real possibility that this could mean the end of Moritan's countship even if he lived. Another House might well decide to take the opportunity to displace Moritan's House, using the excuse that he was unfit to lead.

Because Moritan's daughter couldn't rule – female clan chiefs weren't allowed – the Congress voted to give the Avarch of Delfai control until Moritan died or recovered. My father put forward another candidate, Moritan's brother-in-law, but we were heavily outvoted and forced to concede.

'Somebody's been spending a lot of money,' my father said afterwards, furiously. Only three other Counts, including Courtières, had voted for his proposal, when normally the result would have been close.

'Lexan looks like the cat that got the cream,' Courtières said, pointing over to where the Count of Khalaman sat with a smug look on his face.

'He doesn't have the money to bribe so many people. Either the Domain wants more control or Foryth's doing everything he can to inconvenience—' My father looked at us. 'Foryth! You don't suppose he had something to do with all this?'

'Murder a King for the sake of an iron contract?' We were keeping our

voices low, so as not to be overheard by the Counts next door. The
Congress Hall was a circular structure with its rows of seats divided into
boxes, one for each clan, running around the hall's edge. 'Surely not even
Foryth would do that?'

'The timing's very suspicious, though.'

My father was morose and bad-tempered for the whole of the five days
we stayed there, although he never once showed any grief, not even in
private. The dead King hadn't exactly been his friend, but they'd fought
together and known each other for forty years.

On the last day of the Congress, when the remaining business was
almost finished, we were accosted when leaving the Hall by the Count
of Tamathum, of a clan in the Pharassan faction. He'd voted with us on
Moritan's regency.

'Elnibal,' he said quietly, 'I'm no ally of yours, nor of Moritan's. But I
don't like what's happened here, and I'm giving you a warning. Get
Moritan away from the city, take him to Courtières's hospital at Kula. If
he stays here he'll be dead within the month.'

Before we could ask him anything, Tamathum swung away and was
lost in the crowd. We followed his advice, though, and managed to get
Moritan moved to Courtières's hospital. Aside from being safe, Kula's
hospital was the best in Oceanus.

Before we left, the new King read out a proclamation in Congress in
which he said that heresy was the scourge of the times, and that he would
not tolerate any on Oceanus. He would be giving Avarchs and Inquisitors
more powers to conduct their enquiries and to deal with those who
worshipped false gods. He also decreed that any known or suspected
heretics who put in to Oceanus's shores would be dealt with as they
deserved.

Arcadius stood by and smiled benignly. No doubt the Emperor would
approve of one of his subject kings acting to stamp out that annoying
heresy that disturbed his Imperial peace from time to time.

The proclamation meant that Midian had the powers necessary to
interrogate the Archipelagans before the tribunal. Palatine, Ravenna and
I tried on the way back to think up some way to foil him, but couldn't
come up with anything. My father had brought Palatine along for her
advice, and Ravenna so that Midian couldn't get at her while we were
away.

Now, back in my room in Lepidor, I stared at the wall and wondered what we'd done to deserve all this.

There was more bad news, I learned the next morning. The Archipelagans weren't going to be able to leave for another week; apparently somebody had shoved a rock down the port engine vent of the *Emerald*, causing a breach there and other damage that, if it had gone unnoticed, would have caused a core implosion when the manta got under way. Sagantha had been furious, but there was nobody he could blame – somehow the saboteur had slipped past all our patrols.

Two acts of sabotage, and we still hadn't caught the saboteur, didn't even have a clue who he was.

'This is more likely to be the Domain's work,' Ravenna said. 'Foryth gains nothing by keeping the Archipelagans here.'

'It's not good for us,' Palatine pointed out, fiddling with a blade of grass. It was the end of a hot day, hotter than any for weeks, and we were sitting on the Palace lawn.

'Midian hasn't acted on the proclamation yet, but we have to assume he's going to. Is there any way we could divert him, cause some other trouble to stop him being able to arrest the Archipelagans?'

'But he can arrest us as well now,' I said. 'For obstructing him.'

'Can he now?' said a voice I hadn't heard for years, from behind me. 'He could always try.'

I saw Ravenna's eyes widen in amazement, scrambled to my feet and turned round.

The man standing behind me dwarfed even Palatine – I could remember being stupefied by his size on his last visit, when I was thirteen, and he was no less daunting now. He stood more than seven feet tall, with a frame to match. The Visitor was the biggest person I'd ever seen – or heard of. Almost terrifyingly big, in fact, and despite the smile on his weathered face there was something grim, almost threatening, about him. The green eyes held depths I didn't want to fathom, a chilling, hidden darkness buried within him.

'Visitor,' I said, suddenly embarrassed that I didn't know his name.

Palatine was smiling. 'You know Cathan too?' she asked the giant.

'Why shouldn't I? He's been as much one of my charges as you are.'

'Who are you?' Ravenna asked. Her voice lacked its usual imperious tone – I could imagine that even she found it hard to be haughty in the presence of this man.

'Cathan knows me as The Visitor, Palatine by another name, which I may tell you when I know who you are.'

She didn't seem affronted. 'I'm Ravenna Ulfadha, of Qalathar.'

'Ravenna the mage?'

'You know me, then?'

'I know *of* you. As for me . . . you've heard of Tanais Lethien?'

'From the *History*, yes,' she said, and I saw her eyes narrow. 'He was Aetius's general.'

'I am still Aetius's general, although he found peace long ago, while I'm still looking for it.'

'That was two hundred years ago.'

I was as disbelieving as Ravenna. How could this be Tanais Lethien? He'd been in his fifties at the end of the War, so he'd be more than two hundred and fifty years old now. That was impossible.

'Time doesn't pass at the same speed for everybody,' Tanais said.

'He *is* Tanais Lethien,' Palatine said. 'Take it from me. But what are you doing here?' she asked Tanais.

'I could ask the same of you. It took me months to find out where you'd gone, and before I could come and find you there was some new idiocy in Silvernia I had to sort out.'

'Where I'd gone . . . what do you mean?'

'Don't you remember?'

Palatine shook her head. 'I lost my memory. The first thing I remember is waking up in Hamilcar's house outside Taneth. Some of my memory has come back, but there's so much I still can't remember. I don't even know if the memories I do have are correct.'

'Do you know who you are?' Tanais asked, his face unreadable.

'I think I'm Palatine Canteni, daughter of President Reinhardt Canteni and Princess Neptunia . . . am I right?' I saw uncertainty and concern on her face, and she suddenly looked much younger.

'Yes, you are.'

Palatine let out a shout of joy, alarming birds in the nearby trees. I was glad for her, that she at last knew who she was, and knew that the memories she'd recovered were true ones.

'What about Cathan, then?' she asked. 'He's my cousin, I know that much.'

Tanais's smile faded, and he turned to me. 'Cathan, I'm sorry, but I can't tell you yet.'

Anger flared up in me. 'So you're going to go away for another seven years without telling me who I am? I'm twenty, for Thetis's sake, don't I have a right to know who my real parents were, if you know?'

Tanais remained calm. 'Once I tell you, you'll have to leave Lepidor. There won't be any choice, not for either of you. The difference is that Palatine always knew who she was, and I can't keep it from her.'

'Palatine can't have that many first cousins.'

'You are Palatine's cousin, and you think you know who you are. When this clan is secure, then I will return and tell you. Now, say nothing more on this subject. I've just come on Hamilcar's ship, and I'm leaving again on the coaster in the morning. I'd like to see what you've done to the city.'

I was terribly disappointed, although not as much as I would have been if I'd known The Visitor was coming and had got my hopes up. Yes, maybe I was a Tar'Conantur, the grandson of an Emperor, but why was he so reluctant to confirm it? I already half knew, so what would he gain by not telling me now?

But the giant soldier refused to be drawn or even discuss the subject again, and I didn't press the point. I was too much in awe of him. Aside from his sheer size and presence, if he was, as he claimed, Tanais Lethien, he'd had the most extraordinary life. I learned from him the history Carausius hadn't told.

He'd been born, as I thought, two hundred and fifty years ago in a small village in Thetia, had joined the armies of the Old Empire and risen to be Commander of the Armies under Aetius the Great. He'd stood by Aetius's side all through the darkest days of the Tuonetar War, never giving up even when it seemed Thetia was lost. And, unlike so many of his friends and comrades, he'd survived, even living through the final desperate battle where Aetius and most of his army had perished.

And, it seemed, had lived through the years since the usurpation, the last person left alive from the era of the War. As I realized what that meant, I pitied him. If he was really Tanais Lethien, he'd lost every friend he'd ever had, and had seen the destruction of everything he believed in. Except for the decaying Thetian Empire with its puppet Emperor, a man who didn't deserve to sit on Aetius's throne.

I took advantage of Tanais's presence to find out everything I could about Thetia and, more importantly, Aetius and his companions, my distant ancestors. Even if Tanais wasn't who he claimed to be, he knew a huge amount about the era of the *History*. As the day wore on I grew steadily more convinced that he was indeed Tanais Lethien, however implausible that seemed. Those people who appeared in the book had been flesh and blood to him, people he'd talked to, got drunk with, argued with. He'd know the Empire at the height of its power, in a time when one was free to choose one's god.

When I asked him about the current Emperor, his expression hardened.

'It's something you have to understand about the Tar'Conanturs, that they can as easily turn out bad as good. Even a pair of twins can be mirror images of each other. Orosius . . .' He paused, looking off into the distance. 'Orosius isn't a credit to the name Tar'Conantur. His father was feckless and malleable, but Orosius is worse. He's a traitor and a coward, who couldn't face up to his responsibilities and has turned into a monster. All the more dangerous because he could have been something special.'

'I've never heard him called a coward before,' Ravenna said neutrally.

'There's more than one type of cowardice. Orosius has decided he's not bound by the same rules as the rest of us, that being Emperor exempts him from morality.' Tanais's voice carried contempt, the impression that he barely tolerated Orosius's existence.

Hamilcar had returned with his ship, as promised, bringing the latest news from Taneth. My father's demand for Foryth to keep away hadn't reached there before he left, but he brought other news that was no less interesting. House Canadrath had declared feud against House Foryth in revenge for an unspecified act by Foryth's agents. Canadrath had been the old King's favoured House, and I once again wondered whether Foryth had had something to do with the assassination, even if only indirectly.

There was news from the Halettite Empire too, Hamilcar told us, sipping wine in one of the reception rooms. He looked years younger than he had when I'd first seen him, although still rather worried. House Barca's fortunes were on the rise, and he was making a profit again after years of barely breaking even.

'Reglath Eshar led an army against Kemarea, the last of the independent states, and conquered it in less than a month; they only fought one battle. The Halettites are the only nation south of Taneth now, but of course nobody in Taneth is going to do anything about that. People like Foryth would rather die than give up some of their profits to rebuild Taneth's defences. They're all quite sure that a few miles of open water make Taneth invincible.'

'And you're not?' Ravenna said.

'Let's say I'm sceptical. If Eshar takes Malith or Ukhaa, our gateway cities, the Halettite will have access to a surface harbour for the first time. Most of them may not know what the sea looks like, but I'm sure they can learn to sail. There's no such thing as an impregnable city.'

'How long, do you think, before Eshar attacks Taneth?' Palatine asked.

'A year at the outside before he takes Malith and Ukhaa. After that, I give it five years at most before he attacks Taneth. But whether he'll succeed . . . I don't know. Eshar has no naval experience that I've heard of.'

'He can hire renegades,' Palatine said. 'That's how the Tuonetar did it.'

'That's not an auspicious comparison to make.'

'But it's right. The Tuonetar didn't have a navy at first, and look how much damage they did.'

'The only thing that may give Taneth breathing room is something even worse. Prime Lachazzar wants to borrow Eshar for a Crusade – either against the Archipelago or a heretic clan alliance in Huasa. It's a couple of years off if it happens at all – not even Lachazzar could launch a crusade on the basis of troubles in the Archipelago and discontent in Huasa. But if things get any worse . . .'

'Lachazzar wants to borrow Eshar? I haven't heard that yet,' Palatine said.

'It would mean even more suffering in the Archipelago,' said Ravenna. 'Where did you hear this from?'

'My old legal guardian is a Domain official in the Holy City, and he paid me a visit while I was in Taneth. He thinks I'm a fervent supporter of Lachazzar because I went to a monastic school, so he doesn't guard his tongue.'

'Your guardian was Domain?' Ravenna sat upright on the sofa. 'And you went to a monastic school.'

'That doesn't mean I like what they do,' Hamilcar said coldly. 'No more than you approve of the Tuonetar because you're Tehaman.'

Ravenna sank sullenly back into the cushions.

'Can you pass on anything else he says?' Palatine asked.

'I'm not a rumour-monger, and I'm not going to betray his trust for nothing.'

Every inch the Tanethan merchant still, I reminded myself. I wasn't ever going to trust him fully.

The bell rang for supper, interrupting the conversation.

It was a House supper in the Great Hall, as usual, with one or two of my father's friends on the Council there. My father brought out some of the best wine for Tanais and Hamilcar, and the evening went very merrily.

Towards the end of the meal I was talking to Tanais, on my right, but he didn't seem to be concentrating. He kept glancing in the other direction quite frequently, towards my father on his other side. I couldn't see past Tanais's huge bulk well enough to see what he was looking at. Only when the waiter arrived to refill my father's wine cup did I see. My father was drinking white rather than blue wine, because blue had never agreed with him, so he was specially served.

I stared in horror for a moment – my father was grey-faced and his hands were shaking. Then I pushed back my chair and rushed around, in time to see Tanais pick the waiter up bodily and fling him down behind the dais. There was absolute silence in the hall, broken by Atek.

'My lord?' he said to my father.

Elnibal toppled off his chair and on to the floor.

'Poison!' Tanais roared. 'He's been poisoned! Summon the healer!'

I felt my stomach clench in blind panic and fear.

'Seal the Palace!' my mother shouted above the sudden din. 'Guards on every exit, close all the gates. *Now!*'

Someone shouted the orders on as Tanais picked my father up and carried him from the hall.

I tried to tell myself this wasn't real, that everything was all right, but I couldn't. As the Great Hall of the Palace erupted into chaos I numbly followed the huge man into the ante-room.

Part Four: The Poisoned Crown

Chapter XXVII

Tanais laid my father down on a sofa in the ante-room as the House healer came bustling in. A woman of about forty, married to my father's first cousin, she had some skill with healing but wasn't fully trained. I wasn't sure she'd be able to help.

My father was breathing in short, shallow gasps, and his whole skin had gone a terrible grey colour. Every muscle in his body was rigid, and he was unconscious.

'The poison has affected his breathing,' the healer said, concerned. 'I don't know enough to deal with this.'

'The clan healer's on his way,' my mother said. She seemed calm but her voice almost broke on the last word.

'We may not have that long,' Tanais said. 'Find anyone who knows about tropical poisons and bring them here immediately.' No one dared to question his authority.

'I will,' said Atek, from behind my mother.

'How do you know it's tropical?' the healer asked, looking more than a little intimidated by Tanais's anger.

'I've seen enough death to know what this is.'

Hamilcar, who as a Great House heir had learned about poisons, said he thought it might be a poison called ijuan, which grew in the jungles of Thetia. 'It's very toxic,' he said, 'but it loses potency gradually once it's been harvested.'

The healer did what she could, but that wasn't very much, and for long, agonizing moments we stood by watching, unable to do anything. I prayed silently in my mind, begging every god I'd ever heard of for my father not to die, for the clan healer to know how to deal with the poison.

The clan healer arrived with his case moments later, the crowd parting to let him through, and knelt down beside my father.

'We think it's ijuan,' Tanais said.

'Breathing restricted, grey skin . . .' The healer pulled a leather-bound book out of his bag and gave it to the House healer. 'Check to see if any other poisons have that effect. I think you're right, but I have to be sure.'

We stayed silent, not wanting to break his concentration, while the healer pulled a phial out of his bag, uncorked it and let a few drops fall into my father's mouth.

'Ijuan's the only one that can do this,' the House healer said a moment later. 'The antidotes are temebore and mermaidshair.'

'Temebore!' He reached into his case again. 'This has diluted temebore in it, it should be able to lessen the paralysis a bit.'

He gave my father some of that as well, and moments afterwards I saw his muscles relax, and his breathing get slightly deeper.

'He should be stable for the time being,' the clan healer said. 'But I don't have undiluted temebore or any mermaidshair – it doesn't grow outside Thetia. You'll have to send him to Kula.'

'Is it safe to move him?' my mother asked.

'It has to be. They'll be able to cure him if we can get him there, though he might take a while to recover.'

I managed to find my tongue a moment later, as everybody looked at me expectantly, and I realized that I had just become, for the time being at least, Count of Lepidor.

There was nothing I wanted less.

I looked for Dalriadis and saw him behind Hamilcar. 'Admiral, call out your crew. I want the *Marduk* ready to sail within half an hour. You're in command – get my father to Kula as fast as possible, whatever it takes.'

Dalriadis nodded and ran out as the healer called for someone to go and find the palanquin that was still in the Palace from last year's Festival of Ranthas procession. My mother sent others to get blankets.

'Cathan,' Tanais said to me peremptorily. 'You have to go out into the Hall and tell everyone what's happened, and what you're doing about it. They need to know.'

I wanted to say *Must I?* I hated to leave my father lying there like that. I couldn't tear myself away until somebody took my hand and tugged slightly. I turned to shout at them, but the words died in my mouth when I saw Ravenna's solemn face and Palatine behind her.

'Come on,' she said.

I followed her as far as the door, then she let go of my hand.

'We're here,' Palatine said. 'But you must go and tell them.'

There was a buzz of conversation in the Hall, and people were sitting or standing around in groups, their supper forgotten. The dais was empty, the food on the table pushed aside when my father had collapsed. Several of the chairs had been tipped over, and wine dripped from a knocked-over glass on to the floor.

Silence fell as I walked into the Hall. These were my family, my cousins, my friends, all with more blood links to my father than I had, but they seemed a daunting crowd all of a sudden.

'Count Elnibal has been poisoned,' I said unsteadily, gaining a bit of confidence. It all seemed so distant and yet so real, a reality that I couldn't escape from. 'He is still alive and is being taken t-to Kula, to the hospital there.'

That was all I could bear to say. I stumbled off the dais and back into the ante-room. The palanquin had been brought into the corridor beyond the ante-room and Tanais was carrying my father over to it. A steward drew back the curtains and then Tanais placed Elnibal gently on the cushions that had been grabbed from the chairs to furnish it.

Tanais told two guards to carry it down to the harbour, accompanied by some of the marines who'd poured into the Palace when the news had reached them. It had already gone through the town like wildfire. Then he turned to me.

'Cathan, you go with him; take Palatine and Ravenna with you. No one else, no one at all. Stay down at the harbour until you've seen him off.'

'What about you, and my mother?' I asked.

'We're going to try and find who's responsible. That's why your mother ordered the doors to be sealed.'

We followed the palanquin bearers out of the gate and down the main street. They seemed to be going painfully slowly, but I realized they were being careful, trying not to rock the palanquin too much or trip over any loose stones.

As we walked down to the harbour, the construction sites we passed, deserted at this hour, seemed to mock me. To me they were symbols of the wealth that had caused this, and suddenly I wished I'd never discovered Domine Istiq's searay floating out in the ocean all those months ago, wished that we'd never found the iron.

I did my best to ignore the curious or anxious stares from the people standing on their doorsteps – news had already got around town – as our little procession moved down the street. At the gate to the harbour quarter the guards who'd been carrying the palanquin swapped round with two others.

Dalriadis had done his work at the harbour – the building was blazing with lights and the lift was ready, taking us straight down to the *Marduk*'s level. Dalriadis had marines and crewmen stationed either side of the route from the lift to the gantry entrance, to keep the way clear, and we took the palanquin through, down the gantry and onto the *Marduk*. The captain had a stretcher ready, and we took my father along to the room that had been prepared.

I waited with my father until the healer and his assistant, both of whom would be going to Kula, arrived with their kit.

Before I left the room the healer drew me aside. 'The worst is over, Cathan. He's lived this far, he'll make it all the way. But Kula is the best and the safest place for him to be; Courtières will be able to protect him better than we can. It will take him some time to recover, but you'll see him again, I promise you.'

His words calmed most of my fear, leaving only a smouldering rage. As far as I was concerned, there was only one person who could have done this.

I stayed with my father and the healer until Dalriadis strode in and announced that he was ready to go.

'Get him there as quickly as possible, Admiral,' I said. 'We can repair a damaged core if need be. *Nobody* is to be allowed in this room on their own. Nobody at all, not the healer, not anyone, and I want two guards always on duty at the door.'

'Very well,' he said. 'You'd better go back to the harbour now.'

I went back to Elnibal for the last time, kissed his clammy forehead, and lingered until the healer gave a warning cough. Then I went back along the passageway and out of the manta. Marines closed the door behind us seconds after we'd left, and almost immediately we heard the inner airlock hissing shut behind us.

The *Marduk* undocked and glided off into the darkness of the sea as soon as we were back within the hub. The marines were taking no chances; they formed up around us and kept the crowds at a distance for the walk back to the Palace through the evening gloom.

'Who goes there?' the gate guards said as we approached – there was a full squad there, I noticed.

'Cathan,' I said, as one of them held up a spot lamp.

'Pass through, then, sir.'

There were more marines in the courtyard, which was now brightly lit by aether flares, as we went through, and I wondered if the whole garrison was here – I'd never seen so many of them around as tonight. Only one door was open, guarded by two more marines, dressed in civilian clothes but with their swords and badges prominently displayed.

Inside I found Tanais and my mother, with several of the Council, holding an impromptu court of inquiry in one of the reception rooms. They were sitting in a semicircle on sofas and chairs while the head chef stood in the middle, flushed and looking indignant.

'I do not allow strangers in my kitchen!'

'Nevertheless,' my mother said, 'did you see anyone unusual in the area of the kitchens at any time?'

'No, I didn't.'

'Did you leave the kitchens at all?'

'Very briefly, to go to the pantry. There was an under-chef in the room all the time, and he would have reported any visitors.'

'Very well. You are dismissed.'

The chef walked away, and angry talk broke out around the semi-circle.

'We're not getting anywhere with these questions,' Mezentus said. 'And what right do you have to preside over this, Tanais?'

For answer, Tanais reached inside his plain, coarse-spun green tunic and pulled out a pendant showing the scales of justice with a pair of dolphins beneath, the symbol of a Thetian judge. The dolphins' eyes were tiny black stones. Except for the crossed swords under the dolphins, it was identical to the one worn by the dying Chancellor in my father's memory.

'I am First Marshal of the Thetian Empire. Do you need any more explanation?'

The medallions couldn't be stolen – the black stones held some kind of magic that rendered the medallion unwearable away from its owner. They were very difficult to make, and consequently limited to only the highest ranks of judges – the Thetian Emperor, the Supreme Court, and the Commanders of the Armies and the Fleets, who had ultimate judicial authority over their forces.

Mezentus's eyes widened, then he said grudgingly, 'I recognize your authority,' and talk was resumed.

'It can't have been that chef – too many people have given him an alibi,' my mother said. Then she noticed me. 'Ah, Cathan. We're trying to find the culprit before he can destroy the evidence. Your father's special wine was poisoned after it was brought out of the cellar. There are a number of suspects, but we're narrowing them down.'

I was appalled. 'You mean it was somebody within the Palace that did this? Within the House, even?'

'There aren't too many people it can be,' Tanais said. 'The waiter had nothing to do with it, he was just in the wrong place at the wrong time.'

'Do we have anyone with connections to Lord Foryth?' I asked.

'You think he's behind it as well?'

'I can't see who else stands to gain.'

'Possibly Count Lexan,' Palatine said from behind me. 'He wins this way. Moritan is ill, your father out of the way, so Courtières is the only experienced ruler left.'

'You think he's in danger as well?' my mother said sharply.

'He could be.'

'Is it too late to send to Dalriadis, tell him to pass the warning on?'

'Courtières will think of the same thing.'

'Can we get on with finding whoever did this?' I said impatiently. 'When we do, we can ask him whose orders he was acting on, and then we'll know who to defend ourselves against.'

I realized then for the first time why my father had sent that threat to Foryth, and that he hadn't overreacted at all: I was prepared to do the same. But my father had come within an inch of death for his actions. Whoever was responsible for all this was in deadly earnest, and for all I knew, Lexan and Foryth could be working together. That was a possibility I didn't like to think of.

A councillor got up to give me his chair and I sat down between Tanais and my mother, while Palatine and Ravenna stood behind, looking over my shoulders.

'Bring in the next witness!' Tanais ordered.

As the evening drew on, and the people in the hall grew steadily more impatient, we interviewed everyone who could possibly have poisoned the wine, or seen the poisoner at work. The cork of the wine bottle was examined for punctures where somebody could have slipped poison in, but none was found.

The wine bottle had come up from the cellar an hour before the meal and been placed in the chill room, where it had stayed until my father had arrived. Then it had been uncorked and put on its special shelf by the door until the waiter had used it moments later. Only the cellar keeper, the kitchen staff, the stewards or the waiters could have poisoned it.

But having established that, we came up against a blank wall. We questioned person after person but didn't come any nearer to finding the would-be killer.

By eleven o'clock, with the people confined in the Hall growing restive, we had only three stewards left, and were interviewing the head steward, a man from a House traditionally allied with ours. We'd questioned him on the movement of the other stewards, then asked where he'd been.

'In the hall, supervising the laying of the tables, until just before everybody came in,' he said. 'Then I went into the kitchens to ask the head chef about something.'

'Which was?'

'How many dishes there would be on the high table.'

That matched what the chef and under-chefs had told us earlier.

'Wasn't that a fairly trivial thing to bother yourself with?' Palatine asked suddenly.

'Maybe for you, my lady, but not for me,' the man said, looking as if he resented this intrusion of an outsider. 'That's my job, attention to detail.'

'And you went into the kitchens through the door from the Hall?' Tanais continued.

'Yes.'

'Did you notice the wine on its shelf as you went past?'

'Yes, it was in its usual place. I stopped to make sure everything that should be there was there.'

'Was it properly polished?' Palatine spoke again; this time Tanais gave her an annoyed glance.

'Properly polished? Why do you ask me that?'

'Was it properly polished and cleaned?' Palatine repeated.

'Of course it was,' the man said, aggrieved.

Palatine produced the jug from the table behind my chair. I craned round to see what she was doing.

'Then why lean over and blow on it? Two people saw you, and they thought you were just blowing dust off it. But it's strange how you do that and then half an hour later we find discoloration around the rim.'

'What are you saying, Palatine?' my mother asked impatiently. 'Are you accusing this man?'

'I am saying that if you blew a sachet of ijuan powder across the lip of this jug it would leave marks just like these,' Palatine said, the words coming out in a rush.

I turned back to the man, and saw his expression in an unguarded instant. The others must have done too.

'What do you say to this?' my mother said coldly.

'This is pure invention – you've got no proof.'

'Oh, I think Palatine's just shown that we have,' Tanais said.

I was appalled – I'd known this man for years, he'd served in the Palace nearly all his life. Surely he wouldn't betray us?

And then, as his face twisted with hatred, I realized that he had. He reached down into his pocket, pulled out a black sphere about two inches across, and hurled it towards Tanais, in the centre of the group.

'Die, all of you!'

The sphere hit the leg of Tanais's chair and burst into flames, which spread up the chair and to the rest of the furniture with astonishing rapidity. Someone screamed, and I leaped forward, away from the flames, even as the huge soldier stood up and lifted my mother out of their path. Other people tried to leap out of the way over chairs and sofas that were already ablaze, as lines of flame spread across the room. One of the guards lifted his sword to cut the steward down, but then lost his nerve as the flames advanced across the rug towards him. He and his companion edged round as the flames took hold – within seconds the whole of the furniture was ablaze and the fire was spreading up the wall.

'Cathan!' Ravenna sprinted across the few feet between us. 'There's no time. You've got to help me!' I saw Tanais put my mother down and gesture urgently at me, but I couldn't think why.

Ravenna took my hands, and before I realized what she was doing she initiated the magical contact between us.

'Help me,' she said, inside my mind. 'Release the magic.'

I closed my eyes and let my consciousness flow along the link between us, descending through the layers of the body into the mind, all the way to the edge of the realm of the soul. I was floating in the infinite darkness, the strange realm of the mind that neither of us understood. But I knew what to do.

I rushed through the nothingness towards her, and for a moment, again, I felt that alien feeling of joining that I had when we'd sealed each other's magic away. But this time we moved, a single entity, to break down the barriers that held it back.

It was like a flood, a tidal wave, sweeping through, that within an instant tore us apart again. I felt my body electrified by the power pouring back into it, the strange mixture of Shadow and Water, from my training and my blood.

Then I knew why Ravenna had done this, and abruptly pulled my mind back into my own body. The room was an inferno of fire and smoke, and there was screaming from everywhere. In the middle the steward had become a human torch, his mouth convulsing in a soundless shriek as he was consumed.

I drew on my power, the inborn power of Water I'd hardly used, and emptied my mind for the first time in weeks – it was almost as much of a struggle as it had been at the beginning. I felt outside the burning room, to the calm evening sea, and then brought all the force of a ton of sea water into the room, even as the flames around figures were choked by Shadow. I felt the wave hit me bodily, throwing me back against the wall, and I slipped under the surface, still conscious enough of what was going on to realize I couldn't risk being seen, not if I wanted to live past the evening.

The flames hadn't been from naptha, I saw as I opened my eyes, because the water had quenched them and naptha burned on water. On the other hand, the sudden impact could have snuffed them out.

The water came up to about neck height, and I surfaced again to look round.

The fire was out and the room was lit only by the aether lights from outside the windows; the curtains must have been ripped away. I could see faces and figures – Palatine, the massive figure of Tanais next to my mother, some of the other Council people. There were some missing, too.

'Everybody hold on to something,' Tanais said, his voice suddenly very loud in what had become a much smaller space. He strode over to the window, the water only a little above waist height on him, and held onto the wall with one hand, while with one foot he kicked open the window, allowing the sea water to pour out on the terrace and into the garden. I felt it tug at me, but I was holding on to some heavy object too tightly to be moved; as the water level subsided I saw it was half a table.

Then the doors were opened and light and people flooded into the room. Four or five corpses, which I could see even in the semi-darkness were horribly burned, lay on the floor. The rest of us looked round at each other in dazed confusion. I didn't want to think of the devastation that had overtaken my city in the course of this evening due to the treachery of that single man, now a charred cadaver on the floor. He had been one of our most trusted retainers.

There was little to be gained by keeping the House members and guests waiting after what had happened, so I ordered the marines to open the doors and tell everybody to go home. There was nothing left of the furniture in the room we'd been in, only burned fragments and ashes. The marines, some of them crying openly, had wrapped up the bodies of the steward, their two comrades, and the two Councilmen who'd died. One of them was Mezentus. I wondered what I was going to say to his daughter, a girl no older than me who'd now lost both her parents.

Even then the evening's troubles weren't over. Two minutes after we'd opened the doors, Midian appeared with four priests and a mind-mage, storming into the Palace, and demanded to know what had happened.

I was in no mood for his Halettite arrogance, and his tone was so insulting I barely stopped myself from lashing out at him.

'Several people have died here because of an act of treachery, *Pontifex*. It is purely a matter for me to deal with, in my father's absence.'

'You are greatly mistaken, Escount.'

'*Count* for the time being, Avarch Midian.' There always had to be an active Count in charge of the clan. While my father was ill, I held the title.

'That is irrelevant. Somebody used water-magic tonight, and that is heresy of the foulest kind. My mind-mage will test everybody who was present to find out who was responsible and deal with them.'

'You will do no such thing, Midian. My father has been poisoned and may not live, five of my clansmen are dead, my Palace was always destroyed by fire-magic and only saved by this water-mage, whoever he is. We all owe that mage our lives, Midian.'

'Address me with proper respect, Cathan, and stand aside – or I will have you charged with heresy for protecting this heretic.'

'I would be breaking the Code if I did that.' I was getting desperate. The Code was a set of ancient Thetian laws they'd taught us about at the Citadel, which demanded a far stronger bond of loyalty to the clan than most people ever felt. Only some of the more traditional Thetian clans, including Palatine's, now used it.

'*If* you followed the Code, perhaps. This isn't Thetia, and you can't fool me that way.'

'He is perfectly right,' Tanais growled, an expression on his face that was terrifying even though it wasn't directed at me. '*I* am the one responsible for the water-magic this evening, and I suggest you forget that it ever happened. There is nothing you can do against me.' He gestured to me to say nothing, and I wasn't going to, not yet. He could defend himself better than I could. If he really was Tanais Lethien.

'You are a heretic, and I arrest you in the name of the Domain.'

'Hurl your pathetic little words at me, priest, but be careful because I won't think twice about removing you or anyone who gets in my way. Your men included, Cathan. I suggest you leave this Palace now, priest.'

Midian glared at Tanais, then me, with a look of pure hatred that chilled me to the bone. There was no fear in his face.

'I will see you burn,' he said as he turned on his heel and marched out, the priests following him in stony-faced silence.

I wasn't sure who he was talking to.

Though I was bone-tired, I couldn't go to bed yet. There were two more things I had to do, and I could only put one of them off until tomorrow, if I was going to do it at all. I asked Palatine and Hamilcar to come up to my father's office – now again mine; for the hundredth time that evening I wished it wasn't. Ravenna was nowhere to be seen.

'Hamilcar,' I said, when they'd sat down. The Tanethan merchant looked exhausted, but Palatine didn't seem at all weary, just sombre. 'Do you think Foryth is behind this?'

'He could be,' Hamilcar said warily, 'but I'm doubtful. If he is, he can't have been acting alone. Great Houses get destroyed when they do things like this to clans, so Foryth must have somebody else's support.'

'In less than a month we've had a pirate attack, a native raid, an attempted harbour sabotage, the assassination of the King, and now this poisoning,' Palatine said. 'All these things, coming so close together, must be connected in some way. Everything that has happened has been inconvenient or worse for Lepidor, even the King's death.'

'Foryth would never have done something like that. That's a high-level political assassination, and a Great House simply couldn't cope with the repercussions.'

'But there seems to be a link even there,' I pointed out. 'The feud with Canadrath which started at the same time, Moritan being caught in the raid, the failed attack on Arcadius.'

'If they'd killed Arcadius we'd be heading for all-out war,' Palatine said. 'Orosius would have gone absolutely berserk. I think they never meant to kill him, and attacking him was designed to antagonize the Thetians.'

Hamilcar said, 'If Foryth had a hand in that, they were being used as someone's puppet.'

'Whose? Who has a reason to attack the Empire like that?'

'The Halettites.'

'That's a non-starter.' Palatine was dismissive. 'The Halettites don't have a fleet, the Thetians don't have a large enough army.'

'The Halettites could be hoping the Thetians would blame Foryth and destroy Taneth for them.'

I said, 'Surely not even Orosius would be so stupid?'

'He's a Tar'Conantur.' Hamilcar spread his hands. 'Where they're concerned, who knows?'

'We're not all mad.' I hardly noticed, but it was the first time I'd associated myself with them.

'Most of you are. Always assuming that's who you are. I'm always inclined to be sceptical.'

'Ask Tanais,' said Palatine.

'Elements only know who he is. How many two-hundred-and-fifty-year-olds have you ever met?' Hamilcar said.

'That isn't the point,' she said, 'What do you think Foryth's next move will be?'

Hamilcar's expression was grave. 'He hasn't poisoned Count Elnibal just for the sake of it. He obviously intended to kill, but there has to be some benefit it would bring. I suspect, Cathan, that he'll be relying on your being you and untried. Within the next few days, or weeks, there will be something else. Whoever did this, the timing was too opportune for this to be a coincidence. Within the next few days, a week or two at the outside, this hidden enemy, whoever it is, will strike again. And this time, I think, he means it to be a decisive blow.'

Chapter XXVIII

The next morning was dreadful.

I woke up very early from a restless sleep filled with nightmares, and then remembered what had happened the day before. There was no way I could know if Elnibal was still alive; they wouldn't even have reached Kula yet.

I had no appetite, so I went down for a swim, but that didn't help either. Memories of the previous evening haunted me wherever I looked, and when I dived underwater I suddenly thought I was back in that room again.

When I went back inside, I met Tanais in the hallway, about to set out down to the port to catch the *Parasur* back to Pharassa.

'Are you leaving already?' I asked him.

'I can't stay here, not after what I said to Midian last night. Why did you have to use your magic? I could have dealt with it anyway, and we wouldn't have had the trouble.'

'You're not a mage, what could you have done?' I was still angry and rather truculent.

His patience was infuriating; he didn't even seem to notice my tone. 'My medallion's charged with water-magic. Carausius did it before he died. There's not much left now, but I could have dealt with the fire, and because it came through the medallion the mind-mage couldn't have detected it.'

'How was I supposed to know that?'

'I did shout across to you, and you saw me, but then you were too busy doing that strange ritual with Ravenna to realize what I meant. What was that all about?'

'When the mind-mage arrived we shut each other's magic up so he couldn't detect it. Ravenna was the one who decided to release it last night.'

'She had no way of knowing, but she's put you in more danger than Midian could ever have done. I don't think you've got more than a week before he realizes what really happened. After that, you'll either have to find some way to neutralize him or leave.'

'Thank you very much,' I said bitterly. One more blunder, what was next? 'When are you coming back? Assuming, that is, we're still here and haven't been arrested by the Inquisition?'

'I'll be back within the month. Guard yourself, and remember that no one here is what they seem.' He turned and went out of the door; I didn't bother to follow him.

'What's that supposed to mean?' I shouted at his back, but there was no reply.

So now, thanks to Ravenna and my own blind stupidity, the Domain were going to find out that I was a mage. Even then, I didn't realize what that meant until I remembered Tanais's warning that I'd have to leave. Leave? Leave Lepidor? How could I? There was no one who could take over as Count. For that matter, where was I supposed to go? I'd be branded as a heretic, hunted across the face of the waters. Qalathar might be a safe haven . . . until the armies of the Crusaders arrived, to finish what they had started twenty-three years ago. Damn Ravenna!

There were few people still around at this hour, and a terrible absence where my father would have been, at the centre of the household. I remembered all the times when I'd been up this early, and he'd always been there; even when he was away at the Conference, I'd always been sure he was safe. Now I didn't know if he was coming back at all, and I was the only person standing between Lord Foryth and Lepidor.

I went up to his office, shut the door behind me, and sat down in his chair, staring emptily at the papers on the desk. He'd left himself a note to deal with a dispute between two Houses. I would have to handle that now. Hoping to distract myself by doing something, I pulled across the pile of papers left over from yesterday, left unfinished because of Tanais's unexpected arrival. It was boring, tedious work as usual, but it took part of my mind off the problems facing me.

I worked doggedly until there was a knock at the door. I sat silently for a moment. I knew who it was, and I so desperately didn't want to see her now. But I couldn't put it off.

'Come in.'

'The marines have searched that man's quarters. They didn't find anything,' Ravenna said.

'That was only to be expected.'

There was a strained silence as she closed the door and sat down. 'Has Tanais gone?' she asked.

'He went about half an hour ago. He gives it a week before Midian works out who was really responsible for the magic last night. All he needs to do is check his copy of the *History* to find that Tanais had no magical ability whatsoever.'

'What else could I have done? Stood there and let myself be burned to death?'

'You must have seen Tanais's gesture. I did, but you grabbed me before I had time to think.'

'So? He had no magic.'

'He had. The medallion.'

'Cathan, you can't blame me for what I did. As far as I knew, you were the only person in Lepidor who could have put that fire out. Those flames weren't natural, surely you felt that.'

'No, I suppose I can't. But within a week, I'll have to leave here. Unless we can deal with Midian.'

'Is that my fault as well?'

'I used my magic, so did you. We're both in danger.'

'*You* may be. I didn't use enough of my magic for them to have noticed.'

What was the point of her saying that? Maybe she thought that now she'd got me into this mess she didn't have to do anything about it.

'Well, perhaps you could at least try to help me, even if your own skin is safe. I can't leave the clan, Ravenna. Until my father returns, I'm the Count and there is no one to succeed me. If I leave, my House will lose power and the contract with Hamilcar won't hold. Foryth will have won. And there will be nobody to stop Midian.'

'I never said I wouldn't help you.'

'You implied it. Do you have any useful suggestions, ways to get round this little problem?'

'Short of killing Midian, I can't see what you can do. There's no time to find out if we can blackmail him, and we can't exactly conjure up a storm to keep him sealed in the Temple all week.'

'Is this help or a counsel of despair?'

Her eyes flashed. 'I'm doing what I can, for Thetis's sake. Palatine's the master of strategy, not me. Ask her.'

'Palatine has no magic, Ravenna. You do.'

'So do you, even if it's all inborn and you only have to snap your fingers to get more power than most people can dream of.'

'What does that have to do with it?' I demanded. 'This isn't about where we got our magic from – we're trying to deal with the Domain.'

She stood up from the chair and walked over to the desk, her face a cold mask. 'Surely you can just blow them out of existence, can't you? And anybody who comes to investigate. There's no need to be condescending.'

'What are you talking about? I wasn't being condescending. What did I say?' I was baffled by her sudden hostility; I was sure I hadn't said anything that would offend her, so why was she turning on me like this?

'*What did I say?*' she mimicked, in her flat tones a grotesque parody of my words. 'Are you so oblivious to all us lesser mortals that you don't even bother to watch what you say to us? Oh, of course I've got magic, so I might be of some help to you. Extricate you from this situation you got yourself into because you were too high and mighty to think before you used all that magic yesterday.'

She was almost shouting now, and her voice was losing some of its emotionless control. She was leaning over the desk, looking down at me, and I stood up. The last accusation, groundless as it was, had rekindled my anger.

'You yourself said you acted in the heat of the moment last night. Are you allowed to, then, while I'm not?'

'We mere mortals who have limits to our power have to learn how to control it from time to time. I didn't just let loose so much magic that every mage in Oceanus probably heard it. You used a sledgehammer to crack a nut, and you won't accept the consequences.'

'I saved your life, or have you forgotten that already?'

'Saved my life so that you can use me again next time you need to give the impression of consulting the rest of us before you make your plans.

Of course, there's always Palatine, who's bloody Tar'Conantur like you. She's worthy to consult with, even if she doesn't have Ranthas only knows what running in her blood.'

I tried to say something, to interrupt, but she ignored me, going furiously on. 'Did you never wonder why I collapsed after we linked that first time? You never asked me, of course, because you weren't interested. You were safe from Midian's stake for the time being, until you could think up a way to deal with him on your own. I was merely a tool who occasionally came up with some useful ideas.'

'That's not true!' I protested, wounded by what she was saying. But she raised her voice more, to drown me out, and stared at me across the desk with rage in her eyes.

'You didn't ever think that my collapsing had anything to do with you, with your mind. Your twisted mind, so warped I'm amazed you can ever walk in a straight line. I had to see into your soul-realm, you gods-accursed monster of that blighted, evil family that you come from. You're no different from any of them; from Ragnar, the traitor; Valdur, the insane brother-killer; Landressa, that scheming, murdering bitch who should never have been an empress. Your family destroys everything it touches, even their loved ones. How many of the wives and husbands of those survived with their minds intact? You're rotten to the core, Cathan – even the blood that runs in your veins is tainted.'

It was as if I'd been hit by a hammer. I staggered backwards, clutching the arms of the chair wildly. I tried to say something but I was too stunned by what she was saying; I couldn't understand why she was saying these things. And the most terrible thing was that a part of my mind, the part that wasn't reeling from her onslaught and what I saw as a betrayal, knew that what she said wasn't all lies.

'Cut you to the quick, have I?' she said, her face distorted with anger, but with her icy control still in place. 'Someone at last dared to tell the truth about the Tar'Conanturs—' she turned the word into an insult '—without caring about your temper? You and Palatine and all your ancestors were just the same, let rip at some poor mortal whenever they got in your way. Maybe she does it less, but she's still just the same. You don't need to worry about the mind-mage, because once he's been in contact with you for more than a few seconds he'll go insane, like so many others. Your blessed cousin, the Emperor Orasius, for example.

You're more alike than you could ever realize or admit, and capable of causing just as much death and destruction.'

I slumped into the chair, unable to meet her gaze or even look at her. 'All I wanted was some help,' I said, my voice sounding like a stranger's.

'*Some help*! Of course you didn't. You get that from Palatine and occasionally those who have status, not orphans from Tehama, minions with none of your exalted blood. The only reason you keep me around at all is because you think I'm pretty, and might make rather a good concubine.'

This time I did look at her, and the blood drained from my face. 'No!' I whispered. 'Never!'

'I've had enough of your lies, Cathan. I don't love you, as you may have deluded yourself into thinking. I don't even like you. Drown Midian and all his priests if you want to, but you're not getting any help from me.'

She turned away and almost ran to the door, ignoring my desperate cry. She slammed it behind her and I heard the sound of her running footsteps fading down the corridor.

I didn't look up for long moments after she'd gone. I felt unutterably desolate and alone, as well as betrayed. I wasn't all of those things she'd said, was I?

I wasn't sure what to believe any more. I buried my head in my hands and wept.

A couple of minutes later I heard the door open and someone step softly into the room. I looked up slowly, in case it was Ravenna back again, but it wasn't.

'Cathan?' Elassel said.

'Leave me alone.'

'Those things weren't true.'

'How do you know?' I said, looking up at her again. She came round the side of the desk and squatted down beside the chair. 'You hardly know me, and you're not one of us.' She had heard the conversation, or at least some of it. She knew who I was.

'Not a heretic? Cathan, religion means nothing to me any more. All those things about the Tar'Conanturs . . .'

'Were all straight out of the *History*.'

'Even those aren't true. Think how much she left out, the people who brought honour to the family. Aetius, Carausius, Tiberius. Even Landressa helped defeat the Tuonetar.'

'But there were so many mad ones, Elassel, so many evil ones.'

'It's the same in any family. The only difference is that Tar'Conanturs are famous. I'm not a mage, but even I can see you're not like any of them.'

'Why did she say all that, though? Why did she turn on me?'

'I can't tell you that, Cathan. Only she can. But when she got angry she dragged up everything she could think of. How many of those things have the rest of us noticed? She's using your family history against you, while the rest of us wouldn't even guess you were Tar'Conantur, aside from your looks.'

'Is it that plain?'

'To me it is. Probably not to anyone else. But I'm very good at remembering faces, and I've seen Tar'Conantur portraits.'

'I loved her, Elassel. I didn't always trust her, but I loved her. I even thought that she might feel the same way, or something at least. But now I can see how wrong I was.'

'Somebody who said the things she just said at a time like this isn't worthy of being loved by anyone.'

'Everything has just gone wrong since last night.'

'Cathan, you are Count of Lepidor. I know you must feel terrible, but you haven't the time.' She stood up and walked over to the door, pausing with her hand on the handle. 'I came to tell you something I overheard. I'm going to find Palatine now and bring her up here, because I think she needs to hear it as well.'

Elassel went out, and I sat there, not moving, for a while. After a few moments I brushed my face with one sleeve and sat upright, made myself look presentable. It wouldn't do for the Count of Lepidor to look distraught, but what did it matter? What point was there in looking smart anyway, when I was due for the shortest tenure in history as a Count? Before another seven days had passed Midian would be demanding my arrest as a heretic, and my only option would be to kill him and flee. I didn't see the point in running away any more; there would be no place in the world where I could hide from the Domain for long, and I'd have to abandon those friends I still had. Why bother? Why not just let him seize me and be done with it?

I heard more footsteps coming down the hall, and then low voices conferring outside the door. Almost without realizing it, I used my shadowsight enhancement to hear what they were saying.

'. . . Is inexcusable. Tell Atek that she must be moved out of the Palace at once and into lodgings in the town. She can't stay here after what she's done.'

'Very well. I'll take it as a Count's order.' The other voice was my father's cousin, the new head steward.

The door opened and Palatine came in with Elassel. I waited for them to lock the door and sit down; they were obviously waiting for me to say something.

'Elassel, don't you have a message to give us?'

'Yes,' she said, pushing some hair away from her eyes and tucking it behind her ear. 'Midian's been up to his tricks again; trying to confine me to the Temple, penance to stop my disorderly behaviour. He never learns. Yesterday I slipped into his office; I was going to rig up something that would cause him severe embarrassment at the next ceremony. His robes are kept in a cupboard in there. Anyway, not to go on, I heard him coming and hid in the cupboard. He came into his office with his deputy, that severe-looking old priest. The priest had just got a message off one of the crew of that trader, and they opened it.'

'Do you know what it said?' Palatine asked.

'I'm getting to that,' Elassel said, 'so be quiet. They didn't read it out, but they talked a lot about what was in it. It was a message from somebody in Pharassa to Midian, asking him if he could request his superiors when they arrived to do something about House Canadrath, whoever they are. Midian seemed quite annoyed, but the other priest said that Canadrath had intervened too late to cause any damage to anybody except Lijah Foryth. He also said something about the King taking care of them, Canadrath, I think. That was all.'

'Do something about House Canadrath,' Palatine repeated. 'They're the Great House who declared feud against Foryth.'

Could he ask his superiors? I sifted through the message again in my mind. Midian's superiors could only be Domain hierarchs, but they hadn't bothered to warn Midian because only Lijah would suffer.

Palatine was quicker than me. 'Why didn't I see it before? I can see everything now, except why they're doing it. What are they all hoping to achieve?'

'Who are "they"?' I asked.

'The Domain, House Foryth, and Ranthas only knows who else. They're in this together, Cathan. It's not House Foryth after the iron contract, it's the Domain after the iron, and something else. Foryth are a tool, nothing more.'

'But why assassinate the King, go to all the lengths they've gone to, just to get hold of an iron mine?' Elassel said. 'The Domain may be evil, conniving bastards but they aren't stupid.'

'That's what's missing,' Palatine said. 'There's something else behind this, but I can't think what. It must be something to do with the Empire.'

So everything really had gone wrong, if it was the Domain who were trying to destroy us. The Archipelagans had found, to their cost, that you couldn't oppose them. Still, we might as well go through the motions, even if we didn't have a chance against them.

'There are two places left we can ask for help,' I said resignedly. 'Courtières and House Canadrath.'

'Canadrath will only help us if it's in their own interests.'

'What if we send a message to Canadrath with some of what we've found out and ask for a temporary alliance? They're in feud with Foryth.'

'Would they believe you, though?' Elassel said. 'If you send them some story about Domain plots – even we've had trouble believing this. Why would they?'

'Maybe we should give them some proof,' Palatine said, her eyes brightening. 'Elassel, would you be above stealing that note?'

'Try me.'

After Elassel returned to the Temple, I spent most of the rest of the day in my father's office, working on the documents that had so bored me before. They were still boring, but welcome, because they had nothing to do with Foryth, the Domain, Ravenna or anything else. I appeared at supper and did the rounds of the city to check the guards, but otherwise stayed in the Palace. I was too depressed to have much energy.

There was some better news the next day, when Elassel turned up complete with Midian's message. We hadn't considered the possibility that he'd destroy it, but thankfully he hadn't, anyway.

I ordered Dalriadis's deputy to have three of our five searays manned. One I sent, with an explanation, to Courtières at Kula. The other two were for Canadrath's agency in Pharassa. There was a very real possibility that someone would intercept the message, so Palatine devised a plan to distract them. The first searay, with a dummy message, would arrive in Pharassa and its crew would slink around town for a while, attempting to set up a covert meeting with Canadrath. The second, with the real thing, would sail into the harbour a few hours later and *its* crew would go straight to Canadrath's agency to hand the message over. Before they left, we used an aether console to make some copies of the message, for us to keep in case the first one was somehow lost. I didn't want to send the original, but Palatine insisted that the copies couldn't be authenticated.

From the Palace window I watched the searays leave, seeing the faint trails of their wakes curve out of Lepidor bay and into the open ocean. What few hopes we had went with them. Elassel had told us of a lot of people having private talks with Midian, who seemed to be in command of this end of the operation. I could only assume Lepidor was riddled with spies, and that clan honour counted for nothing any more.

More foreigners had arrived as well, on Bomar's trader. Two Thetians, three Tanethans and a couple of others had disembarked with Tanais. None of them were normal visitors and there weren't usually so many arrivals, so Palatine set clansmen to watch them. Presumably she hoped that at least one person would, for once, turn out to be loyal to the clan and report anything they saw.

Two days dragged past. A searay arrived from Kula bringing Dalriadis's apologies, the *Marduk* was being repaired and he couldn't make it back yet. More importantly, the healers had confirmed that my father would live, although he would be convalescing. They didn't specify for how long, and I wondered whether he'd have a clan to come back to when he was well again.

The men working on the Archipelagan manta *Emerald*, which had been docked on the upper gantry for more than a month now, announced that she would be finished within two days. The Archipelagans had been growing restless, and I sensed that they were impatient to move on. Sagantha had been excellent company, but he too wanted to be going, no doubt to protect his passenger, if she existed.

Surprisingly, Midian hadn't taken any action against the Archipelagans. Had he been ordered not to, I wondered, in preparation for something else? Surely the Domain wouldn't just let them leave like that?

'It doesn't seem right,' Palatine said, when I mentioned it to her. 'Either they'll come up with an excuse to keep them here at the last minute, or they're planning something that will stop them leaving at all.'

'What if they ambush them out at sea?'

'In your waters, it's the Count's responsibility, but Sagantha wouldn't blame you. Out at sea, it could be taken as an act of war. And the Domain don't have the ships to do something like that,' said Palatine.

'I'm sure they could have got hold of some,' she warned me. 'Tell Sagantha to leave in the middle of the night and be on guard against surprise attack.'

I invited Sagantha up to my father's office the evening before he was due to leave.

'It's been a great pleasure staying here,' he said. 'On behalf of the state of the Archipelago, I thank you for your hospitality.'

'It's been a pleasure having you,' I said. With the formalities over, I poured him a drink and we sat down on the chairs in the reception corner.

'With all the trouble we've been having, might I suggest you depart at a different time?' I explained what Palatine had said, and he nodded.

'A good idea. Never trust the Domain. Nobody will like being rousted out of bed at that ungodly hour, but they can settle down again on the manta.' It was clear that Sagantha knew I was a heretic.

'Am I allowed to ask where you're going?'

'We were going to the Northern Islands, to pick up some more people. Now that we've been so long delayed, I think we'll head on to Mons Ferranis instead. I'd like to ask you a favour, which I appreciate you might find awkward.'

'Go ahead,' I said, guardedly.

'I would like Ravenna to come with us. With all respect, Lepidor is not a safe place at the moment, and Ravenna is more important in the Archipelago than she realizes.'

'I can't compel her.'

'Of course you can't. I'm going to ask her before we leave, and I just wanted to make sure it was all right with you.'

'Of course.' Ravenna's words were still burned into my brain; I never wanted to see her again. We were interrupted by the buzz of the comm on the desk. I got up and went over to it. It was the duty harbour master, from his office in the harbour hub.

'Count, there's a manta approaching, demanding permission to dock.'

Something in his voice alerted me.

'Who's on it?'

'Several Domain priests and an Element Prime . . .'

'Etlae?'

'That's her name. They're on a King's manta.'

I wondered what Etlae was doing here, and with other priests in tow. It had to be the Inquisition come for the Qalatharis, but if so, why Etlae? She was on our side.

'Tell them we've got problems with the gantries and they can't dock yet. If they press it, tell them half an hour.'

'You want me to lie to a Prime?'

'She may be an impostor – I have to find out.'

'Very well, sir. But you gave the orders.'

I cut the connection and looked over at Sagantha.

'Can all your people be ready in half an hour?'

'I'll make sure of it,' he said, putting down his glass. 'I'll go past Ravenna's lodgings on the way. Goodbye, and good luck.'

'And to you too.'

He ran out of the door and down the hallway. I switched on the internal comm and summoned Palatine up to the office. I'd no sooner switched it off again than another transmission came from the harbour.

'My lord, they haven't stopped. They're heading for the harbour at full speed, and they've told me you're under arrest for heresy.'

'She's an impostor, then! Barricade the harbour!'

'I can't do that, my lord. Not against a Prime.' He cut the connection and I couldn't re-establish it.

So this was it, then. Even Etlae had turned against me.

As I took the brooch of office from my tunic and laid it on the table, I was surprised at how calm I was.

Chapter XXIX

A couple of minutes later Palatine came running in, but stopped dead in the doorway when she saw me standing by the desk.

'It's an attack, isn't it? They're here.'

'Etlae and her underlings. I've called up the captain of the guard, and he's going to send his men to the harbour to delay them for a while. Enough time for him to find you a hiding place.'

Palatine's eyes narrowed. 'Only me?'

'Only you. I have no desire to go on with this.'

'With what? Life?'

'I've been declared a heretic by a Prime. I can run from here, yes, but where would I go? There's no point in running when there's nowhere to run to.'

'The Archipelago will help you.'

I was growing tired of her arguments. 'Until the Crusade reached them, I'm sure they would. I'd give the Domain the excuse they're longing for. No, there's no point in hiding.'

'So you're going to abandon your clan like this, to the Domain's control?'

'What can I do, Palatine?' I heard footsteps outside. 'Even my own people are deserting me now, and doubtless Etlae's ship is crammed with Sacri. What can two of us do against them?'

'Help save the Archipelago, perhaps? There's no way Sagantha can get out in time. Even if he himself is safe, she'll arrest the others and the crew. At least come with me, for their sake.'

Someone knocked on the door.

'Wait a moment,' I said. Then I spoke to Palatine again. 'I'll lose all respect if I go into hiding.'

'You'll give them hope. Come in!'

A marine came hesitantly into the room. 'I was told to escort you two to a safe place.'

Palatine glanced at me, a wry smile on her face. It seemed somebody else, at least, agreed with her. I looked around the room, my father's office, one last time. My eyes fell on the brooch on the desk, and at the last moment I picked it up and pinned it back on again.

'Lead on,' I told the marine. 'Out of the back gate, so fewer people see us.'

It was late in the evening and word of the approaching troops hadn't spread yet, so we didn't see anybody in the corridors as we ran through them, until we got to the first floor. Just before we reached the door, my cousin Messalus, a couple of years younger than me, came out of his room as we passed.

'What's going on?' he asked.

'The Domain are taking over the city,' I told him. 'There are too many of them for us to resist, and they've proclaimed me a heretic.'

'Are you?'

'Do you think so?'

'No,' he said slowly. 'I don't think so.'

'Then pass on the message through the House that I'm still here, even though the Domain may be in control, and that they won't win. Don't tell anyone who you saw me with or where I was going.'

'I won't. Promise.' My cousin went back into his room and we slipped out of the garden gate and into the street.

'Where are you taking us?' I asked the guard.

'Mezentus's house.'

'Are you crazy? Mezentus was paid by Foryth, though I hate to slander his memory.'

'He was, my lord, but his daughter never agreed with that. There's a hidden room in her house and it's easy to come and go. Besides, the Domain won't think of looking for you there.'

'It makes sense,' Palatine said. The captain of the guard had been efficient, I thought, but then a sudden dreadful fear struck me. How could I know he was loyal? What if he was going to sell me out as well? He'd been my father's trusted servant for twenty years; but so had the steward, and doubtless so had the harbour master who'd let Etlae in a few minutes ago.

What choice did I have?

We ran through the street and reached the back door of House Kuzawa, which was opened, and we went inside. The marine went back to his barracks to await further orders. I noticed that there were no people about in this House, either.

Once the door was shut, Mezentus's daughter, Ilda, turned to us and, much to my embarrassment, knelt before me.

'My lord, I hope my House will protect you, and I swear by Ranthas that *I* will stay loyal to you.'

I wasn't sure what to say, but I took her hand and pulled her gently up again.

'Thank you, Ilda.' She had curly brown hair and a lively, intelligent face.

'I'll show you where the room is.'

She led us up three flights of narrow panelled stairs and another half-flight, then pressed one of the cedarwood panels on the walls on the landing. It slid away to reveal a small room, simply furnished with a couple of narrow beds, a washtub and a chair. There were aether lights on the walls and a small window at one end.

'Why is this room here?' I asked, curious about its original purpose.

'My grandfather had it put in when he built the house, to store his money. My uncle then used it to entertain his mistresses, and after that my father put these beds in in case he ever had visitors he didn't want generally seen. Nobody in my House knows about it any more. These are the back stairs, very little used, so you can get out without being noticed too much. I'll make sure people keep out of this section. I'm sorry you have to share, but there's nothing I can do.'

She explained where everything was, then left us to go and report to her new House head, who'd doubtless be awake and demanding what was going on.

I looked out of the small window, and discovered that it looked out on to the main street, so we would have a perfect ringside view as the Domain's troops marched into the city.

They came about twenty minutes later, two platoons of armoured, helmeted warriors. One group wore the crimson and white of the Sacri, the other the black and green of Khalaman. Lexan's men. There must have been more of them in other parts of the city; you could get far more than two platoons on a manta for a short voyage, and two was in any case too few for the Domain to have been able to rely on in case of resistance.

The aether street lights cast only a faint, cold light, so I couldn't see any faces until another party came along bearing torches. Ten or twelve Sacri on foot ringed a group of Domain priests dressed in black and white, with cowls over their faces. I felt my skin prickle as they walked silently past, and was suddenly glad I hadn't stayed in the Palace. They were Inquisitors.

Behind the Inquisitors, a few moments later, came Lepidor's disarmed troops. Lexan's jubilant men were herding them back to their barracks. They looked downcast and dispirited, but none of them were injured. Such was the power of the Domain that they could force hundreds of men to break their clan oaths without putting up a fight.

The last to pass by were another small group of Sacri escorting four priests. One was dressed in the robes of a monastic order; I didn't recognize which one. Another was a fire-mage. The third was a hooded figure enveloped by a red robe, whose face I couldn't see. There was something familiar about him, though, something I couldn't put my finger on.

And the fourth was Etlae. I heard an indrawn hiss of breath from Palatine as she passed.

'Traitor!' Palatine said. 'So much for her being on our side.'

I didn't say anything, just watched her ride by in mute anguish. Another betrayal. Tanais had been right: nobody was who they seemed. I wondered for a moment whose side Tanais was on, whose side everybody was on. It didn't seem to be mine.

'Is there anyone we can trust?' I said to Palatine. She at least shared my blood, and I'd saved her life in that room the other night.

'We can't trust anyone absolutely. Hamilcar we trust because his profit's at stake here. You met Elassel in Pharassa, before any of this started. I think we can rely on her too. Besides, she can open doors and locks; that'll be useful. Sagantha, well, I'm not sure. I don't think he'd betray us while the Pharaoh's in danger. What about Tetricus?'

'I think so.' He'd been my friend for years, never once leaving me in the lurch, but I was even doubtful about his loyalty. 'The oceanographers would probably give me some help, because they're halfway heretics by trade.'

'We have to get all of these people in one place, decide what to do.'

'That's going to be difficult. We can't meet here, and there's nowhere else in the city we can go.'

'When Ilda next comes we'll ask her what's happened, who's been arrested. Sagantha won't have been, not unless this plot goes far deeper than I thought.'

'Etlae poisoned the Cambressian Exarch back at the beginning of all this,' I said, suddenly remembering the conversation I'd had with Sarhaddon in the park in Pharassa. 'She might think she can get away with it.'

'I can't see that. Poisoning an Exarch is one thing, but openly arresting an admiral? I don't think so, at least not for the moment. I think Sagantha will be free, but they'll have people following him. Hamilcar – well, we don't know.'

Ilda came back about half an hour later, swinging the door panel open suddenly and alarming both of us.

'Sorry to do that,' she said. She had a basket in one hand, which she put on one of the beds. 'I brought you some food, in case you're hungry.'

'What's happened?' Palatine asked her.

'That witch Etlae and her followers have taken over the Palace, the barracks and the harbour. They haven't posted men on the walls, because they don't seem to be worried about an attack by the natives. They arrested Atek, all the Archipelagans except Sagantha, the commander of the guard and the Council.'

'Not Hamilcar?'

'Hamilcar? Oh, Lord Barca. No, he's free to go where he wants. I heard Etlae was very polite to him.'

As she told us everything else she'd been able to find out – which wasn't very much, because Etlae had issued a curfew – I wondered at that. Yes, Hamilcar was a Merchant Lord, but a very minor one who'd probably be ruined by this. So why had Etlae let him go, and been so polite? Then I remembered. Hamilcar had mentioned that his guardian was quite high up in the Domain – and Etlae was almost at the top, and wielded enormous power. Hamilcar's guardian must be very important indeed. Could we trust *him*, then?

'Oh, and one last thing before I forget,' Ilda said as she was turning to go. 'Lexan's with them, the slug.'

So Lexan had come personally to oversee his triumph? All the architects of the plot – except Lord Foryth – were in Lepidor?

'You're right,' Palatine said when I told her. 'All of them here in once place. It means we still have a chance.'

'A chance to do what?'

'Turn the tables. Beat them at their own game. Now, where can we hold a Council of war?'

'We have to get word to everybody, never mind getting them in one place. And we can't send Ilda to do all that, it's too dangerous. Especially contacting people like Elassel.'

'You're too pessimistic.' Palatine got up from the bed she'd been sitting on and went over to look out of the window. 'The Domain control the Palace, the barracks and the harbour. I don't think we're safe anywhere else in the town. And I'm sure Hamilcar's being followed, even if Etlae and her people were polite to him.'

'Is there anywhere his watchers can't go?' I asked. 'Where they'll assume he can't be contacted?'

Palatine said nothing for a moment, then turned round and grinned.

'Cathan, what about a little more swimming?'

I groaned.

As darkness fell the next evening, I crouched in the lee of a small warehouse, waiting for a roving Sacri patrol to pass. Although most of them were defending the three crucial areas of Palace, harbour and barracks, as well as where the Archipelagan sailors and guards were imprisoned, there were enough of them roaming about to make life difficult. It had taken me ten minutes to get through the gate from the Palace quarter to the harbour quarter due to two of Lexan's marines who were checking everyone who went through against descriptions of me pinned on the walls. There were notices all over the city promising a king's ransom for anyone who brought in the 'heretic and worker in evil magic formerly known as Cathan, Count of Lepidor, now outlawed by His Majesty the King in the name of the Empire.' It also stated that anyone found harbouring me or my evil associate 'Paratine of Silvernia' would also be treated as a heretic. I wondered where they'd got their information from. At least some of the traitors were incompetent.

I'd spent the day in an even blacker depression than before, cooped up in the room while Palatine, who wasn't so well known, slipped out to make contact with the few people Ilda had found who still supported us. With luck, Tetricus, Elassel and Hamilcar would all be able to make it to the meeting point. We'd failed to get a message to Sagantha; he was too closely watched.

I pressed myself back further into the shadows beneath a stone ledge as the three Sacri went past, moving with the fluid grace of trained killers, their masked heads turning this way and that. They didn't see me, though.

I gave them enough time to get well up the next street before I dashed across the space between where I was and the moon-pool hut, up against the walls on the other side of the street. It was locked, but I always carried the key for the moon pools on me, along with keys for the Palace and, in my father's absence, for other major buildings. There was nobody to be seen as I let myself in and closed the door behind me. This wasn't the one I'd come up in on my previous expedition, but it was similar.

I collected a waterproof bag, some wetsilk diving clothes and two pieces of equipment from the store, then went down the ladder to the chamber below. I changed into the diving clothes, which were black and, as well as making me harder to see, would keep me slightly warmer. Then I put the clothes in the waterproof bag and strapped it onto my back, secured the pieces of equipment to my diving belt, and climbed down the ladder into the moon pool.

The water wasn't nearly as cold as it had been when I'd jumped into the stream, but I knew that it would be colder as I dived down towards Hamilcar's manta, on the third gantry. As I emerged from under the lip of the rock everything was suddenly much darker, and my eyes took a moment to adjust. To my left the hub loomed large, its lighted windows illuminating the water around. The surface was quite still, not the heaving maelstrom of my last night-time swim. And Ravenna had once said it was so peaceful.

As I swam down past the huge black shape of the *Emerald*, its cabins dark and unoccupied, I found myself thinking about Ravenna again, even though I'd told myself to forget her so as not to become too depressed. I had no idea whether she'd fallen into Etlae's hands or was still at large. I hoped she was free – I wouldn't want any mage to fall into the clutches of the Inquisition. Even one who'd hurt me as badly as she had. Damn her, why had she done it? What had possessed her?

A shape moved near me and I brought my thoughts back to the task in hand. I looked round and saw a couple of fish darting away. I was down below the first level now, swimming as far as I could from the hub in case anyone happened to look out of the window when I was near a spotlight.

I passed the second gantry. Ahead and below, Hamilcar's *Eryx* lay at her moorings on the third gantry, light streaming out from several cabin windows. I had drifted slightly off course, I realized as I approached, and I moved a little to the right, to come in just forward of the port wing, where there were no lighted windows.

When I was within touching distance of the manta's outer hull, I angled down and along, swimming just under the hull as it curved down to the belly of the manta. It seemed to take ages for me to reach the stern, but eventually the hull curved up away again, and I moved back until I was treading water by the outer doors of the port escape-sub bay. I swam along a few feet, until I found the opening side and the arrow that marked the latch, then unslung the pressure opener from round my waist, taking great care not to drop it, and fixed it onto the manta's hull over the seam.

A moment later there was a crack and a grumble as the door began to slide aside, revealing a faintly lit bay dominated by the shape of the escape sub. It only took one kick to propel myself to the surface, then I was breathing air again inside the *Eryx*. I hauled myself out onto the side, then changed out of my diving clothes, towelled myself down with a cloth I'd borrowed from Ilda, and put on my normal clothes again.

Everything had gone well so far, and the other three should be on their way by now. So long as our message had reached Hamilcar and he'd understood it.

I stowed my bag and wet diving clothes in a corner of the bay, then opened the door and strolled out into the ship. This was the cargo deck, below Engineering, so nobody was around. The whole crew were on the ship, but at this hour most of them would be in the mess hall, not wandering around.

If the *Eryx* had the same layout as the *Fenicia* and every other manta

I'd ever been on, Hamilcar's cabin would be on the upper deck, second door on the port side. That meant I had to get up two decks from here, which was hardly difficult. I walked along to the end of the corridor, where there was a ladder in an alcove leading up two flights. There was no one in Engineering, I saw as I climbed past it.

The crewmen must all have been elsewhere, because I saw nobody as I made my way along to Hamilcar's cabin and knocked on the door. Not that they'd have reported me, anyway: they were loyal to Hamilcar and not to Etlae. At least, I hoped so.

'Who's there?' came a voice from inside the cabin. I breathed a sigh of relief.

'The person who sent you that message.'

I heard a chair being pushed back and footsteps crossing the cabin. Then the door was flung open.

'Cathan!' Hamilcar said. 'How did you get here? Do come in.'

'I opened your port escape bay and climbed in from there. The others will be coming in the same way in a minute.'

'So your message did tell me to be on board my ship. I thought that was what it meant.'

'*Remember the Cape.* I was worried it was a bit too cryptic, but obviously it wasn't.'

'Well, it wasn't telling me to beware of pirates or that I'd be helped by black battle cruisers, so I assumed you meant that you were coming on board. I think we should go down to the bay and meet the others.'

A quarter of an hour later, all five of us were sitting in Hamilcar's cabin. Palatine didn't seem any the worse for a day of sneaking round and hiding in corners, Tetricus was his usual lugubrious self, Hamilcar looked as worried as usual and Elassel was massaging her wrists with a wet cloth.

'Before we start,' she said, 'let me make one thing clear. If we win, I get to look after Midian afterwards.'

'Granted,' I said; it was probably a purely academic point. But Elassel deserved it. The moment the Sacri had landed, Midian had had her arrested, chained up and locked in one of the cells below the Temple, accused of aiding and abetting me. It had taken her hours to get free, because she'd only been wearing a nightshirt and most of her escape tools were in various parts of her daytime clothes. Now she was wearing clothes borrowed from Ilda's cousin that were slightly too big.

'I'm very impressed that you've all managed to get here,' Hamilcar said, 'but do you have any plans, or are you just escaping?'

Palatine looked affronted, almost angry. 'Escaping? Of course not.' She explained the idea we'd come up with earlier.

The others looked doubtful.

'There are only five of us,' Tetricus pointed out, 'and more than a hundred Sacri and enemy marines.'

'We only have to worry about the Palace. That's where Etlae and Lexan are.'

'There are about forty guarding the Palace. I wouldn't like to bet on eight to one.'

'You're a real ray of sunshine today, aren't you?' Elassel said to Tetricus, her open manner gone. I noticed Hamilcar's eyes kept straying across to her.

'It's better to be realistic.'

'And do remember they can call for reinforcements from the harbour, say, if there's a serious threat,' Hamilcar said. I had no illusions about why he was helping us; the moment she felt secure, Etlae would break his contract with Lepidor and put in someone from another House as Count; the new man would award it to Foryth. That would probably ruin House Barca, even if it was on the verge of recovery with other customers waiting. A Great House in the Domain's black books was not going to survive long. On the other hand, something wasn't right here.

'Who exactly is your guardian, Hamilcar?' I asked him. 'Etlae was very polite to you.'

The Tanethan looked down at the floor for a minute.

'I don't want any of you to take this the wrong way and think I'm on the other side. I told you earlier on that as far as he's concerned I'm a good son of the Domain and have never been near a heretical text. I don't agree with what he does. My guardian is Lachazzar.'

'The Prime? Old Hell's Cook himself?' Tetricus said savagely. I hadn't heard that epithet before, but it sounded very apt for a man who loved nothing more than sending people to the stake.

'Yes. My father saved his life once, so he feels he has an obligation to my family. Nothing more.'

'I believe you,' Palatine said. Then she turned to the rest of us: 'I lived in his House for three months, and I swear to you he's telling the truth.'

'I'll accept that,' Tetricus said. He seemed to have fallen under Palatine's spell the way everyone at the Citadel had.

'To get back to the problem in hand, what about evening the odds somewhat?' said Palatine.

'How?'

'The barracks are too close to the Palace and too heavily guarded, but the Archipelagan sailors and marines are locked in a warehouse with only a couple of Lexan's men guarding them. They're relying on strong walls and bolts to keep them in. There's nowhere for them to go even if they did escape.'

'But there are only about thirty of them,' Tetricus said. 'They'd be outnumbered, and besides, they aren't as good as the Sacri who'll be defending the Palace.'

'We need to balance things a little. And it won't work if they can get reinforcements.'

There was silence, and I saw the others lost in thought. What could give us a chance? We couldn't really afford a diversionary attack, and those Sacri were so good! The only soldiers in the world said to equal them were the Thetian Ninth Legion, the Imperial Guard, in the old days. And the Sacri were probably more dedicated to their cause than the Ninth had been. How could we even the odds against a band of rabid fanatics who fought like demons and were supported by fire-magic? They were almost a force of nature.

Force of nature? *You can no more stop the storms than the ocean currents . . . it would need three elements working together, Water and Wind and Shadow.* Her voice rang in my mind. Maybe it would need three elements, but what could I do with two? The Sacri hated water; what if I was to increase the power of a storm using my magic, so that it was too strong for the Domain's storm defences and flooded the city?

'I may have an idea,' I said, and tentatively explained my thinking.

'We don't know anything about magic,' Palatine said. 'Surely no one can control the storms, though?'

'I'm not planning to control them, merely harness some of their power. I'm a water-mage, I can make the storm worse by bringing down more water from the sky. The Sacri will keep out of the rain, and in the terrible conditions they won't know their way around. The

Archipelagans have been in the city for a month, they'll at least know where they're going.'

'But even when they arrive at the Palace, what then? The Sacri inside will be fresh and dry, and they can use the people they've taken prisoner as hostages.'

'I should be able to direct it against the Palace, flood some of it.' I was talking about flooding my own home just to gain a slight advantage, but was there another way?

'The sky's clear at the moment,' Elassel said. 'I don't think we can hang around too long.'

'We can probably adapt some of the oceanographic equipment to detect another storm coming. There'll be one within the next few hours,' Tetricus said.

'How can you be so sure?' Elassel asked.

'It's very humid outside, much more so than this morning. That's a sure sign of a storm.'

'Cathan and Tetricus, then, go to the oceanographers' guild to look for the storm,' Palatine said, 'and then back to the hideout. Elassel and I will set everything up for the Archipelagans to break out. And Hamilcar . . . Hamilcar goes up to the Palace, has dinner with Etlae, and makes himself a pain in the neck. Preferably leaves a few doors unlocked.' Her expression was grave. 'If there's no storm this evening, we all go back to our hidey-holes and wait until there is.'

'You won't need to wait,' Tetricus said.

When we finally reached the Oceanographic Guild building, having done our marathon swim and journey across town in reverse, it was deserted. Both of us had keys, though, and letting ourselves in wasn't the problem. What would be difficult was using instruments designed to look at the ocean to predict a storm.

We didn't turn the light on in the darkened lobby but crept up the stairs past cabinets and piles of equipment. I hadn't been in here for several days, and twice I knocked something over with a clang that I was sure must have woken the whole neighbourhood. But there were no shouts in the street outside, no Sacri patrols running towards us at the double.

'You should watch where you're treading,' Tetricus said helpfully.

'You shouldn't leave so much equipment lying around. Where's the Master been?'

'Laid up with a twisted ankle.'

'No wonder it's a mess.'

The sensor room was on the second floor of the building, almost in the centre, with only two small windows. We piled as much as we could up against them before we turned on the light and activated the consoles. They were arranged in a circle facing outwards, with an aether-imaging tank in the middle. We sat down and Tetricus called up the image of Lepidor and its surroundings, on the largest scale we could get. There were observation and aether-imaging stations on the peaks of the mountain around the town, and one, walled up behind the rock, on the peak of the tallest mountain, which faced over the continent. That was the one that gave advance warning of storms.

I pulled back the view until it included the cloud patterns that could be seen – high, wispy clouds in the upper atmosphere, light blue against the darkening blue sky. There were no signs of thundercloud build-ups to the east.

'It's not that close, then,' was all Tetricus said.

'Let's look at the pressure and humidity readings from the stations.' I called these up on the chart and moved the view in closer.

The oceanographic consoles worked in the same way as normal aether pads, controlled by the user's mind, but certain patterns had been stored in them for convenience, activated by separate buttons down the sides. Tetricus pressed one of these and the real-colour view of the city changed, replaced by a false-colour image showing the readings graphically.

'There it is,' he said triumphantly. 'I told you.'

The pressure was much lower than normal, and humidity levels were much higher. Sure signs of an approaching storm.

'Charge?' I asked.

There was a pause, and then another image came up, from a different set of equipment.

'Positive, very positive. I estimate—' he zoomed out again '—about three hours.'

Three hours. I hoped everything was going as we'd planned it. In three hours I would unleash the full fury of a storm against my own city, to gain back the inheritance that I'd lost through my own rashness and incompetence. Elassel had told me, from overhearing Midian, that although the letter to Canadrath had got through, the enemy had somehow learned of its content and launched the attack earlier than intended. Something else that was my fault.

Now we were in the hands of the storms.

Chapter XXX

We shut down the consoles, turned off the lights and unblocked the windows before creeping back downstairs. This time I didn't trip over any of the clutter, and we managed to get to the door without making a sound.

'What do I do now?' Tetricus asked, peering through the windows out onto the street to check whether there was anyone coming.

'Go back home and keep out of the way,' I said.

He looked stricken. 'Can't I be any more use?'

'Tetricus,' I said gently, 'you're not a soldier, you haven't been trained. We'll be fighting some of the best warriors in the world against the odds – you wouldn't last a minute.'

'Isn't there anything else I could do?'

'Fighting and magic are the only things left to do. You've played your part, and I'm grateful.'

He nodded sadly. 'Thank you. I'll go back, but I wish I could do more. It'll be better if I go out of the back door. Good luck, Cathan. May whatever god you worship be with you.' He turned away and went down the passageway, leaving me alone in the hallway.

I waited until he'd had time to get away, checked the street once more, and then let myself out. Luckily this wasn't one of the main thoroughfares, but a side street that curved sharply just beyond the oceanographers' building, giving me the cover I needed to slip across without being seen, into the maze of alleyways between the Houses. I was heading back to the hideout in the Palace Quarter now; I hoped they hadn't increased the guards on the gates.

I heard voices off to my left, and ducked down an alley in the opposite direction, towards the harbour. That was where the Archipelagan delegates were being held, if Ilda's intelligence had been correct. Their guards were in a warehouse a hundred yards further along.

I emerged into a side street that was far too straight for my liking, darted across it and into the shadows of an archway connecting two parts of a House mansion. The sky was dark blue and fading to black, and the aether lights cast only a faint illumination. I was only a block away from the harbour; this wasn't the way I wanted to go. I cursed my sense of direction, which seemed to have deserted me at the moment when it was most needed.

I heard the tramp of booted feet, and looked around for the nearest cover. There was a stone cistern a few yards along, supported on some stone pillars, with a small space underneath it. For once grateful that I was so small, I ran over and wedged myself in as best I could, until I couldn't go any further back. It might be a struggle getting out, but at least I wouldn't be spotted by the patrol as they went past. There wasn't enough light for that.

I saw their feet as they went by, black boots with crimson trousers above them. Sacri, four of them. They seemed to carry a chill with them as they passed, and it was a couple of minutes before I was sure that they were out of earshot.

I twisted round slightly to get out, and felt a momentary panic when I found I couldn't move; my legs were hard against the stonework. I shifted round a little bit more, and this time managed to get enough leverage to push myself out. Once I was standing in the street I brushed myself down and resolved to look for a bigger space next time.

I was so nervous as I made my way further down the alley and up the next one, bare stone with no windows on the ground floor like all the rest, that I kept jumping at shadows. A black cat jumped down from a ledge and ran along the wall; I nearly flew at it with a dagger before I realized my mistake.

'Sorry, cat.' Was I going mad, I wondered, like Orosius? Jumping at shadows, apologizing to cats while I was creeping down the street trying to evade Sacri patrols. Still, it *was* a black cat, a cat of Shadow. I took that as a good omen.

I was still going parallel to the harbour when I reached the next straight side street and cautiously stuck my head out to look in both directions. Almost immediately I pulled back and retreated a few steps into the shadows. There was an unofficial roadblock further up; four of Lexan's men stood surveying the street in both directions. I stood stock-still for a few moments, waiting for the sound of footsteps announcing that they'd seen me, but they didn't come. I cursed; now I'd have to retrace my steps.

I turned back and made my way through the back street again, still on edge. Another patrol passed; again, four of Lexan's men. There seemed to be an awful lot of people in this area all of a sudden. Had somebody tipped them off? My stomach was already clenched and tight, and the thought that one of the people at the Council might have been a traitor made it even worse.

I felt dizzy suddenly and clutched at a wall for support. I'd eaten very little all day, and now I was suffering the consequences. Little as I wanted to, I'd have to eat something when I got back to the hideout, or I'd be in no condition to do the storm-summoning later on. Come to think of it, where was I going to do it from? Was it something I could do from inside, or did I have to be outside? I hoped it was inside, because otherwise I'd get completely sodden.

I reached an intersection of four back alleys and was just about to look out into the one I was crossing to see if it was safe when a shadow moved under a street light in the one ahead of me. I moved back into a blank doorway on the more shadowed side, away from the street light, and looked again. There was definitely someone there, but whoever it was wasn't facing me.

The figure moved, and I heard clothing rustle. I could see his faint shadow on the wall. He was taking something out of his belt: it looked like a small crossbow, one of the double-bolted type that was used at the beginning of a fight and then discarded. There was what looked like a sword hilt under the cloak.

Then the figure moved round, and I caught my breath sharply. It wasn't a he, it was a she, and there was only one woman in Lepidor who'd know how to use a crossbow and was skulking around like this. So Ravenna hadn't been captured after all. But what was she doing? She was facing down towards the harbour, and loading a crossbow. That must mean she meant to fight, but why? She didn't stand a chance against the Sacri. She moved further along the alley and drew her sword.

Suddenly there was shouting and noises of a struggle off to my right.

Steel rang on steel, breaking the night's silence with its harsh tones.

'You're under arrest!' someone shouted. More noises, then silence. I moved along to the corner, kneeled down, and risked a look round at knee height.

Three Sacri, possibly the ones who'd passed me earlier – they all looked the same in daytime, let alone at this time of night – were tying up two prisoners, while another Sacrus leaned against a wall, clutching his arm. I recognized the prisoners instantly: Palatine and Elassel.

I crawled backwards and stood up again, wondering what I was to do. If they were here they were obviously on their way back from dealing with the prison, but I couldn't let them fall into the hands of the Sacri. With my water- and shadow-magic I could probably deal with the four Sacri and get the girls away before anybody else could respond.

But that would mean letting Ravenna make her attack, which would be nothing less than suicide. After what she'd said to me, I was loath to help her, but if that meant letting her die . . . I had only seconds to decide, I realized, as one of the Sacri barked a command and they began to move off towards the harbour.

Palatine and Elassel would survive in the clutches of the Sacri. I wasn't going to have Ravenna's death on my conscience, and I realized I wouldn't be debating the point if it was Palatine or Elassel about to make a suicide run.

I darted across the alleyway, using all the stealth I'd been taught at the Citadel, and covered the dozen or so yards from there to Ravenna within a couple of seconds, just as she lifted her sword and was about to move forward. I encircled her shoulders with one arm, covered her mouth with the other, and dragged her back into an alcove as quickly as I could. After the initial shock, she started struggling, but I managed to knock the sword out of her hand, while her other arm was too tightly pinioned for her to fire the crossbow at me. She struggled like a wild thing, and I felt my grip on her weakening; muscle for muscle, she was probably almost as strong as I was.

'It's me, you fool,' I hissed in her ear, pulling her back as far into the darkness as I could before letting go of her.

She twisted round and punched me in the stomach, and as I doubled over she retrieved the crossbow and pointed it at me, moving over to sit on the other side of the alcove as I gasped for breath.

'You interfering fool,' she hissed, her face distorted by rage. 'I thought I made myself clear last time.'

'I wasn't . . . going to stand . . . by . . . and watch you . . . commit suicide,' I said, between gulps of air. The muscles in my stomach had all been so tense that her blow hadn't hurt as much as it might have done.

'I was trying to rescue the prisoners, you imbecile!'

'On your own . . . without help? Suicide!'

She kept the crossbow levelled at me. 'If I want to commit suicide that is my own decision. I heard that you tried yourself earlier on.'

She must have heard, somehow, about my foolish notion of staying in the Palace to get captured when Etlae and Lexan first arrived.

'Please don't point that at me.' I managed to sit upright again. 'It's got a hair-trigger, and I'd rather not die because you shot me by accident.'

Sullenly she put the crossbow down, looking at me harshly all the while.

'I have the right to die in defence of my people the same way you do.' *My people*: it was a strange thing for her to say, more like a politician's statement than a mage's.

'Why?' I said. 'It's so pointless.' I wondered why I was saying this, I who less than twenty-four hours ago had been prepared to do just that.

'What other alternative is there? To skulk around this godsforsaken city, hiding until some other traitor hands me over to the Domain? Your clan is so full of traitors, it's unbelievable.'

'And I suppose your clansmen are all shining examples of honour,' I said acidly. 'How have you stayed free this long, then?'

'The House who gave me lodging after you so kindly threw me out of the Palace helped me, even if no one else did.'

'Are you surprised I threw you out, after what you said?'

'You're supposed to be my host.'

'The laws of hospitality only go so far. And obviously, there are still people who're loyal.'

'I can't see what there is to be loyal to. We've lost anyway.'

We've lost. At least she still had some allegiance to our side.

'Those of us who haven't been trying to commit suicide are trying to do something. Maybe if you'd been less quick to give up you might have been able to help.'

'Oh, so what is this great idea? Another of Palatine's masterpieces like the letter that brought all this down on us?'

'That was my fault, not hers.'

'Take the blame, then. But how exactly do three or four people plan to defeat a hundred or more?'

I heard the stamp of a patrol marching down the main street, stopping to question someone mad enough to still be out on the streets at this hour.

'I'd be happy to. But could we first call a truce and get out of here? There are a sight too many Sacri walking around.'

'Agreed,' she said, in her usual frosty voice.

Then my heart almost stopped as the patrol turned at the entrance to the alley and started marching down towards us.

Ravenna pushed the sword and the crossbow into the darkest corner and pulled me after them.

'Sorry, if this offends you,' she muttered. 'Play along.'

She kissed me, and I realized what she was doing and put my arms around her under the cloak. I hoped that this would work, that I wouldn't have to use my magic.

I heard the footsteps stop, and then just one man's, but quieter; I guessed they'd sent one soldier on ahead to check the alley. These were Lexan's troops, then. I was facing the wall and Ravenna's face was about all I could see, so I had no way of telling what he was doing.

'Just a pair of lovebirds, Corporal.' He hissed to us. 'You two better get inside, those red automata don't understand about things like this.'

He walked back up the street again and I heard them marching away. I broke free of Ravenna and stared at her uncertainly for a moment. 'We'd best be going.'

She nodded, slid the sword back into his scabbard and hung the crossbow at her belt again, after putting on the catch.

'Where is your hideout?'

'House Kuzawa. Mezentus's daughter didn't share her father's sympathies.'

'You'll know the quickest way there. I told my House I wouldn't be coming back, so they aren't expecting me.'

Listening to her, I realized for the first time that she sounded as depressed as I'd been earlier, and I wondered why. She hadn't lost a city, and she'd been the one screaming at me.

'We don't fight unless we absolutely have to.'

'Agreed.' I hoped Palatine and Elassel were all right.

We set out through the alleys towards the town. This time I headed away from the harbour by the most direct route possible, heading over towards the walls against the Land Quarter. It was the best way to avoid the straighter streets where we could be easily spotted, but it was no less nerve-racking for that. Twice more patrols came too close for comfort but both times we managed to find places to hide.

That had been the easy bit, I knew. Now we'd reached the end of the last alley immediately before the gates. It was after curfew, and no one was supposed to go through. They'd shut the gates, blocking off all three of the arches that led through into the Palace Quarter.

'What do we do now?' Ravenna whispered tensely.

They'd have closed all the towers along the walls as well, so there'd be no going back that way. And if the gates were closed, it would take precious minutes for the Archipelagans to get through when the time came to make their attack. I hoped Palatine hadn't told them to wait for her.

Well, it would alert the mage and bring loads of Sacri rushing to this gate, but I was going to have to use magic. With luck, we'd have time to slip into the alleys on the other side of the gate.

I checked that I couldn't see anyone in the street, walked up to the lock and put my hand on it. Emptying my mind was easier this time, and it was the work of the moment to dissolve the bolts with shadowfire.

'Very subtle,' Ravenna said as she sauntered up behind me, grabbing my shoulder before I could walk in. 'Do these gates have boulder defences?'

I'd forgotten about those. There were holes in the ceiling, above which a roof-space held a couple of tons of rubble to be released on unwary enemies.

'They might have rigged them up.' She directed more shadowfire at the bolts and bars on the gate on the other side, disintegrating them as well. 'Now run for it.'

We sprinted through the six yards or so of the tunnel, pushed open the door and then emerged into the triangular plaza at the other end. Again, we didn't see any guards, but I could hear shouting coming up from the Palace end. We plunged into the nearest alleyway and didn't stop running until we reached the first intersection.

'Never try to creep into the Holy City,' Ravenna said, taking gulps of the evening air, much warmer than usual; another sign of the approaching storm. 'At least, not without an army.'

'Kuzawa mansion is just up here,' I said, pointing to the right. 'Ilda will have left the key in place for us.'

'Who's Ilda?' she asked warily.

'Mezentus's daughter.'

We checked for more patrols before setting off again. There didn't seem to be as many patrols in this area. That was odd, given that this was where their headquarters were, their most important spot. Why were so many people down by the harbour – had they been tipped off?

We reached House Kuzawa without further incident, and we didn't meet anybody inside on our way up. I hadn't realized how tired I was feeling after all that swimming and creeping around; I slumped down on the bed and leaned against the wall. Ravenna pulled her cloak off, unbelted the weapons and sat down on the other bed. The windows had been open all day; I pulled them both to, so that our voices couldn't be heard from below by the men running past to investigate the magic at the gate.

There was an awkward silence.

'Thank you,' Ravenna said, 'for saving my life.'

'Will I ever get an apology for what you said the other day?' I wasn't going to let that go.

'The fault's not all mine there. Maybe I overreacted, but I'm not going to be blamed entirely.'

Anger flared up in me again. 'So tell me, for Thetis's sake, what did I say to offend you?'

'I think you know.'

'No, I don't. Perhaps you'd care to enlighten me.'

'Blaming me for letting your magic out, and then that pretence of asking my help.'

'It wasn't a pretence. I didn't know what to do.' I was as confused as ever; I just couldn't understand what her grudge was.

'You didn't know what to do? Someone of your powers? While the rest of us mortals take years to learn our magic, you can just sail through a year of lessons and call up tidal waves by snapping your fingers.'

And at last I realized what it had been all about, what she'd meant with that savage attack on the Tar'Conanturs. She was jealous of me. I'd been so blind; I'd never imagined there was anything to be jealous of.

She must have seen the belated realization on my face.

'You really didn't know, did you? You didn't see.'

'You seem to think I'm far better than I actually am. I'm not some kind of demigod.'

'I've been learning how to use magic since I was seven years old. I've been to two Citadels, I've learned from the best mages of Shadow and Wind who are alive. You can use Water without even being taught, there's so much of it swimming in your blood. You must be at least half elemental, if not more, and to use Shadow that well you must have some of that too. Things I spent years working on you can do without thinking.'

How that envy must have been gnawing at her over the past year. And I'd always been so much in awe of her, the way she used her magic so much more smoothly than I did.

She had hurt me, but now I understood why my hatred for her suddenly faded away as if it had never existed. I banished it from my mind and told myself it would never return.

'I should be apologizing to you, then,' I said softly.

'No, you shouldn't. It was no fault of yours, and I'm so terribly sorry for what I said. I meant it then, but I don't mean it any more.'

'Forget it, then?'

'Yes.' We embraced, and for the first time it was genuine.

'So what is your plan?' she whispered.

A moment later, when we sat down again, I explained it, and what had happened so far.

'It's rather desperate,' she said. 'If Palatine and Elassel have been taken, will the prisoners still break out?'

'I thought about that. I think we have to assume they will.'

'Do you think we should go and check?'

I thought for a moment. 'No, too dangerous. There's no way we'll be able to get through the gate again; this time they'll have men hiding in the gatehouse. Maybe I can direct the flood towards the gates as well.'

'Even you can't handle the kind of power you're talking about that way. You have no wind magic, which would deal with the gatehouse.'

'You have that, but you don't have the water magic. We don't have any way to merge our powers.'

'But we do.' She smiled. 'We've linked before to direct our magic. There's no reason why we shouldn't be able to do it again.'

'But that was always internal direction.'

'No reason we can't do it externally.' Her eyes were shining. 'Cathan, we can do something nobody in the history of Aquasilva has done before. With Shadow, Water and Wind between us, we can control the storms themselves.'

'But the weather system, won't we be disrupting it?'

'Not now, all we'll be doing will be harnessing the power of this storm, when it comes, for our own ends. We aren't calling up a storm or changing the weather.'

'But if the storm unleashes its full force on Lepidor, there won't be enough of it left to go on out over the ocean, and that'll affect the climate.'

'Do you or do you not want to retake your city?'

'Of course I want to retake it. But if the atmosphere's anything like the oceans, then anything we do here could kill thousands of people elsewhere.'

'Are you sure of that?'

'We can only guess.'

'Guess. On the other hand, it's a certainty that if we *don't* retake the city, all of us are going to die and any new hope for the heresy dies with us. And your people will end up under the benevolent—' she spat the words out '—rule of Midian's puppet.'

'Fine, all right. I see your point. But let's not use too much of the storm's energy.'

'There must be so much power in those clouds it would take a legion of mages to deplete them.'

'You said yourself, I'm a legion all on my own.'

'I didn't mean it literally. Orosius may be, but you haven't got his kind of power. I hope.'

'He probably has far more elemental blood than I have.'

'I wouldn't count on it. I don't think it's possible to have more than a certain amount without becoming an actual elemental, and you've got far too much for your own good.'

'Could we just go back to the plan? How exactly are we going to do this? And where from, come to think of it?'

'How long have we got?'

'About two hours, by my reckoning.'

'I don't think we can really tell how we're going to do it until we try. You've never used water from the clouds before, have you?'

'No, only sea water.'

'I should think the principles are the same. The clouds are made of water, so I'd think all you have to do is summon as much of it here as possible. I'll use the wind to channel it to the place we want.'

'The Palace, the gatehouse, and all the rest in the streets to drench the Sacri. Where does the Shadow come in, exactly? You know more about the theory of magic than I do.'

'You need the Shadow even to begin to work with the storms. The Provost at the Citadel of Wind explained it once, that the atmosphere is tainted with Shadow-magic from the spells cast during the War. It's a sort of magical ghost, but it does strange things if you try to touch it with any other kind of magic. People went mad that way in the early years.'

'Can you be careful not to slow the Archipelagans down too much? Everything depends on their getting to the Palace before the Sacri have had time to recover and improvise a way to keep themselves dry.'

'You look after your element, and I'll look after mine,' Ravenna said reproachfully. But she was smiling.

'And where are we going to be, exactly?'

'Outside. We have to be, or it'll make it even more difficult. Doing something like this for the first time, we've really got to be able to see what's going on.'

'We can't exactly stand in the street and do it. We ought to be on a rooftop.'

'Not this one. We don't want Kuzawa to be punished if this fails. I think from a strategic point of view, the Palace roof is best.'

An hour and a half later, leaving Ravenna's sword behind but taking with us daggers and crossbows, we swathed ourselves in storm cloaks and left the hideout for the last time. Either we'd succeed and regain control of the Palace, or we'd fail and fall into the clutches of the Domain. I only hoped that Midian hadn't taken the opportunity to exact revenge on Elassel.

The wind was getting up, and the air temperature had dropped noticeably; this was to be a cold storm, not a warm one. Not surprising, really; it was mid-autumn, and sometime in the next couple of months winter would descend on us, for a month or two of icy hell. I was glad it wasn't already winter, or there was no way we could have been skulking around the streets like this.

Although all the doors and gates into the Palace were guarded, we didn't have any problem getting past them and into the garden; they didn't have people patrolling the wall circuit. The patrols had disappeared from the streets, presumably pulled back to keep them fresh and out of the storm. By the time we reached the garden gate, it had been full darkness for hours. The lamps thoughtfully left on to help the guards also showed me where one of my ways back into the Palace was: up a buttress on the inside of the city wall – with hand- and footholds hammered in years ago – and down a rope on the inside. Mercifully we were out of sight of anyone at the gate.

We landed softly in a flower bed at the far end of the garden. It was pitch dark here, and there were almost no lights on along the garden side of the Palace, except for the lamps burning where Lexan's marines stood as sentries, one by the outer gate and one by each inner door. They were positioned so each one could be seen by another, I noticed, except the one over to the left who was out of sight because the door was in an inconvenient place.

'That one over there.' I pointed in that direction. While it was unlikely that the sentries could see us out on the lawn, I wasn't taking any chances. We skirted round the edge of it, keeping clear of any loose twigs or shrubs that would rustle and give us away.

However, just past the end of the building itself our cover gave out and we'd have to step into the light. I didn't want to kill anybody, but it was too far to go without being noticed.

I moved back into the shadows of an outbuilding before aiming the crossbow at the man's head. I kept my finger off the trigger for the moment.

It was as well that I did. Seconds later, a sudden brief light flared up and there was a tremendous noise from the direction of the harbour. The marine almost jumped out of his skin.

'What was that?' one of the others yelled from around the corner.

'Beats me.'

There was another thunderclap, and as my ears recovered I heard shouting in the Palace.

'D'you think we're being attacked?' shouted the guard I'd been aiming at. He sounded very young, maybe even younger than me.

'Come here, I can see it!' called the one over on the far side. 'Something burning down at the harbour.'

I watched in disbelief as the others abandoned their positions and ran over to the other side.

'It seems Fate is with us,' Ravenna said as we ran across to the door, which was locked. Not for long, though, once it had met a bolt of shadowfire.

The spiral staircase inside ran up within its own little section, with doors on to the landings every so often. Though we heard shouting as we passed, and the noise of people running down the corridors, nobody saw us or stopped us.

As we emerged onto the parapet amid the trees of the roof garden, I looked over towards the harbour and saw what it was. A fishing schooner was on fire, and above the undersea harbour drifted the unmistakable shape of a manta, illuminated from below by pulse charges and aether torpedoes detonating against its hull. One wing was down in the water; it looked heavily damaged. It had to be the manta Etlae had arrived in.

Then the firing broke off, and I saw the dark water furrowed by the wake of something else moving just below the surface.

Hamilcar wouldn't do something like that, he was too sensible, and there was nobody else free. Somehow, without needing to be told, I knew that the manta leaving harbour was the *Emerald*, and Tetricus was on board.

Chapter XXXI

I didn't have time to admire the view any further. A few yards along, a Sacri sentry stood, watching the harbour impassively from beneath his mask, his cloak blowing in the wind. This time we wouldn't be so lucky. The man turned and reached for his sword.

He never made it. Ravenna had taken the crossbow before she went up, and as the Sacri moved she flipped the catch off and fired. A red stain blossomed on his surcoat and he looked down at the bolt that had pierced his armour. Jerkily he fell to his knees and then forward onto his face, his limbs twitching. She must have hit him in the heart, because he stopped moving a moment later.

'Take that, you butchering bastard,' Ravenna said in a broken tone, and as I looked at her face I realized she was crying. She was stretched almost to her limit.

'What is it?' I put my arm around her shoulders and took the crossbow from her to put its catch back on.

'I hate them,' she said, her control suddenly breaking down. 'My brother. They killed him, and he was only seven.'

Sweet Thetis, I'd had no idea! She clung to me for a moment, sobbing into my shoulder, and I just stood there. There wasn't anything I could say.

When she broke away again she brushed her face with the sleeve of her shirt.

'Thank you.' She didn't say what for.

I pulled my cloak tighter around me; the wind was getting up, and the sky overhead was entirely covered by clouds. In the light from the harbour, I could see a column of people coming up the main street.

'Get down, quickly. We're too visible up here,' Ravenna hissed.

'It's pitch dark,' I objected, but crouched down so I could just see over the parapet. I heard the first faint patter of rain on the slates of roof sections behind us. The garden was specially designed to collect water below the soil and funnel off excess down the storm drains, thus ensuring the extra weight didn't bring the building down every time it rained.

I noticed for the first time a column of people coming up the street; they were the Archipelagan delegation, escorted by ten or twelve Sacri. Their hands had been tied behind them and even from this distance, by the aether lights in the street, I could see the despair on their faces. A number of Sacri and Lexan's marines ran past, heading for the harbour.

'I wonder why she wants them up in the Palace,' Ravenna said, putting up the hood of her storm cloak and pulling the cloth mask over her lower face, so that only her eyes were visible. I did the same; it restricted vision and movement but stopped water from running down our faces and necks and completely soaking us. I unfastened the sleeves as well, slid my hands into them and did up the front. We looked like a pair of Silvernian yeti now. A pair of Silvernian yeti about to unleash on Lepidor the worst storm it had ever known.

There was a muted blue flare all around as the city's aether shields went up, shields that would protect Lepidor from the worst of natural storms – but not from our magic.

We watched in frustration, unable to intervene, as the column made its way up the street and into the Palace courtyard. The gates were closed behind them, and the Sacri retreated into the guardroom where they could watch the gates and keep out of the storm. It was pointless to keep them outside; attacks during storms were too impractical.

It was raining hard enough now for me to feel the drops through my storm cloak, and there was the occasional lightning flash and rumble of thunder. I went over to the door that had given us access and jammed it closed as best I could, while Ravenna did the same with the other door. We'd have a problem if some Sacri came up looking for their friend, though I hoped that he wouldn't be missed in the mêlée.

The light from the harbour had died down now; the burning fishing sloop was gutted, the fire nearly down to its waterline. The manta that Tetricus, if it was him, had fired at had been rescued and was diving, heading out to sea. I hoped that the *Emerald* had enough of a start to get to Kula without being caught.

The storm was getting into its full stride; the lighting flashes over the mountains were becoming more frequent and the rain was coming down in sheets. We wedged ourselves between two trees, hidden from the doors by one of the sections of tiled roof, moss-covered and browned by the elements. We were having to hold on to each other for support, and our cloaks were dripping. It was a fair bet that nobody could stop us now.

Ravenna created a barrier of Air around us, to shield us from some of the worst effects of the wind and rain. The wind eased enough for us to stand up unaided.

'It's all I've got the power for,' she said. 'Ready?'

I nodded. 'Ready.'

We took each other's hands, folding the ends of the storm cloaks over each other to keep out the rain. I emptied my mind, feeling my consciousness floating in the black void as awareness of the outer world faded, and then I initiated the link with Ravenna.

It was something which to the best of my knowledge no one except a mind-mage had ever done, establishing a stable mind-link with some-body else to combine powers. I felt our minds come together, and with that, a sudden feeling of awareness again, as the void faded. We could see suddenly far beyond the darkness of the rooftops; it was more like floating above the city, with a perfect view of everything, despite the blackness of the night and the squalling rain.

The part of the joined entity that was still me heard the sudden outcry in the throne room as the mage, in dismay, felt the magic gathering. I ignored his consternation and reached up to the clouds, piled high above us, deck upon deck upon deck, miles into the atmosphere. To the west of us, as the storm front headed out over the endless ocean, huge stacks rose up with dizzying speed, rearing up like huge avalanches in the sky. To the east, though, was where I would get the water from. Hundreds, thousands of miles of clouds, a storm-belt full of them, all heading towards us.

The Domain defences first, Ravenna's mind said. In the Storm shrine at the centre of the Temple, Midian's deputy stood with his hands on the ruby orb, above a flamewood furnace, that focused the power of Fire to beat the storms back. Beside him two acolytes stood warily, observing.

I reached out to the ocean, gathering energy from its limitless reservoir. More elemental power there than all the fires that had ever existed in all the world. I didn't have my staff, which would have helped, but somehow it didn't seem necessary. As I brought together the raw power straight from the sea its exhilarating energy rushed through me, until I could almost hear my blood singing.

With my enhanced shadowsight, I could see the lines of Fire-magic stretching out from the Temple to reinforce the shields across the city: faint, oscillating traces of power. I drew my will together and sent it along one of the lines as hard as I could, rushing faster than I could have followed it down into the Temple. The ruby briefly flared red, then shattered, unable to cope with the strain. A blue light flared in the priest's face and he screamed, falling backwards as the acolytes looked on in wide-eyed shock.

'What?' I heard a shout from the Palace below, a shout of rage, Etlae shrieking at the mage in the throne room.

'They're using too much power, Your Grace.'

Across the city the curtain of rain thickened, and I saw the trees and plants of the roof gardens bending even more with the wind. A few loose objects flew off, carried hundreds of yards across the city in seconds.

Brilliantly done.

Let's show them.

I turned my attention away from the city, back up to the clouds, as Ravenna's power came into play. All around us, on the mountain slopes and over the sea, the rain was sucked away from its fall, into a vortex concentrated over the gatehouse between the harbour and Palace quarters. I pulled as much down from the clouds and up from the sea as well, drawing on the darkness around us for good measure.

Tons of water, blown by a wind of hundreds of knots, crashed into the tower. The top part simply disintegrated, the bricks falling away like chaff; seconds later the arches and gates gave way too, collapsing in on themselves and spilling into the plazas on either side. Some even ricocheted off the walls of nearby houses or bounced along the streets. Where seconds before there had been a gatehouse, now there was only a shattered ruin.

And power was still flowing through us, as I realized we were losing control. The lightning flashes were almost constant and the thunder a single, continuous, deafening crash. We were using far too much power here, and if we weren't careful . . .

Limit it! We're using too much!

I know, I'm trying! she replied, and I tried to contain the river of energy that was searing through me. It was like trying to dam the torrent that I'd ridden downriver on, or to channel the ocean. I found myself unable to hold, and the walls themselves started disintegrating.

Then, somehow, I managed to partly close it off. The vortex was still in place, as all the rain from miles around poured into the city all at once. I saw winds blow the roof off the warehouse the Archipelagans were being held in, and a protective bubble of air shaped itself around the men inside. The captain of the ship jumped up, seized a weapon from a comatose guard, and ran out to open the weapons chest that Palatine and Elassel had managed to get there. There was a shout from the Archipelagans as they recovered from their amazement at being protected from the storm. Then they had seized their weapons and were running in a ragged group up towards the Palace.

We're almost there, Ravenna said.

Just the Palace now.

Water was lying an inch or more deep in the streets now, we'd brought so much of it down on the Palace and harbour quarters in the last minute or so. Reaching out in all directions, I pulled it in towards me, directing its force towards the gates, even as a black whirlwind swept through the garden and around the Palace, so close to the walls where we were I could almost have reached out and touched it. The glass windows in the guardroom and the corridors around it shattered, bombarding the Sacri with flying shards. Then came the wind and the rain, blowing them through the corridors as if they were nothing more than rag dolls. I saw them thrown against walls, into furniture, their weapons and their training helping not at all in the face of our onslaught. As gale-force winds howled through the corridors of my home, Sacri bodies were dumped around like so much flotsam.

The gate broke, its timbers splintering before the onslaught of the relentless waves coming up the street. Water flooded the courtyard, drowning the paving stones and the plants my mother so liked. I grieved terribly at the destruction I was inflicting, but there was no other way.

And then, abruptly, I felt my control slip away, the river of power dry up, and the vortex that had channelled all the rain vanish. The mind-link was snapped, and I called out in the sudden darkness for Ravenna.

Then I opened my eyes and found myself lying in the pouring rain looking up at the drenched, furious face of the mind-mage.

We were so drained that we had to be carried inside by the Sacri who were with him. At the bottom of the stairs, we were thrown dripping wet onto the floor of the corridor. The Sacri cut away the storm cloaks and hoods – none too gently, either – and tied our hands. Then they hauled us unceremoniously, banging painfully at every step, down the stairs. Every muscle in my body felt utterly devoid of energy, as though I hadn't had any rest for weeks; I was so feeble I could barely open my eyes.

We passed armed guards stationed in every corridor except those on the ground floor, and I saw first-hand the devastation we had caused. Even the paint on the wall had been damaged by the miniature hurricanes we'd sent through the corridors, and the carpets were soaking wet. None of the lights were working, and in the gloom I saw dead or dying Sacri and marines scattered around, slumped against walls or in the corridors. The sight sickened me. Had it been worth all this death and pain, the ruination of my home, just to regain a title? And, in the end, defeat – just as if I'd let them capture me when they first arrived?

Our captors took us by the most direct route to the Great Hall, emerging from one of the side doors that came out in front of the dais. For a moment I was dazzled by the brightness, and then as my eyes adjusted I saw fresh despair in the faces of the Archipelagan delegates and the others who were kneeling over to the right of the Hall, guarded by marines. Palatine and Elassel were among them, and there were fresh bruises on Elassel's face.

We were dumped down in front of the dais, and somebody grabbed me by my collar to wrench me upright again before I collapsed. I saw Etlae sitting on my father's throne, with Midian and the hooded figure on either side. On the right three or four Inquisitors stood in front of the prisoners, gazing impassively down at them; I saw one with a whip clenched in his thin, ascetic hand.

'We have caught you at last, heretic!' Etlae said, her voice pure venom. Her clothes were in perfect order and she looked every bit the Third Prime that she was. 'You will pay a high price for the evil you have wrought today.'

I found it hard to speak with my collar pulled tight against my neck, but I managed to croak, 'In Thetis's name.'

'Your goddess will not help you now, heretic.'

'He is still the Count of Lepidor,' said Lexan, standing over to Etlae's left, confident and triumphant. He was of middle height, with a round, deceptively kind-looking face and coarse black hair rather like a goat's.

'Not for long,' Midian said, with a cold smile on his face that spoke of a long-awaited revenge.

'Until he is formally removed, you will treat him with at least some respect.'

I had no illusions about Lexan's words; he was being careful that the Domain didn't set a precedent for ill-treatment of a clan ruler. If it could happen to me, he knew it could also happen to him one day.

'Let's get on and remove him, then.'

'The forms must be obeyed,' Lexan said quickly.

'They will be,' Etlae said, glaring down at Ravenna and me.

'You never liked the rules, did you?' Ravenna spoke for the first time, nothing but contempt in her voice. 'Unless they suited you.'

'You have no immunity, girl,' Etlae snapped. 'You will be burned at the stake before we even leave this city.'

I think I was the only one who heard the tiny sound of anguish and terror that escaped Ravenna's lips. I looked sideways and saw her eyes squeezed shut, and a single tear running down her cheek.

'Under what law?' I demanded, then remembered that a Prime could dispense justice on his or her own. I was terrified for Ravenna, and cursed in silent, helpless frustration.

'Under the laws of Ranthas.'

I couldn't let them do that to her, to anyone. But what could I do?

There was yelling from the hallway, and a marine ran in, shouting wildly, 'The Archipelagan sailors have escaped, and they're attacking the Palace.'

'Barricade the doors,' Etlae said immediately. 'Lock every one you can. Haroum, I want a curtain of fire over all the doors and windows. And someone call for reinforcements.'

As the mage, who must have been the one she'd called Haroum, lifted his hands, the brief surge of hope I'd felt died. They would be able to defend this hall and hold out until reinforcements arrived, trapping the Archipelagans in the ruins of the courtyard. I felt a terrible, bitter disappointment and then utter despair. We had failed, and there was no way out of this.

'Admiral Karao, I would appreciate it if you called your men to order,' Midian said.

I twisted my head around to look in the direction he'd been speaking, as more Sacri and marines poured into the hall, carrying tables and chests that they stacked up over the entrances. The room suddenly became bright as the upper windows were covered by sheets of flame.

Hamilcar and Sagantha were sitting on their own over to the left of the Hall. Both of them looked tired and worried, and the Admiral seemed a different man from the one I'd known previously.

'I will do that only if it becomes necessary to save their lives, Avarch, not before. They are Archipelagans making an attempt to free the people put in their charge; I cannot and will not interfere.'

'You stray dangerously close to the edge of your neutrality, Admiral,' Etlae said sharply. 'Just being a Cambressian does not give you total freedom.'

Once the uproar had subsided a little, Etlae turned back to me and Ravenna.

'Put her with the others condemned to death,' she said, indicating Ravenna. 'An orphan girl is of no consequence in this.'

Two Sacri grabbed her shoulders and dragged her across the floor, depositing her next to Palatine and Elassel. Oh, sweet Thetis, was she going to burn them as well? There had to be something I could do. *Please*, I prayed, *let this nightmare end!*

But it was no nightmare, it was reality.

'Etlae, I'll sign whatever you want me to sign if you'll let them go,' I said, surrendering any last vestiges of pride I had, and knowing that it could lead me to the stake. 'They were only acting under my orders.'

'So now you're trying to protect your friends. How touching. It is unfortunate that Ranthas in His wisdom does not deviate where heretics such as they are concerned.'

'Etlae, I beg you. I will give up Lepidor willingly, and you will have your legal document.'

She looked down at me in silence, presumably savouring the moment, and I shut my eyes and tried to blank out the rest of the room.

'In the interests of diplomacy, as a representative of Ranthas on Aquasilva, I am offering you a choice. As a heretic, it is more than you deserve, but as a Count, however much of a traitor, you are still entitled to it.'

I guessed before she told me that it would be no choice at all. There were shouts outside, and the noise of running feet and steel hitting wood, but the barricades remained in place. So near and yet so far.

'You can either surrender Lepidor to the Domain, who will appoint a Count from your House, thus saving your own life – although not, regrettably, those of your friends. Or you can surrender it to Count Lexan, and give up for ever your House's right to rule. Either way, your friends will die. You are more useful to us, though, and you will be taken back to Equatoria as a penitent to serve our needs in the Holy City. *There is no other way.*'

Lexan was gloating at his victory-by-proxy in the final downfall of our family, while the others wore cold smiles on their faces. I had never felt as abject, as trapped or as alone as I did then, kneeling down in my own Hall in a city captured by the enemy, being forced to sign my birthright away. And worse than the humiliation was the shame, of having lost and being reduced to bargaining for my clanspeoples' lives in front of Etlae and Midian. I didn't even feel worthy of my own name any more.

Again I closed my eyes and wondered which was worse. Either way, my clan would suffer dreadfully. Thetis only knew how many the Domain would burn, while Lexan, ruling as a puppet here, would be just as bad. And Ravenna, and the others: what could I do? I could tell that everybody in the Hall was looking at me, the Archipelagans with ashen faces as they realized there was no escape. Had I doomed them all?

There was one other thing I could do, to save my people at the cost of my own life, I realized, and shuddered as the image of a stake rose in front of me. It was said to be one of the most terrible deaths ever invented. But how many of my clansmen would suffer it under the Domain's rule? How could I live with that on my conscience, and spend the rest of my days as a slave?

I opened my eyes and said, my voice wavering and shaky, 'Before Ranthas and His servants, I surrender the countship of Lepidor to

Admiral Karao as representative of the Thalassocracy of Cambress.' I'd condemned myself to death.

Etlae's control broke, and she gave an inarticulate screech of rage. 'You cannot do that! I have given you a choice. If you do not follow it you will be burned.'

'As Thetis wills,' I said, my voice breaking on the last word.

Then Hamilcar said, 'I, Hamilcar, Lord of House Barca, bear witness.'

'It is entirely within his rights,' Sagantha said. 'Cathan, I accept your charge in the name of the Thalassocracy of Cambress.'

Etlae looked fit to explode for a moment. Then she recovered and said icily, 'So be it. We will find some way round that little trick later. For now I, as Third Prime of the Element declare that religious law will hold in this city until Cambressian forces arrive to make good their claim.' She turned back to me. 'Cathan Tauro, I find you guilty of heresy in the first degree. You are stripped of all titles, privileges and rights, and I sentence you to be burned to death at the stake. The sentence will be carried out tomorrow morning. Before you are taken away, go and tell the Archipelagans to lay down their arms. We have no quarrel with them; they will be given their ship and sent back to the Archipelago.' She must have noticed my hesitation.

'Otherwise I will send one of the hostages to Ranthas's mercy,' the hooded figure said. And with those words my defeat was complete.

It was Sarhaddon.

He gestured to one of the Inquisitors, who drew a knife and moved over to stand above the boy named Tekraea, the one who'd bridled at Palatine's insistence that there was no such person as the Pharaoh of Qalathar.

'No need for that,' Sagantha said sharply. 'That is against the law.'

'*I* am the law here,' Sarhaddon said softly.

'Don't worry,' I said. Two Sacri pulled me to my feet and pushed me over to the barricade where the attack was the strongest.

'I am Count Cathan,' I shouted, though my voice was more than a little wobbly. 'If you promise to lay down your arms and stop fighting, you will not be harmed.'

'They've got to you, as well!' said one of the officers.

'You have the word of a Prime, witnessed by Admiral Karao and Lord Barca.'

There was silence on the other side.

'Prove it.'

'Admiral Karao, go and tell them,' Etlae said. I heard his footsteps behind me, but he wasn't allowed to come close to me.

'Cathan is telling the truth. If you stop the attack you won't be harmed, although they're threatening to kill Tekraea if you don't.'

'Then we'll stop,' came the voice. As I was dragged back into the Hall, I heard shouted commands and the pounding on the other barricades stopped. The only outside noise now was the rain pounding on the windows and the howling of the wind.

I was dragged back into the hall, only this time placed over with the others to hear Etlae's final piece of treachery.

'All you Archipelagans are also condemned to death. Before we light the flames tomorrow, my mind-mage will use his skills to find which one of you is the Pharaoh. She will be spared; all the rest of you will burn. Guards, take them away.'

Chapter XXXII

The storm hadn't abated the next morning when the Sacri came and unlocked the doors.

There were some small rooms in the Palace cellars that had once seen use as storage vaults, but were now empty. It was down to these lightless rooms, two levels below ground, that we'd been taken by the Inquisitors. Before Ravenna and I left the throne room, the mind-mage had used his powers to put a block on our magic, rendering us as helpless as all the others.

For some reason, I wasn't quite sure what, Ravenna and I were put into the same cell, while the others were separated into groups of two and three and put in the others. Then the Inquisitors got to work; they had obviously brought their collection of shackles all the way from Pharassa and were determined to use them. The room was hardly big enough to lie down in and the door was solid metal and bolted on the outside, but they'd still chained our wrists and ankles, driving a peg from the end of each set of shackles into the wall.

Then they had gone, and left us alone in the darkness.

I'd been feeling strangely calm ever since I'd said the fatal words, but once the door of the cellar closed with a clang and the last footsteps died away, whatever composure I had evaporated, and I froze up in sheer, stark terror. Why had I done it, when I'd had the chance to save my own life? I didn't want to die, least of all at the stake.

Ravenna burst into silent, racking sobs, and I heard the clinking of her chains as she moved closer to me. I felt her brush my arm, and on impulse brought it up and put it round her shoulders, holding her as she cried and I stared into the darkness, feeling literally sick with fear. My throat and chest were too tight for me to make any sound at all.

For a long time we sat in that terrible blackness, as I felt more and more wretched, and nothing I could do could banish the terror or erase that terrible picture of the stake in my mind. I wanted to be sick, but I hadn't eaten very much and my whole body was tensed, my arms and legs rigid. They began to cramp after a while, but there was nothing that I could do about that, either.

I heard Ravenna's sobs dry up as she simply ran out of tears. The walls must have been very thick, because I couldn't hear anything from outside, or from above, or from the other cells; our air came from a vent in the ceiling.

'Why, Cathan?' Ravenna croaked. 'Why are they doing this to us?'

I couldn't say anything, and I felt her other hand take my free hand and hold it.

'What did we ever do to them? What was it that gave them a reason to tie us to the stakes and burn us alive?'

'Please,' I managed to say. 'Don't.' Even mentioning it made everything worse, and I felt my stomach muscles spasm, although still nothing came up.

'I'm sorry.'

I realized that although there was no light at all I could actually see the cell in shades of dark grey. Even without my magic, there were some things that seemed to be inborn. But tomorrow there would be nothing. No life, no memory, nothing to experience. Just nothingness, oblivion. Heretics who died by fire didn't return to their element as elementals, they were utterly consumed by the flames. All that would be left of me was a pile of ashes, and everything I was, everything I'd done, would be forgotten, less than a shadow on the wind.

'Do you think this is why it's so terrible?' Ravenna said, resting her head on my shoulder. 'That you spend hours and hours unable to do anything except think about it, while your mind dwells on the agony, and the heat, and makes it worse and worse?'

'What else is there to do?'

After a moment she spoke again. 'Cathan, for us it can be not so terrible. They have taken away our magic, but we can still retreat into our minds.' She gulped. 'In the void, at least, you won't feel most of the pain.'

'Just life slipping away.'

There was another long silence.

'It isn't going to help – worrying about it, I mean. Forget the agony, please. In our trance we can ignore it.'

'That doesn't make it any easier.'

'Wouldn't you rather die quickly than slowly?'

'I'd rather not die at all!' I screamed, and saw her flinch. She brought her legs round so she wasn't in such an awkward position; the manacles made screeching noises as they dragged on the rough stone floor. It was very cold down here, I noticed, feeling it for the first time. But humid.

'I don't want to die, either. I had as much to look forward to as you did. But that's how they want us to be now, half demented by terror and moaning at their injustice. We don't have to give them that satisfaction. You made a sacrifice none of us did – please don't spend your last night in misery.'

I took a deep breath and forced myself to relax some of my muscles, one by one. I still felt miserable, as no doubt she did, but it wasn't as bad. I still didn't want to disgrace my clan by behaving like a coward now, even if I felt like one.

'What do you want me to do, then? I'm hardly going to sleep.'

'Nor am I.' She smiled wanly, but it wasn't convincing, and I saw how fragile her control was. 'Listen, if I tell you something will you promise not to tell anyone, not even if by some chance we live?'

'Something important?'

'Very important.'

'All right. I swear by the Gods of the Elements that I'll never tell anyone your secret.' It was hardly a formal oath, with the ritual words and witnesses, but it was just as binding.

'You must hold true to it, Cathan. Even with your sense of honour you may want to break it, but please don't, I beg you.'

'What is it that's so crucial?'

'They've been looking for the Pharaoh of Qalathar ever since the *Emerald* arrived. And while they were right that she was in Lepidor, they thought she'd come on the manta. They were wrong. I'm the Pharaoh.'

'*You?*' I stared at her in shock.

'Please, please forgive me, Cathan. I didn't tell you because I've never told anyone. I spent ten years after I left Tehama being moved from place to place, used as a pawn in the nobles' power plays. The only people who ever tried to make friends with me were always spies, or people who wanted something. All that being Pharaoh ever got me was grief, so I told Sagantha that I was abdicating, and I ran away to the Citadel of Shadow, and hid myself, away from all their stratagems and intrigues.'

'So all that time you were trying to get the Archipelagans out of here.' My voice tailed off.

'I know, I know,' she said, almost crying again. 'I shouldn't have done it, but I never really trusted anyone. Even when you came along, and I . . .' She paused, then said, 'I was still obsessed with stopping anybody from ever finding out; I couldn't tell you, because nobody had ever kept my trust. Now, of course, I know you would have, but it's too late, too late.'

'You could have saved your life up there!'

'So could you, but you didn't, for the same reason.'

I wasn't going to hold a grudge against her, not now, not in these circumstances. I didn't want to spend my last night alive at odds with the person I loved.

'You see why you can't tell anyone?' she said. 'I can retreat into the void when the mind-mage scans us tomorrow, and he'll never find me. The Archipelago may lose its Pharaoh, but the Domain won't get their hands on me.'

'I promised I won't tell anyone.' It hurt, not being able to save her life, but I had made the same choice and I wouldn't have wanted her to unmake it for me.

'Thank you. At least I'll get to foil one of their schemes.'

'I only hope Sagantha can do something to protect Lepidor,' I said, moving my hand up from her shoulder and running it through her hair. It seemed totally straight to the eye, but as I stroked it I realized it was actually curly, only straightened by the band she wore and something she put on it. Strange how I was picking up these small details now.

'The Domain are going to kill his wards. He's been a politician for years and he knows when to change sides, but he'll never forgive that. You've left Lepidor in the right hands.'

'But not my father's. I've failed him, I've lost the clan.'

'He won't remember you for that, Cathan. There was nothing you could have done against this, and even then you tried your hardest. He wouldn't have done any better.'

'He wouldn't have been so desperate as to send a letter to House Canadrath, with whom we have no contacts and who could, for all we know, be helping the Domain as well.'

'This invasion was planned long before that. Don't reproach yourself.'

'I can't help it, thinking that if I'd done something differently somewhere, this might never have happened. All those months ago, when I set out from Lepidor, I was so happy because we'd discovered iron and our prospects were suddenly so good. Lepidor was going to be such a wonderful place, I thought, now that we'd have money pouring in. There would be more traders coming, everyone would be happier. You can see how little I knew,' I added bitterly. 'But all that's happened; well, you know. That hooded monster in the throne room was Sarhaddon, whom you met on the *Paklé*. He used to think Lachazzar and his hereticbashers were ridiculous, and now look at him. He'll probably be lighting the torches tomorrow.'

A fresh paroxysm of terror took hold of me, and though I felt ashamed I couldn't stop myself. Despite Ravenna's reassurances, I couldn't take my mind off the flames, and the agony. What if she was wrong, and the mind-mage had blocked my ability to take refuge in the void, as well? I tried it, just to check, and though it took longer than usual to reach the trance state where I wasn't aware of my body any more, I made it.

'See? You can do it,' Ravenna said softly.

I shifted position, feeling the weight of the chains dragging down on me, the metal cuffs chafing my wrists. At least it wasn't for long, it would soon be all over.

'Cathan?'

'Yes?'

'I'm sorry I've been so cold to you. I hope you at least understand why.'

'I can understand, Ravenna. And before you ask, there was nothing to forgive.'

'We could have made a good partnership, you and I. The only people who ever managed to channel the power of a storm, even if it came to nothing in the end. It would have been an entirely new branch of magic, and would have included your oceanography as well.'

'Someone will read about it, and wonder what we did. There must be other ways to do that, other people who can link in the same way as us.'

'I hope so.' She wrapped one of her arms around me as far as the chains would let her, and moved her face towards mine. Then we kissed each other for the first time because we wanted to, without the pretence or the need for disguise, and it seemed to last for ever.

For a moment, a moment only, I forgot that I was going to die in the morning.

We sat together and talked for the rest of that timeless, terrible night, always trying to forget that our lives were ebbing away.

A faint grey light was making its way into our cell by the time they brought us out. I had resolved that, however terrified I was, however reluctant, I wouldn't show it, I would go to the stake with dignity.

As we were driven at spear point up the stairs and through the remnants of the Palace, I saw the others, some looking resigned and proud, others, especially the younger Archipelagans, barely able to hold back their tears. It was still raining hard, and the sky was a mottled grey colour, but obviously the mage Haroum had put shields in place around the market place in front of the Palace, keeping the rain out.

I caught Palatine's glance for a moment, and she gave me a faint shadow of her old smile. She looked much worse than the others, and I wondered why. Elassel looked defiant, although her face was streaked with tear stains.

It was hard to walk with the chains on my ankles, but I didn't trip over any of the rubble, not even when I saw the pyre in the centre of the square. The Domain had built up all the wood they could find into a low wooden mound, from which twenty or twenty-five stakes protruded, at varying heights. There were coils of rope near each one, and plenty of kindling and tarry cordage scattered around to make the flames burn better. Around it, beyond a rope barrier, penned in by Sacri ranked across all the streets, the clanspeople of Lepidor had been gathered to watch their Count die. Etlae and her co-conspirators sat in comfortable chairs in an open space, near where my House were surrounded by six or so of Lexan's marines. Virtually the whole of the occupation force must have been there.

Hamilcar and Sagantha stood over to one side with a couple of Hamilcar's men and the Cambressian sailors. Also with them was my father's guard commander, wearing ill-fitting clothes in Barca colours.

Had even Hamilcar decided to make the best of a bad job and borrow some of our retainers, I wondered?

We were prodded into the area in front of Etlae and ordered to kneel. The paving stones of the square were wet and my chains kept getting caught up in each other.

'You have all been found guilty of heresy of the second degree, and Cathan Tauro with Ravenna Ulfhada of heresy of the first degree. For both of these the punishment is death at the stake, without the choice of recantation. Whichever one of you is the Pharaoh of Qalathar, however, has been called to a higher destiny by Ranthas. Will the Pharaoh come forward?'

There was silence, and nobody moved. Next to me, Ravenna held her head high.

'Then we have other ways of finding out.'

The mind-mage lifted his hammer, and golden light flared around its tip. Then a bolt of energy flared from it, resting on the heads of the Archipelagans at the end of the front line and running along the row from girl to girl with astonishing rapidity. It paused a second on Ravenna, but then went on. After it had scanned the last, the bolt fled back to the hammer, and the light died. The mind-mage turned to Etlae.

'It seems we were mistaken, Your Grace. None of these is the Pharaoh.'

'Are you sure?'

'Quite sure. None of them even know who the Pharaoh is.'

'Well, there'll always be another try.' She turned back to us. 'You are all condemned to die now as heretics, outcasts of Ranthas. Your souls will find no solace in His heaven or roam the world as elementals of His realm. Your names will be cursed for ever, and your fate passed on to future generations as a lesson.'

I was close to tears. *Remember who you are.*

The Inquisitors and a few more of the Sacri moved out from behind Etlae, came up to each person in the front row and unlocked our chains. Then they marched us, at dagger point, across the few yards of square and up some rudimentary steps on the sides of the pyre.

It was slightly pyramidal, part of me noticed, and there was a single stake in the centre at the top, a few feet above the lowest level. Two Inquisitors pushed Ravenna and me up that far and up against the stake;

I was facing towards Etlae; Ravenna, on the other side, towards the gates. With a Sacri sword pointed at my stomach, I could only stand still as the two Inquisitors wrapped the rope around us, lashing us tightly to the stake. They tied our hands to the sides, close enough for us to touch, and we locked fingers as far as we could.

Sweet Thetis, please, I prayed, *if you have ever helped the Tar'Conanturs then help me now, do not let me die like this*. There was no response.

As Palatine, Elassel and some others were bound below us, I looked out over the square for the last time, seeing the crowd, many of them crying, and the woman who had done all this to me.

And I saw Hamilcar raise his head, look me directly in the eye – and make what was unmistakably a thumbs-up sign. What did he mean? Was something going to happen?

The Inquisitors were nothing if not efficient, and as I looked round, not daring to hope, at the Palace and the square, they were tying the last of the Archipelagans around the foot of the pyre. I found myself regretting the amount of rope they were using, which would all have to be replaced.

Lightning flashed over the mountains; it was odd to be here in the square, exposed under the storm, yet not getting wet. Was this the elements' revenge on me for presuming to command them, I wondered? Was Thetis not helping me because I had committed a sin against Her in disturbing the natural balance of things?

The last of the Inquisitors stepped down from the pyre and rejoined Etlae. Sarhaddon stood up, an unlit flamewood torch in his hand. I'd been right, then: he would be the one lighting the pyre. It was all over.

Sarhaddon gestured for a tinderbox. At that moment I saw Hamilcar make a very small hand motion, and my father's marine commander shouted, '*NOW!*'

As Etlae looked over in astonishment, all hell broke out, and time seemed to stand still. I saw members of the crowd produce daggers and rush at the Sacri guarding the exits, who turned to see what was going on. They weren't quick enough. I saw one fall with three daggers in his chest and one through the eye-slits of his mask.

Then arrows arched from the upper windows of the houses around the square and even from the Palace roof, plunging down into the group around Etlae. There must have been twenty or thirty bowmen there, firing arrows as fast as they could. An Inquisitor fell, stuck full of arrows like a pincushion, then another, then Midian shrieked as an arrow hit his arm, and the group ran for cover. But the Sacri were unable to help their superiors as they, too, fell victim to the arrows, as did Lexan's marines. People from the crowd struck out at those still standing, and as they surrounded individual Sacri, I saw their coordination – and realized they were Lepidor's marines.

Unable to move or intervene, I clutched Ravenna's hands tighter in excitement, and looked back over to the chairs. Etlae had taken four arrows in the chest and another in her neck, and she was sinking down onto the ground in a pool of blood. All of the Inquisitors were dead or dying, although Midian, Lexan and Sarhaddon had taken refuge under the chairs.

In the pouring rain, I watched the crowd surge past its barriers and tear the remaining Sacri apart, while marines grabbed weapons from fallen Sacri and ran towards the harbour. As the two mages died, the shield around the market place wavered and collapsed, and I was suddenly drenched by the rain, once again welcome, a friend, and I yelled with glee, a noise hardly heard above all the thunder.

'Miracles happen, Cathan!' Ravenna shouted.

'What a surprise, we're getting wet again.'

'Who cares? Better wet than too dry.'

The deluge of arrows had ceased, and marines were swarming up on to the treacherously wet wood of the platform, slicing through the Archipelagans' bonds, as they looked at each other through the rain gusts and could hardly believe their luck.

And then someone was slicing through our ropes as well; I recognized the marine I'd talked to on the walls the morning after going down the river.

'Strange how things turn out, isn't it, Count Cathan?' he said.

Once we got down to the bottom of the pyre the crowd picked us up on its shoulders, people who normally wouldn't go out in the rain almost dancing for joy as they carried us across the square to the marine commander.

'We owe you our lives,' I said, as the people who'd enthusiastically hoisted me aloft let me down again. 'Thank you.'

'I couldn't fail you again.'

'You didn't fail the first time.' Then I turned to Hamilcar, standing unobtrusively behind the marine commander. I must have been the only one to have seen his gesture, and knew that he'd organized the rescue. His fine robe was soaked through and through, but he looked, for the first time, happy – and terribly pleased with himself.

'Thank you, too,' I said quietly.

'Cathan, I relinquish to you and House Tauro the Countship of Lepidor,' said Sagantha, 'and may your reign be happier than mine was.'

'In the name of House Tauro, I take the Countship of Clan Lepidor,' I replied.

'And I, Hamilcar, Lord of House Barca, bear witness.'

And then we were pulled away and hoisted onto the crowd's shoulders again, Ravenna and I, as they began cheering and calling my name.

'CATH-AN! CATH-AN! CATH-AN!'

Epilogue

Cathan Tauro to Laeas Tigrana.
Greetings.

By the time you read this you should have heard what has been going on here, as Persea was planning to stop off in Liona on her way back to the capital. Doubtless you'll also have heard some garbled account complete with divine intervention and miracles. The reality was not, unfortunately, like that; I could have done with a miracle or two.

Even Persea won't be able to tell you the full story; she left the day after we defeated Etlae, while things were still hanging in the air. Courtières arrived that evening, complete with Kula's marines and a small fleet belonging to House Canadrath. For one of the bigger Great Houses, Canadrath are a friendly lot. Perhaps it's because they're not native Tanethans; the Canadrath heir looks like some reaver from the polar forests, all blond beard and blue eyes.

It turns out the whole thing was planned months ago. Lachazzar desperately wants the services of Reglath Eshar and his army to launch a Crusade, but the Halettites are insisting that Lachazzar pays and arms it. Our mine just happened to come along at the right time for him, and he ordered Etlae to get control of it. She funded Foryth's campaign against us and the King's assassination from the Domain's coffers. If her plan had worked, the Domain would have had all the iron they needed from Lepidor and enough weapons to launch a Crusade. As it is, I think they'll have to postpone the Crusade by two years if not more.

I'm sorry if this letter's a bit messy, but Ravenna and I broke half the windows in the Palace with our little whirlwind, and most of them haven't been repaired yet. Up here, that's not funny, and I can't find anywhere to write that's dry enough.

Anyway, to continue, we've also made sure the two priests who survived,

Midian and Sarhaddon, will keep their mouths shut. Lachazzar won't want this to come out, because it could be a serious blow to the Domain, while Midian and Sarhaddon were only too keen to blame Etlae. The official story will be that she was a heretic trying to damage the Domain, and we were the loyal servants of Ranthas who tried to stop her. Poetic justice, I call it. As for Lexan, he'll be sent back to Khalaman minus his pride and the manta he came on. It was the King's ship, but he'd given it to Lexan. Very short-sighted of him, really.

Everyone is recovering well, at least on the surface. The red marks on my wrists have faded, and I can actually look down at my hands without having flashbacks. But somehow it's worse remembering it than actually being there. All of us are still having nightmares, and I doubt I'll ever be able to forget even the tiniest detail. My father's had those old storage rooms filled in; if only I could block the memory out the same way.

You haven't met Hamilcar, have you? Palatine's known him for two years or so, and even she didn't believe he'd rescue us. He's so much the Merchant Lord, it's hard to believe he actually has a heart sometimes. Ravenna asked him why he did it, and his reply is another thing I won't forget. He said that after we'd all been hauled off, he couldn't understand why I'd sacrificed myself. He realized that there was nothing he would ever do that for, nothing he cared about that much, and that he couldn't sit by and watch me die because I believed in something more than my own life. The Domain had lined up two more contracts for him, so he didn't stand to lose out. As far as I can see, it's the first altruistic thing he's done in his entire life.

Strictly between you and me, though, I don't think Palatine's going to be the same as she was. It was the first time one of her plans had failed like this, and I think she feels she let us all down. She's been very quiet ever since, which may be her way of getting over it, but I don't think so. She isn't as confident and assured as she'd like us to think. I only hope she still wants to get at the Domain, that this hasn't broken her spirit.

I certainly have no intention of leaving things as they stand. Ravenna went through some of my father's records, and she found a reference to something that could be a great help. You'd hardly recognize her, Laeas. She's lost the ice-queen look, and she's stopped using straightener on her hair, so she looks even prettier than before. She even laughed today, the first laugh I've ever heard from her. You and the others were right, I've fallen in love with her, and I think – I hope – she feels the same way.

After the storm we unleashed on Lepidor – about the only successful part of the whole plan – we've decided to form a partnership, the first-ever mages of Storm. What Ravenna found in the records is a reference to a ship, the Aeon. *Aetius used it in the War, and it's supposed to be truly colossal, but most importantly it has access to the SkyEye system. With* Aeon *we could see the storms as well as the Domain do, use the planet itself as a weapon against them. I may be over-optimistic, but this could be a breakthrough. Don't mention it to too many people, but if any of the others know anything about it, it would be a great help.*

Ravenna's just come in, wrapped in a thick cloak because it's so cold, to tell me that the packet ship is preparing to leave. I'll have to break off here. Pass my greetings on to any of the others if you see them. I hope I'll be back in the Archipelago soon, and I'll write when I have more news. Until then, walk in Thetis's path.

Hail and farewell,
Cathan Tauro.